C000082897

The Book Proposal

KJ MICCICHE

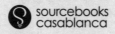

sourcebooks casablanca

Published by Sourcebooks Casablanca, an imprint of Sourcebooks
P.O. Box 4410, Naperville, Illinois 60567-4410
(630) 961-3900
sourcebooks.com

Cataloging-in-Publication data on file with the Library of Congress.

Manufactured in the UK by Clays and distributed by
Dorling Kindersley Limited, London
002-336703-May/23
10 9 8 7 6 5 4 3 2

To the dancing man, who gave me Core Four.

Gracie

Some things never cease to amaze me. Like the Christmas tree at Rockefeller Center. Or the way a good cup of coffee can take the chill out of an early autumn morning. Or how a sunset can paint the clouds like wildflowers, all fuchsia, lilac, and gold.

Or like how the smallest, most meaningless interaction can get into your head and start fucking with you.

Colin Yarmouth was not in my orbit in high school. We shared a zip code, but little else. He played varsity baseball and soccer and ran laps around the field during his free periods. The only place *I* ever ran was the girls' bathroom after a surprise maxi pad leak on a white-jeans day. He had name-brand clothing from the actual *store*, whereas my wardrobe consisted of last season's outlet picks saved for the following year and the occasional trip to Chinatown for knockoff shoes and designer fragrances bottled in six-inch aerosol cans. (*Like Obsession by Calvin Klein? You'll love Preoccupation by Smells by Joe!*) He had girlfriends. Like, beautiful human girls he dated for a few weeks or a few months, ultimately trading up for the next conquest, leaving in his wake scores of used Kleenex to dry the tears of the forlorn. I, meanwhile, had

Ronald. Ronald played exactly zero sports because—courtesy of his chronic asthma—he was better suited for the triangle in jazz band and after-school sessions in front of the television, vicariously working out his suppressed deviant inner life through the controller in *Grand Theft Auto*.

The first time I ever laid eyes on Colin Yarmouth was in freshman biology with Ms. Villani. He was seated in the front row over by the windows, where the sun could caress his stylish mushroom haircut. I sat in the back of the room near the fetal pig jars, which was probably for the best because the over-straightened, half-burnt bangs covering my forehead were not exactly what one would consider an A-game. I studied him longingly, noting his left-handedness and his royal-blue Bic pen. He wore a green fleece vest over a long-sleeved white thermal shirt, jeans from the Gap, and simple black Adidas Sambas on his feet, which he wrapped around the bottom of the legs of his chair-desk combo while he copied down the assignments from the blackboard.

I'll never forget that day's task: Pick a name out of a hat and spend five minutes getting to know your new lab partner. The people in the front two rows of the classroom got to pick the names. The small white slips of paper contained the first and last names of those of us seated in the back two rows.

Ms. Villani was awesome. She was reserved and sweet, and she must have known how nervous we were. (Here, I'm projecting my feelings onto the entire class of freshmen, but I think it's a fair assumption.) She had one downfall though: her cursive handwriting was maybe not as neat as it could have been, so when Colin Yarmouth pulled the name, "Gracelanding," I can understand how he might have thought it was a verb, like the act of going to Graceland.

He was the first one asked to read the name on his slip of paper aloud because of his elite placement in the front corner of the room.

"Gracelanding?" he asked, as if my existence was a question. "Like, Elvis?" he added.

Kids laughed, while I quietly died.

The nickname stuck. The teacher, unfortunately, did not. Poor Ms. Villani was struck by a school bus the following morning and spent the remainder of the year in traction with two broken legs. She was replaced by Mr. Bacharot, a surly older man who came out of retirement to cover her classes. He wore a lab coat every day and seated us in alphabetical order, explaining that whoever sat next to you in class would be your lab partner. Which was fine. Cindy Lee and I were a more appropriate match: both quiet, smart, and good at not blowing stuff up. Colin ended up with Alexis Yacolino, and by October, word on the street was they were getting to third base regularly.

He was my first real crush.

Ever the author, I wrote notes to him and slipped them into his locker in the hallway, signed, *Your faithful secret admirer.* As a freshman, he was recruited to play on varsity teams, so even the sophomore and junior girls noticed him. All that fall, I brought my notebook to the soccer field a half hour before games were scheduled to begin, and while the boys on the team changed into their uniforms right there on the field (alas, there was no locker room), I described on paper the things I could only imagine doing to him in person. Just a quick peek at his boxer shorts could send my imagination into overdrive. His hairless chest set my young heart ablaze.

In November, the soccer season ended, and thanks to Cindy Lee, I learned over a formaldehyde-soaked dead frog that Colin and Alexis were officially porking one another. I stopped writing the letters then. Rather, I stopped *delivering* them. All hope was lost of Colin and I deflowering one another, so I poured out my heart to my journal instead.

But just before Thanksgiving that year, a curious thing happened. I was eating lunch in the cafeteria, and I overheard the boys at the soccer table talking. Scoffing was more like it. The goalie, a thick-necked senior named Gus Nikolaides who always smelled like roasted lamb on account of his dad's (hugely successful) gyro food truck business, was boisterously dramatizing my confidential thoughts, with the remainder of the team and many surrounding tables as a willing audience.

"'If only you would have me,'" he read, in his best attempt at a female voice, "'I would ravage your body with my lips and you would forever dream about the taste of my skin on your tongue as our souls merged, two into one.'"

Billy Gutierrez, a loudmouthed sophomore who rarely got any field time, howled, throwing his head back for effect. "Damn, son! If some chick wrote that shit to me, I would ride her all night long!"

"Don't play yourself, Billy." Gus laughed. "The only thing you know how to ride is the *bench*!"

"Oh!" a chorus of testosterone ejaculated on the lunch table.

My face grew beet red as I watched Gus paw the perfume-sprayed page with his sweaty sausage fingers. His booming voice commanded an audience, and he stood with one foot up on the bench of the cafeteria table, towering over his teammates. I fought back nausea as I continued listening to my deepest fantasies being blurted aloud for the whole cafeteria to hear.

"'I want to feel the touch of your hard body up against me; the slow motion of your fingers as they adeptly unhook my bra,'" Gus went on. "Yo…she used a semicolon. Like for real? Whoever this admirer is got mad grammar skills!"

I glanced over. Colin looked decidedly uncomfortable, despite his outward laughter.

"I'm just sayin' bro, you need to find out who wrote that shit," Justin Gagliardo said, slapping Colin on the shoulder. "If someone wrote me notes like that, I'd definitely do her."

I guess that's how my letters ended up photocopied and circulated among the whole school, until the principal finally put an end to it a few days later. I mean, it makes sense. If the captain of the soccer team says to do something—like, locate a secret admirer by checking the handwriting of every girl in school, you know, like Cinderella and the glass slipper—you do it, I suppose.

Two things changed as a result of my private humiliation though. The first, of course, was my penmanship. I very intentionally began crafting extra small, neat letters, a stark contrast to the giant, loopy scrawl I'd been using in the notes.

Also, I discovered that I might have a future as a romance writer.

I started penning short stories and fan fiction about my

favorite television shows, and by the time junior year rolled around, I chose Creative Writing as an elective. I went to Boston College and majored in English. And now, all these years later, here we are.

It never dawned on me that Colin Yarmouth was the impetus behind my entire life path. I mean, at least not until now.

PART ONE

April

Gracie

Hey Colin,

Long time no speak! How are you? Psych—I don't really
care. I just wanted to tell you thanks for totally fucking up my life in high school by giving me the nickname "Elvis." I found your picture on your company's website, and I wish you were fatter and balder, but for now I guess the fact that you're mildly overweight and your hairline is receding will have to do. I would have contacted you on Facebook, but you don't seem to have Facebook, which, like, how is that even possible?

Anywho, you suck and I hate you, but I also kind of miss you and remember the time you hit a grand slam at the game against Gompers that took us to the playoffs. That was so hot.

Have a nice life—or not—whatever.

Love always,
Elvis

Colin

Whoever started the La-Z-Boy company was a relaxation genius. I feel like it was probably a recently divorced, middle-aged dude who found himself furniture shopping solo, wandering through some overcrowded showroom looking like a deer in head-lights, trying to make his way through the florals and the plaids to find something—anything!—that looked and felt appropriate for a bachelor pad. He probably sat on a dozen couches and realized that, for the first time in his life, he would be tasked with choosing this incredibly important piece of furniture based on the level of comfort experienced by his—and *only* his—ass cheeks.

And, with that realization, suddenly nothing in the entire store was good enough.

I'm sure this entrepreneurial guy labored over memory foams and reclining mechanisms until he discovered the perfect combination that, with scientific precision, could coax any man into a gentle sleep on a date-free Saturday evening in front of the television after 11:00 p.m.

Until the iPhone people came along and fucked it all up by making a wristwatch that vibrates when you get an email.

I rub my eyes and open them, squinting at the blue light emanating from my living room wall. I hate that I'm conditioned to read my emails as they come in. Even on weekends. I've been like this ever since I started working at the firm when my dad was still in charge. It's his fault. He used to send me messages for no good reason, just to time how long it would take me to get back to him. "You've gotta be fast in a customer service industry, son," he would say.

"We're in estate planning," I'd remind him. "We're helping people plan for their *death*, Dad. Why rush it?"

Then he'd roll his eyes, make some noise expressing his exasperation with me, and leave my office.

And yet, despite my clever devil's advocating and the fact that my father has since retired, I'm still waking up to check this message.

I try to focus in on the tiny text, but I can't see it. I reach over onto the end table and grab my cell phone.

Is this some kind of joke?

Grace *Landing*? From high school?

I read the lines of her email on my phone three times. It's not *late*, exactly, just two sketches into this week's new episode of SNL.

Overweight? Is she crazy? I'm down to 13 percent body fat! What picture is she talking about?

And what's this about a receding hairline? I'm thirty-one years old, for Christ's sake! Sure, I sneak Rogaine into my hair regimen (it looks like product, for real—makes my hair look "styled"), but it's not like I have a bald spot in the back or anything. I'd love to meet the ageless Superman *she* ended up with.

She's drunk. I mean, right? She *must* be drunk. Grace Landing never struck me as the kind of girl who'd send alcohol-induced hate mail, but anything's possible, I guess. I only knew her fifteen years ago. Maybe she's different now. Maybe she's a chronic boozer—she could be the kind of girl who keeps a box of wine in the fridge for all I know. Or maybe she's a huge party girl who goes out clubbing every weekend. Either way, insulting a guy you haven't spoken to in fifteen years on his *work* email makes drunk texting an ex look like child's play.

She seemed pretty put together in high school, but people change, right?

Gracie

Ugh.

Hangovers, am I right?

I woke up in an empty bed. Or, I should say, a bed devoid of any other living being…although not actually *empty.* My sleeping companions last night included an almost-finished bottle of red wine (spoiler alert: my sheets are ruined), my kitchen scissors, my dead cell phone, fourteen pairs of thong underwear, all cut in half at the ass strap, and my high school yearbook.

It legit looks like a fucking crime scene.

But today is Sunday—the start of a new week! A new me! Screw Scott and the waify blond event planner he knocked up and left me for. Who cares if the professional pictures of their brand-new baby are posted all over Instagram with hashtags like #bestdayever and #welcometotheworld and #familyfirst. That was a poor excuse to get intoxicated last night, but I'm a forgiver, and so, I forgive myself. Now, I just need to get my body to forgive me too. Advil oughta do the trick. And maybe we'll wash it down with a little—no. No. That was yesterday's Gracie.

Today's Gracie's going out for a jog.

I squeeze my boobs into a sports bra and try not to notice the tiny bit of new back fat that spills over the straps, which reminds me of how Scott used to call me "Lil' Chubs." Ah, the good ol' days. I could laugh it off back then because it's not exactly like he was some prize, with his furry ass cheeks and the carpet full of chest hair he used to ask me to help him shave off on the reg. Also, he'd put a ring on it, so I thought we were down for the long haul—hence my discomfort with him knocking up our damn wedding planner who I paid top dollar to plan *my* happy ending.

Side note—spandex pants are the absolute worst. They must have been invented by Satan himself.

Sneakers? Check. Fitbit? Check. Phone's dead, so gotta let that charge. Old school iPod for tunes? Check.

I leave my building—that's right, I still live in my co-op in Brooklyn instead of the house we were supposed to buy on Long Island—turn the iPod on, and hit "shuffle." *What kind of pump-you-up music does the universe have in store for me?* I wonder.

I look down at the screen when Hillsong United's live version of "Lead Me to the Cross" comes blasting through my headphones.

That's right. Now I remember—the iPod was a gift from a born-again guy I dated like a decade ago.

I shake my head. Dammit. The closest thing I'll find to hip-hop or power pop on here would be that rap song about Jesus and the sheep. The slit in my stretch pants masquerading as a pocket becomes the iPod's temporary new home. I'll throw it back in my nightstand and save it for a future time in my life when I'm feeling particularly spiritual. Today, my church is the bagel store where

I ditch my workout plan in favor of an everything bagel with lox and cream cheese, a giant slab of crumb cake, and a Snapple.

Ha! Maybe I *am* getting in touch with the big guy upstairs— after all, it's a commandment not to work on Sunday. *Message received!* Instead, I head back home to watch *Real Housewives of Somewhere in America* and sink my teeth into this scrumptious breakfast.

On *Monday*, Gracie 2.0 will emerge.

Colin

Ever since Elle and I split, Sunday has become my favorite day of the week. She used to love to sleep in and then waste the day away catching up on work. She'd get bitchy if I got up too early. God forbid I should have to pee and accidentally disrupt her majesty's neurotic sleep schedule. Now that I'm on my own, I can get up as early as I want and go out for a run. It has become a ritual for me—some people go to church on Sunday; I exercise.

Astoria has lots of redeeming qualities, but running space is not one of them—a man can only loop around Astoria Park so many times. Plus, since my car gets no love during the week, lately I've been killing two birds with one stone by doing a tour of parks in Queens. Today I'm off to Kissena Park. It's in Fresh Meadows, over near Flushing. Dom lives nearby, so we're going to meet up at nine and get a little batting practice in since softball starts this Wednesday.

I have about an hour till he gets here.

I started running in the fourth grade. Dad said, "Colin, running is the foundation for all other sports," and I was ten, so I believed him. He enrolled me in a CYO track program, and we ran at Van Cortlandt Park a few times a week. By the time I was in middle school, he had me running track, playing baseball, lacrosse, soccer, and football, and doing gymnastics once a week. I *hated* gymnastics, but Dad insisted it would help with flexibility, balance, and agility. I think any sport that requires boys going through puberty to wear skintight uniforms is just cruel.

I don't know what that man thought I was going to do with my life. Become an Olympian, maybe? End up on a Wheaties box? Compensate for the fact that *he* couldn't go pro?

We fought about it, and I begged my mom behind closed doors to let me cool it with the sports. It took years, but eventually she helped me negotiate a compromise: I had to choose two sports and *commit* to them, and then I could get rid of everything else. That's how I ended up playing baseball and soccer in high school. At the time, I was so happy to be rid of all the excess activities that I didn't realize how much I would miss the smooth, rhythmic running of track: sneakers kicking up dirt, wind in my face, the sound of a steady pace quieting my mind.

Today's run begins at 7:45 a.m. and takes me around a big loop, down a flight of stairs, around a duck pond, and back up the stairs. Repeat twice—five miles in the books. When I'm done, I lie down in the grass, sweating like a beast. I feel healthy, dirty. *Alive.* I look up at the tree I'm under. It has five trunks that all split at the stump. I've never seen a tree like this before. I bet it would be perfect for building a treehouse. I close my eyes and see Elle and the kids we were supposed to have in a backyard oasis with a swimming pool, a swing set, and a kick-ass treehouse, built by yours truly. My son would have begged me to teach him how to use power tools while my daughter practiced cartwheels in the grass.

Nope. Not *my* life. Instead, I'm the guy who got divorced after six months and has little to show for it other than the flat screen TV I got to take and the brand-new car I bought to accommodate our adjustment to suburban living. Elle kept everything else: the house, the yard, my self-respect—you know, the basics—and I moved to a studio apartment in Queens that always smells sort of like souvlaki. I chose that though; even though *she* destroyed our marriage, I still wanted to make sure she was taken care of.

I'm an idiot, I know.

And evidently, a fat balding idiot, according to my inbox.

I take the last swig out of my water bottle. I still don't understand—why would Grace *write* that—out of nowhere, after all these years?

What did I ever do to her?

I check my phone; it's almost nine. I stretch my hamstrings and jog back to my car, where I grab a new bottle of water and my gear.

By the time I get to the softball field, I see Dom crouching next to a bucket of balls, on his phone. He looks up. "Bro, where'd you park? Guam?" he says.

"Nah. By that back entrance," I reply.

He nods, finishes up a text or whatever, and slides his phone into his bag. "Yo, I heard the Tooth Fairies got two new hygienists," he says, grinning. "Bangin'."

The Tooth Fairies are an all-girls team in the league. It's a dental office run by Dr. Macarena Rankin, whose face is plastered on bus shelters and subway platforms all over the city. Dom swears it's a front for either a sorority or a brothel, because she only hires cute girls to work there.

"Nice," I say.

"I'm tellin' you, this is gonna be my *year*."

"Oh, yeah? How's that?"

"Friday night, man. Me and Sparky went down to Fireballs for happy hour, and we met these chicks. Dude—the *outfits*. The one girl wore this belly shirt with, like, undertitty peeking out."

"Undertitty?" *That's a new one.*

"Don't laugh, bro! That shit was hot."

"Did you get her number?"

"You *know* it," he says.

I call bullshit. "So, what happened? Did you take her home? Call her? What?"

"I couldn't take her home," he says, rolling his eyes. "Her friend was a major cockblock."

I smirk.

"She was! She was a double-bagger too. I hate that, y'know? When the busted chick rules the roost and makes sure that if she can't get it, nobody can?"

I laugh. "What are you even saying right now?" This man is an *attorney*. Like, for a *job*. The only reason I can be friends with such a dirtbag is because I know his daddy issues are even worse than mine. Not that he'd ever talk about it—unless you get him good and sloshed.

"You know what I mean," he says. "Whatevs. I texted her yesterday."

"And?"

"She's down."

"Yeah? Down for what?"

"You know. Down for whatever, I guess." He smiles.

"So, when are you seeing her?"

"Not sure," he says, taking a gulp of his coffee. "She said her mom's real sick or something. Said she'd let me know."

Sounds like code for *Please never text me again*. But I nod anyway. "Good stuff, bro. Sounds like she's got real potential."

"You should've come with us, C. Fireballs is the *spot* right now."

Fireballs is a dumpy shit-den where fresh-out-of-college kids go to eat ten-cent wings and drink cheap beer on tap. With zero regard for fire regulations, the bouncers let people in until they're packed shoulder-to-shoulder like sardines, and it often smells a little like a mix of body odor and hot-sauce-flavored puke. For all I know, *Grace Landing* was Undertitty Girl. "Yeah, next time. Hey, what was her name?"

"I forget. Leelee or Lala or some L name like that. Why?"

"Just curious. She sounds real sophisticated, bro." I laugh.

Dom smirks. "I'm sorry, hot shot. What'd *you* do this weekend?"

"Nothing, really. Laundry. Grocery shopping. This," I say, referring to our time right now. I neglect to mention the fact that I was verbally accosted via the Internet. He'd jump all over that.

"It makes sense that you work in estate law. You behave like a dead person."

"I behave like a grown-ass man," I say.

"You know what place is lit right now?" he continues.

I shake my head.

"You ever heard of Waxed? The new underground strip club?"

I laugh. "Dude, are we gonna hit some balls or what?"

"Oh, you'd get your balls taken *care* of at Waxed, that's for sure."

I unzip my gear bag and grab my glove. "You're a real class act, you know that?"

"Fuck yeah, I am." He winks.

I hate to think it, but *this* is the kind of guy who deserves scathing, drunk emails. Not me. I stretch out my arms and breathe in the crisp smell of morning dew, refusing to let Grace Landing take up any more of my head space today.

Gracie

The worst thing about being an author is the self-discipline it requires. Well, that and the fact the money's not so great. You get that MFA and think, "This is it! I'm gonna be a superstar!" and take a knee while throwing your hands up in the air like that old Mary Catherine Gallagher bit on SNL, but in real life you're lucky if you get a five-figure advance and make it onto a few key Amazon book lists. You have to be, like, *so* good at managing your personal finances because if not, you'll end up broke as hell, working a day job at Starbucks because they offer health insurance.

Which is what I'm thinking about on Monday when I *should* be working on my new novel, due to Lindsay Ellerton, my agent, in exactly two months.

Procrastinating is one of my best attributes. No joke. When I die, that's gonna be in my eulogy. "Gracie Landing was a beautiful soul. Her ability to procrastinate set the bar for all of us." I have three favorite ways to procrastinate: 1) watch music videos and pretend that the ingenue/lead singer/booty girl is me, 2) compulsively check my email, and 3) go to the bathroom. Today, it's number two that gets me in trouble. No! Not number two, like on the toilet. Number two on the *list*! (Gross!)

I'm checking email, and of course, my daily Starbucks Rewards message gets me thinking about the solid benefits package I could be having (not to mention all the discounted beverages). When I come back to my senses, I see that I have a new message from Colin Yarmouth.

Colin Yarmouth? As in, the hottest guy on the boys' varsity baseball team in high school? The kid who issued me my not-so-clever nickname, "Elvis," because my name reminded him of Graceland? The boy I used to think about when I was making out with my *actual* high school boyfriend, Ronald, whose cystic acne was surpassed only by his gigantic schnoz?

Why is Colin Yarmouth emailing me?

TO: Grace Landing (gracie222@mail.com)
FROM: Colin Yarmouth (cyarmouth@
    yarmouthaycockpc.com)
RE: yearbook

Dear Grace,

I am in receipt of your email from this weekend. I read it several times and can only wonder if perhaps you were inebriated when you wrote it. In any event, I apologize for any undue stress your nickname caused you, both in high school and now, all these years later. I certainly never meant to offend you,

just as I'm sure that you didn't mean to wish obesity
and hair loss on me in your message.

Best,
Colin

Oh, *no*.

It's coming back to me now. I vaguely recall how Saturday night
ended. We were at the House of Yes in Bushwick, and after trying
my hand at the aerial hoop (which did not end well), my girls,
Tori, Melly, and Alisha sent me home in an Uber. These are my *real*
friends too. Like, since rooming together back at Boston College.

I fell down—that's what happened. No. Wait. I slipped on
my own vomit, and *then* fell down. *Yes*, that's what it was. Okay. I
would've sent me home in an Uber too.

But it wasn't *all* my fault! It was Scott! Why couldn't he just
remove me from following him on Instagram like a *normal* ex-
fiancé would? I couldn't unfollow *him*—that would make me look
like such a loser! Like I care about his stupid baby pictures or his
bimbo trophy wife!

So, yeah. There was extreme drinking. And when I got home,
I cut all my thongs in half because those were the panties I bought
specifically because Scott was a self-proclaimed "ass man." Ass*hole*
is more like it. Whatever—my granny panties are a hell of a lot
more comfortable anyway. And then. And *then*. I played the yearbook game. That's right. The one where you flip through your
high school yearbook and send a drunk text to whoever comes
up on the page you land on. Only I was playing by myself, and

I didn't have Colin Yarmouth's number. Okay, okay. Busted. If we're being completely honest, the page flip might not have been *entirely* accidental. I'd been using my yearbook to come up with ideas for characters for my new manuscript, and it's *possible* that I might have been studying his picture on the varsity soccer page a few days ago. You know, for research.

Oh, *God*.

I reread the email. Is that from his *work* account? What have I *done*?

Well, this is just great. Now I'll *never* get any writing done today.

Except, of course, for a response to this email. But first, let me check out his website. Oh. *Damn*. Yeah, he's still hot. Way hotter than his partner, Gordon Aycock. I can only imagine the nicknames he tosses around that office.

TO: Colin Yarmouth (cyarmouth@
yarmouthaycockpc.com)
FROM: Grace Landing (gracie222@mail.com)
RE: yearbook

Dear Colin,

I am so sorry. Yes, your assumption that I was under the influence is an accurate one. I should not have emailed you. I am mortified. Please go back to your undoubtedly perfect life and forget all about this unfortunate incident.

Regards,

Grace

P.S. You look very athletic, and your hair is well-coiffed. Please disregard any comments to the contrary.

I hit *send* and go back to work. And by work, I mean making myself a sandwich.

Thirty minutes later, I glue my butt to the chair. No more excuses. I flip back a few pages and reread what I wrote on Friday, before the events of my shameful weekend occurred.

Shit. It's literal garbage.

I hate every word.

The story I'm working on is a thinly veiled, fluffy romance where a gorgeous Realtor named Presley suddenly finds herself broke and needs to sell one of her properties quickly. She posts ads everywhere and gets a response from her high school sweetheart, a drop-dead gorgeous beefcake named Connor.

I know, I know. Like I said, thinly veiled.

Anyway, Connor makes an appointment to see the place and Presley tries to seduce him. It's bad. She bakes chocolate chip cookies (referred to in the story as "golden orbs of chocolatey bliss," which is horrible writing but absolute truth, and the recipe I've perfected makes me horny just thinking about them) so the apartment smells sweet, and then she shows him the view and takes him into the bedroom, where they reminisce over their prom night together.

It's funny to read, because man, do I have some imagination.

Colin Yarmouth would never have *dreamed* of choosing me as a prom date. Instead, my *real* prom night was spent with my cousin Jerald, who insisted I attend *the* milestone event of my teen years and drove his slick-looking red VW Jetta all the way down from Connecticut to take me. He's older than me by six years and extremely good looking. I'm pretty sure there were whispers of me having possibly hired an escort.

Anyway, Presley and Connor are in the bedroom, and she creates this moment where there's a pause before Presley pulls him into her. When he kisses her, she compares it to the "sweetness of a Moscato mixed with the raw sensuality of a juicy, fresh-cut porterhouse steak."

I reread that line. Sounds disgusting and delicious, all at the same time. Where did I come up with that? Ah, whatever. That's the beauty of first drafts. They don't have to be polished. I force myself not to fall into a daydream where I have enough money to afford both wine *and* steak in the same meal. Instead, I keep reading.

Presley and Connor go at it with their clothes on, engaging in full-on dry-humping foreplay, which is as descriptive as humanly possible to stir up the loins of all those lascivious readers, per the advice of Shirley Temple (swear to God, that's her real name), the woman who edited my last trilogy over at Grand Imperial Books. We're talking tongues circling, hair-pulling, a detailed paragraph about Connor's ass cheeks, and a case study on his erection. It's smut. Connor is the Colin Yarmouth of my teenage fantasies, like a page ripped right out of an old diary. He's beautiful, sexy, and smoldering, but of course (because every story needs a conflict), he's married to somebody else. The section ends with

Connor's wife, Melinda, walking in on them, and alas—trope of all tropes—we have ourselves a love triangle.

It's textbook. Been done before. The only thing that's different is that in this case, the protagonist (Presley) is supposed to be likeable, despite her motives of seducing Connor so he'll buy her apartment and save her from financial ruin, a move which I think most female readers will agree does not exactly create warm and fuzzy feelings. Also, where exactly is the story *going*?

This is the issue I've been struggling with ever since I submitted the last manuscript.

Once Scott ended things—or, I should say—once the fetus he planted into someone else's womb ended things, I had what Lindsay called a "rough spot" there for a bit. I can usually churn out pages like it's nobody's business. But in order to write romance novels, you need to a) be willing to get down and dirty with anatomical descriptions, and b) be a true believer in the concept of happily-ever-after.

I've got the anatomy stuff down cold, but I don't know how to get my optimism back after what Scott did to me.

Lindsay, who seems to let nothing faze her, suggested I "buck up and try something new." I don't do *new* very well though. So, I guess that's why instead I went backwards—back to high school—back to a world that was less than accepting of my nerdy, awkward self—and figured I'd try to rewrite the ending.

But a girl trying to nail a married guy so that he'll buy an apartment from her? That's not exactly protagonist material. (Let's be real. It's got *man-hating pessimist* written all over it.)

I bang my head down on the keyboard. The sound is so loud that I don't hear the *ping* of my inbox.

Colin

I have a good job. It pays the bills. Hell, it pays the mortgage for the house on Long Island *and* my apartment.

But the job itself? It really sucks sometimes.

My grandfather started the firm in the 1960s, and he passed it down to my dad, who worked there from 1991 until last year, when he technically retired. I say *technically* because he never cleaned out his office. It sits there like a shrine to him, basically a reminder that he can come back whenever the mood strikes.

Like during softball season.

He claps, loudly, three times as he struts through the double glass doors into the reception area. As if we needed an announcement that John Yarmouth was officially in the building. His full head of white hair is covered by a baseball cap, a stark contrast to his tucked in button-down shirt and khakis.

"Hey, hey now, team!" he calls out.

I sigh, push my chair away from my desk, and poke my head out of my office door.

"There's my ace in the hole!" Dad booms.

Poor Daisy—the sixty-six-year-old receptionist—is *on the*

phone, and either Dad's too blind to notice or too egocentric to care. At six foot three, he towers over the reception desk. "I'll have him call you back soon, Mr. Parker," she says with her hand cupped over the mouthpiece.

"Hey, Dad. What's up?" I ask.

Before he can respond, Gordon Aycock power walks his brown-nosing ass right past me and over to my dad. "So great to see you, Jack!"

My father's name is John Yarmouth. Gordon is the only dip-shit who calls him *Jack*.

"Hiya, sport!" Dad says, giving Gordon a heavy-handed pat on the back.

"To what do we owe this great honor?" Gordon says.

I look at Daisy. She rolls her eyes at me and hangs up the phone.

"Team uniforms!" he announces.

Gordon looks around. "Where are they? Are they in the car? You want me to go get them?"

"That'd be great, Gordy. Thanks," my dad says, handing him the keys.

"No prob. Be right back!" he announces, rushing out the door.

"Hi John," Daisy says. "Sorry about that—I had a client on the phone."

"Good to see you, Daisy! No problem at all! Love to catch people working hard." He looks my way. "What about you, son? Busy day, today?"

"Yup. Sure is." *My schedule is literally empty.* "Right, Daisy?"

"Oh, yeah. Colin's got a Zoom meeting in about ten minutes and then a call right after that," she corroborates.

"Well, we better get you your uniform straight away then. Let me get a look at you!" I emerge fully into the reception area. He nods. "Okay, okay. Not bad. What do you bench these days?"

Nope. I run and lift free weights, but I haven't used the bench press since college. "About 180," I say.

"And what do you weigh?" he asks.

Daisy raises an eyebrow.

"About the same, Dad."

"Colin, Colin. Those are rookie numbers! Kids your age should be benching more than a hundred percent of their body weight, you know?"

"I'm sorry. *Kids* my age? I'm thirty-one years old."

"Yeah, I know, but you get my drift. You can push a little harder. Put in a few two-a-days at the gym. You'll be benching at least two hundred in no time." He gives Daisy a wink. She gives me the side eye.

"And what exactly do *you* bench, Dad?" I ask, but I'm interrupted by Ass-Hat-Aycock, who has returned with a big cardboard box in tow.

"Here ya go, Jack!" he says, breathing like he just finished running the goddamned New York Marathon.

Aycock sets the box down at Dad's feet like a sacrificial offering. Then, he grabs scissors off Daisy's desk and slices into the tape across the top of the box. My father reaches down and holds up a blazing red T-shirt. *Kiss of Death*, it reads in cursive writing.

That's our team name.

A few years back, Dad partnered us up with the law offices of D'Aleo and Strauss down the hall. They're divorce attorneys. Their practice is a little bigger than ours, but together we've got enough bodies to create one complete softball team for the Corporate Slow-Pitch League in Central Park.

That was how I met Dom D'Aleo. He became my divorce attorney.

So I guess the team's not a total wash.

They've got Dom, his business partner Richie Strauss (who's about forty and jacked out of his mind), a handful of paras—Jessica, Courtney, and Mark—and two assistants (because Dom doesn't like to share), Rachel and Raoul. They're all young and in pretty decent shape. By contrast, we bring to the table Gordon Aycock (who is about my age but looks like the only sport he might have played in high school was chess), my sixty-nine-year-old father, and my girl Daisy, who packs us all snacks on game days but hasn't had a hit in three years. And me.

We're a fucking dream team.

When Dad took the company over from his father, it was just him and Daisy and a revolving door of paralegals who came and went on their way up the ladder.

Gordon Aycock was one such paralegal. Only he never left.

You would think estate planning was fun, the way he behaved. He was in law school at NYU when I was at Cardozo. On a *scholarship*. Making my family proud, or so you'd think.

I'll never forget the day my dad hired Gordon. He came home from work late (as usual) and, while Mom and I were having dinner, announced, "Colin! I found a diamond in the rough today. He's going to give you a run for your money, son. I can *tell*."

Wondering what the hell he was talking about, I pushed for more intel.

4.0 out of Georgetown, born and raised in Manhattan, went to Bronx Science (excuse me, as if I was nothing just because I didn't go to a *specialized* high school), and just *dying* to study estate law, pun fully intended. I was focusing on law school during the day and working for a construction company off the books on the weekends, so I didn't meet Gordon Aycock until after I passed the bar and started working at the firm as a junior partner.

I assumed, wrongly, that I would be his boss. I quickly learned that Gordon worked for nobody but my father. He was like a feral cat protecting his food source, but with an added layer of passive-aggressiveness reserved for little bitches. He'd smile at my face while misfeeding my copies on purpose, ask how my weekend was while conveniently forgetting to give me my phone messages, and run to Starbucks for my dad without asking if I wanted anything.

He passed the bar the following summer and, to my surprise, immediately earned the title of junior partner as well.

When Dad retired, he left the firm to the two of us. I never thought about changing the name; I was used to it being called Yarmouth Estate Planning from all my years of childhood. So, you can imagine my surprise when Gordon hired a web developer to give us a "rebrand," complete with a new name, new business cards, and new email addresses. It was via *email* that I learned our new name was Yarmouth Aycock, P.C., and when I called my father to discuss that change with him, he responded, "Ah, that's

Gordy for you! Always a go-getter. Always taking the bull by the horns."

I updated the company policy after that. We don't hire paralegals anymore.

"I *love* the color, Jack," Gordy says now.

"You would. It brings out your eyes," I mutter.

Daisy smirks. "Thanks for the outfits, John," she says.

"They're not *outfits*! They're *uniforms*!" Dad says.

"They're great outfits," I sidebar to Daisy.

"Make sure you've all got a shirt that fits, and I'll deliver the rest down the hall," Dad says. Gordy picks out a medium shirt for himself, then holds another up against my dad's chest. "Whaddya think, Jack? Large? Or XL for you?"

"I've got it, Gordy. Thanks though, son."

Aycock steps back and returns the shirt to the box. Daisy walks over and grabs two large shirts, tossing one to me. It barely makes it over the reception counter.

"Sorry," she says.

"Nice throw, Daisy. We just need to work on your form a little before Sunday's game."

She smiles.

"Practice is Wednesday, 5:30 sharp. Colin! Make sure you hit the bench before then!"

"Hooyah, Master Chief!" I say with a mock salute.

"See you on the field!" Dad announces. Then, without asking, Gordy picks up the box, struggles to maneuver it while opening the door, and marches it down the hall. My father follows behind him, saluting me back.

When they're gone, I look at Daisy, who is shaking her head.

"Do me a favor, please?"

"Sure, sweetie. What do you need?"

"Hold my calls?"

"You got it, honey."

I go back in my office and close the door. Grateful for the reprieve from the surprise visit from Dad, I settle into my desk chair and check my email.

Really?

Grace Landing wrote me back.

Gracie

Tuesday. It's a new day. The sun is shining, a rarity in April in New York.

Because I'm an expert at procrastinating, I'm also an expert at getting shit done in short periods of time. Yesterday, I hit my word count by 4:30 in the afternoon and was gratefully celebrating my narrow avoidance of death by hunger with some well-deserved fettucine alfredo and garlic knots: a proper side dish to complement my steak sandwich.

Do you ever feel like food's just so *good*? I've been fascinated with it since I was a kid. I love tinkering in the kitchen, trying new recipes, mixing flavors until I come up with something just (insert chef's kiss) right. And, not kidding, I think food loves me back too, especially when I am the one preparing it. I can get *down* in the kitchen, and somehow everything I cook just comes to life.

Sadly, that's not always the case when it comes to Groupon-discounted takeout. Now, to mitigate the ramifications of all that processed cheese, this morning I'm taking my bloated, gassy self out for a run before I get started on today's word count.

With my water bottle in hand, I'm in the elevator considering which Spotify playlist to listen to, when I'm interrupted by a ding on my phone. It's an email. Probably spam, I figure, so I leave it alone and head out into the brisk air, which turns out to be an issue. The brisk air, that is. Sometimes when there's a sudden change in temperature, my body reacts by developing an instant stomachache as a defense mechanism. Like, "Whoa, get inside somewhere safe before the ice storm begins!" Usually, it passes. Well, sometimes. Okay, rarely. And it always gets worse as my bank account gets smaller, thanks to my creative brain inventing ways to stretch my grocery budget.

The only surefire way to create some relief is to let some air out of the tires, if you know what I mean. So, I glance around, and because there's nobody within a twelve-foot radius, I let her rip. Then, I immediately begin to jog, so as not to be associated with whatever regrettable aromatic situation might be left behind in the airspace in front of my building. It only takes a few steps for me to figure out that something's gone horribly awry.

At first, I assume it's sweat. I mean, let's face it, I'm not exactly in the best shape of my life. But I've only gone a few steps, and why would sweat emanate from my ass before the usual spots, like my armpits or the sports bra crease where my boobs meet my stomach?

Because it's *not* sweat.

Nope.

That would be an alfredo shart.

I recoil once I realize what's happened. Back in the building, I just make it onto the elevator as the doors are closing. An old lady with white hair and a white terrier to match are in the six-by-six space with me. By the time the elevator starts to move, the old lady gives me the hard side eye and the dog starts barking at me. Thank God I only live on the second floor. I should have taken the stairs.

I think this is God's way of telling me maybe I should cool it on the working out. I mean, he *couldn't* be telling me to make different food choices or else he wouldn't have allowed that pizzeria to open after the last one burned down.

Well, message received. And silver lining? It's a good thing I wasn't wearing a thong.

I shower, because, well, *obviously.* Then, I slide into some comfy sweats and sit down at my desk. I let out an audible groan when I see that the new email I got wasn't spam. It was the universe kicking me when I was down.

Yup, you guessed it—Colin Yarmouth.

Why can't he just leave well enough alone?

TO: Grace Landing (gracie222@mail.com)
FROM: Colin Yarmouth (cyarmouth@ yarmouthaycockpc.com)
RE: yearbook

Grace,
    It's okay. It's nice to hear from you. How have you been? (Other than intoxicated?)

Colin

P.S.—Why is the subject line of your email "year-book"?

Wow. First of all, it's barely 10 o'clock in the morning! How *dare* he imply—well, okay, fine, I *was* intoxicated at the point of first contact. But it's not like I have a drinking *problem*. Why is he writing back, anyway? If he wants to know how I'm doing, why can't he stalk me on the Internet like normal people do?

Ugh. How would I respond to this anyway? I'm thirty-one years old with no marriage or even *dating* prospects on the horizon, and unless I go the route of insemination or cavorting with a male sex worker, my chances of motherhood dwindle with each passing monthly cycle. I'm five-six, 145 pounds but still sporting an A-cup, and my prize-winning feature, my long chestnut-brown hair, was interrupted this morning by a wiry white strand that came out of my scalp and pointed itself directly toward the sky like an old television antenna. My friends all live in hip parts of the city, but I can't afford rent that high on my limited book-to-book advances and paltry monthly checks that look more like welfare payments than the "royalties" I'm told they are. My cat, Dorian Gray, is my only confidante—aside from my journal—and my parents keep nudging me to move back home to Westchester. If I do that, it will only be so that I can dig myself a shallow grave in their backyard and jump in headfirst.

It's not like Colin Yarmouth actually *cares* how I'm doing, anyway. I'm sure he's only asking so he's got a funny anecdote to share at some upcoming cocktail party he's been invited to with other *esquires* and their tiny supermodel wives. This is what I get for trying to write about him in my manuscript. The damn universe clearly favors beautiful popular people over average girls like me.

> **TO:** Colin Yarmouth (cyarmouth@
>   yarmouthaycockpc.com)
> **FROM:** Grace Landing (gracie222@mail.com)
> **RE:** yearbook

> If you must know, I was only intoxicated because I was out celebrating with my girlfriends that night.
>   Also, I wrote "yearbook" in the subject line because during the night in question, I flipped to a random page in our high school yearbook and saw a picture of you, which was what prompted my initial email. Again, not exactly my finest moment.

> Stay well,
> Grace

Celebrating—ha! Way to spin an evening of shameful downward spiraling into a "glass half full" situation! Anyway, that oughta do it. Now hopefully he'll leave me alone so I can get back to work.

Evidently not. At lunchtime, I get a response.

> **TO:** Grace Landing (gracie222@mail.com)
> **FROM:** Colin Yarmouth (cyarmouth@
>   yarmouthaycockpc.com)
> **RE:** yearbook

Celebrating what? Birthday? Engagement? Promotion at work? (I assume not pregnancy, given the alcohol involved.)

I haven't seen my yearbook since college. I think it's living in a box in my parents' basement.

Colin

Why the inquisition? I wonder. I won't let him derail me from my word count today though. It's homemade pear and gorgonzola salad with lime vinaigrette for dinner at five o'clock sharp, a glorious meal that won't send me into a gassy oblivion. (Unless the store-brand gorgonzola crumbles have gone bad—an absolute possibility since the tub was on sale as a "manager's special.")

But it's gnawing at me, the knowledge that he just wants to use this whole story to make fun of me. That's all Colin Yarmouth has ever done. He sat behind me in tenth grade Spanish and used to make comments about everything from my small handwriting to my wide back to my perfect quiz grades to—oh. Oh, I see it now. Yep. He was definitely trying to cheat off me in Spanish.

This ends now! I have *enough* going on in my life. I don't need *this* aggravation.

TO: Colin Yarmouth (cyarmouth@
yarmouthaycockpc.com)
FROM: Grace Landing (gracie222@mail.com)
RE: yearbook

Listen, buddy, I don't know why you all of a sudden *care* about my life. All you ever needed from me was a decent Spanish grade—that's right! I figured you out! Cheater!

Now, if you'll please excuse me, I'm sure you have something better to do in your fancy law firm today than chitchat with the likes of me.

Have a nice life,
Grace

Ah, vindication. To know where you stand and get to have the last word. I feel as free as a child experiencing the Sizzler buffet for the first time, going back for thirds and fourths without any consideration for the inevitable implications of mixing unlimited corn fritters and soft-serve ice cream in the same meal. (Sidebar: Why did they ever close the Sizzler buffet? It was a national treasure, and now what are we left with? Crapplebee's? The Cheesecock Factory?) Now I can get back to work on this fine Tuesday, unbeleaguered by useless email exchanges.

In fact, I close my email account tab so I won't even be tempted to look at it. No distractions!

After a quick nap, I get a phone call. It's Lindsay. Weird. She rarely calls—she sends a once-a-week check-in email, but only when I'm on deadline—and that's about it.

"Hello?"

"Grace, are you sitting down?"

"Always," I reply. "What's up?"

"We got an offer."

"For *Reckless Outlaw*?"

"Yes! Cabaret Books offered $500,000!"

Shut the fuck up. This can't be real. "For *that* piece of smut?"

"They think it's the next *Fifty Shades*. They loved it!"

No way. There's got to be a catch. "Are you sure you have your currency correct? They didn't offer, like, five hundred thousand pesos?"

"Yes, I'm sure! I hope you've got some champagne at home, because Karlie London's about to become hella famous, girl!"

"Um, cool! Wow! Of *course* I have champagne in the house. I mean, my whole *life* is just one big party," I say. Really, I have two bottles of champagne left over from my bridal shower that I can't bring myself to drink, collecting grime in the back of my fridge. I keep them just in case the sad day comes when I can no longer afford groceries and need to be resourceful about finding sources of potential sustenance.

"Well, before you pour, there's two little things."

I knew it. Here it comes. "What's up?" I ask, my head spinning like the Gravitron at the annual Our Lady of the Angels carnival back in elementary school.

"Well, first of all, it's not a done deal quite yet. The editor I pitched it to is working on the deal. There's an acquisitions meeting in a few days, and *that's* when we'll know for sure."

"So…we *don't* have an offer?"

"No, no. We do. She's just…working on it. Which brings me to my second point. She wanted to know if you had anything in the works. She thinks they'd be open to considering a two-book deal if you had anything else to pitch to them."

A two-book deal?

"I told them you've been working on a new manuscript for the past six months and it's supposed to be ready in about four weeks. But we can push up the deadline on that, right? Say, to two weeks?"

"Two *weeks*? How come?"

"Well, I mean, you told me you're killing it with your word count. So based on that, I figured you could just grind it out a little harder for the next two weeks and get it done. I mean, it's not like you have a day job or anything," Lindsay points out. "No offense."

"Uh huh." *Super-size offense, bitch.*

"It doesn't have to be polished, Grace. Just give 'em your best shot. I really don't think they're going to say no."

"And how would that change the numbers?"

"Well, if you add in a second book, they said they'd up the advance to seven fifty."

"Oh my God! $750,000?"

"I can't make this shit up, girl. I say let's hop on the surfboard and ride this wave. Who knows when we'll be able to make it rain like this again?"

My eyes cross just thinking about it. I know Lindsay's pushing because she's got skin in the game too—exactly 15 percent of whatever I bring in belongs to her as my agent. And an extra $250,000 for me means an extra $37,500 for her. I also have it on good authority (via Lindsay's chatty assistant, Evan—who, in my opinion, is the best thing about her) that she's been going through some sort of midlife crisis recently. Lindsay's tight-lipped about her personal life, but in this case, her tone says it all: she's hungry for a big payday.

But two weeks?

"Do you think you can hold them off for an extra week?" Because, if we're being totally honest, this new manuscript hasn't exactly been, um, flowing. Of course, I haven't told Lindsay that.

"I can try, but you know the biz. Fickle as hell. I don't want them to change their minds."

"I hear ya."

"Can I say yes, then?" Lindsay asks.

I inhale and shut my eyes. That's the other thing. These are shark-infested waters I'm swimming in. Except I'm not a shark. I'm more like a guppy. And the whole reason I *signed* with Lindsay was because I thought I needed someone shark-y to represent me. Well, that and the fact that she was the only agent who offered. But now, it looks like we're here. This isn't chump change. This is a major deal! They'd definitely give me a publicist, put me on tour, hell, maybe we could even sell a film option. Only a crazy person would say no to this. "Okay," I say. "Go for it."

"Amazing! I'll call you back later with more details! You go write something brilliant, Karlie London."

We hang up, and I'm unsettled. I mean, maybe if I had some decent pages already in the works, I could bang out the rest. But, seeing as how the pages I've got would be best suited for lining a birdcage or picking up dog shit on the side of the road, I can't get myself hyped the way I should be. Also, I love writing, but I don't know if I want Karlie London to become, like, a household name.

Oh, yeah. I should explain. *Karlie London* is my pseudonym.

I mean, after being called "Elvis" for all of high school, y'know. Screw me once, shame on you, and such. Karlie London is sophisticated. Karlie London is a woman for the ages. Karlie London would never shart in public.

Of course, she bears my face, hence my concern.

$750,000. *Damn.* That's a *lot* of money.

Now what? I'm super tempted to call Scott—or better yet—post a picture of myself on IG rolling around in a bed full of dollar bills like Demi Moore in *Indecent Proposal*, because I'm so rich I can just *do* things like that (#bestdayever! #betyouwishyoustayedwithmenowassface!) but then I remember I have $243 in my *actual* bank account at the present moment. So, okay. Maybe hold off on telling people.

If Lindsay needs a new project stat, then I'm gonna need to bring out the big guns.

I go to the fridge and pull an old sugar-free Red Bull out of the bottom drawer. It's my own personal, in-case-of-emergency-break-this-glass trick for churning out pages quickly.

I park my butt in the chair and stare at the laptop. Before too long, it's spilling out of me. The reader gets a rundown of all the properties Presley owns and exactly how broke she is, due to losing all of her high-falutin' city renters during the pandemic. (I have to be careful writing about the pandemic. Lindsay told me nobody wants to even *think* about it, even though the hard-core lockdown phase has been over for almost two years.) Presley put the condo worth the most money on the market—the one she was trying to sell to Connor. As she's reviewing her money situation, she gets a text from him, apologizing for what happened with his wife earlier that day. She ignores it, instead focusing on how to drum up interested buyers. She decides to plan an elaborate open house with what little money she has left in her bank account.

Man, this is a massive disparity from my real life. When I got my condo in Brooklyn, there were no fancy open houses, no balloons, no fanfare. Nope. Only the ghost of Melly's recently dead grandmother, who left behind an immovable, dusty piano, and a sympathetic daughter (Melly's mom), who decided that, instead of dealing with Realtors, she would sell the apartment to *me*, her only child's best friend from college, for well below market value.

If only Presley was so lucky.

I've only written six pages, but by the time I take my next break, my heart is racing, thanks to the eighty million milligrams of caffeine still working their way through my system. My mind flutters about from one topic to the next; thoughts of moving out of Brooklyn and reinstituting doctor's visits for preventative care give way to consideration for a new headshot taken by someone more qualified than the Midwood High School photography club. I want to *talk* to someone, but my girls are working, and if I call my mom, she'll just launch into an hour-long diatribe about how her housekeeper, Sheila, is stealing rolls of toilet paper out of the garage. She's sure of it but hasn't been able to prove it yet. And Dad just corroborates her lunacy, filing it away under his "happy wife, happy life" mantra.

So, I do what any normal person would do under these circumstances. I check my email.

What do you know? I guess Colin Yarmouth can't take a hint.

TO: Grace Landing (gracie222@mail.com)
FROM: Colin Yarmouth (cyarmouth@
      yarmouthaycockpc.com)
SUBJECT: Spanish class

Grace,

You're right. I'm humiliated to say that I did try to cheat off you in Spanish a few times. Lo siento, lol.

You're funny!

Anyway, you never answered my question. What were you out celebrating? Engagement? Bachelor-ette party? Also—when you say *girlfriends*, do you mean friends who are girls?

Write back (for real this time)—
Colin

I don't know. I'm in some kind of mood now. *Friends who are girls?* What is this—fifth grade? And, as to the interrogation that has become this correspondence—perhaps you haven't heard, *Colin*, but I am about to become an *almost-millionaire* thanks to my skillful writing capacity, however misguided its reception might be by the likes of well-bred attorneys such as yourself. So perhaps I was just out celebrating *my awesomeness*! Ever thought of *that*?

Men are so dumb sometimes! I am a *romance* novelist, not a professional email composer. The fact that he clearly found my scathing reveal of his debauchery amusing only goes to show that

I am as charming as I am wealthy. (Or, perhaps, that Colin is as stupid as he is beautiful.) Alas, I *will* write back "for real," if only to elicit more compliments.

TO: Colin Yarmouth (cyarmouth@
   yarmouthaycockpc.com)
FROM: Grace Landing (gracie222@mail.com)
RE: Spanish class

Colin,

I was celebrating a business deal with my BFFs from college. I'm a ghostwriter. It's a very illustrious profession. I can't tell you any more about it or else I'll have to kill you. (Kidding, relax.)

Sidebar: I've opted out on the whole marriage/ kids thing because it feels cliché to me. Like, who *doesn't* have a house in the suburbs and the requisite number of tax-write-off dependents? I prefer to march to the beat of my own drummer. Live life on my own terms. So no big engagement celebrations here, thank you very much.

What about you? I'm sure your wife and children are just lovely. Which New York suburb do you live in: Westchester, Rockland, or Long Island?

Regards,
Grace

Despite my obvious overshare, I hit *send* and close the laptop because I can't sit still. *$750,000.* This calls for a midafternoon pick-me-up! I head out to—where else?—Starbucks, for a venti decaf caramel whipped cream concoction pretending to be coffee (because Lord knows if I have any more caffeine, my heart may literally implode on itself like a sinkhole), with a single cake pop on the side for good measure. Sure, it's seven bucks down the drain, but what's a little frivolity now that there's real money on the horizon?

Colin

Well, this is unexpected. Grace Landing and I appear to be corresponding via email.

I remember the first time I met her. Sort of. We were lab partners, but then our teacher got hit by a truck or something, so some new guy came along and switched everyone around. I ended up with Alexis. *That* girl, I remember. She tried to go down on me during a field trip to the Hayden Planetarium. Not in the planetarium itself, but on the school bus. We kept hitting bumps though—like *big* bumps—and she bit down by accident during one of them.

I got phantom pains every time I saw her after that, so I did what any reasonable fourteen-year-old boy would do.

I broke up with her.

Grace, on the other hand, never struck me as the type to be daring or promiscuous like that. She had nice hair, and I think she was pretty. On the shy side, if memory serves.

Evidently, I scarred her for life.

She's funnier than I remember. I can't believe she called me out on cheating off her in Spanish. I don't exactly remember doing it, but I'm sure she's right, because I *suck* at foreign languages. I tried to use that app, Duolingo, not too long ago, but I nearly broke my phone when I insisted that *Tu madre es una pastel de caballo* meant *Your mother has gray hair*. (Apparently, it does not mean that. Loosely translated, it means *Your mother is a horse cake*.)

I don't try to better myself with that kind of stuff anymore. I stick to things I'm already good at. Running. Working out. Watching television.

I reread her note. A *ghostwriter*? That's kind of interesting.

When I was in high school, I didn't know what a ghostwriter was. I thought it was kind of like the same thing as a secret admirer. Now *that* I was familiar with. I used to get crazy love letters, like dating back all the way back to my freshman year. The first one was innocuous enough. It said something like:

> *Hey Colin,*
>
> *You're so hot. I wish you would make out with me.*
>
> *Love,*
> *Your Secret Admirer*

I didn't pay much attention to it. I figured it was the guys on the team pranking me. They had all kinds of hazing rituals that involved things like shaving heads and toilet-papering houses, but I think the coach told them to take it easy on me since I was so young, so it made sense that they'd start writing me fake love notes.

I kept it though, just in case.

The guys never acted different, and the notes kept coming. Each note was longer than the last and way more descriptive. By the middle of the soccer season, they were looking more like this:

> *Dear Colin,*
>
> *I have never in my young life felt the way I do when I'm around you. My body tingles and my senses come alive. My hands want to feel your skin; my fingers long to graze your lips. The scent of your hair makes me unravel. When I see you change into your soccer uniform, I am left to wildly imagine what you're hiding inside those shorts. I cannot help but think about what I would do to you if given the chance. I promise you, it would be nothing short of exhilarating.*
>
> *Love,*
> *Your Faithful Secret Admirer*

The letters kept coming, sometimes even twice a day, and each one got more and more raunchy than the next. Eventually, they were pages long, depicting entire scenes of me and this mystery girl in bed together, and I realized that either my teammates were amazing writers with ample time on their hands to craft dirty stories, or maybe, just maybe, there was a real-life *girl* behind all of it.

I kept the letters in a shoebox that I hid under my bed

containing a bottle of Jergens hand lotion and a lone *Playboy* magazine I'd found in the trunk of my dad's car. Even though they were weird, they were also kind of hot.

One day, right around Thanksgiving if I remember correctly, I got a letter that was four pages long. I was in the cafeteria with my brown bag lunch and the bell just rang to change periods, but since I had a double period off, I was sitting at the soccer table by myself for a few minutes while kids came and went. I slipped the note out of my bag, thinking I would just read the first few lines.

> *Dear Colin,*
>
> *I'm lying in bed and I can't stop thinking about you. I'm wearing a red lace bra and matching panties, picturing you beside me in only your underwear.*

With an opener like that though, I couldn't bring myself to just abandon ship, so I kept reading. A few minutes later, my fourteen-year-old dong was hard as a rock when a bunch of guys from the team sat down. I couldn't return the note to the safety of my backpack fast enough. Gus grabbed it and read it aloud for the entire cafeteria to hear. I tried to object at first, but I knew that would only make things worse, so I sat in embarrassment while they had their way with my precious reading material. I didn't look up; I was too mortified.

The seniors on the team decided to find my admirer in a mission they dubbed "Operation Hot Pocket." The following day, the note had been copied (and collated and stapled, courtesy of Justin's dad being a manager at Kinko's) what felt like a thousand times. It was circulated everywhere: hanging from bulletin boards, duct-taped to trees on campus, hanging from the walls of every boys' bathroom in school. My friend Joey Jukovic (a sophomore goalie) told me not to sweat it. The notes were doing wonders for my street cred, he said. Even *senior* girls were talking about me.

To my great relief, Principal Nieman shut down "Operation Hot Pocket" after two days. I never received another letter again after that. In fact, I never got my original of that last note back either. I had to take down a copy from one of the bathroom walls so the collection under my bed would be complete.

I thought *that* was what it meant to be a "ghostwriter."

Apparently, I was wrong. Wikipedia tells me that a ghost-writer is "someone who is hired to write literary or journalistic works, speeches, or other texts that are officially credited to another person as the author."

Well. That sounds way more boring, if you ask me.

Gracie

A ghostwriter, huh? That seems like a pretty cool job. I'd be interested to hear more. (Of course, I'm not trying to have you *kill* me.) What kinds of projects are you working on?

No suburbs for me either. I live in a co-op in Astoria. I did live on Long Island for a little while, but I moved back to Queens about six months ago. Where do you live? Are you still local?

Yes—I'm with you on the whole world's expectation that everyone should be married with children by age thirty. I'm an attorney running a successful practice! Shouldn't that count for something?

So, what is the schedule of a ghostwriter? Do you have an office or do you work from home?

Write back,

C.

Colin's email arrived well before 9:00 a.m. Can't a girl even finish her breakfast before being inundated?

Who am I kidding? I'm intrigued. He sounds alarmingly… available.

TO: Colin Yarmouth (cyarmouth@
   yarmouthaycockpc.com)
FROM: Grace Landing (gracie222@mail.com)
SUBJECT: Good morning

Well, you certainly like to get your day started early. To answer your questions, I work from home and so I am presently still in pajamas, which is probably my favorite thing about this job. But ghostwriting is only a part of what I do. That's when you are commissioned by other people to write their stories for them. I completed a book not too long ago about the history of ramen noodles. It sounds horribly boring. (Because it was—lol.) But it paid pretty well. I am also an author. I write fiction—novels, mostly.

That's a coincidence that you recently moved back to the city from Long Island. I was supposed to move out there—at the time, I was engaged. Let's just say that it didn't exactly work out the way I'd planned. I live in an apartment in Brooklyn instead.

Which is totally fine. I'd rather be single and happy
than married and miserable.

What kind of law do you practice?

Grace

I hit *send* and get to work. Fueled by sugar and coffee, I'm
ready to tackle my word count for the day. According to the calendar, my new deadline is May first. May Day. If I'm writing
an 80,000-word manuscript in fourteen days and so far I've only
penned 3,500 words, I've got to write somewhere around 5,500
words per day.

That's about twenty pages.

I take a breath and will the ideas to come.

Where were we? Oh, right. Presley's open house. I describe
it, all the details, all the hard work. I bring in a couple and show
them around, really setting the scene. Next—well, who should
show up but Connor Yates, of course? He has come under the
auspices of "open house," but naturally, he's really there to see
Presley and try to explain himself. I can't make that easy for him,
so I drop in a roadblock—a couple about to have a baby, who are
interested prospective buyers. The wife is horribly type A. Connor
fights me; he wants to be alone with Presley, so he needs to get
these two out of the way. He pretends to call his Realtor and make
an offer on the condo, within earshot of the couple, which, in
turn, makes the type-A girl crazy. She and her husband head into
the bedroom to discuss logistics, and Connor…hmm… Got it!
Connor hides in the front hall closet.

Okay, this sounds like it was written by a lunatic. But I have the prospect of financial security on my mind, so I have no choice. I have to push through and see where it takes me.

So. The couple is in the bedroom and Connor's in the closet. Let's bring the couple back out to talk to Presley. They ask if "the other guy" left, and Presley says yes. Then, they ask if she knows what he was planning to offer so they can outbid him.

A-ha! Connor *texts* her from the closet. Tell her full price, the message reads.

The lady calls the Realtor and puts in an offer for more than asking price. Presley is about to breathe a sigh of relief, grateful for Connor's interference, when…

His wife shows up! "Where is he, you little slut?" she asks.

I can't make this too much like the last time she came. I need to switch it up.

I take a long slurp of what remains of my coffee. Crunchy sugar granules dance on my teeth. My molars grind them up, and mixed with my spit, they become the elixir of the gods.

Block her, I decide. Bring in more visitors, a couple with their Realtor. Connor texts Presley from the closet, Get rid of her. But Presley's at a loss. She texts back, and then…

Ding! His phone goes off in the closet. Connor's wife, Melinda, hears it and all hell breaks loose. She flips out, screaming accusations at him. He tries to call her out for the fact that she's not much of a wife to him anyway; they haven't had sex in months, and he believes the *universe* brought him and Presley back together. The couple with the Realtor sneak out, not wanting to get involved in the ridiculous scene, and then…and then…

Shit. This is a new low for me. Melinda stabs Connor in the ass cheek with Presley's scissors. The ass cheek! I take a few stabs (ha! Literally!) at writing that line, and end up with this:

With an ass that round, Presley almost expected to hear a popping sound, as if it had been one of her decorative open house balloons. Connor twisted his torso to get a better look at the scissors half-submerged in his firm, plump rear.

Ugh. I need a break. Writing action scenes is too exhausting. I scan back over the work and do a quick page count. Not bad. Not bad at all.

All this talk of firm, plump asses awakens my body. I think I need to poop.

TO: Grace Landing (gracie222@mail.com)
FROM: Colin Yarmouth (cyarmouth@
   yarmouthaycockpc.com)
RE: Good morning

Hi,

   Yes, I typically like to get an early start on the day, you're right. There's a gym in my office building so I work out first thing and shower there. I'm usually at my desk by eight.

   I'm an estate planning attorney. It's my family's business—my dad was an estate planner, and so was my grandfather. Since I'm an only child, I was coerced to go to law school to take on the family business, but most days I don't mind it too much. I

never had a dream job—other than becoming a professional baseball player—but I tore my rotator cuff
in college and that was the end of that.

I didn't realize ramen noodles had a history long
enough to fill an actual book. I bet you'll never look
at them as a cheap, tasty lunch again.

I'm sorry to hear about your engagement, but I
agree with your thoughts on being single and happy
vs. being married and miserable. In the spirit of full
disclosure, I was married up until six months ago,
and I can say from personal experience that it's not
all it's cracked up to be. (Neither is Long Island. The
taxes are out of control!)

Tell me about your novels. Anything I might know
of?

Talk soon,
C.

I receive Colin's email after my midmorning snack of charcuterie. No, I'm not kidding. I have a gorgeous cheese board that
I like to use as often as fiscally possible. I roll up some slices of
fresh prosciutto and put out some cubes of cheddar, along with a
handful of grapes and a stack of water crackers, all purchased at
the grocery store yesterday after my writing session. (I was feeling
especially fancy when I chose the water crackers. They were on
sale, prompting the entire idea, but I got carried away and snack
time spiraled into a forty-plus-dollar event. Unfortunately, my

bank account is down to $190 now, but I'm sure I can make that last another few weeks. If not, that's why God invented emergency credit cards. Plus, real talk? It was a spectacular treat.)

I've learned from past mistakes that you should never own something as fun as a charcuterie board and *save* it for "special occasions," because it's highly likely that the people you saved it for will somehow end up not having been worth it in the long run. Then, you'll just end up lamenting all the missed opportunities you had to enjoy the thing all by yourself.

My dating history offers great proof of this point. I spent most of college just playing the field after I started seeing this fraternity boy my freshman year named Jack. He went to Boston University, not Boston College, and we met at a BU frat party that me and the girls crashed. It was loud, sweaty, and overflowing with the unique combined scent of grain alcohol punch and Axe body spray. We danced, and it was glorious. I'd never danced like that with a guy before—his junk grinding all up on my junk, the glazed look in his eyes basically screaming *I love you*. Okay, maybe not. But it *was* fun. We started "hanging out," which I took to mean "going steady" until a few days later when I came to surprise him at his dorm room and a half-naked girl answered the door. She had her hands over her boobs, and he was lying in bed. So, yeah. I learned very quickly that college is maybe not the best place to find a soul mate.

Once college ended, I moved back home and got a job working at *Breaking Bronx*, a weekly local rag that was distributed at the grocery stores and bodegas in my fine outer borough. I was a restaurant reviewer and was responsible for the "Food n' Stuff" column, which ranged from testing new recipes to secret shopping in grocery stores. It paid very little, but I was still living at home, so it didn't really matter. Plus, the beat reporter for sports, Malik Patel-Robinson, was *fine*. He was, like, music video hot, and he taught me the term "badunkadunk" at our first staff meeting together. Afterwards, I invited him to come with me to try out a new Caribbean restaurant, and I taught him the difference between Guyanese black pepper chicken and Jamaican jerk chicken. We started hanging out at work all the time, and he became my first real, adult boyfriend. We went to movies together, went out to eat, and got really creative in the sex department (we once did it on the picnic table in his tiny backyard) because we both lived at home with elderly grandmothers in addition to our parents, and if there's one thing I know, it's that elderly grandmothers are always home. Unfortunately, both of our families were too old-school to accept our relationship as anything other than "cute." I made the mistake of bringing him over for Christmas, where he met my parents and my nonna. There were so many raised eyebrows, Italian mutterings, and signs of the cross from my grandmother that I told Malik she had dementia, just not to have her seem like such a racist old bat. We broke up when he got a job working for a real newspaper in Manhattan and made enough money to move into his own place.

The next guy I dated had great potential, or so I thought. Luke was sweet and attractive but pretty bland. (A great fit for my grandmother, really.) I met him at a church pancake break-fast that I was covering for *Breaking Bronx*. The pancakes tasted like cardboard, but Luke was serving them, and I went back for seconds with fake questions in my mind to ask in the name of journalism. He thought I was funny and "sinfully hot" (his words, not mine) and we stayed together for about two years. Just long enough for him to decide he was called to serve the Lord and join the seminary.

I cannot make this shit up.

After Luke, I had a dry spell for a bit, at which point, my friend Melly suggested I try online dating. "Everyone's doing it," she implored me. I knew she was right, so even though it felt extremely *weird* to post pictures of myself on the Internet in search of a man (my first set of pics looked like I was trying out for a "Missing Persons" spot on the side of an old-school milk carton), I had to suck it up and deal with it. I put myself out there on sites like PlentyofFish, Bumble, and Tinder, and dated a whole lot of train wrecks while trying to navigate my way through this new terrain. If someone were to check my Google search history around that time, one might find such interesting queries as "how to know if you're being catfished" or "how to ghost a psycho."

I tried to focus on *me*, published my first book, saved my money, and moved out of my parents' house and into my current apartment in Brooklyn. Not too long after Melly's wedding, I turned twenty-nine. All of a sudden, with the big 3–0 on the imminent horizon, I began to panic in earnest, thinking I would never meet someone. In reality, Melly was the only one of my friends who was married, but something about the number drove me crazy, and I felt like with each day that passed, more and more guys were disappearing off the market.

I once read that the older you get, the less your eggs care

about which sperm they'll take. So, picture this: Your young, cute eggs are feelin' themselves, and they won't just bring home *any* sperm for insemination. Nope, they want that *good* sperm. Meanwhile, the eggs in reserve sit around aging, and by the time they're old, they'll take basically whichever sperm can make it all the way up the canal. Like the old egg is saying, "Hey, you made it here, might as well let you in," with a yawn and a careless shrug.

This is sort of what happened to me once I saw thirty looming. Convinced there would be nobody left on the market, I began discovering new websites to post my profile on.

I was twenty-nine and two months old (with one foot clearly in the grave) when I met Scott Gross on freezerburn.com, a dating app designed for women looking for love who are also considering freezing their eggs. The site's promise (*Find love in three ovulation cycles or receive a $500 credit towards egg freezing at one of our exclusive partner facilities!*) sounded like a win-win, and sure enough, I was matched with Scott halfway through my second month online. He checked all the surface criteria: 1) he was not living with his parents, 2) he had a full-time job, and 3) he had more hair on his head than on his body. (In fairness, he skated by on the last one. His lower back harbored a situation that he referred to as "peach fuzz," but if I ever saw a piece of fruit covered in long brown curly hairs like that I would assume it had gone very, very bad.) However, Scott's capacity for email was garbage, and it was only because I chide myself for being too hard on people that I accepted his invitation to go out on a date. I'll never forget the message: *Drinx @ mcsweenys? 7pm 2nite?*

McSweeney's, a pub known throughout Brooklyn for its hot

roast beef dip and wide variety of Irish ales on tap, was only a few stops away from my house on the Q train. I wore tight black jeans that showed off my curves, tall black boots, a flowy gray sweater, and a leather jacket. Scott showed up a few minutes late, but one flash of his sheepish grin and I was hooked. He admired my outfit, didn't say a word when I ordered the (technically sharable) cheese fries and ate them all myself, and blew out to the side when he burped after a long swig of his beer (instead of burping in my face). He reminded me of a bearded collie, with his hair pushed back in a trucker's cap, a first-trimester belly that he could still suck in if he wanted to covered up by an old Linkin Park T-shirt, and an average-looking lower half clad in a pair of loose-fitting jeans. He told corny jokes, still smoked weed on rare occasions, and watched football every Sunday with his friends from college at a bar in eastern Queens. He held in his farts when we had sex, but let them out right afterward, always announcing them first. He shared an apartment in Williamsburg with two other guys, so going to visit him was not unlike taking a trip to a fraternity house.

But Scott had a job in Manhattan, working as the tech guy for a small CPA firm, and he liked to watch movies, eat out, and sleep in on the weekends, which made us a pretty good match. I could live with the fact that the toilet seat at his place was always up (and you could bet on finding at least three or four stray pubes lining the rim), or that I could never leave a toothbrush at his apartment because I couldn't be sure it would remain unused by one of his drunk roommates. He was college educated and ordinary, which seemed nonthreatening, at the very least.

After dating for maybe a month or so, we began spending more and more time at my place, and because there was an actual kitchen there stocked with proper supplies like pots and pans, I learned that Scott liked to cook. His propensity for creating fun meals out of cheap household basics (like chicken and dumpling stew made with Bisquick or turkey and cheese rollups baked in crescent roll dough) took our relationship to the next level. *Finally! Some common ground!* I thought. I loved taste-testing Scott's creations, and he would revel in my excitement with that puppy-dog look in his eyes and heavy hints that I could reward him in the sack. *You like my chicken parm? Well, perhaps you'd like a taste of the meat stick in my pants for dessert!* Often, I obliged, because—well, isn't that what you're supposed to do in a relationship?—and I guess that made me a "keeper," because after the requisite trips to visit Mom and Dad on both sides, and after nine months of cohabitating at my place on my dime, Scott proposed to me after sex on my thirtieth birthday.

"We should get married," he said. "You wanna?"

That was it. No ring, no bravado. But I said yes, and it counted as a real proposal. We picked out a ring together, and over a big Italian dinner in the city, I asked Alisha, Tori, and Melly if they would be my bridesmaids. Melly was already married, and Alisha was engaged. Tori was anti-marriage, despite living with her girlfriend of four years. They were all so happy that I had finally found someone who checked off all my boxes, so of course, they eagerly agreed.

I should have taken it as a sign. My married name was going to be *Grace Gross*. The universe was definitely trying to tell me something.

Then, hunting season began. House hunting. Registry hunting. Dress hunting. I tried to keep my cool through it all. Scott could have cared less about any of the details. He felt the wedding was my job to plan, but I dragged him to everything, insisting that it was supposed to be the romantic affair of *our* dreams. We had a budget and my parents had given us ten grand. Melly—my maid of honor—had recently gone through the same thing, only her parents were super over-the-top generous, and she was *not* on a budget, so she enjoyed helping me navigate the "challenge" of dress shopping with financial restrictions. A natural shopper, she also loved reliving the trips to Bed Bath & Beyond with the scanner gun. We put together a binder of ideas, like a Pinterest board but in physical book form, while Scott tagged along, absently surfing the Internet on his phone, giving us the silent thumbs-up whenever we presented him with an idea. In retrospect, I could have suggested that we get married in a vat of green Jell-O, and he would have responded like the human form of an emoji.

About four months before our wedding, we were narrowing down venue options when, out of the blue, Scott's mother recommended a wedding planner. She was the daughter of a friend of the family, but Scott hadn't seen her since they were toddlers. Since she was just getting started in the business, she needed referrals and Scott's mother was happy to help. Scott didn't care—his mom's interference meant it was one thing less for him to do. But *I* cared: Hadn't she seen the binder I made? I was perfectly capable of planning my own wedding! And yet, I obliged, not wanting to piss off my soon-to-be mother-in-law.

Scott and I met Ilana Shapiro on a Saturday, that much I

remember. Scott made first contact on the telephone, and they made plans for us to all get together for breakfast.

Ilana was tiny, with blond, wavy hair, a pointy nose, and pouty lips. Even with heels on she made me look like a gorilla by comparison. She was skittish and giggly, and her voice was reminiscent of a baby.

I hated her from the moment I laid eyes on her.

We met in a diner on Long Island, and while Scott ate pancakes and I ate the meat-lover's omelet, Ilana ordered cottage cheese and fruit. She finished four whole bites of it before pushing it aside, claiming to be full. Then, we rode in her car from one wedding venue to the next. Scott sat in the front because he needed the leg space, and I sat in the back seat like a third wheel. After visiting seven different catering halls, we decided to call it quits for the day, and she dropped us off at the nearest Long Island Rail Road station.

"Well," I said, when we were seated side by side in the train car. "I'm never doing *that* again."

"I thought it was kinda cool," he replied. "Seeing all those places. I kept trying to figure out which one had the best bar setup."

I rolled my eyes. "How about this? You narrow it down to three venues, and I'll choose from the three."

"You sure?" he asked.

"Definitely," I said.

I didn't give it much thought after that. When I told Melly that my fiancé would be spending weekends alone visiting wedding halls with itty bitty Ilana Shapiro, she encouraged me not to worry. "He's marrying *you*. And the way you describe her, she sounds like one of those Minions from *Despicable Me*."

I laughed.

Little did I know, the joke was on me.

After more than two months of searching, Scott still couldn't come up with a top-three list of event spaces for me to check out. I was busy incessantly, between researching ramen noodles, creating a new Pinterest-inspired binder of house decorating ideas, meeting with our Realtor, and endlessly preparing for the details of our upcoming nuptials—which was particularly challenging without the venue booked. I should have thought it odd when he showed up at my place after 10 p.m. after long Saturdays with Ilana, but I chalked it up to him being diligent and genuinely searching for the right place for us to say, "I do." I did not expect that he would be depositing his seed in *her* garden instead, in the back of her stupid Jeep Cherokee, or—worse—in one of the catering hall bathrooms.

That was last July. By August, the stick turned blue I guess, because he told me we should "put a pin in the wedding plans for now." At the time, he cited feeling "confused about things."

Tori made me a voodoo doll of Scott, and I put pins in every part I could think of: through his eyes, in his mouth, up his ass, and in the empty space between his little stuffed legs where his dick should have been.

I kicked him out of my apartment, but, thanks to his own laziness, he never fully moved out of his place in Williamsburg, so he just went back there. He told me she was pregnant just before Thanksgiving, once she decided to keep the baby. Suddenly, his "confusion" made a lot more sense.

I never got a refund back from Ilana Shapiro for "services rendered," and I am now the proud owner of a $1,500 Maggie Sottero wedding gown that I can't return. Beauty and the Beast gave birth to a healthy baby boy, six pounds, fifteen ounces, twenty-two inches long on Friday, April thirteenth. Nobody saw the irony in that but me. And sure enough, they got married on Long Island—Ilana Shapiro was the wedding planner. "For my own wedding!" she boasted on Facebook. They moved into a house that *my* Realtor found for us and completely *stole* my happily ever after, leaving me with a bitter taste in my mouth for all things romance. It got so bad that this year, I bought myself a box of chocolates on Valentine's Day just so that I could light it on fire in my bathtub.

The struggle is real.

TO: Colin Yarmouth (cyarmouth@
yarmouthaycockpc.com)
FROM: Grace Landing (gracie222@mail.com)
RE: Good morning

No, you've probably never heard of any of my novels—I write women's fiction. Well, romance, to be honest.

I'm impressed that you get up so early to work out. I jog sometimes, but I'm not super faithful about it.

Speaking of faithful, that sucks about your divorce. I mean, it's good that you're happier now but it sucks to have to get divorced, especially only a few months into a marriage. I understand what you went through though. My ex-fiancé got our wedding planner pregnant. So yeah, that didn't work out as planned. It was also fairly recent. Their baby was born last week—oh!—in fact, it was the day before my initial drunk email to you. I went out for a girls' night to celebrate not having made the worst decision of my life and had one too many. (So, not exactly a work celebration—you can call me a *mentirosa* if you can figure out what that means—lol!)

Well, I gotta run. I have a big deadline coming up and I should really try and focus on my page count. Hope you have a good rest of your day.

Sincerely,
Grace

Big breath. *Concentrate, Gracie. Connor's been stabbed. Gotta help him out now.*

First, he needs to try and remove those scissors from his ass. Nope, no good. He can't reach. Plus, as Presley points out, blood stains hardwood floors. He's screaming and yelling but Melinda's gone, so Presley's stuck calling 9-1-1. He's whining like a baby—though, in fairness, this isn't exactly a paper cut. Presley asks Connor why he even *came* to the open house, and he says he wanted to see her again. He starts to explain that his marriage is "complicated," comparing it to a "business arrangement," but leaves it at that. The first responders arrive and make a big scene, which includes cutting his leg out of his pants, so Presley gets a good long look at what he's packing inside them. The EMTs are reminiscent of strippers, leaving Presley to fantasize about starring in a porn movie with them.

I shake my head. Ridiculous.

Whatever. I'll edit it later to make it sound less absurd. I don't love what I'm writing, but I guess it's better than writing *nothing*.

I check my page count and then the time. Whoa! It's after four and I didn't even stop for lunch. This never happens. I'm spent from writing, and don't have it in me to cook something healthy, so I order a pizza, because that's the easiest way to get hot food into my mouth without having to wait very long.

Then, I check my email, because… No, you know what? No explanations. I'm a *writer*. Email is just another form of *communication*.

TO: Grace Landing (gracie222@mail.com)
FROM: Colin Yarmouth (cyarmouth@ yarmouthaycockpc.com)
RE: Good morning

Now *I'm* the one who's impressed. Sounds like you've got a great work ethic. Makes me think I should be working on client files instead of sending you more email, but I couldn't just let your last note sit for the whole day without a response.

Your ex sounds like a total douche, if you don't mind me saying so. I'm really sorry you had to go through that. What *is* it with people these days? My ex-wife gave me an STD—it's a long emasculating story that I'm sure you'd rather not hear. Nothing a few dozen years of therapy can't fix though, I'm sure. (Sorry for the overshare. It's all cleared up now, by the way!) Makes you wonder though—doesn't anyone believe in the sanctity of marriage anymore?

Anyway, I completely understand why you might have been as drunk as you appeared in your original email. I would be wasted too if I were you.

Out of curiosity, what is your drink of choice? I don't actually drink very often, but when I do, I'm a whiskey/bourbon/scotch guy. Definitely no beer. Also, no vodka. A nice wine, sure, but only with food. You?

I have a meeting in a few minutes so I'm going to get going—for now. But don't leave me hanging!

Colin

Colin

Practice starts at 5:30 p.m., so after hitting *send* on a response email to Grace Landing, I shut down my laptop and ask Daisy how she's getting to the park.

"Cab, I guess," she says. "I'm getting too old to schlep all this crap cross town on foot." She gestures under her desk, where she's got an oversized L.L. Bean backpack with a metal bat sticking out of the top resting alongside a huge tote bag from Whole Foods.

I smile. "Let's share an Uber. My treat," I say. "What have you got in there?" I point at the Whole Foods bag.

"I baked snacks for practice. Homemade granola bars. Then, I thought maybe that wouldn't be enough, so I threw in a bag of tangerines, just in case anyone got low blood sugar and needed a quick pick-me-up." She shrugged. "Then, I figured we'd need water, so I got one of those twelve packs of tiny water bottles just in case anyone finished theirs and got thirsty. And I picked up some candy in case everyone thought all the snack choices were too healthy."

"So, you essentially packed an entire grocery store into a single bag."

Daisy blushes.

"You're too good," I say.

"I don't know what they like down the hall," she goes on.

"Are you kidding me? Dom will eat whatever. Richie will bring his own four pack of protein shakes. Jessica and Mark are easy. Courtney—not so much."

Daisy scowls. "Is she still giving you grief?"

"Not grief. She's just a wild card, you know? One minute, she acts like we're fine and the next she's crying to Jess that I'm the worst person she's ever met."

Daisy looks at me with an *I told you so* look but doesn't say anything.

"I know, I know. I've learned my lesson. No more one-nighters. At least not with girls from the team."

Daisy's like my work mom. She's known me since I was in grade school, and when I used to visit the firm as a kid, she'd help me with my homework or let me play Spider Solitaire on her computer. In my teenage years, she watched from afar as my dad proudly displayed articles from the local paper about my prowess on the field. She came to my graduation party after college, and when I became a junior partner, she baked me a cake and bought me a money tree for my office. By contrast, when Gordon Aycock was crowned junior partner, she raised an eyebrow at me and muttered, "What is he *thinking*?" in reference to my father. She's steadfast and loyal, and I appreciate that, especially since Gordy incessantly tries to undercut me.

I had a dog growing up. I had no siblings, so for my eighth birthday, my mom gave in to my constant begging and let me choose a rescue dog from the local animal shelter. I named her Chocolate Chip on account of the fact that she had black spots all over her back. Cici for short. Cici was part yellow lab, part Dalmatian, and I remember when they referred to her as a "Dalmador" at the shelter, I thought that sounded like the name of a cool Transformer or something, so I immediately took to her. She was fairly small when we brought her home, but in no time, she shot up and was (in my eyes) roughly the size of a small horse by the time I turned nine.

Cici and I were inseparable until I went to college. She was ten by that time and had slowed considerably. I was about to start my first year as a D1 pitcher for Arizona State. I'd gotten a scholarship and *Baseball America* listed me on their "Ones to Watch" list after I was the 121st pick in the fourth round of the MLB draft that year.

The Sun Devils were killing it my first year of college. We got into the playoffs, which was no surprise. My record was sick—I'd been recruited to the Cape Cod league for the summer based on my stats during the regular season and was flying high.

During the second game of the first round of the playoffs, I was pitching a no-hitter. It was the game of my life. I had perfect control over the strike zone.

It was the fifth inning. I had two strikes on a guy from Cal. All of a sudden, I threw a pitch and I felt something snap in my shoulder. It was swift and excruciating. My arm fell to my side, limp and throbbing.

Meanwhile, 2,400 miles away in the Bronx, my mom had just put Cici to sleep. She had brought her to the vet and found out she was being eaten up by cancer.

The timing was too close for me to chalk it up as being a coincidence.

I had to have surgery on my shoulder, and once my coaches realized the extent of the damage, I lost my baseball scholarship. I transferred back home and started in the prelaw program at Fordham. If we couldn't make it to the big leagues, Dad said, I had better be ready to take over the family business.

I kept up my end of the deal, but somehow, he's still fixated on me playing ball. Like, so much that my poor girl Daisy goes into snack prep overdrive every spring.

I carry her giant bag downstairs to meet the Uber, and we get to the park in about ten minutes. Gordon's already there, along with my dad and most of the D'Aleo and Strauss crew. Only Dom is missing.

"Hey now, slowpokes! Let's get it going!" my dad chirps from the bench alongside the third base line. He claps his hands a few times.

Gordon claps back at him. "Yeah, now, let's hear it for baseball!" he screeches. His voice cracks on the word *let's*.

Gordon is wearing a full uniform and I can't help but notice he has added the word *Captain* to his sleeve in thick, black Sharpie marker.

It is the least official thing I have ever seen in all my years playing sports.

"Nope, not baseball, Gordy," I say. "Slow-pitch softball."

"Eh, baseball, softball, who cares? It's all balls, am I right?" he yells back. He's trying to imitate my dad's attempts at hyping up the group, but I am standing about ten feet away, so the yelling just reminds me of a loud toddler throwing an unnecessary tantrum.

"What's all balls?" Dom says, strutting in with his gear.

"Gordy's Saturday night," I respond.

"Sounds about right," Dom agrees, smirking.

"Glad you could join us, Dominic!" my dad says.

Dom gives my dad a thumbs-up.

Dad barks out some orders, starting with telling Gordy to lead us all in stretches. We gather around him and do jumping jacks, a light jog, arm circles, toe touches, stretches for our hamstrings, quads, shoulders, triceps, biceps, and forearms, Gordy crying out when it's time to count off for the next exercise, but not actually doing the exercises himself—rather, he just "models" the exercise, as if this is second grade PE and he is a retired circus clown. We run karaoke twists, high knees, butt kicks, side shuffles, and sprints, all while Gordy flails about in the middle of our circle like that old children's song, "We're going to Kentucky, we're going to the fair, to see the senorita, with flowers in her hair." See, that's the thing. Even though Gordy's "leading" the group, he's actually just serving the purpose of providing the rest of us with live entertainment. Once the opening act ends, Dad takes back the reins, letting us know which drills he wants to run.

"Colin's got the pitchers," he says. "Girls, practice batting and running bases. You ladies really need to work on hitting the ball on the ground. You pop up too much."

"I'll work with the girls," Dom suggests.

"Good thinking, Dom!" Dad announces.

I shake my head, wondering which firm will handle the impending sexual harassment suit.

"Rest of the guys can run some sprints and do some long toss," Dad declares. "Now, split up!"

I stand at the mound with Richie, who is our only other pitcher. Meanwhile, Daisy, Jess, Rachel, and Courtney all go with Dom. "Nice shorts, Jess," he says, admiring her from behind.

Daisy shoots me a look. I laugh.

Raoul, Gordy, and my dad are left to practice long throws in a triangle in the outfield. That's a threesome if ever I saw one. Raoul is a skinny, short, quiet guy who wears glasses and looks sort of like a Puerto Rican version of Gordon, minus the righteous attitude. I keep an eye on them for a moment, watching as my dad throws a bright yellow softball to Gordon. It sails over his head, and he jumps to catch it, missing by a mile.

"Well, if we win any games, it won't be because of our fielding," Richie says to me.

"Yeah, no shit." I laugh.

He puts on a catcher's mask and heads to home plate. We warm up with a few easy lobs, just to find the strike zone. We switch about fifteen minutes in. Richie's pitches have power behind them—he's showing off, pitching windmill-style. I remember what it feels like to be able to throw that hard. I would remind him this is *slow-pitch* softball, but I'm not in the mood to be the target of a potential roid-rage episode.

Daisy, Dom, and the girls seem to be doing more talking than practicing, which is right on par for Dom. My dad, Gordy, and Raoul are running the bases now. It looks a whole lot like jogging to me. Richie and I get bored after a little while, and I take a break to stretch my arm out a bit more.

Dad notices. "Colin!" he calls out. "You good, son?"

"All set, Dad," I say.

Next, Richie and I split the pitching duties for the team's batting practice. Once everyone's gotten up to bat twice, Gordy walks off to use his puffer, which is the universal signal to my father that we've been at it for ninety minutes.

"Let's bring 'er in!" he yells to the team. The groups trot toward the mound. Daisy gets her Whole Foods bag and offers snacks to everyone. I gratefully grab two granola bars.

"Mmm," I tell Daisy. "So good. What's in these?"

"Yours are baked with extra love," she says.

"I can tell." I nod.

"Okay, team!" Gordy says. His voice is firm, but I detect a slight quiver, the remnants of his narrowly avoided asthma attack. "As your captain, I—"

"Not your job," I say. People snicker.

"Ugh," he replies. "As I was saying—"

"Nope," I say. The girls giggle.

Gordy looks agitated. "Jack? A little help, here?"

"Let him finish," Dad says.

"Of course. Marching orders, sir!" I say to Gordy.

"As your captain, I took the liberty of making us a team cheer."

"Oh, dear God," I mutter.

"At the end of every huddle, instead of saying, 'One-two-three-break!' we'll say, 'Scream and shout and catch your breath for Gordy, Jack, and Kiss of Death!'"

"No," I say.

"Not bad, son," Dad says. "Let's put a pin in that for now. Save it for the playoffs, yeah?"

"We can try it now, before we go," Gordy suggests.

Dom laughs. "Hard pass," he says.

"Good practice, guys. First game Sunday is at twelve sharp. Don't be late!" Dad commands. "And Colin—bring your A-game. No slacking off with those easy swings!"

"Dad—it's *soft*ball."

"No reason for *you* to be soft though, right, kid?"

Dad started this team once retirement began looming about three years ago. I used to hit hard then, until a straight shot to third base during practice hit Daisy in the face and broke her nose.

"Got that right. It's not a *real* game till somebody ends up in the hospital," I mumble. Daisy pats me on the shoulder.

Understanding that our little team meeting has ended, Dom and I turn back towards the bench to grab our stuff. "One, two, three!" Gordy shouts. "Scream and shout and catch your breath!"

My dad pats him on the back. "Not today, son."

Gordy stops, shoulders slumped.

Daisy gives me half the leftover granola bars to take home, and I call myself an Uber. When I arrive home twenty minutes later, I grab a shower and throw a frozen pizza in the oven. I dry off, change into shorts and a T-shirt, and park myself on the couch with my dinner and a bottle of lemon seltzer.

I flip on the television and check my phone. I've got emails from Dick's Sporting Goods, Bed Bath & Beyond Registry (kill me), a panicked client who just got a life insurance policy and wants to make sure the proceeds end up in her will (Sidebar: How *daft* is she? The policy lists a *beneficiary*—it doesn't also need to go in her will!), and a 15 percent off coupon to Besos Burritos, which I fully intend to use, just not tonight.

I binge-watch a miniseries on Netflix about the Heaven's Gate cult, and it's almost 11:00 when my eyes begin to close. Almost an hour later, I'm sound asleep on the couch when I hear a *Ding!* I rub my eyes and check my phone.

It's Grace.

Gracie

There should be a warning label on pizza boxes. Like how the Surgeon General warning lets smokers know their choices are akin to suicide—the same thing should be right on the top of each pizza delivery order.

This is what I'm thinking when I wake up just before midnight, the screen of my laptop a black abyss, my head resting on an actual plate, bits of sauce and crumbs of crust dotting my face like recently popped pimples.

How is this possible?

There was no alcohol. No Thanksgiving-menu tryptophan in my meal. It was just me, my sausage and pepperoni pizza, and Netflix, enjoying a late lunch that lasted from roughly 4:00 until about 5:30, until, as it seems, I fell asleep.

They say carbs will do that.

I get up, navigate my way to the bathroom in the dark, flip on the switch, and look in the mirror. I pull my hair into a ponytail and wash my face, the scent of Noxema cold cream coaxing me awake. (What? It reminds me of my childhood.)

I head back to the scene of the crime. It's okay. These things happen, I remind myself as I wrap up the remaining pizza in tinfoil.

I sit back down at my computer. The clock in the lower right-hand corner reminds me that it's 12:27 a.m. Normal people are asleep.

Where did I leave off? I exit out of *Schitt's Creek* and look at the open windows on my screen.

Oh, shit. I left him hanging.

Well, good for me! Makes me look uninterested. Aloof. Busy. I mean, he *does* sound amazing, between his thoughts on "the sanctity of marriage" (Really? What man speaks like that?) and the fact that he's currently STD-free. Although, that little nugget was an eyebrow-raiser. For. Sure.

So, is it weird for me to write Colin back now? In the middle of the night?

Nah. Not if I'm still technically *working*.

TO: Colin Yarmouth (cyarmouth@
     yarmouthaycockpc.com)
FROM: Grace Landing (gracie222@mail.com)
SUBJECT: Good night

Hey,

Sorry for the delayed response. I got caught up.

Okay, that's a lie. I fell asleep—and I just woke up. Hey, don't judge! I figure if you can tell me about your recent run-ins with the clap, I can be honest about an accidental evening snooze lol.

My drink of choice? I mean, if we're sharing, let's just say you and I would be polar opposites at a cocktail party. You would be all spiffed up in a sport coat drinking a fine vermouth discussing legalese, and I would be by the snack table slugging back anything sour: Midori sour, amaretto sour, even a whiskey sour if no other options exist. I also like mudslides and pina coladas. Basically, I like my alcohol to taste as much like movie theater candy as possible. I'm not a fan of beer and I feel like wine is just people being careless with the sell-by date on what could have been some really good grape juice. And the only reason I'm telling you all of this is because I feel like we have zero boundaries now that I know your nads are infested with pubic lice. Just kidding!!

Anyway, I guess I'll talk to you tomorrow. Or later today, actually.

Have a good night!
Grace

Well. Now what? It's obvious I won't be going back to sleep anytime soon. I guess I should get back to writing. I head into the kitchen to grab a glass of water—anything more than that and my stomach will explode—when I hear a *ding*. My phone is on the desk, next to the laptop. I check it before sitting down.

No way.

TO: Grace Landing (gracie222@mail.com)
FROM: Colin Yarmouth (cyarmouth@
        yarmouthaycockpc.com)
RE: Good night

Hey,

Are you still up?

Colin

If this was Scott, I would've assumed it was a booty call. But Colin Yarmouth is *nothing* like Scott, thank God.

TO: Colin Yarmouth (cyarmouth@
        yarmouthaycockpc.com)
FROM: Grace Landing (gracie222@mail.com)
RE: Good night

I am. What's up?

G.

The response is almost immediate.

TO: Grace Landing (gracie222@mail.com)
FROM: Colin Yarmouth (cyarmouth@
        yarmouthaycockpc.com)
RE: Good night

Can I call you? If so, email me your number. If not, no worries. We can chat during normal business hours if you prefer.

Colin

Um, yes? What fairy godmother has come a-knockin' on my door on this fine April night? My stomach does a flip. It's accompanied by a lengthy fart, but there's nobody listening. Yet.

TO: Colin Yarmouth (cyarmouth@
    yarmouthaycockpc.com)
FROM: Grace Landing (gracie222@mail.com)
RE: Good night

(917) 555-0216.

It rings a minute later.

"Hello?"

"Hey," he says. His voice is melted butter seeping through my phone, drowning me like a decadent bite of lobster tail.

"Hi," I respond, already swooning. The man has said one whole syllable and I've come undone. *Pull it together, Gracie.*

"How are you?" he asks.

Dying. Possibly already dead. For real, we might need to call someone. I think I'm having palpitations. "Good. How are you?" I ask, like a kindergarten child playing that game where you mimic everything the other person says until one child bursts into frustrated tears and/or inevitably bites the other child on the arm.

"Oh, my whole life is just a big celebration."

His response renders me speechless.

"You still there?"

I cough.

"I was kidding. Quoting you, remember? Are you sure this is an okay time to chat?"

I clear my throat. *This beautiful man—nay, this gift from the universe!—is going to hang up the damn phone because you can't behave like a normal functioning adult. Dammit, Gracie! Just be normal!* "Superduper," I respond. Then, legit, I smack myself in the forehead. Who fucking speaks like that?

"I mean, I just figured it's easier than emailing back and forth if we're both awake."

"Totes McGoats," I respond. Good Lord. It's like my mouth is just on autopilot. I have zero control. *Note to self: do not engage in conversations with attractive humans past midnight, when you clearly morph from an intelligent wordsmith into a bumbling five-year-old.*

"Do you always rhyme when you speak?" He laughs.

My sweet Jesus. I laugh aloud. It's better than words. Maybe we can have a conversation like this, where he speaks and I just grunt.

"You seem a little silly tonight. You're not all sauced up again, are you?"

"Nope. Not tonight. That magnificent first impression was a special-occasions-only kind of thing," I say. *Thank God! Actual words!*

"I see," he says, pausing to take a sip of something. "So, are you usually up this late?"

"Hardly ever. I typically keep similar hours to that of a convalescent home. You know, breakfast at seven, lunch at eleven, dinner at four. I'm almost always in bed by eight."

"Stop lying."

"Okay," I laugh. "Usually more like ten. But never like this."

"Yeah, same here," he says. "I like to be up and out early, so I need to get plenty of—"

"Beauty sleep?" I interrupt.

He chuckles. "Something like that."

"So, what's eating at you tonight?"

"What do you mean?"

"Usually when I can't sleep, there's a reason. I lie awake tossing and turning, but it's more mental gymnastics than it is physical. What's on your mind?" I ask.

"Wow," he says.

"What?"

"Nothing, Dr. Landing," Colin says.

"Well? You asked to call me. So here I am," I reply. "Spill."

I wait, but all I hear is him sigh.

"Is it the herpes?" I ask in an earnest-sounding voice.

That breaks him. He laughs and says, "No! It's just nice to chat, that's all."

"Well," I reply, "I agree, but that's no cause for cerebral acrobatics."

"I don't remember you being this funny in high school."

"That's because we didn't talk back then."

"Sure, we did. Remember that science class?"

"You mean the first day of school? When we were lab partners for thirty seconds? Yes. I remember. I think that was the last time we actually exchanged words on purpose, other than the occasional 'excuse me' in the hallway."

"No. That can't be."

"Indeed, my friend. Hate to break it to you, but you've got some rose-colored glasses covering your rearview. You and I"—I lower my voice, like I'm letting him in on a secret—"were not in the same orbit in high school."

"Stop it," he says.

"Colin," I say. "You hung with the cool kids. And I hung out with Cindy Lee."

"Who?"

"Exactly."

He pauses. "Well, my loss," he says.

"Yes," I agree, sounding suddenly emboldened, remembering my love notes and all the passion I poured into them.

"It's good that we're talking now though. I mean…" His voice trails off.

"What?" I ask. He sounds…pensive?

"Can I be honest?"

"I'd expect nothing less at this hour of the day."

"Your email woke me up. But I don't mind. You're really *funny*."

"So, did you call me for jokes, then?"

"Why? Do you have any?"

"Not on the fly like this. I, too, just woke up from a nap, so I'm not as fresh as I'd like."

"Ahh. Hence the rhyming."

"Yes. My conversational skills are rather subpar immediately post-respite. Let's be real though. I'm sure you and—what's your partner's name? Something Facecock?—I'm sure you guys spend most of your days yucking it up in your fancy midtown office, no?"

"Ha!" he exclaims. "No, not exactly. Gordon *Ay*cock is my father's protégé. Sort of like the son he *wishes* he had."

"What?" I ask. "No way. First of all, I will not indulge you in any mournful-sounding conversation about a man named *Gordon*, unless we're joking about his sorry-ass life. For example, we can safely assume that *Gordon* lives above his parents' garage. *Gordon* has never gone past second base with a girl, and that girl was most definitely his sister. *Gordon* spent most of high school stuffed in a locker. I'm just saying. *Protégé* is a nice word for *kiss-ass*, and if you have Daddy issues as a result, it's only because my man *Gordon* is probably a hard-core nerd."

"You don't even know."

"I've seen his *picture*, remember?"

"What? No. How?"

"On your website."

"Ohhh. Yes, of course."

"And let me tell you, you have *nothing* to be jealous of."

"Well, I never said I was *jealous*."

"Please, you're as jealous as a middle-school girl watching her best friend get fitted for a training bra."

"See? This is what I mean! Where do you come up with this stuff?"

"With what?"

"You've got jokes! That thing you said about me cheating off you in Spanish literally put tears in my eyes."

"Well, you're welcome. And as for Gordy, if you want your office to be funnier, just picture him naked. He *definitely* wears tighty-whities."

"Oh, a hundred percent."

"*With* skidmarks."

"Damn. That's harsh."

"The truth is often that way," I say. "For real though? If it wasn't for laughter, I would never have made it through this week. Or this month. Or the past six months, to be honest with you. See, me and Netflix have a deal. As soon as I feel down about anything, I have to watch one full episode of *Schitt's Creek*. It's only twenty minutes. If I don't feel at least a little better after the episode, I have the full permission of the universe to leap off my fire escape into traffic."

"Yikes. No pressure, Eugene Levy."

"The thing is, it always works. Haven't jumped yet," I say.

"Yeah, I guess you're right. But it's different when you're talking to an actual live human being who makes you laugh."

"True."

"How often do you get to do that?"

"Me? Oh, all day. I'm a writer. My characters are ridiculous. They keep me rolling."

"They're not real though."

"Like hell they're not. Everyone I write about is based off something in real life. I can't come up with this shit from scratch. I am *not* that brilliant, sadly."

"So, what are you writing about now? With this 'page count' business that keeps you from returning my emails in a timely fashion?"

"*Timely?*" I ask, awash with faux surprise. "I am *speaking* with you in the middle of the night! And we emailed like four times today!" A moment of self-awareness washes over me. Teenage me would literally die, speaking on the phone with teenage Colin Yarmouth at an hour reserved for late-night talk shows and infomercials.

He laughs, piercing my thought bubble, bringing me back to the present.

"If you *must* know, I am writing about a Realtor who finds herself broke suddenly and tries to sell her condo by seducing her old high school boyfriend."

"Hmm." He considers the information.

My stomach does this weird thing, where it makes a gurgly noise similar to the one that rumbled out of my body just before the unfortunate jogging incident the other day. I clench my butt cheeks together for safety. "What?" I ask. A small gas bubble bursts in my digestive tract and the feeling passes.

"Just trying to figure out how you pulled the story out of real life."

"Oh," I say. "Well, it's not a mirror, if that's what you're thinking."

"So, then I'm wrong to assume that you still speak to your high school boyfriend?"

"Nope. We no longer speak," I reply. "It's weird. My brain pulls together memories and mixes them with current stuff in my life or in the lives of my friends, or even—sometimes—on the news, and poof! A story appears."

"Interesting."

The line goes quiet for an awkward moment. When I can stand it no longer, I say, "What?"

"Just thinking."

"Thinking *what*, Colin?" I ask, exasperated.

"Am *I* in this story you're writing?" He laughs.

Blood rises into my cheeks. "Why would you ask that?" I reply, immediately horrified.

"Because of the yearbook thing, maybe?" he suggests.

I gulp, trying to regain some semblance of composure. "I stand corrected, Colin. Not *everything* I write is based on reality."

"But you just said—"

"Okay, point proven. Clearly, you are one hell of a lawyer."

"Yeah. I mean, you should see how I go rounds with the elderly, assigning their estates to executors and putting their money into trusts. I get *fierce*."

I laugh, relaxing a bit. "I'll bet."

"Well, your story sounds interesting."

"No need for platitudes. It actually sucks."

"Wait. What?"

"Yeah, I hate to admit it, but I've been riding the struggle bus for months."

"You were *just* saying that being a writer is amazing. Now you're saying it sucks?"

"Oh, no. Don't misunderstand me. Being a writer is great. Well, mostly anyway. You get to make your own hours and work in sweatpants. What I'm saying is that my *story* sucks. The one I'm working on."

"Why? What makes you think that?" He sounds genuinely concerned, which is unexpected and sweet.

"Well." I sigh. "The sad truth is, my plotline is a mess."

"How come?"

"The protagonist—the Realtor—she's behaving like a gold digger. Protagonists are supposed to be likeable. And, I don't know," I add, "I just can't see through it to the end. I can't figure out how to get to a happy ending."

"Can you change it?"

"I'm not sure. My agent put me on a really tight deadline. I've got a publisher interested in my work. Like big-time interested."

"How do you know?"

"They offered my agent a six-figure deal," I say. "Or, well, they're about to." The words linger in the air, taunting me, as if now that I've said them aloud, they—and the money they represent—will surreptitiously disappear.

"That's awesome! So obviously that means you're a great writer, doesn't it?"

"Maybe I *was*. But that was *before*. Y'know, before everything with Scott destroyed my joy."

"I understand that feeling. My world was pretty rocked when Elle and I split."

"Elle?"

"My ex-wife," he says. "She's a literary agent, actually."

"Really?" I consider this. I've never heard of an Elle Yarmouth in the industry before. Maybe she's in children's lit. "Small world."

"Yeah," he says.

"So how do you handle the hard times?" I ask.

"Huh?" he says.

"Now that you and Elle are splitsville. Do you drink the pain away, like me? Or do you have some other kind of secret weapon to get through the lonely nights?"

He laughs. "No," he admits. "It's not easy. I just keep telling myself that it wasn't meant to be."

"Does it help?"

"Not really."

"Does it spill over into your work?"

Colin pauses. "Maybe a little. I can do most of this stuff on autopilot, I've been doing it for so long. But yeah, I guess. I mean, every now and then I'll talk to clients who are elderly and have been married for decades, and when they share their end-of-life wishes, I can just feel how much they love each other," he says. "I don't know. I thought that was how marriage was supposed to be."

His voice is soft when he says this. The sound—the softness—is more attractive than any physical attribute of his I can remember. "I agree," I say. "I was expecting the same thing. Or at least hoping for something similar, y'know?"

"Yeah. I completely understand," he says. "But, so, explain. How is it affecting your writing?"

"Ugh," I begin. "I just can't think of anything creative that's not ultimately fueled by my anger. And romance novels are supposed to be sexy and fun. *Light* reading. Not angsty and morose. I used to love writing them. But now...well, now, I just feel like I'm suffering from a never-ending case of impostor syndrome."

"How do you figure?"

"Like, who am I to even be trying to write this stuff? It's clearly not any indication of how my life is turning out."

"Hmm."

"What?"

"Nothing."

"No. Tell me."

"Help me understand. When you say 'romance novels,' are you talking about the little shiny paperback books with the half-naked firemen on the front?"

I laugh. "Sometimes, yes."

"So, you feel like an impostor because you're not currently hooked up with a jacked-up fireman?"

"Or a cowboy, or a man of the law, or—"

"Or an old high school flame?" he interjects.

"That'd be a hard pass." I laugh, but the comment feels the tiniest bit flirty.

He pauses, then recovers. "I always wondered about those books. Do people actually *buy* them?"

"You'd be surprised. Lots of people love them."

"Huh."

"My guess is they're not all estate attorneys—and probably not men—but, yeah. People read them."

"Do you like writing them?"

"Usually, I really do." I think about this. "Well, I *used* to. Since Scott..." I leave the remainder of the sentence inside my mind, where I can't consider it as a reality.

"What *would* you like?"

"To write? Good question. I don't know." I take a breath. "A story about someone who's been hurt, maybe? And how she recovers from it."

"Like *How Stella Got Her Groove Back*?"

I stifle a laugh. "Personal favorite of yours?"

"No. I just don't live under a rock. I know about movies, thank you very much."

"I'm not mad, I'm just noticing. Plus, *Stella* is a classic."

"So then why not just write that instead?"

"Well, because of the deal on the table. And the crazy deadline. Despite how upper echelon I may sound, I'm not exactly rich, Colin."

He laughs. "I get it. Hey, I have an idea."

"What's that?"

"Why don't you send it over and let me read it? Maybe I can help you come up with something."

"Seriously?"

"Yeah. Why not? If your writing is anywhere as hilarious as your speaking, I bet I'd really enjoy it."

"I don't know," I say, thinking about the names I've used, the physical descriptions—any likenesses that relate directly to Colin Yarmouth.

"C'mon. How long is it?"

"So far? It's only like thirty-five pages."

"That's nothing. I can breeze through it in a day. Then, we can talk about it tomorrow."

"I don't know," I say again. "It's stupid. And a little raunchy."

"I'm a grown-up, you know."

I inhale. "Okay," I say. "But no judgment. At least nothing too harsh. The exercise here is for you to help me come up with a way to salvage this mess—not for you to tear me apart. Deal?"

"Why on earth would you think—?"

"Sorry. I don't know. I haven't shared my work with anyone blind like this since grad school."

"I'll be easy. I promise," he says in that soft voice again. *Mmm.* He could ask me to fly to the moon in a rocket ship naked and I would do it if he used that voice.

"Okay," I finally concede.

"It sounds like fun."

"Reading a plotless introduction to a romance novel sounds like fun to you?"

"What? It does!"

"Of course, Colin. As does your work," I say.

Colin laughs. "Yes. Death planning. Real riveting stuff."

Here, we both pause, fresh out of banter. "Well," I finally say.

"This was nice," he says.

"It was," I agree.

"Same time tomorrow?" he asks.

"Are you out of your mind?" I say.

"It's possible."

"I can't commit to a phone date with you tomorrow anytime past ten."

"Oh, so now it's a *date*?"

Asshole! Why'd you have to use that word? "Yes, because *I'm* the one who hit you up for *your* number in the middle of the night," I retort.

"I'm just saying. If it's a *date*, I can do better than just a phone chat."

"Really? Are you propositioning me for phone sex now, Colin? What is this—the turn of the century? Should I check my caller ID and write down your 1-900 number?"

"No, wise guy."

"This explains the herpes."

He laughs. "You're ridiculous."

"You love it," I say.

"I just might," he says. Chills soar through my body, up my neck, and into my cheeks, somehow rendering them burning hot.

"I'll send you the manuscript. Then, it's your turn to email me."

"I know."

"So, write me tomorrow."

"Oh, I plan to."

I giggle, but mostly it's just nerves. This guy is *smooth*. "I guess I'll talk to you then."

"Sweet dreams. And thanks for the chat. It was great."

"G'night."

Click.

Damn.

I send over the manuscript immediately, with *Be nice!* as the subject title but nothing in the body of the email. Then, I sit at my desk, staring at the blackness of my computer screen in disbelief for what feels like an eternity, replaying as much of the conversation as I can remember over and over again in my mind. When I can stand it no longer, I go into the bathroom, strip down, and run myself an extra steamy shower. One of the luxuries I afforded myself when I got this place was one of those removable handheld showerheads.

That thing is worth its weight in gold.

Colin

Well, that was surprising. She sounded flirty and cute, but not in a ditzy way. Smart, with all those jokes.

And something about her made me feel…I don't know. I can't put my finger on it.

I wish I could remember what she looks like.

I open the Amazon app on my phone and look up Grace Landing in the search bar. Hmm. That's curious. I can't find anything written by her.

Maybe she's anti-corporate and only sells her books at those indie bookshops. Elle used to go on and on about how important it is to support the small guys—how they're the backbone of the industry and yadda, yadda, yadda. But, I don't know. Doesn't *everyone* sell their books on Amazon?

I do a Google search next. I search the images—I mean, really, no sense in beating around the bush. I already know she's got a fun personality, but if she's a wildebeest, then I deserve to know that up front.

There's one small grainy image on a now-defunct Myspace page that shows up. It's got to be at least fifteen years old—probably her very first attempt at social media. I peer at it. She's got really long hair, and her body looks curvy. She's cute. The picture jogs my memory and reminds me that she had a pretty face back in high school.

This whole thing is so bizarre.

The phone dings, and an email comes through with the subject line *Be nice!* and an attachment.

I smile. *Cool. This'll give me something to read tomorrow.* Right now, I'm beat and my shoulder hurts.

I pop an Aleve and hit the sack. For the first time in a while, I'm actually looking forward to going to work in the morning.

Gracie

I write a group text to Melly, Alisha, and Tori: SOS!!!

What's up? Alisha answers.

Big developments, I say.

??? Melly adds.

Do tell, Tori says.

Remember Colin Yarmouth? From my high school?

Obvi, Melly says.

HE CALLED ME LAST NIGHT, I write, adding a mind-blown, yellow-faced emoji.

Stop it!! Tori says.

Really? Alisha says.

OMG, Melly says. How'd you swing THAT?

We've been emailing, since that night at House of Yes.

You were emailing at House of Yes? Alisha asks.

Nooo, afterwards. When I got home. I was not in a good place, and I wrote to him. At his work email.

KYS, Tori says with a hand-slapped-on-face emoji.

Tori!! Alisha says.

Anyway, he wrote back and turns out he's not only hot but nice too. Pretty surprising for a dick jock from high school.

Go for yours, girl!! Melly adds an eggplant emoji.

So now, we're like, talking, I think.

That's cool, Gracie. I'm so happy for you! Alisha says.

Try not to fuck it up! (Said with love), Tori adds.

Send pix, Melly requested.

You can find them on his company website: www.yar-mouthaycock.com.

DAMN GIRL, Melly says.

If I was into dudes, Tori says, I'd hit that.

Yeah, he's really cute, Alisha says.

Thanks! I'll LYK what happens.

Def, Tori says.

Good luck! Alisha says.

Xoxo, Melly says.

TO: Grace Landing (gracie222@mail.com)

FROM: Colin Yarmouth (cyarmouth@
    yarmouthaycockpc.com)

RE: Be nice!

Good morning,

How did you sleep? I actually was able to get right to bed after our conversation last night. It was really fun chatting with you. I hope you enjoyed it as much as I did.

I'm looking forward to reading what you sent over. I'll start it at lunch, and if I don't finish it then, I'll finish it up at the end of the day before I head home.

If you write more today (which I feel like you might?), feel free to shoot it my way and I'll add it to the end.

Either way, I hope you have a productive day. I have a client at nine, so I'm going to go grab a fresh cup of coffee and mentally prepare myself to discuss who gets the cat if my client dies first.

Talk to you soon,
Colin

TO: Colin Yarmouth (cyarmouth@ yarmouthaycockpc.com)
FROM: Grace Landing (gracie222@mail.com)
RE: Be nice!

Hi,

I also went to sleep not long after we spoke. I took a shower first—you know, just in the off-chance that I might've caught a little something from you over the phone! Lol, only kidding. And yes, I had a great time talking to you as well.

Thank you again for offering to read for me. I rarely rely on alpha readers, but in this case, I really do need some help. I don't love feeling this vulnerable, if we're being brutally honest. But I guess I would rather hear that it's complete garbage from you than from a publisher.

Good luck with your client and their cat. I have

a cat. His name is Dorian Gray. Perhaps you'd like to write a will for us in your free time.

Do you have any pets?

Okay, I'm going to try and get started on some work now. Wish me luck. I'll check my email when I take a break a little later on.

G.

It's so hard to write when you know who your audience is. With every sentence, I picture Colin, hoping he laughs at the funny parts and isn't too grossed out by the sex scenes.

I have Connor removed from the building via stretcher. Presley goes with him. He gets stitches and a tetanus shot, and they change him into scrubs because they couldn't send him out of there with shredded pants or else he'd get arrested for indecent exposure.

Meanwhile, Presley's starving, so she tries to leave Connor and get something to eat, but he's afraid to go home, so he suggests they go somewhere to eat together. She agrees because he offers to pay for the meal, and (for reasons I'm not entirely sure of) she picks an expensive Italian place. Which is maybe not my most clever decision, given the fact that he's dressed in scrubs, but whatever.

She comments on his outfit, and he says that if the place she's forcing him to limp to is any good, there will be a long wait and they'll just end up grabbing a pizza and heading back to the condo. I like Connor. He's outwitting her.

It turns out he's correct too. The wait for a table is over an hour and they are both starving. They grab a bunch of slices and walk back to the condo, which is only like two blocks away. The apartment is basically empty—no furniture or anything—but the remnants of open house snacks are on the counter and Presley grabs at them while reheating the pizza in the oven. He makes a joke about not having taken the Vicodin he was prescribed at the hospital because he wanted to be "fully present" in case this moment were to present itself. He starts trying to work his magic on her with some sexy talk, then walks towards her and gets ready to plant one on her, but she turns away. "Don't kiss me," she says. He kisses her neck instead, making her swoon, and says he can wait until after they eat.

And, oh my God. This line comes out of me: *His hands landed on her hips, and he pulled her groin into his, grinding his stimulus package into her sugar cookie only once before releasing her.* I can't. I'm dying. Real-life tears are falling out of my eyes. Colin's going to think this is hysterical—I hope!

Presley avoids *falling prey to his pelvic sorcery* (man, sometimes I'm so good) and takes the pizza out of the oven. She serves it and tries to create a comfortable spot on the floor for him to sit down. Connor lights the fire in the fireplace and turns the living room lights down, setting the mood. They eat while savoring the view out of the floor-to-ceiling windows. The lights of the 59th Street Bridge twinkle in the darkness. And then, it takes me a few minutes to finish the section, but eventually I come up with this: *The azure hue spilling in through the giant panes of glass stood at odds with the warm glow of the dimmed lights and the orange flickering flames of the crackling fire. It was a standoff: hot meets cold. The slick strip of moisture in Presley's panties foreshadowed which side would win the inevitable battle.*

I can't believe I'm going to send this to Colin. It feels like the equivalent of sending him one of my passionate love letters from back in the day. You're safe when you're a *secret* admirer, just like you're safe when you have a pseudonym. You can say whatever you want, and nobody knows it's you who said it. Also, I never, ever wrote about him making my panties wet back then.

Back when I had some dignity.

Now, I just write soft-core porn for hormonal women and people who aren't afraid to read about them, and I can't even do *that* without help! But who knows? Maybe Colin and I will come up with some amazing solution. We'll fix the book, I'll get it in on time, Lindsay will love it, and all will be right with the world. I can just picture the copies flying off the shelves of Stop & Shop, thrown into shopping carts alongside kids' Lunchables and eight-packs of Honest Juice.

Mmm. Lunchables.

I need a break.

TO: Grace Landing (gracie222@mail.com)
FROM: Colin Yarmouth (cyarmouth@
    yarmouthaycockpc.com)
RE: Be nice!

Hey,

Just letting you know the morning totally got away from me. My 9 o'clock stayed until almost 11. He was trying to turn our appointment into a personal therapy session, which happens every so often when clients have to change their wills for big life reasons. In this case, his wife just died (spoiler alert: he got the cat), so I tried to be sensitive. But if we're being honest, I really just wanted to read your stuff! And then Gordon and I had to meet with a guy for an interview. We're looking for a new bookkeeper. Doing anything with that guy is the absolute worst. Before I knew it, it was noon. Good news is I'm going to grab a sandwich and then lock myself in my office so I can read. I promise I won't derail your deadline.

If you wrote anything new, feel free to send it over and I'll add it to this thick stack of paper I just printed out.

Hope you're having a good day!

Colin

TO: Colin Yarmouth (cyarmouth@ yarmouthaycockpc.com)
FROM: Grace Landing (gracie222@mail.com)
RE: Be nice!

Hi,

Yes—I wrote some more this morning. It's attached.

Sorry to hear about your client. I hate when my time gets hijacked by something unexpected like that. Well, I won't take up any more of yours right now. Enjoy your lunch and thank you again for reading!

Talk to you later,
Gracie

I hit *send* and stand up, lifting my arms over my head to stretch out my back. I look outside. It's sunny. *I should take a walk*, I decide. I slide on my sneakers and grab a hoodie sweatshirt.

I live in an area of Brooklyn called Sheepshead Bay. It's not close to anything, really. I mean, you think *Brooklyn* and maybe you think of huge slices of foldable pizza or steaming hot bagels or Italian meatballs and Sunday sauce. Or maybe you picture the Brooklyn Botanical Gardens, or the trendy, laid-back vibe of Prospect Park. Maybe you think about the Promenade, where many a first date has walked hand in hand, gazing starry-eyed at the Manhattan skyline and the pair of bridges that can get you there. It's possible you consider Coney Island, the Cyclone roller coaster, and the original Nathan's five-cent hot dog. Or if you're a die-hard Jay-Z fan, you contemplate the Marcy Projects where he grew up.

But I'd be willing to bet you a slice of Junior's cheesecake you don't think of Sheepshead Bay.

It's sort of an anomaly, really. The Belt Parkway draws the southern perimeter of Brooklyn along the edge of Jamaica Bay. And there's this one little inlet at exit nine. On one side of the inlet is Manhattan Beach, and on the other? Sheepshead Bay. It's quiet, by Brooklyn standards, home to a heavy Eastern European population. Lots of attached houses and small buildings like mine. On Emmons Avenue, where the inlet lies, there's a waterfront strip lined with charter boats, fishing boats, party boats, and a handful of waterfront restaurants that are good for special occasions. Lundy's, which was a famous restaurant known for its seafood, was the cornerstone of the area for dozens of years. But it closed long before I got here.

Anyway, Emmons Avenue is dotted with a row of old-fashioned streetlamps painted blue, and there's a footbridge you can cross to get to Manhattan Beach. Some people fish off the footbridge, despite the fact that it's pretty narrow. It's romantic though: a sweet little wood-planked bridge in one of the busiest-city-on-Earth's outer boroughs. Not what you'd expect. Once you cross it, you enter one of the most remote locations Brooklyn has to offer, marked by opulent, oversized detached houses that cost anywhere between one and five million dollars. There are three things about Manhattan Beach that I love: 1) The heart of it is the Manhattan Beach Park, which features a small beach with actual sand where I spend hours writing in the summertime. 2) The houses are so big and beautiful that when you walk through the area, you feel like you're somewhere else—maybe in Florida minus the palm trees, though I've never been there so I can't say for sure. 3) Melly's parents live right near the park on Kensington Street—which is how I came to learn about the area back in my old college days.

Melly—Mela Andronikashvili—and I met at freshman orientation the summer after I graduated from high school. We bonded over both being New York kids (her from Brooklyn, me from the Bronx), making fun of Bostonians who couldn't pronounce the R sound correctly and openly judging the lack of good bagels in Massachusetts. We also shared some heritage: my mom is from

Albania, to the west of the Black Sea, and her parents are from Georgia (not the peach tree state down south, the independent republic on the eastern border of the Black Sea) so we found solace in being familiar with ethnic foods from the same region. We also both grew up speaking lots of other languages: I learned a smattering of Albanian and Italian, and Melly spoke Georgian and Russian. We shared a bunk bed for three years, until our senior year when we moved off campus with our other suitemates, Alisha and Tori.

During Parents' Weekend in September of freshman year, I met Melly's mom and dad, Boris and Natasha. (I am not making this up—I swear those are their government names.) I learned that Mr. A owned a successful limousine company in Brooklyn and Mrs. A was a traditional stay-at-home Eastern European mother, which meant that Melly grew up doing three things all the time: eating home-cooked meals, studying, and suffering through piano lessons.

Melly was (and still is) a skinny girl. She's tall too, about five-eight, and probably weighs a hundred twenty pounds fully dressed. She used to joke with us during those first few meals in the dining hall about how nice it was to consume a meal without being scolded for not eating enough or body-shamed by her mother for being too skinny. On Parents' Weekend, Melly's mom packed an Igloo cooler full of food: a big tray of meat and cheese blintzes, at least three to four pounds of kotleti (which are sort of like flattened chicken meatballs), several logs of piroshki filled with potatoes and mushrooms, and two giant tubs of borscht. Mrs. A tried to serve us a meal out of the cooler—she brought plates and utensils, and Melly was the only one of all of us to have brought a microwave from home. Melly was, of course, mortified. But I felt bad, and also hungry, so I gratefully accepted her warm, loving attempt to bring us a taste of home. In response, Mrs. A said in her thick, throaty accent, "I like this one. She is strong and meaty. Ready for winter."

Over Thanksgiving break, Melly invited me to her house for the Wednesday night before Turkey Day: the biggest party night of the year. We met at her Manhattan Beach mini-mansion at 8:00 p.m., where we put on makeup, got dressed in our tightest, shortest dresses, counted our money, and made a plan for the night. At around 9:00, we came down the stairs, and I couldn't help but notice the dining room table was set with two places. Glass plates were piled high with meats, some fried-looking thing, and a cooked cabbage dish, adorned with a side bowl of borscht and a glass of red wine.

"Wow—your parents eat dinner kind of late, huh?" I asked Melly.

Just then, Mrs. A appeared. "No, no! *You* eat. She too skinny, no?" She nodded fervently at me for approval. I shrugged. "You come. Have second dinner," she said. "Keep you warm in this tiny dress."

Melly lashed out at her mother in a language that I later learned was Russian, words flicking off her tongue like a frog catching a fly or a snake attacking its prey. Quick. Deliberate. Angry.

Mrs. A responded in kind. Having no clue what either of them said, I felt super uncomfortable. But then, Mrs. A pulled out a chair and motioned for me to sit down. "Have some wine. It is good for your heart."

Melly sat too, sulking like a little kid. I cleared my plate and enjoyed a second serving.

We never made it out to the club that night, likely on account of my poor tolerance and overstuffed belly. But I made a new friend—Mrs. A—who has looked out for me ever since.

After graduation, Melly moved back to Brooklyn to share a rental loft in Greenpoint with Jake, and I was a common couch-surfer there on nights when we went out. Melly and Jake got engaged four years later and began searching for a house, like real grown-ups, so I got the hint that it was time for me to consider getting my own place as well. Melly's babushka had recently passed away, and when Mrs. A heard I was looking for a place to live, she sold me her mom's apartment on Avenue Y for tens of thousands of dollars less than what it was worth. "The rent is too damn high!" she proudly announced when she signed the paperwork. When I moved to Sheepshead Bay, she let me use their garage to store a beach chair and a few boxes of books. So now when I walk to the beach, I don't have to carry a chair the whole way. I punch in the garage code, grab my chair, and go.

Which is exactly what I do today.

I find myself a nice stretch of sand near the jetty and unfold the chair. I settle in and pull my phone out of my pocket, content to bask in the warm glow of the sun. It's about sixty degrees out, but the beach is empty, with the exception of a group of toddlers swinging merrily at the playground. I should be writing, but I feel like I'm at a standstill until I have Colin's response to work with. Anything else I do now will be futile.

"Yoo hoo!" I hear in the distance. I open my eyes and see Mrs.

A in a velour track suit the color of a ripe plum coming towards me with a travel mug in her hand.

I laugh and offer a friendly wave. "*Zdravstvuyte*, Mrs. A," I call out. (In English, this *sounds* like *zraz-vut-ee-yuh*. It means *hello*.)

"Hallo, my Gracie!"

I stand up and she gives me a sloppy kiss on the cheek.

"I heard the garage. Is too cold for beach today, no?"

"No." I shake my head. "It's nice in the sun."

"Ah, well. I bring you borscht." She hands me the travel mug. Because truly, nothing screams "beach day" like a mug full of hot beet soup.

Still, I take a sip.

"How are you, my *devushka*?" (This means *girl* in Russian.)

"I'm good," I nod. "*Khorosho*." (Russian for *good*. As you can see, I picked up quite a bit of the language from Melly's family. Just add it to my long list of talents.)

"Yes?" she asks. She looks at me with a pitiful gaze. "I saw on the Facebook that Scott has baby now, yes?"

"Oh," I say. "Right. Yes. A week ago."

"She looks like gremlin to me," Mrs. A says.

"Who? The baby?"

"No, no. The girl." Mrs. A's voice kills me. It sounds like she's saying *Ze girl*.

I laugh. "You're sweet to say that."

"How baby even came out of that? She looks like baby herself. So small, like foolish demon child."

"I love you, Mrs. A," I say, smiling.

"Mela says you went home in Uber. From sickness."

"Oh. Yeah. I drank too much last weekend."

"No, there is no such thing as 'drink too much.' There is only 'not eat enough bread.'" She reaches into the pocket of her jacket and hands me a buttered roll. Purple pocket lint is stuck to the edge of it. "Here. I bring you bread."

I accept it, even though it's a little gross. Mrs. A is like that grandmother who shoves all the crackers from the diner into her purse, forgets about them, and then rediscovers them at the most inopportune times, like in the middle of a funeral. You wonder, *What in the world is happening right now?* as she's snacking on her found treasure, crumbs flying everywhere—but you love her just the same. I take a bite of the bread.

"Maybe you come to my house. Is too cold for beach. You need lunch."

"Oh, I ate already," I say.

"So, you come have second lunch," Mrs. A says.

I hold up the travel mug. "But you just *gave* me second lunch! Soup and bread. Delicious."

"Gracie," she says, shaking her head and making a *tsk, tsk* noise. "Soup and bread is only snack."

"Of course," I say. Because if there's one thing I know, it's that you don't argue with Melly's mom when she's trying to feed you.

I dutifully fold up the beach chair, and we head back to her house.

Once inside, she motions for me to sit down at the table, and she immediately begins buzzing around the kitchen. Before I know it, a plate featuring a mountain of pelmeni is in front of me, smothered by a giant scoop of sour cream and sprinkled with freshly chopped dill.

"For you, Gracie. Dumplings for my best dumpling." She smiles and pats my hair, like one might pat a good little dog.

"Thank you," I say, sinking my teeth into the thick pasta shell hiding the mixture of ground meats inside. The whole point of taking a walk was to try and be healthy. This is just proof that the *calories* find *me*.

Mrs. A sits across from me at the table. "You are sad, yes?"

I shrug. "I'm okay."

"Then why you sit on beach in winter like homeless?" she asks.

"It's warm today. April's not winter—it's spring!"

Mrs. A shakes her head. "Where I come from, every month is winter," she says.

I can't help but laugh. My phone dings.

"You have message," Mrs. A comments.

"It's okay," I say, waving it off.

"You check. You know what they say, 'Opportunity knocks only once.' You check. Could be good news."

I pull out my phone. It's an email from Colin. I don't open it. For one thing, if he read my work and hated it, I want to be alone when I find out—and preferably near a toilet in case second lunch decides to repeat on me. And if he loved it, I want to be alone so I can bask in his praise. It's this potential basking that I'm thinking about when Mrs. A calls me out.

"You see? It is happy message. You are smiling."

"It's just an email," I say, popping a dumpling in my mouth.

"No. You make face like this, is not 'just email.' Is somebody special?"

I shake my head. "Just an old friend."

"Is boy, this friend?"

I nod, chewing. "From high school."

"Ah. In my family, we have saying. 'Best way to forget is drink Goldschläger.'"

I laugh at the ridiculousness of this family mantra.

"Means like American saying: 'Best way get over someone is get under the bed.'"

Now there are tears coming out of my eyes from laughing so hard. "I'm sorry, Mrs. A. I think you mean, 'The best way to get over someone is to get under someone else.'" I wipe my cheeks with a napkin.

She points at me with her wise, knowing red fingernail, nodding her head, considering these words. "Ah, yes. This very wise. You do that. This boy, he is handsome?"

I nod. "I think so, yes."

"He has job?"

"He runs a law firm."

"Oh my. Then, yes, my Gracie. You call him back now. You go. You get under him. I pack this food for you."

I shake my head as Mrs. A takes the half-eaten meal away from me and spoons it into an empty Tupperware container. She wraps the container in three rubber bands, places it in a plastic grocery bag, and hands it to me. I stand and give her a hug. She smells like heavy perfume mixed with fryer oil.

"Remember, Gracie. The first pancake is always lumpy."

"Um, thanks," I reply.

"Is mean, you keep trying. The right one will come."

"Thanks, Mrs. A. And thank you for the food. You're the best," I say. I mean it too. She's right, after all. The first pancake *is* always lumpy. And I should know. Pancakes are one of my top three fave breakfast foods.

TO: Grace Landing (gracie222@mail.com)
FROM: Colin Yarmouth (cyarmouth@
    yarmouthaycockpc.com)
RE: Be nice!

Hi,

Okay—I read the pages you sent. I have SO much to say, lol—it would take me hours to write it all down. Are you free to talk on the phone tonight instead?

Let me know,
Colin

P.S. Do you prefer to be called Grace or Gracie?

TO: Colin Yarmouth (cyarmouth@
    yarmouthaycockpc.com)
FROM: Grace Landing (gracie222@mail.com)
RE: Be nice!

Ugh—now you've got me all nervous! I hope you didn't totally hate it.

Yes, of course I can talk on the phone tonight. What time were you thinking?

My friends and family call me Gracie. Now that you've basically seen me naked (which is what reading a first draft of a writer's work is akin to), I guess you should call me Gracie too.

Let me know about the phone call.

Thanks,
Gracie

TO: Grace Landing (gracie222@mail.com)
FROM: Colin Yarmouth (cyarmouth@
    yarmouthaycockpc.com)
RE: Be nice!

No, I definitely didn't hate it! I'm sorry, I'm not trying to make you nervous. Just have a Zoom call at 3pm so I'm a little pressed for time.

As for tonight—how is 7:30? I should be finished eating dinner by then.

And I'm going to leave that comment about seeing you naked alone—for now. ;)

Colin

TO: Colin Yarmouth (cyarmouth@
    yarmouthaycockpc.com)

FROM: Grace Landing (gracie222@mail.com)
RE: Be nice!

Okay, 7:30. Looking forward to it.

P.S.—I obviously didn't mean it the way you're taking it! Pervert!

TO: Grace Landing (gracie222@mail.com)
FROM: Colin Yarmouth (cyarmouth@
yarmouthaycockpc.com)
RE: Be nice!

Excuse me, I am not the one who wrote a story where every other page is about erections. Who's the real pervert here? Lol!
7:30 it is. Can't wait.

C.

Wow. With five hours left until my chat with Colin, I have no clue what to do with myself for the rest of the afternoon. For someone who works from home, you would think that I'm always bored, but this is actually rarely the case. In fact, because of deadlines and awful attempts at first drafts, I usually keep myself quite busy. Even since Scott's been gone. I mean, there's definitely more of a lull than there used to be when he was around all the time, but still. I'm a great procrastinator but I'm also a workaholic in many ways.

The thing is, in those rare moments where I *can't* work—like if Lindsay is reviewing a draft, for example—I get stir crazy. I can't sit still. Add to that the anxiety mounting in my body from my impending phone date, and I have two choices: 1) induce vomiting to evacuate the butterflies from my stomach, or 2) clean the house.

I choose the latter. First, I collect all the laundry strewn about my bedroom and take it downstairs to the laundry room. When I return to the apartment, Dorian Gray is hiding under the bed. He's a smart kitty. He knows there's a storm brewing.

Next, I tackle dishes. I'm not a slob, but I hate doing dishes. I even hate loading and unloading the dishwasher. As a result, dishes pile up in my sink rather frequently. I roll up my sleeves and tell Alexa to play some house cleaning music. She mistakes this for *house* music, and suddenly my ears are assaulted by the electronic fire of dance beats that feel equivalent to an auditory strobe light. I correct Alexa, explicitly ask for songs by Ariana Grande, and let the warm water run over my forearms as I rinse and load the dishwasher with stacks of plates, bowls, and silverware while expending energy bopping around from side to side. (When intoxicated, I *dance*. Sober, I just bop.) I wash the pots and pans by hand, then I wipe down the counter.

While Ariana belts out songs about sexual positions (she's super subtle), I'm interrupted by my phone ringing. I check the screen and dry my hands on a dishtowel. It's a 212 number. Probably spam, but I answer just in case.

"Hello?"

"Grace?"

"Yeah?" It's kind of hard to hear with Ariana in the background begging the listener to "fuck me till the daylight," but I don't immediately recognize the voice, so I'm still not convinced it's not a telemarketer.

"It's Colin."

Oh, shit. "Alexa, stop!" I yell.

He laughs. "Having a party over there?"

"If laundry and dishes are your idea of a party, then yes. A hundred percent." I check the time. 3:30. "What's up? I thought you had a Zoom call?"

"I did. It just ended. I just, um," he begins.

I wait, eyebrows raised.

"I think we should have dinner tonight," he blurts out.

"You do?" I ask. "You mean, like, together?"

"Yes," he says. "Together. I feel like it will be easier to work on your manuscript if we're sitting at the same table."

Easier for you, maybe. I, meanwhile, will probably not hear a word of what you say if you're anywhere as good looking as I remember. Or if you use that soft voice. My God, I might just melt into a puddle on the ground. "Um, okay. Sure." My heart is racing. I think I'm actually having a coronary. There is a sudden intense pressure in my rib cage.

"Say around seven? I can come pick you up."

"From Astoria?"

"Sure. I'll go home and change real quick, and then I'll drive over to get you."

"You have a car?"

He laughs. "Yeah. Don't you?"

"Nope. I thought about buying one when I was supposed to move to the suburbs, but over here I really don't need one."

"Fair enough. I bought mine when I moved to the island, so yeah, that makes sense. But I kept it because driving is a nice luxury every now and again."

"I'll bet. Do you know your way around Brooklyn?"

"Not really, but I'll figure it out."

"Okay, well, just a warning—it's a hike. It might take you over an hour in rush hour traffic."

"That's okay, Gracie," he says. "I think it'll be worth it. I'll leave the office early."

I wonder if you can text 9-1-1 operators while you're in the middle of a phone call. Like Emergency. I'm having a heart attack. The hottest guy in the whole school is asking me out. Please come. My chest pounds and I try to breathe and remain composed. I picture their response. Ma'am. You're thirty-one. You haven't been in high school in over ten years. You should be ashamed of yourself for wasting taxpayer money by requesting a response to an embarrassing text message like this.

I swallow. "'Kay."

"One job. You pick the restaurant. Something nice."

"What kind of food do you want?"

"How do you feel about Italian?" he asks.

Good. Better than Mexican, which'll have me farting all night. I can pick something relatively safe at an Italian place. "I love Italian," I say.

"Okay. Pick a nice Italian place and I'll see you at seven. Email me your address."

I gulp. "Uh huh."

"You okay?" he asks.

"Yepperoni," I say. *Oh, fuck. Not this again.*

He laughs. "See you soon, Gracie Landing."

Colin

I asked her out to dinner.

I could have asked her out for drinks instead, which is more of a typical first step, but after reading the pages she sent me, I don't know. Like, talking to her on the phone and over email, she was really funny—but reading her work was kind of *hot*. Definitely not what I expected. So, I figure if this is a girl who can nail funny *and* sexy, she might be someone worth having dinner with.

Plus, I haven't been out on a real date since before I was with Elle. And yes, I realize I could just take her out for drinks instead of committing to a meal, but Gracie doesn't seem like the kind of girl you'd pick up at a bar.

I don't want to be one of *those* guys, anyway. A guy like Dom, who tries to lay his swagger down on random strangers over beer and loud music. Been there, done that, and I'm not a fan. Those girls are usually sloppy and overdone. Plus, it's dark—and what looks good in the dark might not look quite as appealing in the light of day. I figure by meeting up for dinner, I can basically kill two birds with one stone: I can see if she's nice looking *and* get a good meal.

I honestly prefer to have a girlfriend. I realize that's not a very macho thing to say, but it's true.

The best girlfriend I ever had was this girl named Caitlin, who I met the summer after freshman year of college. I had just come back to the Bronx from my stint in Arizona, and I got a summer job at Brophy's Hardware Store so I could start saving money. Caitlin was the owner's daughter. She was studying to be an elementary school teacher at Marist College in Poughkeepsie, and she lived in a huge house in Larchmont. Her dad owned *seven* hardware stores throughout the Bronx and Westchester. She was forbidden fruit (being my boss' daughter) and so was I (being an employee of her dad's). Also, I don't think it helped that I lived in the Bronx, given how rich her family was. We had lots of stuff in common, namely a similar taste in all things media. She came into the store one day in August claiming to have an extra ticket to a Counting Crows concert in Wappingers Falls, a little town in Dutchess County.

I was never really the type to think that things are "meant to be," but this particular concert was being held at a minor league baseball stadium.

In exchange for my free ticket, I drove Caitlin there, and on the way home, it was so late and we were both so tired that we pulled over in a McDonald's parking lot and slept together. Literally. We took a nap, holding hands. She was my girlfriend after that. We saw each other every weekend. She'd come visit me one weekend, and I'd go stay with her the following weekend. We went back and forth like that until graduation, when she moved to Hawaii as part of a teacher placement program offered by her school. Neither of us wanted the relationship to end, but after one visit to Hawaii (which involved two layovers, took about twenty hours of travel time each way, and cost me a whole month's worth of paychecks from the hardware store), we came to terms with the hard truth that it wouldn't exactly be feasible for us to maintain something long distance.

She's married now, according to social media.

After Caitlin, I became a serial dater, thanks to spending a little too much time with Billy and Bobby from high school. We met girls wherever we could find them: bars, clubs, even restaurants (I dated three different waitresses, all of whom responded favorably to the whole "phone number on the receipt" pickup line). My relationships lasted anywhere from a few weeks to a few months, but nothing serious.

Once I got older, I got my own place in the city, which made me a hot commodity on the dating circuit. Billy was still living at home and Bobby was renting a basement apartment in a sketchy area of Queens, and every single weekend, they'd hit me up to go out. But I was tired of the scene.

I was twenty-eight by the time I met Elle. We met at the Strand (which is to bookstores what Urban Outfitters is to clothing stores, in my opinion). I was there in search of a birthday gift for my mother. Elle was there for a book launch for some author whose name I can't remember. I noticed her browsing the tote bags. I went over and asked her if she could help me choose a nice one for my mom, and she did. I think she thought it was cute that I gave a shit about my mother's birthday. She asked if I wanted to stay for the reading. I had no interest, but I told her I'd stick around if she'd have a drink with me after. I was fresh off a breakup with Heather, the receptionist at the accounting firm my father used for our annual audit, and I guess my game was pretty on point because she smiled and said yes.

Elle explained that she was an assistant at a swanky literary agency and that the author was represented by one of the agents she worked under. Part of her job involved making sure the big-name authors were "taken care of" at events like this. She sat up front, and I hung back because I understood about not mixing work and personal stuff (especially now that we had to find a new accounting firm to do our tax returns).

Afterwards, we went to a bar nearby. I ordered a Jack and Coke and she got a Sex on the Beach, which basically was like a green light to take her back to my place. Little did I know, she was down for whatever—like, surprisingly. The girl wasn't even drunk and it was a Tuesday night, but somehow I was able to get her between the sheets before ten o'clock. I think it was the apartment, if I'm being honest. She told me she was sharing a place with two other girls in the West Village and was happy for a night away from them, even if it meant doing a train ride of shame the following morning.

We started dating. She loved my place and, without much warning, began hanging out there all the time. She said the quiet was perfect for reading manuscripts. I'd grab takeout on the way home from work, and she would meet me there. We didn't have much in common, but the sex was good, she didn't make me watch a bunch of girly television shows, and she was meticulous about cleaning. I'm a pretty clean guy, but she meant *business*. I never saw countertops sparkle like that.

Wife material, right? That's what I thought. After eighteen months, I proposed. Saved up some money, gave her a fancy wedding, and bought her a house in the burbs. She could scrub to her heart's content.

Six months later, I was at the law offices of D'Aleo and Strauss seeking representation for my divorce case. Courtney had just been hired as Dom's paralegal. I made the mistake of joining Dom and his team for happy hour *one time,* and now the girl can't look me in the eye without becoming an emotional train wreck.

So, yeah. I've learned my lesson about mixing business with pleasure. Won't be making that mistake again, thank you very much.

Gracie's a safe bet though. She's from my *high school,* for God's sake.

What could go wrong?

Gracie

I hang up the phone and check the time again, like a neurotic person. It's 3:35 now. All of a sudden, the meaning of time
has completely shifted. Like how on Christmas morning, when
you're a kid, if you have to wait until 6:00 a.m. to open the gifts
and it's 5:30, those minutes just drag by so slowly—but, if you're
a grown person hitting snooze on the alarm clock on a Monday
morning, thirty minutes can go by in a snap.

Panic ensues as I realize I only have three hours and twenty-
five minutes to get ready for a monumental, once-in-a-lifetime,
dream-come-true kind of event. I look in the bathroom mirror.
Oh, man. This is going to take some serious strategizing.

My hair hasn't been colored in well over a month, and there's
no way I can pull off all that root growth looking trendy, or even
intentional. Thank God for L'oreal Excellence. A two-pack of
6G—Light Golden Brown—which, in reality, always comes out
like chestnut brown with dark blond highlights, is living under
my bathroom sink. Another win for procrastination; I meant
to color my hair two weekends ago but instead decided it was
more important to YouTube how to make a red velvet cake from

scratch. (Which, side note, came out sinfully delicious.) And we all know what happened to me *last* weekend.

I roll on the cheap plastic gloves, unscrew the caps, and mix up a bottle of the dye. "Alexa, continue!" I yell, knowing I'll need some good get-in-the-mood-for-a-hot-date music to pump me up. It takes about ten minutes of careful application to cover my roots. I gather all of my hair up in a big plastic clip on top of my head and crack the bathroom window to let out some of the toxic fumes.

Then, while that sets, I run a bath. I take off my sweats and slide my hands along my legs. *Damn.* It's been a minute since I broke out my razor. I begin to entertain the internal tug of war. *If I shave, I'm assuming there's a chance he might be getting me out of my pants tonight. If I don't shave, there's no chance at all because I won't let his first encounter with my skin be reminiscent of a* Planet of the Apes *movie.*

So, yes. Definitely need to shave.

I haven't bought actual shaving cream since I was a teenager, but a healthy palmful of conditioner seems to do the trick once I glide down into the bathtub. I'm not a hairy girl—my body hair is thin and light in color—but still. When we were in high school, Colin Yarmouth dated some of the best-looking teenage girls on the planet. I'm sure their skin was smooth like rose petals or menthol cigarettes, not all sprouted like some science experiment where you track what happens to an old potato with toothpicks stuck in it. *Dammit. This is what I get for not shaving all winter.*

I am slow, methodical, and careful with the razor because I notice there's a bit of rust along the edge, which means this will only end badly if I rush. I get through both legs and then find myself face-to-face with a grave decision.

What to do about the fuzzy butterfly in between?

I have never been waxed. Like I said, I'm grateful for my body hair situation. And something about the idea of having some undoubtedly gorgeous, Scandinavian-looking bombshell come anywhere near my undercarriage with a bowl full of candle drippings just terrifies me. Like, for real. It's the stuff of nightmares and horror films.

To be fair, my downstairs isn't completely terrible. When Scott and I first dated, I used to use a pair of nail scissors to keep things trim. Once we were basically living together, I upgraded to his haircutting kit, using the same electric razor that I used for his biweekly fades to keep my own hedges tight. Every few weeks or so, I'd mow the lawn using a number one cutting attachment. By the time we were cohabitating for about a year and a half, I got the sense that he really didn't care, so after swimsuit season, I gave up on that and grew it out. Scott never complained, but then, of course, Ilana came along, and she probably never sprouted a pubic hair in her life. I'm sure I looked like a woolly mammoth by comparison, and he left me for her, so yeah, it's probably best I handle this situation lest I remain single for all eternity.

Since he no longer lives here, I don't have access to his electric razor anymore, but I know I can't go at this mess straight on without a solid trim first. So, I stand up, drain the bathtub, dry off my hands, and fumble through my makeup case for the old nail scissors. I move onto the toilet and begin to snip away at the jungle, Ariana's encouraging "Thank U, Next" permeating my airspace.

Once I can see the light at the end of the proverbial tunnel, I check my phone and turn the shower back on to heat up for my impending rinse. Now, I have a real choice. I have to guess if Colin prefers a total smoothie or just a well-groomed patch. I reach for the Gold Bond ultimate super-healing hand lotion that I use only in the dead of winter when my thumb skin cracks open like fault lines during an earthquake. I squeeze a hefty drop of it onto my forefinger and rub it in. I work the razor around the edges. *God is a woman, like the song says. Let's leave a little something down there to remind him of that.* I opt for a wide landing strip.

The way I was taught, when shaving a sensitive area, always work top down, in the general direction of the hair growth. Well, I'm doing that, and things are looking good. I finish up the most visible area and grab my compact mirror from my makeup case to check out my artwork.

I am a vagenius, I tell myself, smiling.

But how does that saying go? Never mistake arrogance for intellect? That's what I *should* be thinking when I decide to take the haircut to the next level and shave underneath.

Bad idea. Very bad.

In fact, here's a fun riddle for you. What do you get when you cross a rusty razor with an inflated ego? Yup. A lacerated labia.

Holy. Sweet. Jesus.

Blood drips into the bowl as I moan aloud. I hop into the shower, smearing blood onto the toilet seat and dripping some on my bathroom rug. It's running down my leg like a biblical river—surely, one of the plagues has befallen me. I cross my legs tightly and unclip my muddy bun, rinsing the dye so I don't end up overprocessing and frying my hair with chemicals. This is a horrible idea. A noxious stream of 6G makes its way directly to my crotch, as if pulled there by a magnet, only to incite a riot among nerve endings already under siege.

I rinse, and rinse, and rinse some more, until finally the water runs pinkish-clear again and my body goes into that shock of when the pain is so much that you can no longer feel it. I scrub down everything except the *one* part that should be the cleanest with a bar of Dove soap and then wash my hair with shampoo and conditioner.

Finally, after what feels like an excruciating eternity, I wring out my hair and step out of the shower. I dry off with a white towel (mistake number three) and notice there is still fresh blood. Unsure of how to proceed, at least for the foreseeable future, I grab a Band-Aid and affix it horizontally across both lips, sealing them shut like the world's tiniest chastity belt.

Hopefully, it will clot.

Now, to the bedroom to try and figure out an outfit. *Oh, shit. I need to put the laundry in the dryer.* I throw back on the sweatpants, almost losing my Band-Aid more than once, slip a hoodie over my freshly colored head, slide on my sneakers, and head back downstairs.

In the elevator on the way back up, I consider our dinner options. I feel a lot like Presley in the story—should I try for a fancy restaurant or just go with pizza? I don't want to look like the kind of girl who needs a man to take her out to an expensive dinner, but, if we're being honest, I'm still a little scarred from the pizza incident from last night. The only place I can think of for *nice* Italian is Luna Bella, a waterfront restaurant on Emmons Avenue. It's kind of romantic, but maybe that's okay. I mean, this was *supposed* to be a phone call. *Colin* is the one who upgraded it to a full-on date.

Luna Bella it is. I go back into my apartment and call them to make a reservation—a table for two at 7:15 overlooking the water.

Since the laundry is in the dryer and there might be something in there worth wearing, I head back into the bathroom to dry and style my hair, an operation that—when I care about how I look—can take upwards of an hour. The blow-drying part takes about twenty-five minutes, largely because I have so much hair. I use a round brush and section it, and to be honest, I typically do this while sitting on the floor reading a book. But seeing as how my bathroom presently looks like a murder scene from CSI, I realize I need to clean it first.

Twenty minutes later, after the toilet, sink, and bathtub have all returned to their proper shade of white, I'm seated on the ground, and instead of a regular book (I just don't have the headspace for that right now), I drag my laptop into the bathroom and open up my manuscript.

When you're a writer, sometimes you reread your work and wonder what spirit took over your body and wrote the things on the page. Like, am I *really* capable of turning the features of a condo into the basis for dirty talk? Did I *really* put a guy in the closet and then have his wife stab him in the ass with a pair of scissors? Did I *really* refer to potential sex as *pelvic sorcery*? Worst of all, did I really use the not-so-clever name "Connor Yates" for my main male character and then *send* the story to Colin? Who allowed this to happen? I even made Connor the star of the high school soccer team and then went on to describe his backside in full detail. *More than once.*

I think I need to consider a lobotomy. I am clearly a danger to myself.

I close the laptop when my hair is dry. I look like Diana Ross—even though I try to work my mane with the brush, the only thing that can get the natural curl out is my straightening iron. I plug it in to let it heat up, and then go back into my bedroom to assess the situation there.

The bed is unmade, which is fine, because I own exactly two pairs of sheets and I plan to put the fresh ones on for this special occasion. For insurance, you know. Just in case we end up in there (assuming my botched labiaplasty heals in time). It's like how you should always have a box of condoms in the nightstand. Which I do. They were Scott's but once I realized *I* was the only one he was using them with, I decided I should be allowed to keep them when we split. Take that, Scott! That's nine dollars back in my pocket!

I strip the bed and shove the dirty sheets in the bottom of my closet for the time being. I replace them with the clean sheets and make the bed. Since I don't have time to wash the comforter, I spray a healthy amount of Febreze on top and light my cinnamon-scented Yankee Candle to freshen up the room a bit.

Next, I head back to the bathroom to handle my hair. I try to focus on my breathing. Tori's girlfriend, Kiki, teaches yoga, and she always says, "Conscious breathing is the body's most natural form of meditation." I am an awful meditator. I just can't get my mind to shut down like that. In order to try and think about nothing, I close my eyes and try to focus on my immediate surroundings, and then I'll remember something totally irrelevant and asinine, like how the man stretching next to me has an obvious ingrown toenail and how maybe he should invest in a pair of yoga socks so as not to visually violate the rest of us with the inflammation protruding from his nail bed. And then, I start to giggle. Usually uncontrollably. Kiki tells Tori that she really likes me but has cordially uninvited me to participate in her classes. It's not personal, I know that. I can't help it if my brain is ticklish.

Since I am not a well-trained deep breather, I'm finding it awfully hard to calm down right now. I tell Alexa to put on zen spa music, which she sees as an opportunity to remind me that I might want to order more maxi pads. (Who programs Alexa, anyway?) I finish my hair in silence, listening to the thumping of my clogged arteries and wondering if this is all some elaborate scheme from the universe to shit on me like a jealous seagull circling a beach picnic.

I head back down to the basement of the building to get my laundry, the Band-Aid reminding me with every step of my earlier bathroom blunder. I fold my clothes in my apple-pie scented bedroom and try to decide on an outfit.

A dress? No. Too fancy.

Nice jeans? Hmm. Too casual?

A skirt? Nope. Makes my hips look too wide, like I'd have no problem birthing a small calf.

Slacks? Sure, if the date is with my grandmother.

I go back to the jeans in my closet. I thumb through the

pile and remember, I have one pair of black jeggings—you know, those pants that are half jeans, half leggings. Super stretchy and comfortable. Good for eating Italian. I can dress these up, for sure. And if I drip sauce on myself, these will hide any potential stains.

Yes.

Thank you, God, for these black jeggings.

I choose a black tank top over a black push up bra. I gently and carefully remove the Band-Aid as I change into my only pair of black lace panties—full coverage, because all the thongs are gone, but still sexy enough. Over the black tank top, I put on a sheer metallic gold sweater that accentuates my padded boobs and healthy curves, and that matches my gold sparkly belt. For shoes, I'll go with the trusty tall black riding boots so I can wear socks underneath and not feel like my feet are going to explode with blisters if I have to walk a block or two. I add big gold hoop earrings, a few bangle bracelets, and a spritz of perfume on my wrists, and check the mirror. *Amazing. I look like a real human woman.*

I refold the contents of my closet, which are now strewn about all over my bed. Gotta keep the bed neat! Then, I head into the living room to see what cleaning needs to be done in there. Dorian Gray is asleep on the couch. Asleep! At a time like this! A dog would have picked up on my mega-nervous vibe by now. A dog would try to console me. Hell, a dog might even try and talk me through this crisis. But not Dorian Gray. He opens one eye and closes it again. I grab the vacuum and go over the carpet. *That* wakes him up and sends him running. I love Dorian Gray, but sometimes he's a little bit of an asshole, if we're being really honest.

Once the rug is free of crumbs and I've wiped the dust off the surfaces, I take a breath and check the time. It's 6:15. Unbelievable. I use the remaining forty-five minutes to put on makeup and nervously pace my apartment until, at 6:50, my phone dings.

Hey, the text says, I'm here. Should I park the car?

Breathe. It's going to be okay. No, I'll come down. Be right there, I write.

Okay, he responds, with a winky face emoji.

I put on my jacket and my black and gold crossbody purse, check myself one more time in the mirror, grab my keys, and head out.

Double parked in front of the building I see a white SUV. A man hops out of the driver's side. He is taller than Scott by at least two inches. His thick brown hair is styled with some type of product, and it's definitely long enough for me to run my fingers through. His eyes are flanked by dark lashes and well-groomed brows. As he walks toward me, I recognize him, but not just from school and not just from the picture on his website.

Holy shit, I realize. *I recognize him from my manuscript.*

When I write, I create visual pictures of my characters in my mind. This is an exercise I learned in college—it helps me feel like I know them more intimately if I can picture them, like you might picture a friend or a relative.

I created Connor Yates—and he looks *exactly* like Colin Yarmouth. That outfit—the khakis with the white collared shirt, the muscular legs beneath, and *oh my God* that perfect ass—it's all right there in front of me. Like I dreamed it into being.

And he's smiling. His wide friendly grin forms tiny crows'

feet on the sides of his eyes, and his allegedly unused laugh lines outline his cheeks as his arms open wide to embrace me in our very first hug.

"Hi," he says.

He is strong, and he's not afraid to show signs of genuine happiness about our unexpected reunion. The feeling is so incredible, I could cry. I swear, after Scott left, there was definitely a small part of me that thought I would die alone. Just me and Dorian Gray, who couldn't even show an ounce of emotion when I was freaking out all afternoon. I never thought another guy would look at me, much less a guy who looks like *this*.

"Hey," I half whisper.

He releases me. "You look great," he says, still smiling.

"Um, yeah, you do too," I say, dumbfounded. *This is a dream, right?*

He steps away and takes a long look at me, like someone who cares about art might look at a painting. (I'm not that girl, unfortunately, so I'm merely hypothesizing.) "You look sort of the same, but also different. Don't get me wrong, you were cute in high school, but now—"

Well, here it is. I knew the other shoe would drop if I waited a minute. "I know," I say. "I've looked into adult orthodontics. I just don't have the money."

He laughs. "You're ridiculous. I was gonna say—"

"It's hereditary, you know. Bad teeth."

"Will you shut up and stop interrupting me?" he says. "You look beautiful."

Inside, I die. Outside, I laugh, and I'm pretty sure I snort a little.

We get in the car and stumble through the first few lines of small talk as I direct him towards Luna Bella. There's no valet because it's a Thursday night, so he parks the car and grabs a file folder with a pen affixed to the outside from his backseat.

Inside, the hostess seats us by the window, and I'm careful to give Colin the seat facing the footbridge to Manhattan Beach. It's the prettier view. She hands us menus and we discuss the options. When the waitress comes, Colin orders the chicken parmigiana and I order the shrimp francese, each with a ginger ale and a house salad.

"No Midori sour tonight?" he asks, after the menus are gone and we're alone again.

I chuckle. "Nope. This is a business meeting, right?"

He nods, picking up the folder and setting it in the space where the cloth napkin is. "Yes," he agrees. "I conduct all of my business meetings by candlelight."

My chest gets tight. "So?" I gesture at the folder. "Scale of one to ten. How bad is it?"

He shakes his head and takes a sip of newly delivered ginger ale. "Nope. That's not how this is going to go."

"That bad, huh?" I joke.

"Yes," he nods. "It was so bad that I couldn't even tell you about it over the phone. I had to come to Brooklyn to soften my comments with salad and shrimp. That was the only way," he says.

"Will you please just tell me?" I say straight-faced, the smile in my heart undoubtedly illuminating my face.

He clears his throat. "You're really talented," he says. "And, my God, *so* funny. Some of the phrasing—I mean, where do you come up with it?"

I shrug.

"But I know *you* don't seem to think it's great. You said on the phone something about the protagonist. And I genuinely want to help. So, explain to me, now that I've read it, what the problem is." He carefully unbuttons each of his shirt cuffs and slowly, methodically rolls up his sleeves, putting his distractingly muscular forearms on display.

"I don't like Presley," I say, gulping.

"Well, sure. I mean, I don't like her either. She actually reminds me a little of my ex-wife."

"Really? Is she a Realtor too?" (Lots of literary agents have a side hustle, so this wouldn't surprise me.)

"No," he says. "But I get the sense that she married me for the money. It's not like I'm loaded either. But I have a solid job and I *had* a decent savings account, until I bought her the house that she kept when we split."

"Hold on. She still *lives* there?"

He sighs. "Yup."

"But you're a *lawyer*! How could you—"

"I—" He shakes his head. "Let's focus on this, first," he says, tapping the folder. "I'm sure we'll get to all of my relationship mishaps at some point."

I don't want to push or make him uncomfortable, so I let it go. "Okay," I say. "Sorry."

"Don't be," he says, stirring the ginger ale with his straw. "So, you and Presley—interesting name choice, by the way—how come you're not jiving?"

I blush. "Well, I just feel like none of it's believable," I say.

"I mean, I'm sure there *are* girls out there who would sleep with someone to sell a condo. I just don't know anyone like that. And I feel like Connor is stupid."

"Hmm," he says. "That's interesting. I actually don't agree. I understand Connor's motivation."

"To *cheat* on his *wife*?"

"No. Don't misunderstand me. His wife seems like a straight-up she-devil, for sure. But he seems, like, sorry. Sad." He takes a slice of the warm Italian bread out of the basket between us. "I don't want to say *pathetic*, but close. Like Presley was the one that got away, and that's amplified by the fact that his wife—Melinda, right?—is just awful."

I nod.

"So, I feel like he's trying really hard to look like he's got his shit together, y'know? Like he's got a solid A-game, when really, he's completely insecure?"

"I guess."

"I mean, I don't think he deserves to be *stabbed*, but I'm only going by the thirty-five pages I read. I'm sure you know more about these two than I do."

At this, I nod.

"The thing is, when I read it, I felt like it was, I don't know." He pauses. "Recognizable. Relatable."

"Really? How?"

"He just seems like he's been through a lot with the wife. At least, that's how I read it." Colin licks the tiniest bit of butter off his lips. The sight of it nearly knocks me on the floor.

"Yeah," I say. "Sure, I suppose. To be honest, I haven't really thought too much about the backstory around his situation. I mean, I've considered it—obviously, they're not in a *good* place— but I don't know exactly why that is. I think I kind of thought it was *his* fault Melinda was so horrible. He's a playboy, don't you think?"

"Maybe. I don't know. It looked to me like there was more than just a horny guy there, like, when you scratch the surface."

"Wait—you mean *all* guys aren't just pigs, nothing more than testosterone and sexual demands?" I joke, sort of.

"Yikes," he says. "Someone's a little sore."

I laugh. "Yeah. I guess that's pretty obvious." I take a breath. "Scott definitely did a number on me."

"I can see that," Colin says. "It's okay. We're all just damaged goods, right?" He smiles, but not exuberantly. More like someone accepting a sad truth.

"I guess so," I agree.

He raises his glass. "Well, here's to damaged goods. You and I wouldn't be here right now if it weren't for us getting our hearts broken, right?"

I clink my glass against his. Our fingers are close enough to touch. We take a sip. I try not to focus on how his perfect lips suck on the plastic straw.

"Does it still hurt?" I ask.

"What?"

"The breakup?"

He shrugs. "Sort of?" He nods in my direction. "What about you?"

"Yeah, sometimes. Like, it's weird. Sometimes I could care less. I mean, really. Fuck him, right?"

"Totally."

"But then I wonder what it says about *me*. Why'd he have to choose *her*, y'know? We were *engaged*. It's not like we were just dating or something."

"I completely understand."

"I often consider a life in the nunnery," I say.

"Are nunneries even a thing anymore?" he asks.

"I don't know. I think so. Maybe later I'll ask Google. I'd hate for my backup plan not to be a solid one."

Colin smiles. "Gotta keep those options open."

The waitress brings our salads. We busy ourselves eating. He chews quietly, his napkin folded in his lap. Scott would never have eaten salad, for one thing, and I am almost a hundred percent sure he never put a cloth napkin in his lap. Colin, by contrast, makes a comment about how the salad dressing might be the best balsamic he's ever tasted, and gratefully accepts my cherry tomatoes when he notices me eating around them. He uses a second piece of Italian bread to mop up the shallow pool of dressing at the bottom of the bowl.

"I'm sorry," he says. "I'm starving, and this is delicious."

"Don't apologize. It's yummy, I agree. And I eat like six meals a day usually, so I get it."

"Really? Are you one of those girls who portions out the food really tiny and eats snacks instead of meals? I forget the name of that meal plan."

I shake my head. "Oh, no," I laugh. "That's definitely not me. If there's one thing I can do—and do well—it's eat. Mostly because I love to cook."

"What kind of food do you cook?"

"Everything. I love trying new stuff out in the kitchen. When I was a kid, my nonna lived with us, and she was always cooking. She never followed a recipe either. She was big on tasting stuff," I say. "You know how some people are born with a silver spoon in their mouths?"

He nods.

"My spoon was wooden. I learned all about spices and flavors and how to mix random stuff together to make all kinds of foods."

"Well, cheers to that. I love a girl with an appetite who's not afraid to indulge."

"Meanwhile, look at you. You look like one of those guys who has incredible metabolism and can eat whatever he wants."

"Nope. I wish!" he says. "I work out. It keeps me sane. I honestly don't know what I would've done after the breakup with Elle if it wasn't for the gym. It was a great way to channel my anger."

"I know the feeling. Ilana was lucky she was pregnant. I could definitely have considered assault otherwise. Although, I don't think I'd do very well in jail."

"Yeah? Why's that?"

"They only give you three meals." I smile.

He grins. "Okay, so let me ask you something. I don't read romance novels—at least, not typically. Does there always have to be a female protagonist?"

"Hmm," I think aloud. "No. But typically, the rule of thumb is write what you know. It creates authenticity if you can relate to your narrator," I say.

"Could you go the other way?"

"And have a male narrator?"

He takes a sip from his water glass. "Yeah."

"I don't know," I say. "I mean, I could certainly *try*."

"Well, let's think about it as an argument. You said that the publisher, or your agent, or both, are pushing you for a second novel. Right?"

"Mm hmm."

"Then, they're hungry for you. They'll likely be open to reading whatever you submit to them, I'm sure."

"I don't disagree. I think they'll *read* whatever I send in. But that doesn't mean they'll publish it. Walk me through your thought process though. Like, all the way."

"If you would be comfortable switching over to Connor's point of view, and write the whole thing from his side, I could help."

"Really? How?"

He nods. "You said you're stuck because you don't like the narrator."

"Uh huh."

"Well, do you like *me*?"

I can feel the heat rise up to my cheeks again. "Yeah."

"So, would *I* be a likeable narrator, then?"

I smile. This could actually be a brilliant idea. "Sure, I guess."

"Then, all you need is Connor's side of the story," Colin says.

"And I'd need to rewrite what I've got."

"Is that awful?"

I shake my head. "No. Not at thirty-five pages. If it was a whole manuscript, that would be tough given the deadline I'm on."

He nods. The waitress delivers our meals.

"Whoa. This is huge," Colin says.

The waitress shreds fresh parmesan cheese over our meals, as if she's sprinkling dairy-based fairy dust over the evening.

"Brooklyn Italian," I say, winking. "Queens doesn't hold a candle to it."

He takes a bite of his chicken. "Damn," he moans. *What I wouldn't do to be the chicken on this beautiful man's fork.*

I start in on my meal too, savoring the fresh flavors. He offers me a taste of his food, which I accept. I reciprocate in kind. The exchange feels intimate, like we've been doing this for years instead of minutes. He keeps his mouth closed when he chews, another thing Scott never did. He orders another ginger ale and offers me one too, which I accept.

"So," he says, when his plate is about half-empty, "Connor."

I smile. "Yes. Your thoughts, please."

"Well, hang on. Before we go all into plot lines and all that, I have some comments."

"Oh, boy." I bite my lip.

"First of all, I had no idea romance novels could be so…" He pauses, looking for the word.

"Sexy?" I offer.

"Yeah. Like, my goodness. I was *not* expecting to read some of the detail that you went into."

"What did you think it would be like? I mean, it says it right there in the genre. It's *romance*."

"When I think of romance, I think of flowers and candy. Maybe a fancy dinner or, if we're going really crazy, a Lexus commercial. But what you wrote—"

I cringe, waiting for him to call it porn. "Smut?" I offer instead.

"Not at all. It was just a lot hotter than I expected it to be."

I exhale, grateful not to have to defend the heat level in my work. "I guess I'm just chock-full of surprises, huh?"

"Are all romance novels like that?" he asks.

"Nope. My agent refers to it as the bedroom door. Some authors keep the door shut tight, so the reader can't see anything. Others keep the door wide open, so the reader can a hundred percent be a fly on the wall. It's not black and white. There's gray there too."

"Fifty shades of it?" Colin laughs.

I shake my head, smirking. "I forgive you for that awful joke."

"You left the door wide open for it."

"Oh my God. Please stop." I laugh.

He nods, swallows a forkful of neatly coiled angel hair, then dabs at the corner of his grin with his napkin.

"Anyway, I guess I should have warned you. I just thought everyone knew that romance novels involved sex. Not all of them, but a lot of them."

"Noted," Colin says. "Like I said, I enjoyed it. I just wasn't expecting it at quite that level, that's all."

I nod.

"So, okay then. My man Connor. He needs a backstory. If he has to be likeable, then the reader needs to understand why he's okay with the idea of cheating on his wife."

"Agreed."

"It's easy, really," Colin says. "The wife cheated first."

"Go on."

"What do you mean? Isn't that *enough*?"

"Well, I mean, in *real* life, sure. But these kinds of stories are high drama. It needs to be unexpected. Like, if Melinda cheated on Connor with Connor's brother, then maybe that could work."

"Connor has a brother?"

I laugh. "I don't know. I'm just saying."

"What if Melinda cheated with a woman?"

"Okay," I say. "I'm interested. Elaborate for me, please."

Colin takes a long deep breath and looks me dead in my eyes. "What if Melinda brought home a woman for Connor's birthday? Like, as a gift. You know, for a—" He lowers his voice. "Threesome," he whispers.

"This is good stuff. Can I borrow your pen so I can take notes?"

He shakes his head. "No need. I won't forget."

I shrug. "Okay. Continue."

"So, Melinda brings home a girl she says she met online. Connor wonders if maybe she's been paid to engage in this escapade. But he's just so excited about the idea of it that he doesn't think to ask at that exact moment."

"Uh huh." I lean in.

"So, one thing leads to another, and they get things started. And Melinda seems to be really enjoying herself. Like, more than Connor expects. She's crazy into it. *Way* more than she's ever been into things she's done with him." He gulps. "She's bold. She obviously knows what she's doing. He wonders if maybe she's done this before. Like, before she was with him." He shakes his head very slightly. "Anyway, there comes a point where Connor sort of realizes that she and this girl are going at it pretty seriously and he's not really…necessary, I guess?" He looks down, contemplating his chicken. Hard.

"Colin?"

"Yeah?"

I don't say anything. But I know. And he knows I know.

"And then, uh, y'know. The girl gives them both chlamydia. Because nothing says, 'Happy birthday,' like an STD from a sex worker your wife hired for herself."

"Colin," I say softly.

"Yup," he says, nodding. His eyes are glued to the votive candle burning in the glass jar beside the window.

"I'm so sorry," I say.

He chews on his lower lip and nods a few times before finally meeting my gaze. "Thanks," he exhales. "She really did a number on me."

"That's awful. Like, really and truly. I don't even know what to say."

"I'm sorry. I'm not trying to ruin our dinner."

"Are you kidding? It's fine. I already told you what Scott did. At least the birthday surprise didn't knock up your wife."

He takes a sip of water. "Guess that's true." He swallows. "Anyway. I thought maybe you could use some of that." He shrugs.

"I mean, yeah—it's incredibly dramatic, and definitely would make for a hell of a backstory if I made Connor the main character. But I don't know, Colin. I don't feel right using something like that. It's so—"

"Fucked up?" he asks.

"I was going to say *personal*."

"Didn't you say everything you write somehow relates to something in real life?"

"Yeah, but not at the expense of hurting someone I—"

"Someone you what?"

My heart flutters. *Jump, Gracie.* "Someone I like so much." He smiles, thank God. *The night is not completely ruined.*

"I like you too," he says, running his forefinger along the rim of his water glass.

I die inside for the millionth time this evening. I try to do that breathing thing from Kiki's yoga class to slow my heartbeat. It doesn't work. I grin like the Cheshire Cat in *Alice in Wonderland* and put my hand over my mouth.

"What?" he asks. "It wasn't obvious?"

It takes me a moment to find my composure. "It's just," I say, "you're Colin *Yarmouth*."

He laughs. "Guilty as charged."

"You don't get it," I explain. "You were like a god in high school."

"Ha! That's some revisionist history."

My mouth hangs open. "You *were*."

"Okay, agree to disagree. What does that have to do with anything?"

I clear my throat. "I was a nobody."

He makes a confused face. "No, you weren't."

"Oh, I definitely was."

"I think you're wrong. But even still. What does it matter? This isn't high school, Gracie."

The waitress appears with dessert menus. "Can I get you guys anything else?" she asks.

I'm grateful for the interruption. I need a second to calm down.

Colin looks over the menu. "How do you feel about tiramisu?" he asks me.

"Sure," I say.

"One tiramisu with two forks, please," he tells the waitress.

She smiles at him and writes down the order. "You got it," she says and walks away with our empty dishes.

"Listen to me," he says. "I want you to use the story I gave you. I mean, if you can. It'd be nice if *something* good could come from it."

"I understand that," I say.

"It's settled then. The idea is yours. And now we don't have to talk about it anymore."

I nod. "Thank you."

"For what?"

"That was really personal. Thank you for sharing it with me."

"Thank you for emailing me."

"When?" I ask.

"When you were drunk. You've made me laugh so much the past few days. You have no idea how nice that's been."

I smile, and we slip into more conversation about which outer borough has better desserts as the waitress returns with our tiramisu and the check. Colin pays without a word, and I don't fight him about it, but I graciously thank him. We leave the restaurant and head back to his car, where he opens the door for me.

We drive the few blocks back to my place, and, once we're double parked outside, I say, "Would you like to come up?"

He looks at the time on the dashboard. It's almost ten. "I want to, and thank you for the offer, but—"

"Right. Of course," I say. "I'm sure you're super, um, tired."

He laughs. "You're nuts, you know that?"

I look at him. "Why?"

"I *want* to come upstairs. But I know—and you know—what will happen if I do."

I lower my chin. "And would that be so bad?" I ask quietly.

"Yes—because I have a meeting tomorrow morning. And that would mean I wouldn't have time to cook you breakfast."

"I can skip breakfast," I whisper, as he places his left hand on my cheek.

He leans his face in closer. I smell the garlic on his breath, but I don't care. I lick my lips, pushing away any concerns about what my mouth might taste like.

"But I make a killer eggs benedict," Colin whispers, and I see his eyes close as he moves his face in to meet mine.

His kiss is transcendent. I am lifted out of my own body, floating in the air somewhere, completely weightless. His tongue is gentle but firm. He moves his hands slowly, reaching one across the center console of the car to hold my waist and running the fingers of the other one through my hair, lightly massaging the back of my scalp with his neatly trimmed nails. I feel exhilarated and exhausted all at once, like a runner who has reached the end of a marathon and finally crosses the finish line. I want so much more from him, but in this moment, in this vehicle, on this Thursday night, I am wholly satisfied.

"Mmm," he says, slowly pulling away in order to take a breath.

I open my eyes. It's real. He's still here. This actually happened. It's not cystic acne Ronald in front of me—it's Colin Yarmouth, genuine flesh and bone. I don't know what to say, but I feel my mouth form a smirk, and before I know why, I begin to laugh.

"What's so funny?"

I shake my head.

"What? Do I taste bad?"

"Oh my God, no," I say. "Not at all."

"Then, what is it?"

"You have no idea how long I've wanted to do that for."

"Yeah?"

I nod. "I used to daydream about kissing you."

"Really?"

"Uh huh," I say, sheepishly.

"And? How did the real thing measure up?"

"Good. *Very* good."

He nods. "I'm glad. Can I call you when I get home, or will you be asleep?"

"You can call," I say. "You should call. Definitely."

"Okay," he says, licking his lower lip. "Then I definitely will."

"It's probably a good thing you're going," I say.

"Why's that?"

"Because I lied to you before."

He looks at me, confused.

"I could never skip breakfast," I say.

He kisses me again, says good night, and waits in the car until I am safely inside.

Colin

TO: Grace Landing (gracie222@mail.com)
FROM: Colin Yarmouth (cyarmouth@
 yarmouthaycockpc.com)
SUBJECT: Last night

Good morning,

Sorry for the early email. I hope I'm not waking you! I know I said this on the phone last night, but I just wanted to reiterate that I had a really great time with you on our date. I hope the story I shared with you will help your writing. I'd be happy to read the pages you come up with as you go, if that's helpful. I don't know enough about the writing process to offer lots of advice, but at least I can be a sounding board. I don't know. It's just an idea.

Another idea: Are you free to go out with me again sometime this weekend? I know you're working to meet your deadline, but I would love to bring you to my neck of the woods for a taste of Astoria.

Let me know!
C.

P.S.—I just reread that, and I think you're rubbing off on me. "Taste of Astoria" sounds at least marginally sexual. Lol!

TO: Colin Yarmouth (cyarmouth@
    yarmouthaycockpc.com)
FROM: Grace Landing (gracie222@mail.com)
RE: Last night

Wow—you weren't kidding when you said you had to be up early. I know you have your whole morning workout thing, but I didn't expect to get an email from you before 6am. That's *extreme*, in my opinion.

Yes—although my social calendar is brimming with events this weekend (and by events, I mean binge-watching Netflix, getting Chinese takeout, and trying to hit an insanely high daily page count), I would be happy to go out with you again. When are you thinking? And I feel awful to make you drive all the way to Sheepshead Bay only to turn around and have to drive back to Astoria—that just seems like a waste of gas. I can take the train. It's no big deal.

Good luck with your morning meeting. Talk to you soon!

Xo,
G.

P.S.—If it doesn't work out with estate law, you could definitely try your hand at romance novel writing. I think you'd be a natural. Your debut book could be called *Taste of Astoria* and could feature two gorgeous Greek people who run the trope of enemies-to-lovers into the ground with their competing spanakopita food trucks. For sure, you're sitting on a gold mine.

She's kind of adorable. Not in that first-grader-with-pigtails-and-no-front-teeth way, but in that I-wonder-what-you-look-like-naked sort of way. Her smile is incredible, and her hair is so soft, and—

Fuck. I was *not* expecting this.

I knew I was in trouble when Gracie invited me up to her place and I said no. I never say no—not unless I'm catching feelings. Only then might I say things like, "I think our first time should be *special*," and other shit like what was running through my head when I kissed her in the car.

Daisy caught me this morning when she came in, too. She

said "Good morning," and I said, "Good morning," but I must have said it weird because the next thing she said was, "Somebody got lucky last night," in this weird singsongy voice.

"What are you talking about?" I asked.

"Well, first you left early, and then Gordon said he overheard you giggling."

"I wasn't *giggling*. I was *reading*. My God, Daisy. I don't *giggle*." I could feel my cheeks turning red though. I *may* have been giggling. The manuscript had some funny lines in it. "Fuck Gordon, anyway. Like he knows anything about getting laid."

"I think the lady doth protest too much," Daisy said. I could hear the smirk in her voice.

I got up and went over to the reception area. I tried to glare at Daisy, but my smile crept through.

"Are you going to tell me who she is? Or do I have to guess?"

"And risk messing up what we have, my queen? Never. My lips are sealed."

She grinned, nodding. "You look happy this morning. That's all I'm saying."

"Well, thank you. You look happy too," I said.

"I am," she said. "Gordon's not coming in till ten, so I have more than an hour to enjoy my breakfast in peace."

"Excellent," I said. I started to head back into my office, and she called after me, "I'm here, you know, in case you want to talk."

I sat down in my chair. "Thanks, Daisy," I said. "When there's something to talk about, you'll be the first to know."

"Fair enough," she said. "Do you need anything for your meeting today?"

"No. It should be straightforward enough. I figure I'll leave here around ten."

"Avoiding Gordon, are you?"

I laugh. "Always."

"Did you drive in?"

"I did. The roads should be okay midmorning. And the meeting starts at eleven. An hour should be enough time to get me there."

"Sounds like you've got it all figured out."

"Assuming everything goes smoothly, I'll be one step closer to freedom."

Daisy rolls back in her chair. I look up and she's standing in my doorway, holding her mug of coffee.

"That's good, Colin. I think this is long overdue."

"Yeah," I agree. My tone shifts from silly to solemn, and I hope she doesn't notice.

"Letting go is never easy," she continues. *Of course she noticed. That's Daisy for you.*

"I know. I say that to my clients all the time."

"Well, you'll like Lydia. She's the best. She sold my co-op in five days and got me top dollar for it," she continues. "I know it's scary to make big life changes, but I think it's time. Just my two cents," she shrugs.

I nod, trying not to get in my head about this meeting. "Thanks again for the referral, Daisy. *You're* the best."

"Anything for you, kiddo."

She winks, turns, and goes back to her desk.

Gracie

Buzzing off the leftover bits of adrenaline from last night, my promise to the universe on this fine Friday morning is to focus up and give my story's new direction a bona fide try. I brew a large pot of hazelnut Folgers and swear to myself that I will take only two breaks between now and lunchtime, and they can only be to pee and/or to refill my coffee cup. At lunch, I can check my email again.

I open up the laptop. The cursor mocks me. *You can't do it, Karlie London*, it says.

I take a breath and stretch my arms up over my head, cracking my knuckles towards the sky.

Like hell I can't, I whisper to the screen.

Where were we? That's right. Presley and Connor are eating dinner on the floor in front of the fireplace—pizza slices and a chicken roll—and we have to experience this through Connor's eyes. Okay. He feels sad—no, *pathetic*—like as if it's not enough that his marriage had morphed into a sham, he's finally back in front of his first love but is nursing an ass wound on top of her coat. He laments his choices, specifically the choice to stay with

Melinda and try to take care of her instead of hiring a hard-nosed lawyer who could have cut that cord swiftly, precisely.

Hmm…why would he have done that though?

I think about this. Ah. Of course!

Embarrassment. She had emasculated him, not just during this incident, but over and over again for the past year, starting with his birthday (of course) and happening God knows how many times since then.

I write my little heart out. I make it so that Connor is telling this whole sordid tale to Presley, totally spilling his guts to her. I describe how Connor puts on airs of machismo, sleeping around with random women to make himself feel better ever since Melinda destroyed their marriage. I take great pains to describe her in his voice. I say they met in college. That she was beautiful, popular, president of her sorority. I give her some backstory; I imagine her as a debutante from the South whose Daddy owned a restaurant that went under, and when her family lost all of their money, she didn't want to go back home. Like, ever. So, when she graduated from college, she moved in with Connor and let him take care of her.

It's amazing how my creative juices can flow once I get into a character. I'm not sure why, but I begin to flesh her out, paint some goodness so my readers will understand what he saw in her in the first place. I make her get a job. She helps young Connor pay for small things, like groceries and the Internet bill. Connor pays for their studio apartment in Queens, and while he acknowledges that she would like to help out more, he genuinely enjoys taking care of her. It makes him feel strong. Manly. After a while, things begin to shift. Connor gets a hefty promotion—he's a senior analyst now—and Melinda gets laid off from her entry-level marketing job. He makes *big* bucks, like almost $500,000 a year. But he doesn't tell Melinda, because she wants them to upgrade to a place in the city and he wants to save as much money as possible before doing that.

Because he wants to marry her.

Meanwhile, Melinda can't find a new job. She takes a job as a hostess and a telemarketer, and these don't stick. Until. *Until.* She gets a job at a massage parlor. Answering phones. Booking appointments.

Here it comes. Let the other shoe drop.

The massage parlor is a fairly shady establishment where men come and pay lots of money to have their needs satisfied. Connor finds out (later on, in marriage counseling) that Melinda has been paid lots of cash to engage in some girl-on-girl action for clients there. The men can look but not touch—only the girls involved can touch Melinda. Connor, meanwhile, is working crazy hours, banking big money, getting ready to propose. He is thirty years old by this point. He buys a gorgeous three-bedroom apartment in Manhattan and brings her there to show it to her, completely empty. And he proposes, right there in the middle of what will become their future living room. She says yes, of course, and decides to quit working at the massage place, now that all her dreams are coming true.

Especially when she finds out how much money he has.

They get married in an elaborate affair at Gotham Hall in New York City—a place typically reserved for celebrity weddings.

Melinda is more than happy to spend Connor's hard-earned money on whatever tickles her fancy: designer clothes, bags, haircuts, shoes, you name it. They're rich! Gone are the days of her attempting to help support their household with her paltry paychecks.

Then, for Connor's thirty-first birthday, he comes home and finds his lingerie-clad wife in bed with another woman. "Surprise!" she says, when Connor gets home. "Happy birthday, sweetheart! I got you a threesome!"

At first, he likes it, because he is a *man*, after all. But once it's over, he asks where the girl came from, and Melinda says she's an old work friend.

The following week, he catches them in bed again. They invite him to join them, but Connor gets the feeling they are patronizing him. He tells Melinda he is no longer comfortable with this, and she starts an argument about it. The result? She stops having sex with him altogether.

Months later, he comes home from work in the middle of the day because he isn't feeling well. He walks in on Melinda and this girl having sex in his bed. And that is the official beginning of the end.

Connor explains that the reason he is looking to buy Presley's apartment now is because he's looking to purchase it for *Melinda*. It's a settlement—to get her out of his hair and make sure she's taken care of well enough for her to leave him alone.

Presley understands now why Connor had been so brazen with her.

Hmm. Now what? I envision a heavy sex scene coming on, and my fingers are starting to cramp up.

I check the time. It's almost noon. I haven't stopped at all. My silenced phone offers me all kinds of information: I missed a call from my mother, along with two texts from Melly checking in to say hi, and I have a swollen inbox that needs to be addressed.

Now is as good a time as any to take a break. Plus, I have a Tupperware full of Mrs. A's leftovers with my name on it.

TO: Grace Landing (gracie222@mail.com)
FROM: Colin Yarmouth (cyarmouth@ yarmouthaycockpc.com)
RE: Last night

Hi,

I hope you're being productive so far today. My morning has been a disaster, lol. (More on that some other time.)

I can totally drive into Brooklyn to get you. I don't need you taking the train for hours each way to come to my neck of the woods. Besides, I barely ever get to use my car anymore. All I ever do is move it from one side of the street to the other, so I don't violate alternate side of the street parking rules.

Anyway, how is Saturday for you? We could meet up in the late afternoon, grab dinner, and then see where the night takes us?

C.

TO: Colin Yarmouth (cyarmouth@
yarmouthaycockpc.com)
FROM: Grace Landing (gracie222@mail.com)
RE: Last night

Saturday sounds great! I would be happy to go a few more rounds with you about the driving, but you seem like you have your mind made up.

This morning was productive, from a page-count perspective. I like replacing Connor as the narrator. He's definitely way more likeable. I was wondering if you would be willing to read the pages I wrote, to tell me what you think. If you have time, of course. I know you're super busy over there waiting for people to die. (Totally kidding!!) Let me know!

Xo,
Gracie

P.S.—A disaster? I hope everything's okay! I'm happy to listen if you need an ear.

TO: Grace Landing (gracie222@mail.com)
FROM: Colin Yarmouth (cyarmouth@
yarmouthaycockpc.com)
RE: Last night

100%. Send them. I'll get them back to you ASAP.

(Assuming none of my clients kick the bucket, of course.)

And I'll pick you up at 4pm on Saturday. I think we might be going for Greek food, if that's okay with you. Your joke from this morning got me in the mood for it!

Everything's fine, no worries. I'll fill you in when I see you.

C.

TO: Colin Yarmouth (cyarmouth@ yarmouthaycockpc.com)
FROM: Grace Landing (gracie222@mail.com)
RE: Last night

Perfect. They're attached. Thank you!!

4pm it is. You can be my personal Uber. I'll pack extra Tums in my purse. Can't wait! Xo.

While my leftovers are reheating in the microwave, I respond to Melly's texts. Her mom was kind enough to inform her that I was loitering on the beach in the cold, so she wanted to make sure I hadn't slid into a dark place. Then, I call my mom back, without bothering to listen to her voicemail. She always calls to check in on Friday. That way, she says, if she calls any other day, I know to immediately panic because it's an emergency. Similarly, if she doesn't call on a Friday, I should also panic because it means that she and my father have been assaulted and left for dead.

We have quite the system.

It's funny too; one might have thought that after my parents moved out of the Bronx and up to Westchester about ten years ago that Mom would have mellowed out a little. Well, one could not have been more wrong. I grew up in an attached row house in an area of the Bronx called Morris Park. We lived with my elderly grandmother (an Italian woman who made the world's most delicious Sunday sauce) because my grandfather was killed in the Vietnam War in 1969, and my father—at the ripe old age of fourteen—pledged to take care of his widowed mother for the rest of her life. Now, I love my grandmother dearly and still visit her at Riverdale Assisted Living once a month, but I wholeheartedly blame my mother's neurotic behavior on her.

I will never forget my first day of freshman year of high school. After Colin christened me "Elvis," I came home, dumped my bookbag on the ground, kicked off my shoes just inside the front door, and marched straight back through the house to my bedroom, slamming the door behind me. In a row house, it is hard to go unnoticed. The only windows are at the front and back of the house, and a long hallway, marked with bedroom, bathroom, kitchen, and pantry doors, runs the entire length of the space. Since there was no way to tiptoe to my room, I indulged my teenage angst in a full-on stomping march, the perfect opening act to my feature performance of flailing my limp body on my bed in complete meltdown mode.

"I *hate* my life!" I screamed, loud enough for all the other families on our block to hear.

Cue my mother.

"Honey, what is it?" she asked in a melting pot accent of Albanian-meets-New-Yawk that is unique to her. Her big blue eyes peered out from under her thick bangs and blinked in concern.

"Our name is so *stupid*," I wailed into my pillow.

"What do you mean?" she wondered.

"Our *name*! Today in school, the cutest boy I ever saw in my *whole life* called me 'Gracelanding,' like as if my name was a thing you would *do*, and then asked out loud *in front of the whole class* if I was, like, Elvis or something! It was awful!" I cried. "I'm never going back to school again."

"That's a bit clever, actually," she replied. "I never thought of your name that way."

"It's not *funny*, Mom!"

"I'm sorry, Graciebear. I wasn't making fun of you." She smoothed my hair and handed me two Oreo cookies from her apron pocket. "Here. Cookies make everything better."

I gratefully accepted them and began to munch, catching my breath. "Mom?" I asked. "What kind of last name is *Landing*, anyway? I've never met an Italian person with a last name like that. Why can't I have a *normal* name, like Russo, Rossi, or Ricci?"

She looked around like a thief getting ready to swipe the diamond out from under the nose of the sleeping guard in a Disney movie. "You're right, baby. Landing is a silly name. My last name was Hiri."

"See? *That* sounds reasonable. Grace Hiri," I said, trying it on for size. "I could be okay with that."

She sighed. "Oh, my little one." She shook her head. "*Hiri* means *grace* in Albanian."

"So, if my name was Grace Hiri, it would actually translate to *Grace Grace?*"

My mother nodded. "This is why we named you Grace. After my family name."

I shoved my face back into the pillow and let out a scream.

She gently rubbed my back and put a third Oreo cookie in my hand. "It's okay. It is just a name."

"I can never look at Colin Yarmouth again," I wailed.

"Who?" Mom asked.

"Colin Yarmouth. He's the boy who called me...Elvis." I popped a whole cookie into my mouth and chewed voraciously.

"He doesn't have such a great name. *Yarmouth.* I don't like it."

"It's better than Landing."

"Relax, Gracie. Let me go get you more cookies. You rest."

Mom opened the door to my bedroom and went down the hall to the kitchen. I sat quietly on my bed, breathing deeply and savoring the chocolate mixed with the partially hydrogenated goodness in the center. I wasn't crying, but I could still *hear* crying, which made me think I was going crazy, until I realized the tears I was listening to were not actually mine.

"Nonna? Are you okay?" my mother asked. "Why are you holding your rosary beads?"

"I pray for this house, that my Joseph does not strike lightning upon us all," my grandmother said, each word laden in an Italian accent as thick as cannoli cream.

"Why would you think such a thing?"

"You talk about his name as if it was some curse. *Landing,* this beautiful name, it means *the end of a voyage.* It was *Landin* in

French from my Joseph's father, and they changed it to *Landing* when he came to the United States. And you mock."

"No, no, Nonna. Don't misunderstand. Gracie had a bad day in school because someone made fun of her name."

"I never blame Gracie. She is still a baby. But you—you should teach her some respect."

"I apologize, Nonna. I have only respect for—"

"You live in my Joseph's house, God rest his soul. He bought this house for us in 1958, when little Joey was still a boy. This is a *Landing* house."

I could hear my mother get the Oreos out of the pantry. The crinkle of the wrapping was unmistakable. "I'm sorry, Nonna," she said.

"Have some respect," she repeated quietly. "Our Father, who art in heaven," she prayed.

This was how both my mother and I knew the conversation was over.

Mom brought the cookies to my room and placed them on my nightstand. Then, without a word, she went into her bedroom and stayed there until my father got home from work. I never mentioned Colin Yarmouth or complained about my name in that house ever again.

The lesson? Never, under any circumstances, should a woman have to cohabitate with her mother-in-law. Side lesson? Three Oreos is never enough.

I'm reminded of this story as I listen to the phone ring at my mom and dad's house.

"Hello?" Dad answers.

"Hey, Dad. It's me."

"Oh, Gracie!" he says. "Emina!" he yells. "It's Gracie!"

"How do you guys live without caller ID?" I ask. "I could be one of those identity theft scammers. I could be calling to make you go out and buy thousands of dollars in gift cards to send to my alleged captors."

"But you're you," my dad replies. "Please," he whispers. "Tell your mother it's normal to pay the landscapers in cash. She thinks they are overcharging us."

"How much are they charging?"

"$25."

"To cut the grass?"

"Yes."

"That's nothing," I say.

"I know! So, you tell her," he whispers. "Here, Emina! Gracie called for you."

"Love you, Daddy."

"*Ti amo*, Grape Juice. Here's Mom."

My mother takes the phone from my dad. This is the phone still connected to the wall by an actual cord in their kitchen. I'm sure of it because it's the only landline phone in the house. I don't know how they got the phone company to install such an obsolete contraption, but it's my mother's favorite thing in the house. She hates all technology, including the Internet. Her idea of social media is sitting in the breakfast nook with the cord stretched across the room, as if this is a publicly acceptable thing to do in this day and age.

"Hi, Gracie. I called you," she begins.

"Yes, I know. That's why I'm calling you back," I say. "How are you?"

"Another week, you know. We're fine. I walk in the driveway. It's nice to get out," she says.

"Another week...meaning..."

"We're still alive!" Mom says.

"Ah, yes, of course. Well, that's great news, Mom."

"I'm telling you, ever since they planted that bat flu in America, I just watch the news and wait for the next major pandemic."

"But not this week," I remind her.

"That's right. This week, I have bigger problems to deal with."

"Oh?"

She sighs, lowering her voice. "It's the gardeners."

"Ah. You know, it's totally fine for them to get paid in cash."

"Daddy says the same thing! But it feels wrong to me."

"Then, maybe get new gardeners."

"I may have no choice. I can't be complicit."

"Of course," I say, silently shaking my head. "What else is new, Mom?"

"Nothing, honey. Nothing at all."

"What do you mean, you walk in the driveway?" I ask.

"Oh, you know. For exercise."

"Just up and down the driveway?"

"Mm hmm," she says, cheerily, as if this is something people do.

"Okay. How come you don't go to the park?"

"Because it's spring. The hoodlums come out."

"The hoodlums?" I ask.

"Yes. There is a band of them in my neighborhood. They accost people."

"Is that right?"

"They ride their bicycles in packs—big packs, Gracie. One time, I counted eleven of them."

"And how do they accost people?"

"They take up the walkway, and you have to move into the grass. They just have no regard for anyone."

"So, you can never go to the park again?"

"I can go back in the summer. That's when they go to the pool instead. The walkways are safe beginning in late June."

"Okay. Well, this has been nice, Mom. I'm gonna get going."

"But wait! You didn't tell me about *your* week."

"Oh. Yup. Everything's fine here. No complaints."

"Anything exciting happen in your professional life?"

My mother loves to brag to her friends that I'm an author, but she never goes any deeper than that. I have no doubt in my mind that she's completely embarrassed by what I write. (In fact, I've heard her lie and say that I write children's books.) My father refuses to speak about it. I'm pretty sure he's still waiting for me to get a real job. He quantifies a "real job" as anything with health insurance.

Starbucks, here I come.

Her question lures me like bait. I haven't told anyone—other than Colin—about the deal that's in the works, and even though my mom's a little bit cuckoo, she's still my *mom*. I feel sort of like she should get first dibs on the news. But I know it's a fine line I'll be walking if I tell her anything remotely interesting, and then she won't let it go for the next five phone calls, minimum.

This is a real *Sophie's Choice*. I decide to do the honorable thing and tell her the truth.

"Well, there is one sort of cool thing happening."

"Oh? Tell me. Or like they say on the TV, 'Dish, girl.'"

"Nope. Please, never say that again."

She laughs. "Okay. Go ahead."

"It looks like I might have gotten some serious interest for *Reckless Outlaw*."

I hear her clapping. "Yay! You go, girl!"

I shake my head. "Yeah. And the publisher would like to see a second manuscript, to try and bundle it into a two-book deal."

"Is that right?"

"It's exciting. I'm excited. There's just one problem."

"What?"

"I've been having trouble with the second manuscript."

"What kind of trouble?"

"Just, writing it in general has been really hard. I'm struggling to come up with plausible ideas. My protagonist was a mess, and I didn't like her at all. But I'm working through it," I say. "I actually had a very weird thing happen."

"What?"

Hmm. How to word this? "An old friend from high school and I have been talking, and he's been helping me break through my writing issues."

"Oh, is it Ronald? Such a sweet boy. Not exactly easy on the eyes, but he always really liked you."

"No. Not Ronald. Another boy. You never met him."

"Gracie, I remember high school. When you only have one

child, all the images are burned in your brain," she says. "Ronald was the only friend you had who was a boy."

"That's not true!" I say.

"What is this boy's name?"

I inhale. "Colin Yarmouth," I say, quickly.

"No! Grace Marie Landing, how could you?"

"How could I *what*? Speak to the most gorgeous guy in my class?"

"You remember what that did to Nonna?"

"Mom, Nonna's like a hundred years old. There is no way she would remember that. And I'm not telling her! I'm telling *you*!"

"And now I am an accessory."

"This is not a crime!"

"Oh, to Nonna, this would be worse than a crime. Familial treason. Punishable by endless shaming."

"Then don't tell her."

Mom sighs. "I have nothing else. What am I supposed to speak about when I see her next Wednesday? I have nothing!"

"Tell her about the gardeners."

She is quiet for a moment. "I suppose."

"Because they're definitely stealing from their company. It's totally illegal to pay landscapers in cash," I add. "Nobody *ever* does it. Really? They should probably be thrown in jail. Wild criminals."

"I *knew* it!" she cries.

Today's lesson: Go with your gut when talking to Mom. Only tell her important stuff when it's a totally done deal. Example: If Colin Yarmouth and I decide to get married one day, or if I become pregnant with a Yarmouth grandchild, *that* is the appropriate time to tell Mom about it.

I should write that down somewhere so I don't forget it next Friday.

———

After my leftovers (which, in case you're wondering, only taste half as good the next day), I decide it is in everyone's best interest if I take a shower and get dressed like an actual human person, given the fact that it's just after one in the afternoon. I don't know that I'll be able to write much more before talking to Colin about what I've already sent to him today, but I can certainly daydream/ brainstorm about where to take my characters next.

As the water runs down my back and I revel in the scraping of my fingernails against my sudsy scalp, I think about the little switcheroo we're pulling in the new version. Connor is the protagonist now and Presley's the love interest. Following the expected arc of "Boy meets girl, boy gets girl, boy loses girl, boy gets girl back," she's got to do something fucked up to lose him. Not necessarily in an antagonistic way though. More like by accident. *Melinda's* the villain, not Presley. But Presley's selfish and has questionable-enough morals that she would try to sleep with someone to make a sale. So maybe that's it. Connor comes to Presley all vulnerable and openhearted, and Presley pushes him to buy the condo without being honest about the fact that she's broke.

I mull this over while the bubbles gather at my feet. If Connor's the main character now, then he needs a clear motive. I slather on the conditioner. The gentle massaging feels so good. I close my eyes and enjoy it, wondering what it would feel like to have Colin rub my head like that.

I felt like garbage after Scott chose Ilana over me, so my guess is that Connor feels impotent too. Taken a step further, maybe Connor thinks he *turned* Melinda into a lesbian. Men are stupid enough to think things like that, so why should Connor be any less prone to making such a foolish assumption? That's his motivation then. He doesn't just want to feel attractive (which, since he's been sleeping with a bunch of randoms for the past however-many months, he already feels)—he wants to feel macho. Tough. Strong. He wants to be a provider. We already know this because he was trying to take care of Melinda for so long. But not just *any* provider; he wants to be the world's best provider. God's gift to women. More specifically, to one woman: Presley, the one who got away.

So, what's at stake then? His *manhood*, which will make it even more crushing when he realizes Presley is using him for his money. Even though she has genuine feelings for him, she'll have to do something completely over-the-top to win him back.

I like it, I decide, rinsing myself one last time before turning off the shower and wrapping myself up in a big fluffy beach towel. I dry off, moisturize my face, roll on some deodorant, check to make sure my labia wound is healing (thank God it is), and put on some clothing. My hair is wrapped on top of my head, making my neck strain to stay straight.

I grab my phone off my nightstand and check it. *Ugh*. I missed a call from Lindsay. That makes sense. It's Friday. She's probably checking on my progress.

I call the agency and Evan picks up. "Vision Board Creative Group, this is Evan. How may I direct your call?"

Evan is the best thing about Vision Board. Agents come and

go like the seasons at this company, and I'm pretty sure a good amount of money has been spent on legal fees to keep potential scandals under wraps over the past few years. (According to Evan, anyway, who told me about the agent who posted a video of herself topless on Instagram lighting one of her client's books on fire. For what, you might ask? I have legit no idea.) Suffice to say, the place has no shortage of HR drama. Lindsay's fine, I guess, but she's super uptight and professional, and if we're really trying to call a spade a spade, I am just…not. I get my work done on time and I'm professional when it counts, for sure. But I don't know. When I signed on the dotted line, I had this secret hope that my agent would be someone who I'd end up becoming tight with, like a good friend. Not so much with Lindsay. But Evan's a *great* consolation prize. He's a total gossip—which I love, because he not only dishes about agents and editors but also about the Hollywood set, thanks to the agency's huge involvement in selling film rights. Evan's also stylish, funny, he's got a huge heart for animals, and is extremely smart. He reads most of the subs that come in to weed out the garbage and participates in those Twitter pitch contests on behalf of the agency. His job is fast-paced, and I would imagine it's pretty stressful, but Evan is the picture of composure at all times. Also, his boyfriend, Oliver, is hot as hell, and they have the cutest little rescue pup named Trixie, who came from the animal shelter where he volunteers on Saturday mornings.

I know all of this about Evan in large part because Lindsay is so buttoned up about herself that when I started having to call the agency on a fairly regular basis, I'd feel so unsatisfied when I got off the phone that I took to asking Evan unnecessary questions, like how his day was going or if he'd had any celebrity sightings of late. He *loves* talking to me. He says most of the authors don't even give him the time of day. Little do they know, he was probably their first-round gatekeeper in the industry.

Not me though. Lindsay was actually my first-round gate-keeper, because she *was* Evan before she was promoted to being an agent. I originally queried someone else at the agency, but then that lady got canned for cooking the books on one of her clients' royalty statements, and Lindsay moved up. I came out of a slush pile of "potentials" she'd been holding on to and was upgraded to client status. The industry is funny that way—people shift and move and there's all kinds of drama—although I've noticed it happens *a lot* at Vision Board. But I think that's what makes Evan *perfect* for his job.

"Hey, boo boo," I sing.

"Shut. Up. Gracie?" he says in a hushed tone.

"Yeah. Unless you have a new boo?"

"Um. No. You're my one and only queen bee. I am *so* glad you called."

"Why? What's up?"

"*Such* dirt. Okay, so you know Angie?"

"You mean Angela Drake?"

"Yep."

"She's a VP, right?"

"Not anymore."

"Stop. It. What happened?"

"Apparently, someone outed her for offensive tweets she posted back in, like, 2015."

"Really? What did they say?"

"She made comments about the cleaning staff at a hotel she stayed at during a conference. I can't repeat them, at least not right now. But it was Not. A. Good. Look. So, yeah. Bye, Felicia."

"Damn."

"Right? Ugh. I feel so much better, now that I got that off my chest. It literally happened like just a few hours ago. I texted Oliver and he was all, 'Angie who?' and I had to stress-eat a beautiful fucking donut from Sacco's Sugar Shop to get over the fact that he had no idea what I was talking about. Like, my *God*. Listen much? I swear to you, Gracie, he's legit only with me for my body."

"You *are* the better looking one."

"Thank you. I know," Evan says.

"Anything else exciting going on?"

"The shelter took in a potbellied pig. Some asshole left the poor thing in a crate on the doorstep. Like Little Orphan Annie. So I might be fostering a pig soon." He sighs dramatically. "Now I won't be able to eat bacon ever again."

"You know they don't kill those little pigs to make bacon, right, Ev?"

"Obviously. But I'd feel guilty. Like, sorry, piglet. I just ate your grandpa in my breakfast sandwich."

"You're crazy."

"Hard truth. Oh, and there's another big thing going on. But I can't tell you."

"Or else you'd have to kill me?"

"Something like that. I *will* tell you in like a month-ish. But right now, I can't. It's gigawatts-huge news."

I laugh. "I love how you're testing my patience, Evan."

"Ha! Me and the rest of the publishing industry, am I right? Anyway, boo, trust. It's *worth* the wait."

"Okay. If you say so," I say. I'm grinning, and I know he can hear it in my tone of voice.

"All right. I need to get back to it. There are *so* many queries this time of year. It's like spring fever all up in my inbox. I'm going to need reading glasses soon instead of just my blue-light ones."

"Aw. Good luck."

"Thanks, lovie. I'll pass you through to Lindsay now. Good timing too. She just got in like an hour ago. I love how people just make their own hours around here."

"Fashionably late Friday," I say.

"Ugh. Exactly. 'Kay. Muah," Evan says, blowing me a kiss goodbye.

I wait, and another phone rings. My stomach always gets a little tied up in knots when I'm waiting to talk to Lindsay. I feel like I'm on an endless interview—I'm forever terrified that I'll say the wrong thing and she'll just opt to drop me as a client.

"Vision Board, this is Lindsay," she says.

"Hi Lindsay. It's Grace," I reply. "Sorry I missed your call. What's up?"

"Hey, Grace. Psyched to hear from you. How's the writing going?"

"Good," I say. "I got a burst of energy over the past few days."

"Excellent. Glad to hear it."

"Have you heard anything else from the publisher?"

"Nope. But no news is good news. They're patiently waiting, just like me."

"Okay. Well, yes, it's coming along."

"Feel free to send pages if you want me to get started on reading. You know, with a deadline this tight—"

Hard to tell if that's a suggestion or a demand.

"I will," I say. "Soon. Just not quite yet. I'm working through some ideas with a friend of mine who's helping me."

"Oh, yeah?"

I feel myself blush. "Yeah. It's been pretty cool. He's got great suggestions."

"He?"

"It's kind of, um, a new guy I'm seeing," I say.

"Nice. Well, just make sure he doesn't steal your focus."

Nope. Only my heart, I think, and immediately laugh at myself for such a vomit-inducing line. "Don't worry," I say.

"Keep me posted, okay? And, like I said, send me stuff. You know, when you're ready."

"Okay. Will do."

"We've got a lot of money on the line," she reminds me.

"I know."

"Well, have a great weekend. Check in whenever," she says.

"Thanks, Lindsay. You too."

I hang up the phone, shaking off the feeling of someone looking at me and only seeing a payday. I've never personally experienced this feeling before—but, man, does it make me feel bad for Connor Yates.

Use it, I tell myself.

Use every ounce of it.

Colin

TO: Grace Landing (gracie222@mail.com)
FROM: Colin Yarmouth (cyarmouth@
yarmouthaycockpc.com)
RE: Last night

Hi,

I read your stuff. You nailed it. Really. It was scary; it felt almost like you were in my head. And I appreciate you leaving out the STD part. But you made Melinda seem just as skeevy. You almost don't need the STD thing on top of it—I think it would be too much.

So, what do you think is going to happen with Connor and Presley now?

P.S.—I can't wait till tomorrow night either!

TO: Colin Yarmouth (cyarmouth@
yarmouthaycockpc.com)
FROM: Grace Landing (gracie222@mail.com)
RE: Last night

Hi,

Wow—that was quick! Thank you for reading it so fast. I'm glad you felt comfortable with it. I didn't really feel like I could continue unless it had your stamp of approval.

I'm not sure what's going to happen with them yet. I feel like it might be too soon for them to have sex...although, she really wants to sell him that apartment... What do you think?

😉 Gracie

TO: Grace Landing (gracie222@mail.com)
FROM: Colin Yarmouth (cyarmouth@
         yarmouthaycockpc.com)
RE: Last night

I say go for it. He wants it. She wants it. Why not?

C.

TO: Colin Yarmouth (cyarmouth@
         yarmouthaycockpc.com)
FROM: Grace Landing (gracie222@mail.com)
RE: Last night

Well...maybe he has a morning meeting.
    (mic drop lol)

TO: Grace Landing (gracie222@mail.com)
FROM: Colin Yarmouth (cyarmouth@
    yarmouthaycockpc.com)
RE: Last night

Oh, snap! I might need to go to the hospital because
that was a sick burn! (How do you like my dad humor? Not bad, eh?)

Okay, big talker. Change of plans. I'll be at your
house in an hour. Be ready.

TO: Colin Yarmouth (cyarmouth@
    yarmouthaycockpc.com)
FROM: Grace Landing (gracie222@mail.com)
RE: Last night

An *hour*?? Are you kidding? And ready for what, exactly?

Ha! This is going to be *fun.* She's freaking out, and that certainly isn't my intent, but after the day I've had, I deserve a little
bit of fun. Plus, I have so much new stuff to tell her, and I'm *sure*
she can work it in to the story.

Elle's such a dick. I know it sounds like a terrible thing to say,
but after the stunt she pulled today, I am just completely *over* it
with that girl.

I get in the car and start driving. Something inside me stirs.
I feel like a kid again before a big baseball game or something. It
almost feels like butterflies. The promise of possibility.

I recognize it. *Hope.*

Man, it feels good.

The late-day sun beams through the front window of my car, warming my forearms as I drive.

I could chase this feeling to Brooklyn and back a hundred times.

I just hope Gracie feels it too.

Gracie

I refresh the email on my phone several times, but Colin doesn't write back. I wait a few minutes, casually cleaning up my dishes just in case he wasn't kidding. He *must* be kidding though, right? I mean, who *does* that? Who shows up in the middle of a Friday afternoon for a date that's supposed to be on Saturday night? And for what reason? Because I made *one joke*?

I might throw up. I burp and can taste the leftover pelmeni, most notably the very particular flavor of dill and sour cream. Thank you, heartburn. A warm puff of air escapes my lips. *Whew!* That is *not* a fresh smell.

In fact, I realize as I move through the kitchen, *I think this whole house smells like an Eastern European catering hall.*

Oh my God. What if he comes here and I look like a drowned rat, with my wet hair dripping down my oversized T-shirt, leaving marks like leaky breasts on a sleep-deprived mother? And he takes one step into my apartment and is like, "No, thanks," and ducks out immediately because the odor of mixed chopped meat and onions overpowers his nostrils? Why can't I just be like one of those put-together girls who always smells like strawberries and french vanilla?

Breathe, Gracie. Don't get your skivvies in a twist, I tell myself. *Call his cell phone. See if he's really coming here.*

I inhale and count to ten in my head. Exhale. Dial. Wait.

He picks up, and I hear the Bluetooth kick in on his end of the line. "Hello?" he says amidst what sounds like windy background noise.

"Colin, it's Grace."

"I know, silly. What's up?"

"Are you really coming here?"

"Why? Do you not want me to?"

"Colin!" I whine. "Are you serious right now?"

"I mean, I can turn around if you don't want to see me."

My pulse races. "Where are you?" I ask.

"On the parkway," he says.

"Which parkway?"

"The Southern State. Heading towards the Belt."

"Stop. You're *not*."

"Oh, I am."

"But—" I protest.

"But what, Gracie Landing?"

"I'm not ready!"

"Not ready for what, exactly?"

"Not ready for you to see me looking like crap! I just got out of the shower!"

"Then it sounds like you're completely ready, in my opinion."

"Colin! I'm serious!"

"All I'm saying is if I were you, I'd stop chitchatting on the phone and go *get* ready."

"I hate you!" I laugh.

"I know. I hate you too, princess. Now, off you go. GPS says I'll be there in about thirty minutes."

"Colin!" I moan.

"Can't wait!" he says.

"Ugh! Goodbye!" I exclaim.

I can't believe this is happening. I slam the phone down on the counter and go into the bedroom. I try to consider what I should wear—he's given me absolutely no idea of what we're doing or—*oh. Wait. A. Minute.*

Is Colin Yarmouth coming over to have *sex* with me? In the middle of the day?

Holy shit! When I said I just got out of the shower, he said that sounded like I *was* ready...

I'm dying. My house smells like mixed meats and sour cream.

I run back to the kitchen and grab the Febreze from under the sink. I spray it everywhere: in the sink, on the counter, in the airspace all around me. I bring it to the living room and spray the couch, the curtains, and the carpeting. I spray the bathroom rug and the towels. I drench my rumpled, unmade bed with it and then begin pulling the sheets up and fixing the pillows, smoothing out the comforter on top. I light the three jar candles I have on my dresser—their scents all conflict (Champagne and Caviar, Summer Leaves, and Cinnamon Toast)—but it sure as hell beats "Dill meets Febreze," which is the current aromatic name for this house.

Now, what the hell am I going to wear? I wonder. I've never gotten a *Hey, u up* email in the middle of the day. I've actually never had a booty call, ever. This is a real first for me. What do people wear in this kind of situation?

I empty my underwear drawer out on the bed. *Goddamn it! Not a thong to be found!* I have a few lacy bras, but let's be real: am I *really* going to answer the door in a bra and underwear? No! I have dignity. Self-respect!

I dig through the mountain of undergarments until I find a sealed plastic Ziploc bag. *Holy sweet Jesus. I forgot all about this.* It's a costume I bought for Scott for our first Halloween together. I only wore it once, and I remember it didn't stay on for very long. I take out the getup. The black patent leather squeaks against itself as I remove the bustier from the bag. It's accompanied by a pair of shiny black thigh highs and what I remember referring to as "ass-less" spandex booty shorts, which bear a resemblance to a thong but actually have the butt cheeks cut out of the back of what otherwise would fit as a full-size panty. I remember the very first time I saw them, I thought it was a design flaw. But no. That was all intentional, courtesy of comeandgetmekitty.com, an online sex shop that I frequented one time only but have received spam from up to twelve times a day ever since.

I have black heels that would pair nicely with the thigh highs, and since my hair is drying wild all over the place, I might as well just leave it out and curly. I pump some mousse into my palm and rub it through my damp mane. Hopefully it won't look too ridiculous. In the bathroom, I apply a few quick dabs of concealer and a layer of powder, and then go extra hard on black eyeliner, green eyeshadow, and black mascara. I purse my lips and paint them blood red, which makes my teeth look super white.

I squeeze my body into the outfit on the bed and opt to leave the pleather whip in the Ziploc. I wouldn't want to give Colin the wrong idea. I dig a pair of black high heels out of the bottom of my closet and slide them on. Then, I hastily dump all the underwear back into the drawer and return it to the empty space in the dresser where it belongs.

Finally, I take a look at myself in the full-length mirror.

Hmm.

It's possible that I may have overdone it with the eye makeup. My face kind of looks like a cosmetology student's dummy. Or maybe a vampire, thanks to my lips.

Easy fix! I quickly move through the house and turn off all the lights. The sun still beams in through the windows, but at least it's a little bit better.

The buzzer alerts me that someone is in the downstairs lobby. I catch my breath. "Who is it?" I ask in my most sexy, nonchalant voice. It's bad. I sound like an elderly smoker.

"It's Colin," he replies. "Should I come up, or do you want to come down?"

Come down? "Um, you should come up. Definitely."

"Okay. Be right there," he says. I buzz him in.

I pace back and forth. *Why would he ask me if I wanted to come down? Is this* not *a midday mounting?*

I'm all confused and nervous when the doorbell rings. *Guess someone used the stairs—#MVP.* I laugh.

I look through the peephole. He's just standing there, looking all cute. Dressed in jeans and a hoodie, it looks like.

Shit. I think I read this situation wrong.

And this is when panic ensues.

"Um, hey," I say, through the still-closed door.

"Hey. You gonna let me in?" he asks.

"I don't know if I should," I reply.

"What? Why?"

"It's just, I, um. I may have misread this impromptu little get-together." My palms begin to sweat.

"What are you talking about?" he asks. "Open the door, crazy."

I look through the peephole and see him smiling.

"Okay, but just know that I've never done this before." I muster up all my courage and unlock the chain.

"Never done what?" Colin asks as I pull the steel door towards me. I hide behind it and poke out my head. "Oh. You look… different."

He comes inside the entryway of my apartment. There is nowhere to hide as the door shuts, leaving me standing there in front of Colin Yarmouth, scantily clad in a dominatrix outfit and drag makeup for what I am suddenly realizing might *not* have been an afternoon-delight Netflix and chill.

"Holy shit, Gracie!" Colin's eyes pop open wide, as if he was just stung by a hornet. "What…are you wearing?"

My face is lit on fire by the blowtorch of his expression. I have no idea how we got here. Without a clue of how to proceed, I say the first thing that enters my brain. "Surprise!"

"Um, yeah. This is a surprise all right." His eyebrows imply concern, but his smirk suggests something else. Enjoyment, perhaps? Appreciation?

I do a quick spin. "What do you think?"

"Gracie, what happened to your ass?" he cries.

"What do you mean?" I lean backwards to try and look at my butt.

"It's...*out*!"

"Oh, that! Yes, that's part of the outfit," I assure him.

"You're a total nut job, do you know that?" he asks.

I shrug, embarrassed and a little confused, but happy to see him and thrilled that he hasn't run out the door yet.

He puts his arms around me and squeezes me in a hug. "I was having an awful day, and you just turned it completely upside down."

"Really?"

"Mm hmm," he says, burying his nose into my hair.

"What happened?"

"No," he says. "First of all, I can't have a serious conversation with you when you look like this. We either need to move into the bedroom or you need to go change, and maybe wash your face. My God! That's not even why I called you!" he says. "Shit! Did you really think I came here for sex?"

"Well, I mean—" I begin. Then, I smack him on the arm. "You asshole! You changed the plans on me so last minute! And said I 'sounded ready' when I told you I just got out of the shower! What was I *supposed* to think?"

"Okay. So, to clarify. If I want to hit you up for a booty call, I will be way more explicit in the future. Now, I'm not suggesting that I *don't* want to engage in"—he waves his hands up and down in front of me—"all of *this*, but not for our first time together. I'm not a complete dickhead," he says. "I actually like you, Gracie. I'd like it to be—"

"Special?" I ask.

"Yes. Special," he says.

"Terrific. I'm so glad we're on the same page," I say. The heat rises into my chest, and I am almost a hundred percent convinced that I am breaking out in hives all over my body. "Go sit down," I say, waving my hand towards the couch in the living room. "And please close your eyes so I can walk past you without you seeing my bare ass again."

He laughs. "Sure," he says and walks in front of me to the living room. He sits, closes his eyes, and as I walk into my bedroom, I hear him ask, "Hey, why is the couch wet?"

"Wet? Or just damp?" I call out, wrestling my upper half out of the stupid bustier.

"I guess just damp," he says.

"It's Febreze," I reply. "I'm sorry. I'm a complete shit show today."

"You're fine," he assures me. "I smell it, now that you mention it. But you know what your house really smells like?" he asks.

Oh, God. "What?"

"Like a Yankee Candle store. Have you ever been in one?"

"Ha! Yes, I have. Super overpowering." I put on a regular pair of underwear and a white cotton bra. Then, I wonder aloud, "So, we're *not* having sex today then?"

Colin laughs. "What?"

"I'm just trying to get dressed here and want to make sure it's fine if I wear normal underwear!"

I hear him laughing, but no answer.

My phone dings. I grab it from the dresser and check it. It's a text—from Colin. I open it. I see a picture of what appears to be red, black, and white plaid. "What the hell is this?" I yell.

"It's my underwear. Clearly, you're having a tough time figuring yourself out today. I'm wearing boxers, jeans, a T-shirt, and a sweatshirt. Coordinate accordingly, if you like," he calls back.

I shake my head, smiling. I'm reminded of the line Melly always says: "If you're gonna be a mess, at least be a *hot* mess."

After washing my face and applying a regular amount of makeup, Colin and I head out to his car and begin the sojourn back to Astoria, where he tells me he's taking me to the world's best Greek diner. Because it's before 4pm, there's still not much traffic, and when we arrive, Colin's lucky enough to find a parking spot close by. The diner is small, with compact booths and linoleum floors, giant, thick menus, and a bakery case full of house-made cakes, pies, cookies, and other dessert treats.

A waitress named Ginger brings us glasses of water and directs us to look at the chalkboard wall for today's specials. "No need," Colin says. "Can you please bring us a dip and spread sampler to start?"

I raise my eyebrows, impressed.

"Sure thing, honey. Any drinks?"

"Two ginger ales, please," he says. "You good with a gyro?" he asks me.

I nod.

"Then, can we please have two gyros with extra tzatziki on the side? And a plate of fries to share."

"Anything else?" Ginger asks.

"That's it for now. Thanks," he says, handing over his menu.

I hand her mine and watch Ginger speed walk over to the kitchen window and pass the order slip to a heavyset line cook. "That's the first time anyone's ordered a meal for me since I was a kid," I say.

"The thing about this place," Colin replies, "is that the menu is huge. Everything's good, don't get me wrong, but you can't come here and not get the dip sampler, a gyro, and baklava. At least the first time." He takes a sip of water.

"Well, I'm psyched," I say.

"I know you mentioned you ate not too long ago, but even if you just have a little bit of the stuff we ordered, you can wrap up the rest and take it home."

I shake my head. "I don't think you know who you're dealing with," I say. "It's 3:45—that's perfect timing for second lunch."

"*Second* lunch?" he asks.

I nod, grinning. "It's a thing. Believe me."

Colin laughs.

"So, what happened to you today? I thought you'd be in the office, but evidently I was wrong. You said you had a meeting, no?"

"I did. I got up early and went to the gym, and then I *did* have a meeting, but it wasn't for work," he says. "I ended up taking most of the day off."

"Oh," I say. "That sounds nice. So then, how come you're having a shitty day?"

"The meeting was with Elle."

"Your ex-wife."

"The one and only."

"Yikes. What about?"

"We're selling the house."

"Well, that's good, isn't it?"

He sighs. "Do you have anyone in your life who, like, it's just never a dull moment with?"

I think about that. "Not really. I mean, my mom's kind of a pain in the ass but she's pretty harmless," I say. "Why? What happened?"

"Okay," he begins. "Remember how I told you about the threesome with the woman who gave me"—he lowers his voice—"the STD?"

I nod. "Thank you for reminding me about that." I smile.

"Shut up," he laughs. "Well, anyway, not long after that, I found out Elle had been regularly hooking up with her, which explained why she seemed like she knew what she was doing during my birthday surprise. I'll spare you the intimate particulars, but I learned that they met on Tinder. Let that sink in. She was married to me, living in a house I bought so we could start a family, but swiping right on some chick from Tinder." He sighs. "Anyway, Elle and Sandy—that's her name—"

"Like the hurricane?"

"*Yes*," he says. "They had been dating for about three months by the time of the birthday sex incident. I offered to try counseling with her, but it was pretty obvious that she was happier—physically—with Sandy than she was with me. Which would have been great information to have found out before she went ahead and married me." He swallows.

"I'm sorry," I say. I reach across the table and give his hand a squeeze. The feeling of his skin under my palm gives me goose bumps.

"Thanks. I hate even talking about it because it's so humiliating. But, anyway. Later, after I moved out, Elle had our nice big house all to herself. I told her she could keep it for as long as she wanted, as long as she paid her half of the mortgage payments and all of the bills. I took the stuff I wanted to keep, and everything else—furniture, appliances, all of it—was hers."

"Okay," I say.

"We've spoken a few times since the split. You know, there are legal matters to deal with, and one time, the toilet overflowed and she didn't know what to do with herself. But I never asked about her and Sandy because quite honestly, I didn't want to know."

"I get that."

"So, check this out. Today, we had a meeting with a Realtor because Elle said she wanted to sell the house and move back to the city. Which is fine. The deal is, if we sell, no matter how far into the future that may be, we split any profits on the house fifty-fifty," he says. "Which is why I had to be there."

I nod as Ginger delivers a triangular wood board with ramekins of hummus, Greek baba ghanoush, and feta cheese spread at the corners and a pile of pita bread triangles loaded up in the middle. It looks and smells incredible, but I try to ignore it and pay attention to Colin's story.

"Eat some. Please," Colin says, releasing my hand, picking up a piece of bread and dragging it through the dish of hummus. "Mmm. So good."

I follow suit. It tastes like what I would imagine Greek food in *actual* Greece to taste like. The pita is warm and so soft, and the hummus is smooth, creamy, and drizzled with fresh olive oil. "Delicious," I say, chewing. "Go on."

He swallows. "So, we met the listing agent at her office. We're using a woman who my assistant, Daisy, set me up with. Her name is Lydia." He takes a swig of ginger ale. "I got there at eleven, which was the agreed-upon time, and we're waiting and waiting for Elle to show up," he says. "Finally, she gets there, and she's a total mess. Disheveled, looks like she hasn't slept in days, thick sunglasses on. She looked worse than I've seen her look in a *real* long time. But I'm not trying to get involved in whatever drama she's bringing. I'm just pissed that she's late."

"Uh huh."

"Lydia begins explaining how the listing would work, the fees involved, all that normal stuff, when all of a sudden, Elle bursts out in tears."

"Why?"

"She asks me if she can speak to me outside for a minute, and I'm just so embarrassed that I'm like, 'Sure, whatever.' I just want to move the whole thing along, y'know?"

I nod again, tasting the feta spread on another piece of pita. *Home run. This place is legit.*

"So, we go outside, and she's sobbing—loudly—so, I suggest we sit in the car. Then, she proceeds to tell me the most fucking ridiculous story I've ever heard in my life."

I take a deep breath. "Okay. I'm ready."

"She starts off by saying, 'Whatever you do, please don't judge me.' So, right away I know I'm walking into a dumpster fire."

"Yikes."

"Then she tells me she woke up this morning and all of the TVs in the house were gone."

"What? Really?"

"There's more. The engagement ring I got her is also gone, and mysteriously, so is Sandy—all of her clothes and things have vanished—poof!—into thin air. So, I'm like, 'Wait, Sandy was *living* with you?' because I didn't know, and she said that she was, but only for the time being because she was in between jobs at the moment. So, I ask what kind of work she does, and Elle says she was a delivery driver for Amazon."

"What happened? Did she get one of their vans in an accident or something?"

"Nope. Brace yourself. She got caught mishandling packages."

"What does that mean?"

"That's the terminology Elle uses to tell me this. So, I asked her to clarify. Evidently, she got arrested for stealing people's deliveries."

"No way. Really?"

"Right?! So, I'm about to lose my shit, because I'm piecing together in my head how it is that this *thief* gave me the god-damn clap in my *own fucking bed* and then, to add insult to injury, ran off with a $10,000 ring that I bought and three flat screen televisions."

"Holy shit," I say. "That's wild."

"Wait! It gets even worse!"

"No way."

"She takes off her sunglasses and, I swear, she looks like a drug addict, her eyes are so bloodshot. Then she grabs my face and tries to kiss me!"

"Oh, no!"

"Yes! She launches into this diatribe about how she made a huge mistake and how she never should have left me and that she's not into girls anymore and she just wants a second chance. You don't understand—she was *hysterical*—saying that she can't be alone in that house because Sandy has the key and what if she comes back and tries to steal more things?"

"So, what did you do?"

"Well, first, I pushed her away. And then, I told her to change the locks and that this is her own damn fault for getting involved like that with a stranger she met online. I mean, really—I'm fine with online dating, but if someone sounds shady, you don't *move* them into your brand-new house!"

"Damn. That's nuts. So, then what happened?"

"I went back into the real estate office, apologized to Lydia, and told her we would need to reschedule. Then, I called a locksmith and told her to go home and meet him. That's it. Then I left," he says. "I was going to drive back to the office, but I was hungry and royally pissed—"

"Mmm. Never a good combination," I say.

"Seriously. So, I went to a bagel store, got something to eat, and read your pages." He laughs. "Which made me feel surprisingly better."

I nod, chewing. "I can see how maybe you're not having the greatest day," I say between bites of bread and dip.

"Right?" he says. "I mean, I'm trying not to consider the fact that all the televisions that I bought—and there were three left after the one I took!—are all gone. And the ring! My God, that thing cost me almost a month's worth of take-home pay," he says. "But it's just money. It can't buy you happiness, Lord knows."

"Amen," I say.

"I'm just reeling with disgust. First, her 'gift' gives me all kinds of unsavory symptoms in my downstairs. Then, my house gets robbed. Worse, she thinks she can throw herself at me and fix everything?" he asks incredulously.

"Normal doesn't understand crazy."

"You ain't kidding."

"I'm sorry though. That all sucks."

"Thanks. It's been a day, that's for sure."

Ginger delivers the gyros but leaves the platter in the middle of the table so we can continue to pick at it. She sets the plate of fries down next to it. The ceramic plates are enormous, and the portions are out of control. The food smells amazing though, and I know if I pace myself, I can at least make a dent in it.

"Well, you wanted a story, am I right?" he says.

"Huh?"

"This crazy-ass story!" he says. "Feel free to use it. It's a hell of a plotline, right?"

"I mean, maybe. I've never written anything like this, but—"

"But it's good, right? You should totally use it."

I pause. He seems intent, which is weird. *I* wouldn't want to put my personal shit on blast like this. I'm not sure what his angle is.

"Are you sure, Colin?"

He nods. "Definitely."

"Why? That's your private life, all out there on display for the whole world to see."

"But no one will know that it's me. And anyway, *I'm* not the one who's crazy. So it's less embarrassing than you'd think," he says. "I mean, sure, if *I* brought home a criminal and she robbed my whole house, I wouldn't want that published. Hell, I wouldn't want *anyone* to know if it happened to me. But it didn't—it happened to *her*. My ex-wife, emphasis on the *ex*."

I bite the gyro and savor the taste in my mouth. Colin follows suit, and we sit together, silently chewing through the moment.

Swallowing, he sighs. "I'm sorry, Gracie," he finally says.

"For what?"

"For being such a mess."

"Are you *kidding* me? May I remind you of what I was wearing when you showed up at my house?"

He laughs. "Good point."

"So, we can be messes together," I say.

"Messes together," he repeats. "I like that." He wipes his hand on the napkin in his lap and then reaches across the table, palm side up. I place my hand on his and he interlocks his fingers with mine. Electricity runs up my arm and into my chest, sending shockwaves out into my brain and my lady parts all at the same time.

"Thank you," he says.

"For what?"

"For letting me vent."

"My pleasure," I say.

"I feel bad."

"About what?"

"Well, I sprung this date on you and stole you away from your work," he says. "I know you have a deadline."

"Yeah," I say, thinking. "But I wouldn't be here if I didn't want to be."

He smiles. "Thanks. I still feel bad though. So, how about this? After we're done eating, why don't we go for a walk to try and digest all this, and then I'll take you home so you can finish up your writing for the day?" he offers. "Did you have plans tonight?"

I consider the question. "Not really. I probably would have gotten takeout and sat on the couch."

"Well, this was better than takeout, right?"

"My God, absolutely. This is incredible," I say, picking at the french fries.

"You get the leftovers then. As fuel for later. And, if you're available, I'll make it up to you tomorrow night with a proper date. We haven't had one yet. Not really, anyway."

Intrigued, I ask, "What's a *proper* date?"

"Well, think about it. Yesterday, we went out to eat at a place you chose to talk about your story. That's not how a date should go. That's a business meeting. With perks." He smiles. "And today I kidnapped you in the middle of the day to eat at a diner with me. Also not a proper date."

"What do you have in mind then?"

He looks up at the ceiling, thinking. "I don't know. Something special. How do you feel about the city?"

I shrug. "It's good. I don't go very often, but I like it."

"When was the last time you went to a Broadway show?"

"It's been a long time. I don't exactly have the resources for that type of luxury on the reg, you know."

"Well, there you go. Dinner and a show in the city. We can dress up. I'll look online for tickets tonight. We might have to sit in the nosebleeds or way down front, depending on what I can find. But it'll be fun." He grins as he takes a final bite of his gyro. "Sound good?"

"Sounds great," I say. "But, just so you know, this is great too."

"Nah. You deserve better." Another thing Scott would never have said to me. I feel heat rise into my cheeks.

"Exactly how dressed up is 'dressed up'?" I ask.

"For you? I don't know. A dress and boots? Or a shirt and nice pants with heels? Whatever makes you comfortable."

"So, *not* assless pleather hot shorts?" I laugh.

Colin almost chokes on his water. His eyes bug out. He coughs twice and then sputters. "Maybe after," he says, wiping his mouth. "But cut me some slack. I'm trying to be a gentleman here."

"I appreciate that."

He coughs once more. "Just so you know, though, you don't make it easy."

I nod, hoping he can't see the way my insides are lighting up.

Colin

Okay, maybe I haven't been quite as forthcoming as I could have been. The publishing industry is like a rural town in the sticks. It's *small*. And incestuous. Everybody knows everybody.

The other thing I know about publishing is that if a house is willing to put big money behind a book, that means there will be a budget for marketing. So, if Gracie is going to get a six-figure, two-book deal, then her house is going to put some real dollars behind her work to make sure it sells.

Which means there's a higher likelihood that Elle might see it. In my mind, her reading this story—or even hearing about it as an aside in some staff meeting or whatever—would be the equivalent of me walking in on her sleeping with somebody else in our bed. The thought of her business being put on full display, knowing there's not a chance in hell she'd sue for libel because she would *never* let the world know that she was such a scumbag in our marriage, is an unfortunate delight. It brings me great joy to consider her indignant scowl awash with the realization that her life could potentially be optioned for film.

Does that make me a horrible person? I wonder.

I ruminate on this for a moment.

Nah, I decide. Other guys would never speak to the girl again. Would have kicked her ass right to the curb. Not me though. I'm the sucker that gave her a damn house so she could basically turn it into her own private wayward home for convicts.

I hate feeling this angry, but it almost doesn't register, seeing as how I spent the afternoon with the only person I've ever met who can listen to stories about a crazy ex and *not* openly judge—a trait which is pushing me to fall even harder for Gracie. I was too caught up in the empathy in her eyes while she listened to me, the whiteness of her teeth when she smiled, the way she softly sang along with the radio under her breath during our natural quiet pauses. The joy in her laugh.

She's a beautiful girl, but I think her laugh is the most beautiful thing about her.

It's messing me up too. I'm *supposed* to be rebounding still, right? It's only been six months since the whole debacle happened with Elle. There are at *least* another three Courtneys out there calling my name, right?

Of course, those girls are probably hanging out with Dom at the bar.

Shut up, I tell myself.

You have a date to plan.

Once I get home, I immediately get on the computer and search for Broadway shows with available seats for Saturday night. Almost everything is sold out, but I manage to score a pair of second-row tickets on resale for *Wicked*. I pay through the nose for them, but I don't care. I call in a favor with Alex Murphy, the manager at The Secret Garden in the theater district (I wrote his will)—I need a romantic table for two for tomorrow at five. He finds a way to move some reservations around and squeezes me in at 4:45, which I happily accept.

It's going to be epic.

TO: Colin Yarmouth (cyarmouth@ yarmouthaycockpc.com)
FROM: Grace Landing (gracie222@mail.com)
SUBJECT: Friday night

Hi!

Just wanted to thank you again for the delicious meal and for forcing me to come back home and work tonight. I got a lot done—enough to send a sample over to my agent to read. She's been on my case about the deadline, and I really wanted to shoot something off to her before the weekend actually started. (I cut it a little close, but oh well!)

I can't wait for our "proper" date tomorrow! I'm really looking forward to it.

Thanks again for everything. I would have called or texted, but I figured (hoped?) you might be asleep by now.

Sweet dreams!
G.

Gracie

I have never been on a date like this before.

When Colin picks me up, he's wearing a sport jacket over a shirt and tie. His slacks have been pressed and his shoes are shined. He hands me a bouquet of flowers at my door. They are thick and lush, with colors so vibrant they almost look fake.

The only time Scott *ever* dressed up with me was for his grandma's funeral. And even at that, he looked all rumpled, like that was his one "funeral outfit" and it hadn't been washed, or even hung properly, since that last time someone in his family died. There were flowers that day too, but they weren't from Scott, and they weren't for me. They were for the shriveled old lady in the open casket whose depressing condition made Scott feel it was necessary to go smoke a joint in the parking lot with his cousins, laughing at a wildly inappropriate decibel while the corpse inside continued to slowly rot away.

May she rest in peace.

By contrast, Colin's had his car washed and waxed (as if it wasn't already clean when I rode in it yesterday) and he holds my hand across the center console while we drive through the Battery

Tunnel into Manhattan. When the sun gets in my eyes, he offers me the Ray-Ban sunglasses in his glove compartment to keep me from squinting.

We arrive at The Secret Garden Conservatory—one of the hottest restaurants in Midtown—for our reservation at 4:45. It's breathtaking; it feels like dining in a tropical rainforest minus the humidity. Our table for two is dressed in crisp white linens with fan-shaped cloth napkins and enough cutlery set out for four people to dine comfortably without ever running out of forks.

We order our meals: Chilean sea bass with fingerling potatoes and sauteed asparagus for him and bacon-wrapped filet mignon in bordelaise sauce for me. The steak melts on my tongue like butter; I have never tasted bacon so perfectly smoked. We get drinks: a whiskey sour and a seven and seven. We make funny small talk over a fresh bread basket and our shared crab cake appetizer. He compliments my outfit, my hair, and my sense of humor, holds doors for me, and wraps his sport coat around my shoulders when I get cold in the theater later on. We sit in the second row, close enough to see the sheen of sweat forming on the actors' foreheads. The singing gives me chills that rival the tingling sensation that runs up my arm when Colin squeezes my hand. He laughs at all the right times, at just the right volume, and other girls look at me with jealousy when he comes back from a trip to the bathroom at intermission with a drink for me in a keepsake glass. *No one mourns the wicked*, it reads, with a picture of Elphaba's pointy witch hat etched into the crystal. "It's perfect," I say, and I mean it. It subtly references Scott and Elle and celebrates new beginnings. I will keep it always as a souvenir of the first "proper date" I've ever been on in my whole life.

He drives me home, and I invite him upstairs. This time, he says yes.

I make him say yes over and over again that night.

Colin

It is the best sex I have ever had in my entire life.

She's sensual and generous, and she looks at me as if she really *sees* me, right through the skin and into my soul.

The first time is electric, magnetizing. I cannot have her fast enough. I will myself to slow down, but Gracie pulls me into her with a heat that is irresistible. I've been wanted by girls before, but something about her touch lights me up in a way that I've never felt before. She grips my back with her fingers, she whispers my name into the darkness. She *needs* me, and it is my undoing.

Her body is unbelievable, with skin as soft as falling snow and curves that seem endless. My hands ache to memorize every inch of her. She is not tiny or weak. I am not afraid to crush her under my weight. She is like a perfect painting, a piece of art. She is a woman in every sense of the word.

When it ends, we lie in bed together, panting and sweaty, and her face is so beautiful it almost pains me to look at it. She doesn't make any jokes. She runs her fingers through my hair and rests her head on my chest. My heart pounds into her eardrum.

Gracie waits silently, and I watch her chest rise and fall with each breath she takes. Neither one of us can speak. Finally, she rolls onto her side and wordlessly begins to have her way with me again.

Three times.

Gracie

The smoky scent of pan-fried Canadian bacon mixes with the aroma of hot coffee to coax my eyes open. I roll onto my side and survey the scene: the sheets are wrinkled, the pillow is unfluffed, and on the nightstand, there's a note.

Breakfast will be ready shortly, it reads. *Stay put and I will bring it to you.* There is a heart drawn next to the word *you.*

I stretch my arms up over my head and close my eyes, calling to mind images from last night. Those lips, baby soft and sweet but firm and assertive when necessary. Those eyes, warm and inviting, appreciative yet seeking affirmation. Those strong, talented hands. Mmm.

Colin Yarmouth is here in my house, cooking me breakfast after making love to me four times last night.

"Good morning, sleepyhead," he says quietly, padding into the room holding a mug of steamy coffee. "Light and sweet, right?" he asks, handing it to me.

I smile and open my eyes. "Mm hmm," I say. "Good morning." I gratefully accept the mug from him and take a sip.

"Figured you might need this after that workout last night," he says, smirking.

I shake my head, pressing my lips together. "You loved it."

"I *did*," he agrees. "I hope you enjoyed it too."

"Are you kidding?" I ask.

He shrugs.

"It was incredible," I say. "You were insane."

He laughs.

"I'm serious. That thing you did with your tongue? You need to put that on your resume under 'special skills.'"

Colin puts his hand on his forehead, shaking his head. "You hungry?"

I grin. "Always."

"Would you like me to bring you breakfast in bed?"

"Nah. Only because I'm a sloppopotamus. It'll end up everywhere."

"Got it. Well then, come on out when you're ready. I'll go set the table." He turns to leave, gifting me with the view of his ass muscles taking turns flexing through the thin fabric of his boxers as he walks out of the room.

I use the bathroom quickly, brush my teeth, and splash some water on my makeup-free face. I look in the mirror, trying to see myself through Colin's adoring eyes. I don't know how he did it, but he made me feel like I was the only woman in the entire world worth looking at. Interestingly enough, this morning, I don't feel the need to criticize every wrinkle or strand of hair out of place.

I hear that's called *afterglow*.

I slip on a T-shirt and a pair of sweatpants and head over to the table. It's set for two, replete with glasses of orange juice and a mason jar in the middle filled with spring daisies. I take a seat and Colin sets a dish down in front of me. It's picture-perfect eggs benedict, with orange slices adorning the edge of the plate for decoration.

"Wow. This looks amazing," I say. "Thank you."

He sits down opposite me, setting his own plate on the table. "You're welcome. I hope it tastes as good as it looks."

"That's what she said." *The Office* quote makes me snicker.

Colin laughs. He takes a bite and nods appreciatively. "I had a great time with you last night."

"Me too," I say, tasting the hollandaise sauce on my fork. "This is yummy. Did you make it from scratch?"

He nods.

"And where'd you get all the food from?"

"So, there's this thing they have in America. It's called a *grocery store*."

"Okay, jackass." I laugh. "You really went out this morning?"

"I woke up early." He shrugs. "Plus, I didn't want to hype up my culinary skills and then not come through in the clutch."

"I get it. Well, mission accomplished, my friend. You definitely proved yourself."

"Does that mean I can sleep over again?" he asks.

"Indeed, you may. Although, I feel like maybe next time we do this, it should be at your house. I make the world's best chocolate chip pancakes. From. Scratch."

Colin laughs. "A regular Julia Child, ladies and gentlemen."

"They're no joke. I've been perfecting the recipe since I was about eight years old. I even have a secret ingredient."

"You do?" he asks.

"Yes, sir," I say.

"Well,"—he grins—"I would eat your pancakes any day of the week."

"That sounds serious. We're not even exclusive yet," I say, teasing him.

"Then, maybe we should be."

"Should be?"

"Exclusive."

"Are you asking me to be your girlfriend?" I say.

"I think I am, yes."

"Well, I'm sorry, but I'm going to need you to do it 'properly.'"

He chuckles. "How's that, now?"

"I mean, at the very least, you can get down on one knee."

"I suppose that's fair."

"I mean, given the fact that I got down on my knees last night for you, I just think—"

"My God," he interrupts. "We're just a classy pair, now, aren't we?" Colin stands up and takes a single daisy out of the mason jar. Then, he kneels down in front of me and holds it out to me, dripping.

"Gracie Landing, will you be my girlfriend?" He blinks his eyes for effect.

I accept the daisy. "I suppose I can slum it with you until something better comes along," I say.

"Perfect," he says. "I'll have to write down that line."

"For what?" I ask, smiling.

"I don't know. I might want to read it when I give the toast at our wedding." He grins.

I die inside, wondering what I ever did to make the universe finally smile on me after shitting on me so hard for the past six months.

Colin

I *want* to stay, and I honestly wish I could, but it's Sunday, and Kiss of Death has a doubleheader with Doctor Murvin's Magic Feet. Dr. Murvin is a podiatrist from another building on the block, and his team lineup consists of three medical assistants, two young receptionists, two older women in the billing department, Dr. Murvin himself, and his three grown sons.

I sometimes wonder if the slow-pitch softball league was created as a place for father-son issues to work themselves out. Like, "Hey, don't spend a fortune on therapy! Just spend a quick hundred sixty-five bucks per person and take all your issues to the field!"

I was tempted to invite Gracie to come with me to the park, if only because I found having to peel myself away from her excruciating. But she had to write, and I was not in the mood to have to explain her to my father, or Gordy, or Dom. Or, for that matter, to have to explain *them* to her, despite the fact that she would probably come up with a million jokes about Gordy alone.

Also, I didn't want to add any fuel to the Courtney fire.

Because I tend to be a planner, I packed my softball gear in my car yesterday afternoon, along with my team shirt and extra bottles of water. I kissed Gracie goodbye, begrudgingly, and promised to call her later.

I want Gracie to stay as perfect as she is to me in this moment, I think en route to the field. Her smile when I delivered her breakfast in bed was just as intoxicating as our night together. Well, almost.

While she slept this morning, I went out to the store, got some ingredients, and cooked her eggs benedict, my favorite meal from my youth. I was never allowed to order it at the diner as a kid because my father always said, "Eggs benedict is a grown-up meal, Colin. You won't like it," and then he would order me french toast and bacon off the children's menu instead, along with a large glass of plain milk, which I hated, but he said that I had to drink it so that I could be strong.

The very first time I went to the diner with friends in high school, I was a freshman. It was nighttime. A group of us had gone to the movies, and afterwards we hit up the diner because it was one of the few places we could go to sit down, shoot the shit, eat, and stay for pretty much however long we wanted to.

I ordered eggs benedict that day. Because I *could*. The other kids looked at me a little like I was crazy.

"What?" I said. "Breakfast is served all day."

They shrugged, ordered their chicken tenders or fries with gravy or mozzarella sticks, and when my meal came, I studied it. It was an english muffin, toasted, open-faced. Canadian bacon sat on top. Eggs—runny-ish (because they were *poached*, but I didn't know that at the time) on top of that. And all this yellow sauce. I ran my finger through the pool of thick hollandaise and tasted it.

It tasted like defiance. I loved it.

I chose to cook it for Gracie this morning because I have since perfected the recipe and I wanted her to have a meal worth remembering. Just the act of being with a girl like Gracie—someone so vastly different from Elle—is my own personal act of defiance.

My father *loved* Elle—thought she was perfect in her sorority sister, homecoming queen kind of way—although he never expressed any feelings towards her one way or the other while she was *actually* my wife. Only once she was gone did I suddenly have to hear about how perfect she was and how I had flushed my chance at happiness down the toilet.

"Why would you choose to move to *Queens*, Colin?" he asked.

Because I am allowed to *live* wherever I want. Just like I am allowed to *eat* whatever I want. To sleep with whoever I want. To develop feelings—quickly—for whoever I want.

Now, if only I could figure out how to be allowed not to have to play slow-pitch softball against Dr. Murvin's Magic Feet with my father and his kiss-ass protégé and a one-night mistake for my entire Sunday, I'd be in great shape.

When I get to the field, Dom nods at me. "Damn, son!" he says. "Almost thought you weren't gonna make it." He taps his watch.

"Nah, I'm here," I say, pulling my glove out of my bag. "Let's go warm up."

He follows me to the outfield, telling me about the three girls he met at the club last night in great detail. "You missed a good time, bro. One of them—I forget if her name was Keri or Kelly—or maybe Katie?—yo, she had—" He gestures with his hands in front of his chest, fingers spread wide on his free hand. "Let's just say, I might have been able to hold one of them with my baseball glove."

"That big, huh?"

"*Huge*, bro. I could suffocate in that motorboat."

I can't help but laugh. He's a pig, but an entertaining one at least. Plus, I have it on good authority that all the tough-guy bravado is just a front for his teddy-bear bleeding heart. He had a serious girlfriend once, but she left him to go perform on a cruise ship and he's never fully recovered. "Did you bring her home?"

"Nah," he says, shaking his head. "But she let me touch one." He grinned.

"Sounds like you're living out the fantasy of a twelve-year-old boy, dude."

"Don't judge me." Dom scowls. "Jealous prick!" he says, tossing the softball at me.

I catch it over my head. "I *am* jealous, man! I *wish* I was as good with the ladies as you are." I laugh.

"Damn right." He smiles. "When's the last time *you* got any action?"

"Me? Oof. It's been a *while*."

"See? Take a note from the master."

It's too easy. "Master-bater," I mumble, making myself laugh.

"Hey now, hey now!" my dad calls out. He's walking toward the field with—oh God. You've got to be kidding me! My *mother* is here?

Well, this day just morphed into a new, unusual kind of torture.

Don't get me wrong. I love my mother. Honest to God I do. But I have absolutely no idea why my father would put her through the agony of watching not one, but *two* seven-inning games of slow-pitch softball on this reasonably mild spring day. Mom used to play ball in college, and from what I recall, she wasn't half bad. Watching our ragtag jizzaster of a team is akin to watching a slow, agonizing game of tiny tots soccer, where more time is spent chasing butterflies and picking dandelions than actually playing. Why would he bring her here? Does he *hate* her?

"Colin!" She sits down and waves from the front row of the bleachers. "Halloo!" She is wearing a straw hat and oversized sunglasses, a pink blouse with a white cardigan over it, and a pair of pressed khaki capri pants. She should be at brunch, not on a dirty softball field.

I wave back and toss the ball to Dom. "Hang on. My mom is here," I say, jogging over to the bleachers.

"Aw!" I hear Jess and Rachel say. I shake my head and shoot them a look, which only makes them follow it up with, "So adorable!"

"Hey, Ma. What are you doing here?" I lean in and give her a kiss on the cheek.

"Daddy said he had a surprise for me," she explains. Then, she lowers her voice. "He said he was taking me someplace special."

"I see. That explains your outfit."

"Well, I figured, it's Sunday morning! We must be brunching!"

"Joke's on you." I smile. "Guess you're stuck here for the day."

"Do you really think it will be the whole day, honey?" she asks, her smile flattening.

"Knowing Dad?"

Mom sighs and looks down at her hands. "I'm starving," she whispers. "I purposely didn't eat."

"No worries. I'll hook you up. Daisy made carrot muffins. They sound gross, but they're really delicious."

"That sounds amazing, actually. Thanks, baby," she says, squeezing my hand.

I trot over to Daisy, who loves my mom and is more than happy to deliver the muffins herself.

That's just like him. I remember once when I was turning five, I begged him for a pony for my birthday. He said, "Sure," I guess assuming that I would forget about it since five-year-old kids typically have the attention span of a fruit fly. Then, finally the day came, and in the late morning, he blindfolded me and put me in the car, then took me somewhere and told me to sit down. It was cold and dark and smelled different than I expected a horse farm to smell. He took off my blindfold and whispered, "Surprise!"

We were in the movie theater. He took me to see *Field of Dreams*.

It had nothing to do with horses.

I spent the rest of the day waiting, hoping that there would be something else. Another surprise trip somewhere. Mom threw me a birthday party at the candlepin bowling alley, and there was cake and ice cream and square slices of bowling alley pizza, which was nice.

Then, at the end of the day, Mom was tucking me in and I asked if I could talk to Dad. She got him for me, and he sat on the edge of my twin bed.

"What's up, squirt?" he asked.

"Dad?" I asked in a small voice. "What about the pony?"

"Colin, please. We live in the Bronx. Where would we put a pony?"

"I don't know. In the backyard?"

"Our backyard is the size of a postage stamp."

"But you said—"

He raised his eyebrows.

"You *said* I would get to dress up like a cowboy and that you would get me a real horse to ride! You *promised*!" I felt little-boy tears sting my eyes.

"You can be a cowboy for Halloween. *You*, Colin—*you're* going to be an *athlete*."

"But Halloween just passed! You made me be a baseball player!"

He shrugged and said, "You're fine. It was a great day. I *gave* you a surprise. The movie was fun, right?"

I cried into my pillow until he left the room.

I heard him yell at my mom through the closed door. She yelled back. "He's *five*, John! Why did you have to upset him on his birthday?"

The following weekend, Mom took me out to Long Island to a petting zoo with pony rides. She bought me five tokens, which got me five long trips around the ring.

"One for each year," she told me, kissing my forehead.

I wondered, growing up, why she put up with him, why she didn't just leave and take me with her like I sometimes wished she would.

Instead, she tried to make things good. She got me Cici for

my eighth birthday. She helped me limit the sports so that I wasn't enrolled in everything. She pushed for me to come home from ASU after my shoulder surgery.

Now, here she is, chatting with Daisy like old pals, eating carrot muffins together. I pull out my phone and order a bacon, egg, and cheese on an everything bagel and a mixed fruit bowl through Grubhub from Mannino's on 62nd and Fifth Avenue, with detailed instructions regarding delivery location, all the way down to my mother's outfit so the food finds its way to her. I add a $20 tip to the bill.

The first game starts. It's slow and boring, until Dom hits a two-run homer in the third inning and I follow that up with a triple to deep right. Daisy bunts (not on purpose) and I make it home, even though she gets tagged out at first. Then, Courtney strikes out and the inning ends, and literally nothing else happens until the seventh inning, when I catch a grounder and throw it to Richie at first, and he throws it to Gordon at second for an attempt at a double play.

The ball bounces off his cleat, right into his junk.

Gordy yells out in pain and falls to the ground, sweat (or possibly tears) running through his eye black.

My mother watches from the sideline, munching on her fruit.

The ump calls time out and Dad jogs over to Gordy from the outfield. "You good, son?"

He holds one hand up, indicating that he needs a sec. The other hand clutches his balls.

The rest of the team (myself included) surround him, buzzing with injury energy. I feel bad because it sucks to get hurt, but it's killing me not to laugh. He's being so dramatic about it, whining and moaning like a baby on the ground.

Dad tries to get him up, but Gordy is legitimately sobbing.

"Well, if he ever had a shot with any of the girls on this team, that's gone to shit now," Dom whispers to me.

"Good news," I whisper back. "He never had a shot."

Dom laughs under his breath.

Suddenly, my mother is out on the field. "John? Colin?" I hear her call. I see her shimmying across the field in her oversized sun hat. I walk over to her. "Should I call an ambulance, honey?" she asks me, cell phone in hand.

"Gordon? My mom wants to know if you want her to call 9-1-1 for your busted nut?" I holler.

"I think you should, Linda," my dad says. "This isn't right. Usually when you take a shot to the sack, it hurts, but the pain goes away shortly after."

Mom nods, takes a few steps away, and makes the call.

The ambulance comes in minutes. Paramedics check his vitals and carefully move him onto a stretcher.

"What happened to him?" I hear my dad ask the driver.

"Looks like he stabbed himself in the testicle with a pencil," the driver says.

"A *pencil*?" I say. "Why the hell did he have a pencil in his pocket?"

"I was *keeping* the *book*!" Gordy screams from the stretcher. Then he makes a sound like an animal who's been hit by a car. It's deafening. EMS gets him into the ambulance, leaving the back doors open. "Anybody going with him?" the one guy asks.

"Jack!" he wails. "You gotta come, Jack!"

"It'll leave us short," my dad says to me, trying to stifle the panic in his voice.

"It's fine," I say. "It's not a big deal. I can bring Mom home. You should go with him."

"Colin," he says under his breath, "we would have to *forfeit* the game."

"So what?" I ask. But I know John Yarmouth. *Forfeit* is not in his vocabulary.

He glares at me. "Richie—go grab me the roster, quick. And a pen."

Richie runs across the field and pulls the roster off the bench. He returns it to my dad with a pen. My dad scribbles a name on it and hands the roster to me. "You handle this, Colin. I'm counting on you." He walks toward the ambulance. "I'm coming with you, don't worry," I hear him tell Gordy.

I look down. Is he fucking *serious*?

He added the name *Linda Yarmouth* to our roster.

I shake my head as the ambulance doors close.

"Lemme guess," Dom says, sidling up next to me so the umps can't hear, "he called in a ringer?"

"Fuck my life, dude," I reply, shaking my head. I slap the roster into Dom's hand and go over to my mother, who is lamenting Gordy's injury with Daisy.

"Hey, Ma?" I say. "What kind of shoes are those?" I point to the strappy wedge-looking things attached to her feet. Her polished toenails are the same pink as her blouse.

She looks at me, confused. "They're Eileen Fisher espadrilles, honey. Why?"

"I hope you can run in them," I say.

"Run in them? Where?"

"Dad just added you to the roster, Ma. So we wouldn't have to forfeit the game. We've only got nine players."

Her face registers surprise, followed by the kind of annoyed, expected resignation that can only come from almost forty years of marriage to a self-centered control freak. I've seen it in my clients' faces. It's a specific, nuanced brand of disappointment.

But Mom is funny. She looks up at me and starts smiling like a goofball. "You got an extra glove?" she asks.

I pull her gently to the side and look her square in the eyes. "You don't have to do this," I whisper. "We can easily forfeit. It's basically bar-league softball, Ma. Nobody gives a shit."

"Are you kidding? This is amateur hour over here. I can play."

Now I am the one with a confused look on my face. "Ma, I appreciate that you've played before, but you're not exactly a spring chicken anymore."

"Come on, honey. It'll be fun." She raises her eyebrows up and down.

"I don't need you getting hurt, Ma."

"Colin, sweetie, I'm not the one you need to worry about getting hurt."

"What are you talking about?"

"Don't you remember?" she asks.

"Remember what, Ma?" I ask.

"When you were a little boy, and you were learning all about sports, your father put you in Little League. Remember?"

"How could I forget?"

"Don't you remember the Slip 'N Slide?"

Holy crap, I think. *I forgot all about that.*

"The summer you joined, you couldn't figure out how to slide into a base to get under a throw."

"So you bought me a Slip 'N Slide and taught me to practice in the water first."

"You know why, don't you?"

I shake my head.

"Your father couldn't do it. He was always afraid he'd hurt himself."

"Wait. Dad couldn't *slide?*"

She laughs. "Are you kidding me? That man can do a lot of things, but he wasn't much of an athlete."

"Well, sure, because he got hurt," I say. My entire childhood was predicated upon the notion that I was supposed to live out the big dream of going pro because my dad watched his shot go up in smoke when he tore his ACL.

"Honey, he will tell that story until he's dead and gone. About his great big missed opportunity and all that." She puts the words *missed opportunity* in air quotes.

My eyebrows stitch together, wondering what she's talking about.

"Daddy tore his ACL running to an accounting class in college. He woke up late for his final."

I audibly gasp. "Stop lying," I say.

"I'm not surprised he never told you. It's the same reason we never talked about my big win in college."

"What big win?" I ask.

"Honey," she says. "When you're married, sometimes you learn to leave well enough alone. But you know I played softball in college."

"Yeah," I say.

"Well, look up the 1982 UCLA Bruins softball team when you have a chance," she says with a wink. Then she trots over to Daisy, and I hear her ask something about a shoe size.

Rachel supplies Mom with Nike running shoes in her size. (Thankfully, Rachel brought cleats today.) We get Mom an extra shirt from Gordy's bag, which she slips on over her blouse, and she gets my dad's glove, which is still sitting in the grass in the outfield. She trades in the sun hat for an extra flat brim that Dom wore to the field.

"Yo, bro, I'm not sure how I feel about your *mom* wearing my lucky hat," he says to me.

The black baseball cap has *FBI: Fat Booty Inspector* stitched on it in white.

"Yeah, you and me both, dude," I reply.

I ask her where she feels most comfortable playing and she offers to take Gordy's position at second base. "Better to keep me in the infield," she suggests. "I don't know if I can track fly balls anymore."

The end of game one is a sight to behold. A grounder is hit straight to my mom, and she fields it super clean, with the flawless mechanics of an experienced ballplayer. It's the third out for Dr. Murvin's Magic Feet. "Just like riding a bicycle," she whispers to me on our way back to the bench.

The second game ends within an hour after we mercy-rule Dr.

Murvin and his bush-league crew of bunions and hammertoes. Something about playing without my dad and Gordy around gives everyone the chance to loosen up a little and have some fun. We all rally around my mother. Even Courtney laughs when Ma says, "Those Murvin boys are as crusty as an ingrown toenail."

Later on, after I drop Ma off at home and share the entire story with Gracie over the phone, I type *1982 UCLA Bruins Softball* into my Google search bar. The first result is an article from the *L.A. Times*. The title reads, "Inaugural NCAA WCWS Crowns UCLA Bruins Women's Softball Champs." I read on to learn that my mother was a catcher in the first ever NCAA-sponsored Women's College World Series—and her team won.

You were one hell of a ringer today, I text her.

Now you know where you get your athletic prowess from, she writes back with a winky-face emoji. But don't mention it to your dad!

Secret's safe with me, Fat Booty Inspector! (Lol!)

Never call me that again, she says.

I laugh so hard that I almost start to cry.

Gracie

It's Monday morning. A new week! Gracie 3.0 laces up her sneakers. Grace with a boyfriend. And not just *any* boyfriend. *The* boyfriend, I think, as I grab my headphones and head downstairs.

That's right! It's happening! I'm going for a jog!

Well, maybe not a *jog*. But a walk, at the very least. Walks are healthy! And it's a beautiful day outside! The sun is shining. The birds are chirping. I got laid this weekend by the man of my dreams and I! Am! Radiant!

I've got a spring in my step, good tunes in my ears, and energy to burn. I walk down to Emmons Avenue, past the fishing boats, the party boats, and the random men with buckets and crab traps trying their luck in the water. I walk over the footbridge and down to Manhattan Beach. I stroll along the sand and come back up through the playground, smiling at the little ones as they joyfully chase one another down the slide and into the sand pit. I marvel at the clear blue sky and the emissions from an airplane painting a thin streak of white clouds across it. *Every day should be this glorious,* I decide.

Heading back to the footbridge, my phone rings. Hoping it's Colin, I pick up without checking who the caller is.

"Hello?"

"Gra-cie, boo," I hear the voice say in a hushed tone.

"Evan? Is that you?"

"Listen. I can't really talk," he says, "but I've got *major* tea to spill."

I stop walking by the bridge and sit down on a bench overlooking the water. My heart's pounding, a mixture of adrenaline, caramel macchiato jitters, and real-life physical activity threatening to take me down at any moment. "What is it?" I ask.

"So, check it out. I was just sitting here, minding my own business, when who comes storming past me in a fit of rage?"

"Who?" I ask.

"Lindsay. She looks *crazy* pissed, and she's carrying her bag and wearing her coat like as if she's headed out for the day."

I check the time. "It's only 10:30," I say.

"I *know*! But I'm not going to be the one who gets in her way. So I'm all, 'See you later, Lindsay,' and she must have lost her footing or something because before you know it, she's just sprawled out on the ground."

"She *fell*?"

"Yesss! It was *so* embarrassing! She spilled a manuscript everywhere, so she looked like she was drowning in a sea of pages. Anyway, she collects herself, stands back up, and yells at me. Like *legitimate* yelling!"

"Oh my God, Evan! For what? And what did she say? You didn't, like, trip her or anything, right?"

"No! Of course not! She goes, 'Clean up this mess! And just fucking toss it! It's all garbage, anyway!' and I'm like, 'Your wish is my command, your royal highness,' and she fucking storms off. Papers *everywhere*."

"Ugh. I'm so sorry, Evan. That sucks."

"Gracie, I don't *care* about all that. I'm calling you because I'm worried about you."

"Worried? Why?" I ask.

"Boo, those were *your* pages."

"Really?"

"I collected them, and when I saw your name on the manuscript, I was like, 'Oh, hell, no! That's my *girl*.' So, you bet your ass I didn't throw it away. In fact, now I'm *dying* to read it. I'd love to know what turned her into such a salty little potato chip."

My head spins. "I have no idea. It was good stuff," I say. "I mean, at least I thought it was." What could have bothered her enough to make her lose it like that? Was it the male protagonist spin? Not enough sex? It was just a *sample*, for God's sake.

"Who knows?" Evan asks. "Maybe it's Shark Week for her."

"Huh?" I ask.

"Crimson tide. Maybe she's on the rag. Or, worse—maybe she's off her meds."

"Oh. Yeah, maybe," I say. "I just don't get it," I think aloud. "Evan, have you ever seen her get like that before?"

"Honestly, no. But there's a first time for everything. Plus, it's just Dramedy Central over here. And she's been acting weird lately. Remember, I told you she came in late this week? That day I spoke to you?"

"Yeah."

"She was in a mood then too. So, try not to stress. I just wanted to give you the heads-up before you got blindsided."

I sigh. "Thanks for looking out," I say. "You're the best."

"Let me know when you hear from Princess Frostybox."

"Sure. I'll keep you posted."

"Talk to you later. And remember, *you're* the talent. Don't let her try to convince you otherwise." Evan hangs up the phone.

I'm stunned. What the *actual* fuck?

TO: Colin Yarmouth (cyarmouth@
    yarmouthaycockpc.com)
FROM: Grace Landing (gracie222@mail.com)
SUBJECT: Can you talk?

Hey,
    Do you have a second to chat? I need some advice. Please give me a call whenever you can.
Thanks. Xoxo.

The phone rings almost immediately.

"Hello?"

"Hey. What's up? Everything okay?"

I take a deep breath. "I'm not sure. I just got this super weird phone call."

"From who?"

"A friend of mine at my agency. He's like the assistant to a few of the agents."

"Okay."

"He said Lindsay called my manuscript garbage."

"Who?"

"Oh, sorry. Lindsay. She's my agent. She had been on me to get her some pages, so I sent a sample on Friday night, after our date. So then, Evan—he's my friend—just called and said that Lindsay was storming out of the office in a 'fit of rage'—those were his actual words!—and she tripped and my manuscript went everywhere and she told him to just throw it out because it was garbage. Garbage! Can you *believe* that?"

"Wait. Your agent's name is Lindsay?"

"Yeah. Lindsay Ellerton. Why?"

There's a pause on the line. Then, "Oh, shit."

"What?"

Nothing.

"*What*, Colin?"

"That's Elle."

"Huh?"

"That's *Elle*. My ex! Lindsay *Elle*rton. Elle was my nickname for her."

Have you ever had one of those moments where you feel like you're suspended in midair? Where the world is closing in on you and there's nothing to do but surrender to the fact that you're about to fall—hard—right on your face?

The last time I had a moment like that was when Scott told me Ilana was pregnant. I was in the grocery store, picking up fruits and vegetables because I had been trying to eat healthy and lose those last few pesky pounds so that I could fit into my wedding gown comfortably. My phone rang, and I answered it, and he told me, and all of a sudden, I felt like my legs could no longer support me. Like I was for real going to pass out. So, I leaned into a display of apples, and as I breathed into the gravity of the situation, my body collapsed onto the ground. Red, ripe apples rained down all around me.

I ate mostly takeout for the next three months. I was too embarrassed to be seen in the produce section of Stop & Shop, where I assumed everyone was undoubtedly referring to me as Applesauce Landing or some other equally hideous nickname.

"Are you still there? Gracie?"

I cough.

"Gracie. Lindsay Ellerton is my ex-wife."

I hear the words. I know they're bad. Time stands perfectly still, frozen in the white noise of emptiness.

And then the apples come.

"Are you *kidding* me? You and your *fucking* nicknames! Why couldn't you just call her *Lindsay*?"

"Whoa! I'm sorry! I didn't *know* she was your *agent*!"

"You told me your ex was an agent, but I never heard of an agent named *Elle Yarmouth*! And the publishing world is so small, Colin! I just assumed she was in nonfiction or kid lit or something unrelated to my work!"

"I didn't think it was a big deal because I didn't think she was *your* agent. I knew all of the names on her client roster."

A carefully assembled bunch of Granny Smiths barrel down onto me.

"My pen name is Karlie London," I say on a whisper of breath.

A sack of Honeycrisps pile right on top, threatening to bury me.

"Fuck," he mumbles. Then, silence permeates the line. Finally, he says, "Well, how was I supposed to know that?" He's getting worked up. "And why'd you need a pen name, anyway?"

A single Red Delicious is pitched like a fastball straight to my face.

"Because *you* called me *Elvis* in high school!" I scream. My voice is so loud that several of the fishermen on the footbridge turn and look over at me. "Because you called me Elvis in high school," I repeat again, quietly.

"Gracie," he says softly.

An apple is lodged in my throat, like a pig on a spit.

As I roast in the fire, there is nothing left to do but cry.

Colin

I should have asked her sooner.

I *knew* it was weird that I couldn't find her books online.

Now, Karlie London—*that's* a name I would have remembered.

When Elle and I first started dating, she was a literary assistant at Vision Board Creative Group. She spent her days poring over query letters from would-be authors, reading sample pages, requesting partial or full manuscripts if she thought someone might have potential. It was a thankless job, seeing as how even if she did find a diamond in the rough, there was no percentage cut for a paltry *assistant*, no thank-you gift with *her* name on it FedExed to the office, no listing on the acknowledgements page of the author's debut novel.

It was grunt work. She knew it and I knew it. I likened it to my time working at Brophy's Hardware Store. "It's an apprenticeship," I explained. "No one ever got hired by Mr. Brophy as anything more than a stock boy. Once you mastered that, you could learn the register. After register, you could learn how to deal with the vendors. Everyone got to learn from either Brophy or one of his sons." It was the same thing at Vision Board. Elle worked directly for the agency's founders, Sean and Kathleen Jamison, a power couple who had both started off at other agencies and decided to launch their own company once they got married. She scheduled appointments for both of them and answered their phone lines, but Kathleen represented mostly women's fiction and romance, so Elle handled most of her queries.

I am a firm believer that hard work pays off, so I tried to quietly encourage her. I brought home food almost every night because she didn't like to cook, and I kept the apartment—*my* apartment—quiet for her in the evenings so that she could focus on reading manuscripts.

Every now and again, she'd ask to read me something, to get my two cents on whether or not it would sell. Not entire manuscripts, of course. Just a paragraph or two to get a sense of the narrator's voice. Sometimes, she'd read me lines that she thought were funny or awful. She valued my opinion. Or, at least, I *used* to think that, before the whole threesome-STD-birthday episode.

One night, I got home from work and found her curled up on the couch with a pencil in her mouth, a common position for me to find her in back in those early days.

"You have *got* to hear this!" she exclaimed as I closed the apartment door.

"What's up?"

"This writer! She's *incredible*. Her stuff is so…hot!"

Hot? I thought. "Really?" I asked.

"Yeah. Listen to this: 'Kelsey stood between Damian's legs, holding her ground as he leaned back against his desk nonchalantly. "What do you want from me?" he asked her. She considered the question. *I want your tongue in my mouth*, she thought. *I want your hands in my hair, your skin under my nails. I want to pull your shirt up over your head slowly, so I can savor every inch of your stomach, chest, and arms. I want you to pull me in by the hips and stop trying to pretend you don't give a fuck.* She gazed at his eyes, looking into him, piercing the façade and diving into his depths. *I want you to pull up my skirt and feel how wet you make me.* "What do you think I want?" Kelsey asked in return. Damian smirked a little, the corners of his mouth rounding like a mischievous child. Then, he stood up, closing the gap between them. He placed his sturdy hands on her waist and lifted her up off the ground. Kelsey's heart caught in her rib cage and, without her even realizing it, her legs wrapped around him. He took three steps forward with her clinging to him and stopped when Kelsey's back gently hit the wall. Only then did Damian move his lips in to hers. But, just before kissing her, he whispered, "I don't know. Something like this, I'm guessing."' Can you believe that?"

I swallowed. "Damn," I said.

"Hot, right?"

I reached into my pocket and adjusted my semi. "Yeah. Who wrote it?"

"This new girl, Karlie London. Mark my words, Colin. She's going to be *huge*."

She was right. She pitched Karlie's debut to Kathleen and begged her to read it. The following Monday, Elle got the promotion that landed her a position as an agent.

Karlie London was her first real client.

I swear, shit like this only happens to me.

Gracie

Damage control: *Action taken to limit the damaging effects of an* accident or error.

After hanging up the phone with Colin, I try not to have a full-on panic attack. I'm out, which is probably for the best, because the brisk walk back home forces me to burn off some of the adrenaline that might otherwise pump my fragile heart into an early stroke. I'm tempted to call Lindsay, but also terrified. Still about a week away from my next paltry royalty check, I need to know what this means for the *Reckless Outlaw* deal. One can live from paycheck to paycheck for only so long.

I stare at her name in the contact list on my phone, but I can't dial the number. I'm just too scared.

Instead, I draft an email. I sit at my desk, stress-eating Cheez-Its right out of the box, contemplating every word of every line. I work on it with the same fervor one might muster when toiling away at a query letter seeking agency representation for the very first time. I never hit *send* though, because every time I think it's done, panic ensues and palpitations shoot through my chest. The email sits in my "drafts" box, being worked and reworked until the lines all blur and the words stop making sense. When you chew gum for too long, it eventually turns into a flavorless rock. That's my letter. It mixes an apology with a meeting request with an explanation and is cloaked in self-deprecating desperation, with rainbow sprinkles and a cherry on top.

My nervous breakdown is interrupted by a phone call from Colin. Our previous call ended rather abruptly, with me saying something along the lines of, "I gotta go. I'll call you back." Because, in my humble opinion, there's really nothing worse than full-tilt meltdown sobbing in the middle of the street.

"Hello?"

"Hey," he says. "I spoke to her."

"Lindsay?" I ask. "Er—Elle? Whatever you call her?"

"Yeah," he says.

"How did that go?"

"Um, not well, as I'm sure you can imagine."

"I actually *can't* imagine. So please, enlighten me," I say.

"Well, I told her that we—you and I—are a couple now, and that I gave you the story that you wrote."

"And?"

"She accused me of trying to sabotage her career. She said she could sue me for libel, but I reminded her that I'm an attorney, and nothing has been published, so that quieted her down a bit," he said.

"She's never going to speak to me again." My stomach churns.

"Gracie, you didn't know. *I* didn't know. Nobody knew we were all part of the same fucked-up little circle."

"Can you explain one thing to me, please?"

"Of course."

"Why did you want to put that story out there in the first place?"

He pauses, contemplating the question. "Revenge, I suppose. I mean, I didn't think—not for a second—that she was *your* agent. But I know the publishing world is pretty close-knit, and word spreads fast. I thought maybe she'd see it in print somewhere and read it and maybe, just maybe, she'd feel like an asshole when she saw it from a bird's eye view like that."

"Uh huh."

"She *hurt* me. I don't know. I think I just wanted to hurt her back," he says. "To give her a little taste of her own medicine, you know?" My heart's immediate reaction is to break a little because I am intimately familiar with that feeling.

"I understand," I tell him.

"But, my God, the last thing I ever wanted was to jeopardize your career."

"No, I'm sure," I say. "How did you leave things?"

"She hung up on me."

"Ahh. Wonderful."

"I'm sure she'll call you," he says.

"I mean, at some point, she has to."

"I'm sorry, Gracie. I never meant for any of this to happen."

"I'm sorry too," I say.

Our words hang in the air, suspended like particles of dust floating aimlessly in a ray of sunlight. My head is too dizzy to digest them or understand their implications, so instead of speaking, I remain silent, listening to the sound of his breathing on the other end of the line.

Finally, Colin speaks. "What does this mean for us?"

"What do you mean?"

"Are we still…" His voice trails off.

"Together?" I ask.

"Yeah."

"Let me just figure out what's going on with her first—"

"Right. Of course," he says.

"It's not that I don't—"

"No," he interrupts. "I get it."

"Colin—"

"No worries, Grace. Just let me know when it's all straightened out."

"Right."

"I'm here if you need me, of course."

"Of course," I echo.

"Okay," he says.

"Okay."

"You should probably go."

"Yeah," I agree, though my mind is still floating. Still in shock. Still trying to piece together how this happened. I want Colin to drop everything and drive to my house, curl up in bed with me, and hold me while I cry. Run his fingers through my hair and tell me it will all be okay.

Instead, I let him go.

After we hang up the phone, I go over to the couch and lie down, covering myself with a throw blanket Nonna crocheted for me when I was a kid. I close my eyes, willing myself to fall asleep, which has been my defense mechanism of choice ever since I was in high school. I'm like a possum in that way. Whenever a possum feels threatened or is about to be attacked, its first instinct is to play dead. Most human beings don't do that—they go into fight or flight mode. Not me. I channel my inner possum and try very hard to pass out.

The upside to this is that sleeping helps time pass quickly. The downside, of course, is that when you try to sleep your problems away, you wake up and for one split second you forget that the problems even exist. Then you remember, and you suffer the realization of the issue all over again. It's kind of like peeling a scab off a healing wound. The wound reopens and has to start healing all over again.

Cheez-Its help a lot, believe it or not. In fact, any kind of carbs, eaten quickly, make it much easier for me to drift off to sleep. So, as I lie here, teetering on the edge of a Cheez-It-induced stress-coma, willing my mind not to think about Colin or Lindsay or my uncertain future with both of them, my mind does this funny thing.

It brings me back to—of all people—Ronald.

Ronald Cummings and I met on a yellow school bus that went through Parkchester, Westchester Square, Morris Park, and Pelham Bay to get to Bronx Gardens High School. He was a sophomore and I was a freshman, but despite his advanced age, he still sat at the front of the bus, instead of at the back with the jocks and the cool kids. He was loud and often obnoxious, but also smart and funny, and he would verbally spar with the other front-of-the-bus nerds about all kinds of things I found useless at the time: politics, current events, comic books, video games, and, occasionally, music. He was far from attractive; he had a lazy eye that was just off enough that you could never be a hundred percent sure of whether or not he was actually looking at you when he talked to you. His nose had been broken in an unfortunate accident at a roller-skating birthday party as a kid. (His lack of sporting ability and generally poor balance led him to fall, and while on the ground, a superfast teenager on roller blades tripped over Ronald's face.) It never healed right, leaving him with a prominent bump that he joked was a "battle scar." He had awful acne: red, raised pustules lined his cheeks and neck, and he used to nervously scratch and pick at the scabs in his thick brown hair, which he parted to the side without any particular style. He had braces on his teeth that would occasionally catch food particles in them, changing his otherwise-average smile into an unsightly potential advertisement for dental floss. He wore clothes from JCPenney, because his mom worked at the Bronx Center mall and was able to use her employee discount there. As a result, he had a plain Champion sweatshirt in almost every color of the rainbow, and he would cycle through them weekly, always paired with a turtleneck in either white or black and a pair of loose-fitting Levi's jeans.

Ronald wasn't one of those nerdy kids who knew his place in the world, like me. In fact, he was quite the opposite. He thought highly of himself, dominating the other geeks at the front of the bus with his loud opinions and musings on life and the world around him. He sat alone on the vinyl bus seat meant for two, his oversized backpack occupying the window space beside him, his knees pointed out into the aisle so he could chat with whoever was close enough to listen. This often included our bus driver, Sam, whose poor ears were assaulted daily with the noisy ruminations of an egotistical fifteen-year-old.

For the first half of my freshman year, I sat next to Maya, a friend of mine from junior high school who I had art class with. She was quiet and unassuming, and we were both content to sit side by side and listen to our respective Sony Walkmans without interacting too much. But one day, Maya was absent, and Sam got a call on his CB radio that another bus had broken down midroute. We were the rescue bus, so in an attempt to make space for the kids on the other bus who we went to pick up, Ronald parked himself and his bookbag-luggage in the empty space next to me.

"What are you listening to?" he asked.

"Hmm?" I replied. I was not used to having to engage in chitchat with my seatmate.

"What are you listening to?" he repeated, louder.

I took off my headphones. "Notorious B.I.G," I said.

He nodded. "So, you like old-school East Coast hip hop."

I shrugged. "I guess. I mean, I also like Tupac and Dr. Dre, and I think they're both from the West Coast."

"You see? This is *exactly* what's wrong with the youth of America."

"Huh?"

"You're totally *blind* to the implications of your choices."

"What?" I looked at him, confused. To this day, I think it was Ronald who gave me my first wrinkle, a small perpendicular crease right between my eyebrows borne out of all the times he'd say something I didn't understand.

"Forget it," he said, shaking his head.

"I also listen to Jay-Z and DMX. What difference does it make?"

"And Justin Timberlake?" he asked.

I nodded.

"Ugh," he said with disgust.

I didn't particularly *care* about his personal feelings on music, but I was bothered by the conversation and the fact that he was cutting into my quiet bus time.

"Ugh, what?" I said.

"Nothing. You just don't know music, that's all."

"How do you know what I know? You don't even know me!" I replied.

"You know what I listen to?" he asked.

"No," I said. *And I don't really care*, I thought.

"Tribe Called Quest. Beastie Boys. The Roots," he listed.

"Good for you," I said.

"That's *real* old-school hip hop. Don't get me wrong, I'm a fan of Biggie as much as the next guy, but all that radio crap is just so played out."

"Okay," I said, wishing the conversation would end.

"I mean, really. Does Justin Timberlake even know what he's *saying*? 'I'm bringing sexy back—yeah!'" he sang. Yes, *sang*. Out loud. On the *school bus*. In *high* school. I contemplated launching myself out of the locked window onto the moving pavement below.

"Sshhh," I implored him.

"What?" he asked. "I'm serious! What does that mean—'bringing sexy back'? Like, where did it go? Does Justin Timberlake, with his unnaturally high-pitched voice, think that sounding like the human equivalent of Mickey Mouse is the key to delivering 'sexy' to the masses?"

"Oh my God," I said. "Can you please lower your voice?" My cheeks were turning fire-engine red.

"Just tell me what it means, and I'll drop it," he replied, grinning. It was obvious that he was getting off on embarrassing me.

"I think it just means that people think he's sexy, and he's calling himself out as a sexy singer of his generation—like, maybe the equivalent of Britney Spears during her 'I'm a Slave 4 U' period. Okay? Can we stop now?"

"Okay." He shrugged. "I guess. Though it's far from surprising that you would bring up Britney Spears."

I *hated* that conversation, but if we're being genuinely honest, the reason I remember it with such vivid detail is because it made me laugh so hard on the inside.

Ronald started sitting next to me after that. I got on the bus a few stops before him, but Maya got on after him, so she ended up sitting across from us, in his old seat. The first time it happened, she shot me a look that was code for, "Are you okay? Do you need rescue?" and I shrugged uncomfortably, but as time went on, we both got used to it.

This went on for about six months. Ronald would—in his very *Ronald* way—share his views and beliefs (and occasionally, his breakfast) with me, and I would listen and laugh at his absurdity. Maya would chime in if she felt like it, and the three of us became something of a group of bus buddies. Since Ronald was a sophomore, we never had classes together, but we'd say hello if we passed each other in the hallway.

Colin, meanwhile, was a thing of the past, as he had cycled through Alexis Yacolino and about a half dozen other equally gorgeous girls by that time, and my secret romantic overtures were also history. I still gazed at him longingly in biology and on the soccer field, but I was beginning to understand my place on the sociological cafeteria map. Cindy Lee and Maya—those were my people. And Ronald.

I never would have thought anything of my friendship with him had it not been for a New Year's Eve party at Maya's house. A small group of neighborhood kids who went to junior high were invited, along with Ronald, since he was our only "older" friend. We played tame versions of games like Truth or Dare while we crunched on Cheez Doodles and sour cream and onion–flavored potato chips and drank Fanta out of paper cups. Once Maya's parents announced they were going to turn in for the night, she turned the lights down and took the empty Fanta bottle and placed it on the floor in the center of the living room.

"Spin the Bottle!" She giggled, gathering everyone around to sit on the carpet in a circle, in a formation reminiscent of our kindergarten games of Duck, Duck, Goose and Hot Potato.

As the hostess, Maya spun first. She landed on Ronald. He grinned, revealing braces dotted with orange cheese powder, and she planted a juicy, wet kiss on him.

All of a sudden, I felt something. None of the feelings I expected bubbled up inside me: not disgust, repulsion, or even pity for my friend.

I was *jealous*.

It took me several days to work through the complicated,

hormonal, teenage emotions I was feeling. I gave Ronald the cold shoulder for no good reason. He didn't understand why I was being such a bitch. He couldn't leave well enough alone either, and one cold January day he must have left his house at the ass crack of dawn because he showed up at my bus stop.

"We need to talk," he said.

"What do you want?" I asked.

"Why are you being like this to me? What did I do to you?"

"Nothing. It's fine. I'm fine," I said. I couldn't believe he walked the four bus stops in the dead of winter to have this conversation with me on a street corner so early in the morning.

"You're not fine. Just tell me what I did."

"You didn't *do* anything!" I insisted.

"Then why do you have such an attitude with me?"

"I don't have an attitude!"

"Yes, you do!"

"No, I don't!"

"Will you please just tell me what the hell I did to make you *be* like this?" he pushed. "I don't *like* it. We're *friends*! If I did something to hurt you, just *tell* me so I can fix it!"

My blood was boiling, and the bus was nowhere in sight. I was stuck, trapped on a corner with no answers and a quickening pulse. He kept asking, and asking, until finally I couldn't take it anymore. "Why did you have to *kiss* her?" I yelled.

"Kiss *who*? Maya?" he asked.

"Yes," I said, deflating like a popped New Year's Eve balloon.

He was quiet. "It was just a game," he said.

I kicked a pile of snow. "I know."

"Did you—?"

"What?"

"Did you want it to be you?" he asked.

"No!" I objected.

But I was lying. And Ronald could tell.

"I call bullshit," he said. Then he moved in close to me, put his gloved hands around my waist, and leaned in for an awkward smooch.

It was my first.

Over the next two years, we navigated the uncomfortable terrain of "firsts" with each other, slowly rounding the bases until the night of his high school graduation, where we went to another party—not at Maya's house but at a rented beach house on Long Island—and ended up sharing a bedroom together. With deep bass thumping in the background, we went all the way amidst the smell of cheap beer and cigarette smoke. I knew there was no way he was going to stay with me when he left for college in the fall. We loved each other, but he loved himself more, and that was no secret. Still, I wanted my first time to be with someone I knew and cared about, and the prudent part of my teenage self believed it made sense to lose my virginity to Ronald. When he broke up with me two months later, it hurt. A lot.

But in a muddled state of fear about starting my own senior year, I did the only thing I could think of. I focused on the things I could control. I concentrated on the tasks I had to take care of, like filling out college applications and writing essays. I put my feelings in a jar and closed the lid as tightly as I could, and then I put that jar in the back of my freezer, hidden behind the ice cream and frozen chocolate bars.

In short, I let him go.

Kind of like what I'm doing now.

Colin

Don't panic. Everything's fine.

I try to breathe, but I feel like the air is thick. Like it's choking me.

You're such a fucking dick sometimes! Why didn't you just ask if she had a pseudonym?

And who the hell goes around spilling every detail of their fucked-up love life to someone they barely know? You might as well have posted the story right on Instagram, complete with pictures and hashtags and the whole nine.

Asshole.

Okay. This feels like a complete meltdown. I'm pacing back and forth in my office. I can't focus. Can't think about anything other than this giant mess I've gotten Gracie into. This poor, unsuspecting girl from my childhood who happened to drunkenly stumble back into my life could potentially lose her income as a result.

What do I have—the reverse Midas touch? Does everything I touch always have to turn to shit?

There's a knock at the door.

"Come in," I say.

Daisy steps into my office. "No, Colin. I don't think you have the reverse Midas touch."

"Huh?" I ask.

"Honey. You know you're talking to yourself, right?"

"Sorry." I shake my head. "I didn't realize."

"Such a cute little quirk. You've been doing that since you were in nursery school," she comments. "So, what is it? What's eating at you?"

"It's this girl."

"Courtney?"

"No."

"The new one?"

I nod. "Her name's Gracie."

"Something's wrong *already*?" she asks.

"I screwed everything up," I say. I hate the sound my voice is making. If Dom was here, he'd tell me to quit being such a punk bitch and go out and get under the next female pulse available.

"So, fix it," she says matter-of-factly.

"This was a biggie, Daisy. I'm not sure I *can* fix it."

"Have you tried yet?"

"Sort of."

"Nope. Not good enough. Try harder. Try with everything you've got."

"What if it's not enough?"

"Keep trying. You're a good guy, Colin. Whatever it was, I'm sure it wasn't as bad as you're making it out to be."

"You have no idea," I say.

"Hit me with it then," she says.

"Let's just say I may have destroyed Gracie's career."

"Really? How?" she asks.

"By royally pissing off her agent."

"Her *agent*? It's not Elle, is it?"

"The one and only."

Daisy shakes her head. "Oh, dear."

"Exactly."

"I didn't know your new love interest was an author."

"Yes. The operative word being *was*."

"What did you do, exactly?"

"I shared all the sordid details of the demise of my relationship and told her to use it in her manuscript. So, she wrote all about it and sent it straight to the inbox of my ex-wife."

"Oh, wow. And you had no idea she was Elle's client?"

"None. I should have asked. I couldn't find any of her books online, which led me to believe she was working under a pen name, but I was so caught up that I never asked."

"So, where is she now?"

"Who? Elle?"

"No. Gracie," Daisy says.

"She's at home, I think."

"Then why are you still here?" Daisy winks.

I sigh. "She needs space, I think. This was a huge deal. I may have screwed her out of a ton of money."

"So then, it's like I said. You need to fix it."

"I *know* I need to fix it. I just don't know how."

"Speak her language," Daisy says.

"What does that mean? She only speaks English."

"No, you dingbat. She's a writer. So, *write* to her."

I'm struck by the idea. It's so simple. "You're smart, you know that?"

"Like a wise old owl." She smiles. Then she says, "Get to it," and shows herself out, gently closing the door behind her.

I sit back down at my desk, take a deep breath, crack my knuckles, and begin typing.

Gracie

Lindsay's phone call wakes me up from my state of hibernation. I don't want to have to call her back, so I put on my best attempt at a normal-sounding voice and answer the phone.

"Hello?" I say.

"Grace," she says. There's none of her usual pep, no inflection, just my name, a single syllable, a guttural utterance of her diaphragm.

My throat constricts and I fight my gag reflex. "Hi, Lindsay."

"Let's skip the small talk," she says. "I'm sure you've talked to Colin."

"Yes," I say. I sit up on the couch, trying to monitor my breathing.

"I don't appreciate what you did."

"I didn't know, Lindsay."

"He told me that, and I believe you."

"I'm sorry."

"I believe that too. But there's no way we can sell that book. I won't do it."

"No. Of course. I understand," I say.

"And I don't think I can represent you moving forward."

"Wait," I say, panic and bile combining to travel backwards up my esophagus. "What?"

"I don't think it is in your best interest or mine for us to continue our working relationship moving forward," she says.

"What about *Reckless Outlaw*?"

"I've got a call in to Danielle at Cabaret Books. I'll try to sell it as a single title. Hopefully, she still wants it."

I purse my lips, willing the contents of my stomach to stay exactly where they are. "And then what?"

"And then I think it's best if we part ways," she says. "I can't work with my ex-husband's new girlfriend. Especially if he's ghostwriting his misinterpretations of what happened in our relationship into your work. Fifteen percent is not enough of a commission to put myself through a nightmare like that."

"I swear, Lindsay. I swear, I had no idea that *you* were the subject of his stories," I say, her words—*best if we part ways*—digging into my intestines. I picture myself agentless, having to start from scratch to try and find new representation. The sleepless nights, the query letters going unanswered, the constant checking of email and praying for full manuscript requests. I imagine going through all of that again. It was torture the first time around. How would I explain myself? My agent dropped me because I slept with her ex-husband? Shit, I would drop me too.

My career is over. Reckless Outlaw *will be the last book I ever sell in my life*, I think.

"It's fine, Grace. What's done is done. Do I have your permission to try and sell it as a single title?" she asks.

"Yes," I mumble, stunned. "Yes."

"Good. I'll have Evan be in touch. In fact, from now on, it's probably best that you reach out to me through him."

"Okay," I say.

She hangs up, and just like that, it's over. Afraid I won't be able to crawl back into my hole on the couch easily, I go to the bathroom, take two Benadryl, and practice playing possum for the rest of the afternoon.

Colin

I stay late at the office, writing an email to Gracie. I do my best with it. Lord knows I am *not* a writer.

I compose entire paragraphs—only to delete them moments later.

I am not sure what to tell her. I start with a lengthy story about how I gave Lindsay the name Elle—about how when she was a kid her father called her *Linzer Tart* but he went to jail for some white collar crime when she was seven years old and, ever since then, she *despised* the name Lindsay, because it always inevitably ended in the nickname *Linz.* So, I intentionally called her Elle starting very early on in our relationship; it began right after she told me that story, in fact. She loved it. It was chic, she said. She wished she could start fresh in life so that everyone could call her Elle.

Delete, delete, delete. Irrelevant.

I try again, this time with humor. I mean, Gracie made me feel better just by making me laugh, so I figure maybe I can return the favor. The only problem is, I'm not that funny. I resort to looking up jokes online that have some variation of the word *Elle* in them and start typing them out. That looks a little something like this:

What's gray but turns red?
An embarrassed "elle"phant!

What is an energy provider's favorite dance?
The "Elle"ctric Slide!

What do you call a shrimp who only cares about himself?
Sh"elle"fish!

So, yeah. More d"elle"ting. (By this point, I feel like I'm fresh out of good judgement, almost to the point where I fear I may never finish this email and leave my office.)

I close my eyes and lean back in my chair. The message screen is blank, taunting me.

Being a writer is hard work, I decide. This feels like one of Gracie's page count exercises.

Thinking about her working makes me sad. I realize I may have just flushed months, even years, of her creativity down the toilet with this mistake.

I type the word *misunderstanding* in the subject line.

It's a start.

Gracie

Waking up hours later, I feel hugely discombobulated. It's dark in my apartment. There's an empty box of Cheez-Its on the coffee table next to me. My stomach is rumbling, and my eyelids feel heavy.

I check my phone. It's 4:00 in the morning. Too early for breakfast, I decide. I take a much-needed trip to the bathroom to relieve myself, then I run the shower, because I'm not sure what else to do. I don't have any missed calls or texts from Colin, and I'm afraid to check my email, because what if there's nothing from him there either?

You know that saying, *If something seems too good to be true, it probably is?* I feel like that's what's happening with me and Colin. I try to put it out of my mind while I scrub my hair and lather up my body. The warm water soothes me, washing the yuck of an all-day nap off my skin. I breathe in the steam and tell myself that everything is going to be okay.

I get dressed and towel-dry my hair. The phone is taunting me on the edge of the sink, so I finally give in and check it.

Oh, thank God.

TO: Grace Landing (gracie222@mail.com)

FROM: Colin Yarmouth (cyarmouth@
yarmouthaycockpc.com)

SUBJECT: Misunderstanding

Hi Gracie,

I'm writing to you because I wanted to check in and see how you're doing, but I also want to give you space if that's what you need right now. (I'm not really sure how you are when it comes to stressful situations.)

Have you heard from Elle yet? If so, how did it go?

I can't tell you how awful I feel about everything. I keep replaying it all over and over again in my head. Honestly, if I had known that you were one of her authors, there's no way I ever would have responded to your original email. In fact, I probably would have avoided you like the plague, labeling you guilty by association with Team Crazy.

So, in a way, I'm grateful for your pseudonym because without it, we wouldn't have reconnected.

Do you know what I was thinking about today? Don't laugh. I was thinking about the first time we met, back in science class on the first day of high school. Do you remember that? I forget the teacher's name—the one who got hit by the bus—but what I do remember is that when we sat next to each other, you asked me the most interesting "get to know you" questions and then scribbled down notes in your binder on my answers. I only recall one of the questions—*If you could have a superpower, what would it be?*—and I chose teleportation. I asked you the same question, and you said you would want to be able to eat whatever you wanted and never get a stomachache. I laughed at your answer—not at *you* but at the answer itself—and thought that you would be a funny girl to have as a friend. But I never had any friends who were girls, so I didn't know how to go about becoming friends with you. And then that got all screwed up when the new teacher came.

I also remember our Spanish class (I know you do too, thanks to our recent emails), and how I used to try and talk to you, but we were only allowed to speak in Spanish, and I was terrible at it. So instead, I tried to strike up fast conversations with you a few times before the late bell rang—like by complimenting your handwriting or some other stupid thing. I had no idea how to talk to people back then. It's a wonder I made it to adulthood.

I guess what I'm trying to say is that I really missed out on the opportunity to become acquainted with you back then. I think we might have been friends if I hadn't been such a moron. And I'd even go so far as to say that (if I had gotten to know you) we might have been the kind of friends who would've remained close through college and the real world beyond it.

I don't have any friends like that. I mean, don't get me wrong—I obviously have friends—but nobody from all the way back in high school. I knew lots of people back then, but we all lost touch over the years. And to be honest, most of those friendships were really just based on convenience. (That happens a lot when you play sports.)

I just reread everything I've written in this email, and I realize now that I'm rambling. I'm sorry. All I'm trying to say is that I really care about you, Gracie. I feel like I screwed up the chance to get to know you in high school, and I don't want to screw it up now. I'm so sorry about this huge misunderstanding with Elle. I wish there was something I could do.

I'll think about it and try to come up with a solution. But, in the meantime, I'm here if you need anything.

Colin

P.S.—I'm going to stick to email for the time being to try and give you some space. I hope that's okay. You can call me anytime though, day or night. I'm not going anywhere.

Whew. Okay. So maybe it's not *all* bad.

When you're a writer, you appreciate words. At least, that's always been my experience. Like, if you don't get me a gift on my birthday but you write me a beautiful card—we're good. The written word is a gift in itself.

So, Colin's email makes me feel better, even if only for the moment.

I brew a pot of coffee, then sit down at the kitchen table with a blank piece of computer paper folded in half and a bowl of Cocoa Pebbles. It's just after 4:30 in the morning, but I have some major problems to solve, and sugar and caffeine can only help. I begin scribbling a list:

Things I Need to Do to Fix My Fucked-Up Life
1.   *Write a new manuscript*
2.   *Find a new agent*

I tap my pencil on the table. Everything feels so monumentally in disarray; this *can't* be all I need to do in order to fix it. But then—a new manuscript? I could barely even work my way through the *last* manuscript without a significant assist from Colin. And it was far from done by the time this whole fiasco happened. I guess this is in keeping with my last list that went by the same title, written approximately six months ago. It read:

Things I Need to Do to Fix My Fucked-Up Life
1.   *Find a new fiancé*
2.   *Get a house*
3.   *Have a baby*

Well. Perhaps list-making is not my strong suit.

I need to really clear my mind and think about this. *How can I clear my mind?* I wonder. *How can I get to a Zen-like state of relaxation so that the answer can take shape before me, like a cloud that develops out of thin air?*

Of course!

Yoga!

I check the schedule online. Kiki's teaching in her studio in the village today. Her first class is at 6:30. This is perfect—I have just under two hours to get myself together and get into the city.

I brush my teeth, feed Dorian Gray, and change into workout clothes. Then, I tie my hair up into a bun and put on just enough makeup not to look ghastly. I grab my rolled-up yoga mat from the closet and head out for the subway. I take the B train into Manhattan. I'm surprised by how many people I see on the subway so early in the day. I feel like one of those super-healthy people who works out before going into some swanky Manhattan office.

This must be what Colin is like in the morning, I think, smiling.

When I get to the studio, Kiki is *not* happy to see me, but I explain that I'm going through something right now and I really need to relax and I *promise* I'll take it seriously this time, so she lets me stay. Which is no surprise. Tori would kill her if she cast me back out into Washington Square Park in my fragile condition.

Exactly one hour and dozens of poses later, I am basking in the sunshine of another gorgeous spring day, and I actually feel okay. The stretching coupled with the calming music miraculously eased my nerves a bit, it seems. I spot a smoothie café across the street and decide that Gracie 4.0 deserves a healthy treat. I choose a Green Detox, which looks a little suspect on the menu board but touts its powers of rejuvenation and clearheadedness. The young hipster in the rainbow apron hands it to me with a smile that says, *Cheers to you, Gracie.*

I pluck the top with a straw and take a sip. *Ugh!* It's horrendous—the explosion of kale in my mouth makes sperm taste good by comparison.

I can't believe I just spent nine dollars on this garbage.

Nine dollars is a lot of money to spend on one's health, and since I know that not *everyone* would find such a concoction repulsive, I decide to do something generous and nice with it.

I head back down into the subway and grab the 6 train uptown. I figure I'll surprise Colin with a Green Detox smoothie as a thank you for his sweet email and to show him that we'll be okay, even though I'm in a bit of a crazed state at the moment. By the time I get to the law offices of Aycock and Yarmouth, it's just after 8:30, and I'm greeted by an elderly, but pleasant, receptionist.

"Is Colin here?" I ask.

"I'm sorry," she replies, checking his calendar on her computer. "It looks like he won't be in until this afternoon. Did you have an appointment scheduled?" she wonders.

"No, no," I say. "I didn't. I was just stopping by to surprise him with a smoothie." I lean in and whisper, "I'm his girlfriend."

She smiles. I don't know her name, but I feel like he told it to me once. She looks like someone who should be named after a flower: Rose, Iris, Lily, or the like. "I can put this in the fridge for him, if you'd like me to," she offers.

"That would be wonderful," I say. "Thank you."

She nods and gives me a wink, taking the perspiring cup from me.

"Have a great day," I say.

"You too, dear," she calls out after me.

Well, that was nice. I'm beginning to see things more clearly. All is not lost. I'm a good writer. I'll find a new agent. I'll have a solid nest egg from *Reckless Outlaw* and that will buy me some time. Plus, I have a great boyfriend who is funny, kind, gorgeous, and can write one hell of an email when he wants to.

Everything is going to be okay, I tell myself, walking out of the building and into the sunshine.

Colin

The alarm goes off at 5:00 a.m. The first thing I do is check my phone.

Nothing.

I guess my email attempt isn't going to cut it.

Tempted to wallow, I take a breath and stretch my arms up over my head.

Nope, I decide. *Not this time.*

I will not *let this one go without a fight.*

Gracie

Free of any imminent deadlines (other than new, self-inflicted ones), I decide to text the girls on the train ride home. It's time for another celebration, I write, adding a series of balloon, party hat, and confetti emojis.

I'm always down to party, Melly writes back.

Celebration? Kiki said you were a hot mess this morning, Tori chimes in.

When is Gracie NOT a hot mess? Lol, writes Alisha.

I'm fine, I say. I have big news, actually! One of my books is maybe sorta about to sell for a cool half-million dollars, I add, finishing the line with a series of dollar sign emojis.

Word??? Tori says.

Guess you're buying drinks!! Melly says.

Really? Damn, girl, Alisha adds.

R u guys free on Friday night to celebrate? I ask.

I'm still trying to live down our last night out, Alisha says. Neil made it pretty clear he wasn't cool with his wife going to House of Yes without him. Can we keep it a little more low-key?

Sure, I say. Honestly, I've been sleeping weird. So a chill night out works for me.

Y'all are so old, Tori says. But I'm down.

If it's just gonna be an easy night, why r we waiting till Friday? Why not tonite? Melly asks.

I can meet up tonight, Alisha says. In fact, that would prob be better for me.

Worx 4 me—Kiki's got classes late tonight, Tori writes.

Great! I say. Where should we go?

How about dinner at Rollicks in Soho? Melly suggests. We could get in early for happy hour. Their apps are killer!

U think we need a reservation? Or is it too late? I ask.

Don't sweat it. I got the hookup, Melly writes, with a winky face emoji.

Lmao who? Tori asks.

The bartender, Mike, Melly says. He def has a crush on me.

OMG, writes Alisha. Some things never change lol!

I can't help it if he has good taste! Melly retorts. 6pm good?

Done deal, I write. Can't wait to see you guys!

Don't puke this time, Tori says.

I won't, I promise. I'm in a MUCH better place now.

Several more texts full of emojis and x's and o's fly across my screen, and I get off the train at my station.

I have so much to be grateful for, I decide.

A second shower and quick snack later, I'm cleaning off my kitchen table, daydreaming about ideas for new stories, when my cell phone rings. It's Lindsay's office number. I take a deep breath and swallow, willing the sesame bagel and cream cheese I just ate to stay down. *She didn't want to deal with you anymore*, I remind myself. *She said to talk to her through Evan from now on, remember?* I say a silent prayer, hoping it's Evan on the other end of the line.

"Hello?"

"Happy Spiral Tuesday, friend," I hear. *Thank God.*

"Evan." I sigh. "I'm so glad it's you."

"Listen, boo, I can't talk because it's like full-tilt armageddon over here. Real end-of-days stuff." His voice is more serious than I've ever heard it before.

"What? What are you talking about?"

"I just wanted to give you the world's fastest FYI. I'm pretty sure your girl is done," he heavy-whispers.

"Lindsay?"

"Mm hmm. I'm not exactly sure what the story is, but she threw a chair through the glass wall in the conference room."

"Shut up! Why?"

"She was meeting with some guy, but I don't know all the deets because I was in the bathroom. My body's still working through a new sushi place I regret having tried this weekend."

"Gross," I say.

"Yeah, well, all I know is that there's yelling going on. I feel like we're all frozen, like that moment in *Jerry Maguire* where Tom Cruise goes off the deep end. This is, like, breaking news right now."

"Why would she—?"

"No idea, G. But she's in with Sean and Kath right now. And

you know that's *never* a good thing. Oh, shit! I gotta go. I'll keep you posted." *Click.*

What the hell?

I can't sit with this kind of news and not talk to *someone*. I want to call Colin, but his secretary said he wouldn't be in until after lunch and I remember he's been dealing with the Realtor, so I don't want to interrupt him if he's already stressed out by that. I consider emailing him, but we're in sort of a weird place right now and I'm sure the last thing he needs is more drama concerning his ex-wife. Nobody likes that.

I decide to go grocery shopping. I should be brainstorming, but now that the Cheez-Its are gone, there are no emergency snacks in my house, and I typically brainstorm solutions to life-altering situations best with empty carbs on hand.

I pull on my shoes and get the reusable shopping bags out of my front hall closet. I grab my credit card and house keys, and nearly leave without my cell phone. Dorian Gray gives me a look of pure disdain as I grab it from the windowsill where he's having a sunbath. I shove it in my back pocket. "Lucky you're cute," I mumble at him.

I'm putting together a mental grocery list when I open the door to my building and breathe in the late morning air. The scent of dirt and mulch lets me know the landscapers are doing their thing along the front of the building. A car alarm in the distance fails to drown out the sound of two birds chirping in the tree above. Spring is really here, bringing with it all sorts of hopeful promises for the bright days of summer that lie ahead. I walk with my head held high, breathing in the aromatic fragrances of budding trees mixed with bus exhaust. I get to the crosswalk at

Ocean Avenue and wait for the *walk* sign to signal my safe passage through the intersection. Up ahead, the Stop & Shop promises an abundance of treats to fuel my creativity.

It is as I am crossing the street that I consider a new heroine: an ingenue not unlike myself, an independent young woman with strength, good looks, and a big heart who suffers the misfortune of poor communication with a new lover, resulting in his ex-wife somehow throwing a monkey wrench into their relationship. It's all too common, but I have lived it now, so certainly I could embellish and exaggerate the romantic interludes to excite my readers. I could give her an exotic name, like Diamonique or Philomena, and she could—

Oh, shit! Ow!

I don't see the curb.

In fact, the next thing I know, I'm flat on the ground, my reusable bags parachuting in the wind to the side of me. The heels of my hands are scraped and my chin hurts. I touch it with my finger; I can feel the blood.

"You okay?" a driver, stopped at the light, hollers out his window at me. I hold my hand up to wave, then pull myself up onto all fours and survey my surroundings. A black metal grate with oval-shaped holes is clearly the culprit: I must have tripped on the edge of the sewer.

I'm so glad I took two showers today, only to launch myself onto the ground alongside one of New York City's most horrifically filthy underground attributes. Home to water rats and giant cockroaches, I am close enough to its entrance to hear the sewage running like a spring brook several feet below me.

Ugh. I pick myself up, more embarrassed than anything, and try to wipe some of the street dirt off my clothes.

Faced with the decision to continue on my way to the store or to go back home and clean myself up, I decide, in true Brooklynite fashion, to just keep it moving. *Nothing to see here, folks!* I wipe my chin off on the inside edge of my sleeve so I don't appear too mangled. Once I am off the corner and almost to the entrance of the grocery store, I decide to check my reflection in my phone just to make sure I'm not actively bleeding down the front of my shirt. I reach my hand into my back pocket, feeling around, palming nothing but my own backside. Panic rises in my throat, and I nervously pat down the front pockets of my jeans. The credit card and keys are right where they should be.

But my phone is gone.

I run—yes, *run*—back to the corner where I fell. I look around frantically. It's a black rectangle in a neon pink zebra-striped cover. Shouldn't be too hard to find.

The sound of the water flushing septic waste beneath Ocean Avenue mocks me. *I've got your phone*, it hums. *I took your lifeline to the outside world AND your dignity all in one fell swoop!*

I am living inside of a nightmare, I decide.

With little recourse, and now facing the direction of my building, I take one final look around, and when the street reveals nothing to me other than a random Taco Bell wrapper and a pile of old dog shit, I decide it's in everyone's best interest if I just go home.

—

Thank God for my laptop.

After my third shower of the day and the determination that my chin might need stitches but fearing the potential medical bills a trip to urgent care would result in, instead I slap a Band-Aid on it. I sit down at my computer and draft an email to my girls giving them the heads-up that I am temporarily off the grid but will definitely be at Rollicks at six tonight. Then, I open up a new email window and take a deep breath before beginning to type.

TO: Colin Yarmouth (cyarmouth@
yarmouthaycockpc.com)
FROM: Grace Landing (gracie222@mail.com)
SUBJECT: Dead zone

Hi,

Your email from last night was really sweet. I appreciate everything you wrote, and I agree—I'm sorry too, for my part in all this craziness. I can't believe you were trying to be friends with me in high school, but that's a debate for another day.

Today, I'm sort of in crisis mode. I was on my way to the store and tripped over the curb and I'm like 99% sure that my cell phone ended up in the sewer. So, I'm going to go out to Cell City and try to get a new phone this afternoon. I just wanted you to be aware of this new episode in the dead zone of my life, so that if you need to get in touch with me and I am unreachable, at least you know why.

I hope you are having a better day than I am! I'll be in touch (hopefully) soon.

Xo,
Gracie

I never knew that getting a new phone could become an all-day affair.

After sending my emails, I grab an expired protein bar from the back of the (basically empty) pantry and check the time on the stove—2:10—before heading back out. The walk to Cell City takes me about twenty minutes, and I am extra careful not to let my mind wander lest I should trip again. My job is to put one foot in front of the other, look out for major cracks or unlevel spots on the sidewalk, and carefully cross each of the side streets.

There are several people waiting to be helped inside the store, and their disgruntled, generally unhappy-looking faces suggest that the customer service representatives on duty today might not be running their A-game. I peruse the new phones, looking for something in the price range of between zero and fifty dollars, and am sorely disappointed to find that the cheapest phone that doesn't fold in half is listed at a whopping $250.

It's okay, I remind myself. *Hopefully, you'll be rich soon enough, and then you can pay off all your credit card debt and not have to worry about trivial matters like emergency phone purchases.*

Once I've decided which phone I want, I am directed to sign my name on a clipboard and wait with the others in rows of red plastic chairs. This feels not unlike a doctor's office or, maybe more accurately, a trip to the DMV.

I chew my protein bar quietly while I wait, watching the other patrons who are all staring at their cell phone screens. I'm reminded of my first cell phone, a T-Mobile Sidekick with a blinged-out case that my parents bought for me when I left for college.

They're called "Massholes" for a reason, my father said, referring to the sweet moniker worn by Massachusetts assholes, of which (he was convinced) there were plenty. *You keep this on you at all times.*

Similarly, my mother bought me a rape whistle and a can of mace. I'm not sure what they thought was going to happen to me on one of the nicest campuses along the eastern seaboard, but alas, we are Bronx people, and Bronx people know their way around a self-defense plan.

Or so I thought.

On Halloween of our freshman year, Melly, Alisha, Tori, and I decided to dress up as slutty playing cards. (Any costume was fair game as long as it was slutty. In our case, we took tight white T-shirts and decorated them with the four aces in a card deck. I was the Ace of Clubs, largely because Melly insisted on being the Ace of Hearts, Tori wanted to be the Ace of Diamonds, and Alisha had never played cards before.)

Coupled with black spandex pants and boots with heels, we strutted off campus to a party Melly heard about up on South Street. It was on the early side—around 10:30 pm—and we hadn't been able to pregame because nobody had a fake ID or access to any upperclassmen that early on in the school year. We walked as fast as we could in our heels and were freezing, because you don't wear a *jacket* to a college party, especially on Halloween. We all looked extra cute with our hair and makeup way overdone, our padded boobs stretching our hand-drawn Sharpie marker aces out across our chests, and our pre-freshman-fifteen asses stuffed into those leggings.

We were rounding the reservoir on our way to South Street when our very own Ace of Spades was struck by an errant egg, one which missed some young kid hiding in a row of bushes across the street. Unbeknownst to the four of us, we had stumbled into a Halloween street war, and before we knew it, another egg flew our way, followed by a stream of silly string and shaving cream. Alisha screamed like a boiling teakettle and Tori screamed in one of the kids' faces, but they all got away, racing down the street on bicycles they'd left hidden in the bushes, laughing like a pack of hyenas.

And wouldn't you know? Not a single one of us had remembered the rape whistle—or the rhinestone-laden cell phone, for that matter.

It's almost an hour by the time my name is called. At least it *feels* like an hour—could be more, for all I know. I explain what happened to a young man who looks like he might still be in high school. He sells me the new phone and informs me that I can keep my number the same but without a SIM card, all access to the contents of the phone, including my contact list and photos, are alive only in the cloud storage backup system, which I do not have the time nor the luxury of accessing at this particular moment.

For now, I will have to deal with a blank slate of a phone, which will be about as useful to me as trying to hit my people up using two cans and a string. I'll also have to set up my email again—but that's fine, I say, I can do it later.

Looks like all the important things in my life will be starting over from scratch today.

At least it can't get any worse, I think, after I've spent over three hundred dollars on the phone, a sparkly case for it, and a screen protector. I refuse the insurance because, well, I'm a glutton for punishment, I guess. Or maybe just a grade A knucklehead, as my dad would say.

It's well after four by the time I get home, and I'm a bit aggravated but also in too much of a hurry to sweat it. The only numbers I know by heart are my parents' house in Westchester and the number to the Chinese food restaurant, so I program those in quickly before changing into appropriate dinner clothes, brushing my hair, putting on makeup and a fresh chin Band-Aid, and carefully placing my new phone in my purse, along with my wallet, keys, and lip gloss.

On the subway, I'm trying to set up my email on the phone when I realize that I have a voicemail message. No, wait. *Two* voicemail messages.

I hit *send* on the voicemail icon and plug my ear with my finger so I can hear better.

"Holy. Fucking. Shit. Gracie, I need you to call me back like *yesterday*. Lindsay's *done*. She just stormed out of here in a full-on rage with all her shit. I think she got *fired*."

I hang up before listening to the second message. My new

phone's got an unlimited data plan, so I'm able to pull up the Vision Board website and grab the number from there. I check the time. It's past five, so Evan might be gone, but sometimes he works late to read through subs.

It rings. *Please pick up*, I think.

"Vision Board Creative Group. This is Evan," he says cheerily.

"Evan? It's Grace."

"Oh, thank you, sweet Jesus! I have been *waiting* to hear back from you *all day long*! What the fuck took you so long?"

"I'm sorry! I dropped my phone in the sewer—it was a whole, long thing. But forget about that. What *happened*?"

"Your girl is *gone*. I told you about how she trashed the conference room, right?"

"Uh huh."

"Well, I got the 4-1-1. Turns out she had a surprise visit from her ex today."

Oh God, I think.

"He came here to try and talk to her about I'm not sure what but *not* like your typical divorce stuff. And she flipped on him! She threw the chair and shattered the glass and Sean and Kath were legit *furious* and now they're threatening legal action against her!"

"Holy shit," I say. My head spins.

"Yeah, it was the most drama I have *ever* seen in this place. I only wish I had been there for the chair toss. Fucking bad sushi," he grumbles. "Do you have *any* idea how much money a video like that could have made on the Internet?"

"I'm sure," I utter. Then, something dawns on me. "Hey, Evan. What does that mean for her deals?"

"What do you mean?"

"Lindsay was working on a deal with Cabaret for my manuscript."

"This new one? From yesterday? The one she called garbage?"

"No, a different one."

"Because, sidebar? It's not garbage at all, boo. It's fucking spectacular."

"You read it?"

"Um, *yes*. It's so *scandalous*."

"If only you knew," I say under my breath.

"What?" he asks.

"Nothing," I say. "But the other one—*Reckless Outlaw*? What happens with that if she's been fired?"

"Did you sign anything?"

"No. Lindsay said she was working on a deal—something about them having to go to an acquisitions meeting—and originally they were thinking about offering $500,000 for the one manuscript and $750,000 if I could give them a second one for a two-book deal. So, I was working on the second one—that's the thing you read—but she hated it and I have no idea what the status was on the deal." A woman with about forty shopping bags and a scarf wrapped around her head gives me a dirty look. I lower my voice. "Evan, I don't even know the last name of the editor she was talking to at Cabaret."

"Okay, hold up. Explain this to me. Lindsay was working on a deal, but it wasn't finalized?"

"Correct."

"Do Sean and Kath know about it?"

"I don't know if she told them," I say.

He pauses, and I hear him swallow. "My guess is no, because if they knew, they'd be doing immediate damage control and you would have already received multiple calls from them."

"But my phone—"

"Right. It was floating upstream in the underground waterways of New York City. Still—I know them. They'd be up your ass so deep you'd taste it in your throat."

"Gross image."

"You're welcome. G, when you signed with Vision Board, did you sign with the agency or with Lindsay?"

I sigh. "I signed with Lindsay. It was part of the arrangement. She was new and was trying to build her own list."

"Shit," he seethes. "And now she's kaput."

"Exactly. Which leaves me here totally freaking the fuck out, Evan! What am I going to do? I need that deal!"

"Well, you know I hate to be the bearer of bad news, love, but if you didn't sign anything official with Cabaret then there is no deal. And if she's gone…" His voice trails off.

"I'm fucked," I mumble. The weight of the revelation feels like an axe through my ribs.

"At least through Vision Board you are. I mean, unless you petition yourself to Sean and Kath and try and get one of the other agents here to rep you. Although, Lindsay is—was—the only agent really working in the romance space anymore. But if you have someone *else* represent you, that person could revisit it for you." He sighs. "But, I've got to be honest with you. Sean was just saying how he can't afford any more bad publicity. Having an agent be fired so dramatically because she got violent? It's a bad look for them."

I begin to hyperventilate. Shopping bag lady eyeballs me. "Ev, I gotta go."

"Okay, but for real, I'm *obsessed* with this new manuscript of yours and I totally think you should keep at it."

"I *can't*," I say, trying to control my breathing.

"Why not?"

The subway doors open and a large man wearing giant headphones squeezes into the seat beside me. I can feel my blood pressure rise with each audible thump of the bass from his blaring rap music. It hits me: Lindsay's *gone*. Like forever. She threw my career out the window as if it were nothing more than a chair in the conference room at Vision Board.

"Because the story is all about Lindsay. The guy? Her ex? I went to high school with him. And we've been sort of *seeing* each other."

"Shut. Up. You. Whore! He was hot too!"

I'm unraveling. I'm going to pass out right here on the subway, and my fate will be forever linked to Shopping Bag Lady and Headphone Guy deciding whether or not it's even worth it to call 9-1-1.

"His name's Colin. He helped me write the new story. It was all based on the awful shit she did to him."

"I can*not* believe this! You're so *bad*, girl. Who knew little Gracie Landing had it in her?"

"I didn't *know* he was her ex. I didn't even know they knew each other!"

"Really, boo? How is that possible?"

My insides feel like they're on fire. "He has this thing with nicknames. He called her Elle, like short for Ellerton. I had no clue it was Lindsay."

"Damn. That's the kind of unfortunate that's usually reserved for red carpet fails at the Emmys."

"Ev, I really gotta go."

"Wait. One more thing. If you want me to try and talk to Sean or Kath for you, I will. But I wouldn't be surprised if they didn't want to touch you with a ten-foot pole. Especially if you were only *hoping* for this handshake deal to come through. Honestly? They might not even believe you. The agents around here have really made a mess of this place lately."

I groan.

"But don't lose hope. You won't have a hard time finding someone new. You're amazing, G."

"Right now, I think I just need to drink myself into oblivion."

"I hear that, girl. You do you. Let's touch base soon though, okay?"

"Okay. Thanks."

"Bye," he says and hangs up the phone.

I look up. Still in Brooklyn. Thank God the B train runs above ground.

I do a search online for *Yarmouth Aycock, P.C.* The number comes up and I double click it to place the call. It's 5:35. The phone rings four times, until an answering machine picks up.

Fuck.

Fuck, fuck, fuck. What am I supposed to do now?

Headphone Guy is spilling over the seat divider into my personal space, making me feel next-level claustrophobic. Still, I can't relinquish my seat because I'm too busy on my phone. I decide it's in my best interest to take the few remaining minutes before the subway careens into the below-ground tunnel and set up my email on my phone.

I am not technologically savvy. Like, I'm not completely useless on a laptop, but I am probably the only human person under the age of forty who still pays bills using actual, real-life checks and balances a checkbook. I don't *trust* myself with the Internet. I'm afraid if I put my bills on automatic bill pay I'll end up broke and starving. Granted, I'm not far off from broke and starving right now, but that's why God invented credit cards.

When cell phones went from having actual buttons you could press to just being a flat touch screen, I thought I was going to chop off my thumbs in frustration. I could not for the life of me figure out how hard to swipe or push "buttons" that would come up on the screen. I missed zillions of calls the year I got my first touchscreen phone, simply because I couldn't get the hang of swiping the big green phone icon that would come up when someone was calling me. Texting was a nightmare. I tried hand lotions. They only made things slippery and greasy. I tried those gloves with the different-colored forefinger and thumb. That just made my hands sweaty. For a while, I found I was okay if I just used my knuckles to swipe at things, but I saw myself do that once in the reflection of a Dunkin' Donuts window and *my. God.* It was like watching an ape play with a cell phone. I was so mortified that I immediately went home and spent the rest of the night texting and emailing myself until I could figure out the exact pressure to use with the touch screen to make it work.

So, as one could probably imagine, setting up my email account on a moving train with a wannabe emcee sweating all over me and a bag lady staring me down is not the easiest feat. But I remain focused, and I am able to respond to simple prompts, including what my mother's maiden name is, what street I grew up on, and what my favorite movie is. And with moments to spare, I am able to unlock the Pandora's box that is my email account on my phone.

New messages pour in. They are mostly spam because I am a nobody. There's a forward from my mother of kittens wearing sweaters that makes me seriously contemplate ending it all right now, just smothering myself with Headphone Guy's flabby upper arm.

But then I see I have a message from Colin.

TO: Grace Landing (gracie222@mail.com)
FROM: Colin Yarmouth (cyarmouth@
    yarmouthaycockpc.com)
SUBJECT: Call me

Hey,

I know you said you're trying to fix your phone situation (sorry to hear about that, by the way), but as soon as you do, can you please give me a call? It's important.

C.

For a smart guy—a *very* smart guy—a *lawyer*—you would think Colin might realize that if he's asking me to call him and my cell phone is in the sewer, there's a good chance that I don't have his number anymore. Sadly, this is not the case.

The space around me goes dark and the pressure suddenly changes in my ears. We're in the tunnel. Now I have no service, so I can't write Colin back. I check the time. It's 5:50. As soon as I get off the train, I'm going to have to run right over to the restaurant. Everything else will have to wait.

I lean my head back against the window, willing the universe not to add the acquisition of head lice to the endless list of momentous events happening to me today, and close my eyes. I inhale the scent of Headphone Guy's sweaty armpits mixed with traces of deodorant he likely slathered on hours (or days) ago, mixed with the familiar urine smell all New Yorkers expect from the subway. I consider the gravity of what has happened and draw a picture in my mind. Colin went to Vision Board to try and talk to Lindsay. Lindsay freaked out and threw a chair through the window, thus getting herself fired and losing my book deal.

Essentially, my new boyfriend sabotaged my whole career.

Stop it, I chide myself. *He was trying to help. He couldn't have known she would explode like that.*

Oh, really? my cynical side asks. *He just told me, like, a dozen stories about the level of crazy that she is. How could he think she would be anything OTHER than clinically insane?*

My schizophrenic brain volleys this birdie back and forth over the net of my patience. By the time I get to the Broadway-Lafayette station, I am ready for a drink.

The girls already have a table at Rollicks, no doubt thanks to Melly's low-cut, skintight dress and this obsequious *Mike*, who thinks she's all that. They wave me over when they see me enter the restaurant, which is busier than I'd expect for a Tuesday night.

"Girl, you look tore *up*," Tori says.

Alisha smacks her in the arm. "Stop it!" she says. "Gracie, are you okay?"

"Yeah, what happened here?" Melly asks, pointing her finger in a circle in front of my bandaged chin. "This is not a celebration face."

I sigh. "Did you order drinks yet?"

Melly sits up straight, putting her hefty C-cups on full display. "First round's on Mike," she announces proudly.

"Yeah? That's fantastic," I say. "I'll take a double shot of Malibu."

"Uh-oh," Alisha says. "Something *is* wrong."

A waitress comes over and I repeat my order.

"Spill it," Tori says.

"Before I even *begin* to tell you about my day, I need your phone numbers." I pull out my new phone and pass it to Tori. "Please just program them in for me. I can't deal with that thing right now."

"What happened to your old phone?" Alisha asks.

"It's probably washed out into Jamaica Bay by now," I say. "I dropped it in the sewer when I fell and split open my chin earlier today."

"Oh, honey," Melly says.

"That's not even the worst of it," I say.

"Yikes. What else?" Alisha asks.

I shake my head. "I don't even know where to begin."

"We got you, girl. Just say it real fast, like ripping off a Band-Aid," Tori says. "I mean, don't *actually* rip off your Band-Aid." She laughs.

"Very funny." Melly rolls her eyes.

"I lost the deal," I say.

Alisha's face scrunches up so she looks a little like a french bulldog. "Huh?"

"The half-million-dollar deal with Cabaret books," I explain. "It's over. Not happening," I say. My insides twist. My drink is set down in front of me and I gulp it back gratefully.

"How?" Tori asks.

The rum hits me quick, and I eagerly welcome the social lubrication. *I'm tired of being Gracie the loser, Gracie the fuck-up, Gracie with the cheating ex-fiancé, Gracie who slips in her own vomit at the club, Gracie who still lives in Brooklyn because her life's such a mess. I'm so over it!*

"Remember I texted you about how I was talking to Colin Yarmouth?"

"Uh huh," Melly says.

"So, I didn't really share *how* exactly that came to pass."

"Yeah, you did," Tori says. "You said you hit him up when you were wasted."

"After the club," Alisha adds.

"Right," I say. "But there's a little more to the story than just that."

"Go on," Melly says.

"So, I was feeling shitty about everything with Scott, and I'd been thinking about maybe using Colin as a model for the love interest in the story I was working on." I hear my own voice echoing amidst the din of the restaurant. Even *I* can hear that I sound like a girl who's full of shit.

"What does that mean, exactly?" Tori asks. "Thinking about *maybe* using him?"

"Oh, boy," Alisha says, under her breath.

"This is the kid from high school?" Melly asks. "With the love notes?"

I nod weakly.

"G, as I recall, you've already written *volumes* about his ass," Tori says.

"Fine! Busted," I say. "I was already writing about him. Anyway, I emailed him, he emailed me back, and whatever, one thing led to another, and we saw each other a few times this week."

"Like, how?" Melly asked.

"He took me out. One dinner, one late lunch, and one—" Tears sting my eyes thinking about our *proper* date. Its perfection rivaled any date I had ever gone on before that and, honestly, probably any date I'll ever go on again. "One *other* date." I blink the tears away. I will *not* cry about this in public. "I need another drink," I announce.

"Damn! Okay, girl! How Gracie got her groove back," Melly says, ignoring my beverage request, arms raised in the air. "Did you—?" She makes a lewd hand gesture, her pointer finger penetrating her other hand, which is balled up like a fist.

I smirk, and they all start laughing and cheering.

"But listen, listen," I say. "I just found out his ex-wife is my agent. Or, *was* my agent." I swallow. "We had this big misunderstanding. Colin was helping me write my new story—giving me ideas, you know? He kept telling me about all this crazy shit that his ex-wife did. So, I wrote it all into my manuscript, and submitted it to her, and she lost her mind and basically divorced me as a client."

"Harsh," Melly says.

"Yeah, but it gets worse. Colin went over to her office this morning. I'm guessing he wanted to try and smooth things over, but she threw a chair through a window and got fired. So, my deal that was in the works—for $500,000—is no more."

"Shit," Tori says. "You can't talk to somebody else up in there?"

I shake my head. "I did," I explain. "You remember Evan—the one who I'm actually friends with? I spoke to him about it. He said that there's a good chance that Lindsay never told the bosses about the deal. That may have been because she was negotiating and nothing was set in stone yet."

"And if Lindsay just got fired…" she trails off.

"Then there's no reason for her to say anything about the deal, especially because the only person it will benefit is the person she hates most in the world right now—me." I hang my head in my hands.

"So why don't you go and talk to the boss people? Tell them what was up. Maybe *they* can figure it out," Tori suggests.

"Yeah. Evan said he would intercede on my behalf if I wanted him to."

"So, there you go," Tori says.

Melly pulls her dress down a bit in the front, revealing a thin edge of black lace along her cleavage. "Well, if you're really *not* buying drinks tonight, I'll get the next round," she says, winking at me.

Melly's something else. She's married, and I don't really think she'd ever touch anyone else, but the girl *loves* to flirt. I think it makes her feel like she's still got it.

I stop counting drinks after six, only because I can no longer mentally compute numbers at that point. We toast to new opportunities, old mistakes (good riddance!), and the eternal sisterhood of our friendship. At some point, I know that I try to ask Mike if he would ever destroy his girlfriend's career, and he says he doesn't have a girlfriend and winks at Melly.

I eat too. Buffalo wings with bleu cheese dressing. A chicken avocado sun roll (which is like an egg roll pretending to be healthy). Something called tornado shrimp, which is sweet and spicy and nestled in a bed of lettuce. Halfway through dinner, I order fried Oreos, and when I'm done with those, I order a pear and goat cheese salad with house-made cheese bread on the side.

It should come as no surprise to anyone when I excuse myself to go to the bathroom and end up vomiting on a birthday cake being delivered to a family by a brigade of servers.

Next thing I know, I'm right where I was a week and a half ago, sitting in the backseat of an Uber, being driven home as a punishment for my indiscretions.

Out the window, the world whizzes by. Streetlights flash so quickly that they make me uncomfortably dizzy. I fish my phone out of my purse and look down at my lap, unlocking the screen to maintain my focus on anything other than the spinning sidewalks outside of this fine Toyota Camry driven by a man named Rolf, who I casually mention has the same name as the piano-playing dog from *The Muppets*.

Rolf is not amused by this, so it appears he is done speaking to me.

My $300 cellular device informs me that I have four missed calls, all from the same number. I do not have this number programmed in my phone. I try to call it, but my thumb is too rough with the screen, so nothing happens. I try again with a gentler touch, and voila! Success. I put the phone to my face and listen to it ring.

"Hello?"

I know this voice. "Colin?" I ask.

"Gracie! Where have you been? I've been trying to reach you all night!"

"I have been out celebrating!" I declare.

"Really?" he asks. "Celebrating what?"

"Why, the death of my career, of course! And I have you to thank!" I announce. Rolf looks at me in the rearview mirror.

"About that," Colin says. "I am so, so sorry, Grace. I went in there to try and talk some *sense* into her—"

"But instead, you destroyed the tiny bit of hope I had left in my life. Really, Colin, well done," I say.

"I'm sure it's not that bad," he says.

"Not that bad?" I cackle. "Colin, do you know that I have about $46 in my checking account at the present moment?"

Rolf shakes his head, undoubtedly concerned about the

overdraft fees I'll be accruing in order to pay him for our time together this evening.

"No," he mumbles.

"Well, it's true. I'm just a heartbeat away from homelessness, you could say. And the *one* thing I had going for me—a book I wrote *without* your help—was supposed to sell for $500,000! I was getting ready to *retire in style*, Col-in!"

"I didn't know that," he says.

"I didn't *tell* you because it wasn't important. I'm a grown woman. I can take care of myself without divulging the details of my bank statements to you. And maybe I was afraid that if I did express my momentary impoverished status, you might classify me with the likes of *Elle*—a financial geologist mining the trenches for buried treasure and such."

"I don't think you're a gold digger, Gracie."

We hit a bump, and I feel half-digested food shift in my over-filled stomach. I burp aloud. "Excuse me, Rolf," I say. He makes a disturbed face. "Bottom line, Colin. I was walking a fine line when you reentered my life. I'd been to hell and back and was holding myself together by a thread." My voice keeps getting louder. "And you, my friend. Well. You"—I consider my metaphors—"are the scissors in my ass."

"You don't mean that," he says.

"Oh, but I do. You ruined what little glimmer of hope I had left! Now I have literally nothing!"

"I can *help* you with money, Grace," he says. "And it wouldn't be like it was with Elle! I know you're working hard. I *know* you're not looking for a sugar daddy."

"I don't need your *charity*," I seethe. "In fact, I think you should really quit while you're ahead."

"What are you saying?"

I hiccup. "I think you've done enough."

"What does that mean?" he asks in a small voice.

"It means we're finished here."

"What? Why?" Colin asks. He sounds frantic.

"Because you cast your flawless, all-county MVP spell on me and turned my life to *shit*, that's why. I should've left my fucking yearbook locked up in the top of my closet. I don't know what the hell I was thinking. The past is *done*, Colin. Just like us. I was a fool to think this could work."

He doesn't respond to this.

"Goodbye, Colin. Have a nice life—or not—whatever," I say.

I drop my phone in my purse. Then, I throw up on the water-proof floor mats in the back of Rolf's Uber.

Colin

Fuck.

What a complete and total shitshow.

Leave it to Elle. Just when I think it can't get any worse with her, or that there might be a light at the end of the tunnel, she manages to destroy any chance I have of finding happiness with someone else.

I can't believe she threw a fucking *chair* through a plate glass wall of windows.

I can't sit still. I don't even *blame* Gracie for being as mad as she is. It's not like this is just a job; it's her entire *career*! I may not love my work, but if Gracie somehow figured out a way to make me lose my job, I'd probably be mad too.

And to think! We were *this close* to working through it. She brought me that god-awful green drink thing today. Nobody has *ever* just dropped by my office to bring me a treat. *Ever.* Daisy even commented about it.

"I like her, Colin," she said. "She's so different from Elle."

"I know, right?"

"Yes! She *smiled* at me. She looked me in the eye. When she asked for you, she even blushed a little."

"Really?"

"Really," she confirmed. "This one's a keeper, for sure."

Daisy's right. There's an honest-to-god connection between me and Gracie. Nobody had to swipe right or jump through all of the awkward hoops that are synonymous with online dating. I was at that point too, where I was practically ready to swear off the idea of ever getting married again for good. Then, out of nowhere, a girl from fucking *high school*—of all places!—hits me up, and she's funny and sexy and kind and, well, gone.

Gone.

Fuck my life. Seriously.

I gotta move. I gotta get the hell out of the house. I throw on a pair of jeans and boat shoes. The shoes were a gift from Elle— who told me I needed more style. I never thought I'd be the kind of guy who would own a pair of boat shoes. But to be fair, I also never thought I'd be the kind of guy whose marriage only lasted six months because his wife realized she wasn't into men anymore and left him high and dry with nothing but an itchy dick to show for it.

There's a bar down the block from my building. It's a dive bar, but in my opinion, every bar is a dive bar on a Tuesday night. I walk in, survey the place real quick, and grab a stool near a flat screen with a constant stream of ESPN highlights. I order a double shot of Jack Daniels. It burns my throat, but I take it like a man. I follow it up with a Jack and Coke, careful not to push myself too hard too fast. I just want to forget this whole debacle. The double shot helps. A lot.

All I wanted to do was fix it. I thought if I went to her office and talked to Elle face-to-face, I could remind her of how forgiving *I'd* been despite all the torture she put me through. But the second she saw me, she dragged me into the Vision Board conference room and just came at me like a rabid dog. She stood there, barking, drooling, spitting words at me rapid fire, trying to break through my skin and rip me to shreds, when, if you think about it, *she* was the reason I had all those stories to share with Gracie in the first place.

Elle did *not* like being reminded of that.

I should reopen our divorce case and take her cheating ass to the cleaners in court.

The baseball highlight reel starts to look a little blurry by the time I order my fourth Jack and Coke. I go to take a piss and sort of miss the urinal. I get back to my seat at the bar and watch the bartender, who's giving me a little bit of side eye and kind of looks like my father when he does that—if my father's forearms were covered in faded tattoos and he was about three inches shorter and had a crew cut instead of a comb-over. So, yeah. Really nothing like my father at all.

When I feel the ice in the glass clink against my front teeth, he approaches. "Settle up, brother. We're closing down." He slides me the bill.

I try to check my phone for the time, but the numbers are dancing a little. There's a two and a one and a seven but I have no idea what order they're supposed to be in. I look around and I'm the only one left at the bar.

"You need me to get you a lift somewhere?" he asks.

"Mmm," I reply. I'm pretty sure I shake my head no. I can't

read the bill either, but I put down three twenty-dollar bills and figure that oughta cover it. He takes the money and delivers some change, which I leave on the bar as I try to stand up.

I make my way towards the glass door under the glowing red exit sign.

"You sure you're good?" the bartender asks.

I wave without turning around.

Outside, a blast of cool air hits me hard. Something's different out here. I look up. Drops of rain shoot straight from the sky directly at me, as if God is holding a machine gun loaded with raindrops inside of my very own personal thunder cloud.

It's cold, and I'm wet. I accidentally step ankle-deep in a puddle.

My right boat shoe is ruined, I think.

Then, everything turns black.

Gracie

It's amazing how the universe can kick you when you're down.

Ten days ago, I woke up in a bed oddly similar to the one I'm lying in now. Today's crime-scene evidence is different though. Instead of snipped thongs, I am surrounded by glossy pages, torn hastily from their binding and ripped to pieces. Young smiling faces are shredded and strewn about, as if a wild animal inhabited my bed last night. I close my eyes and try to patch together the remains of what I can remember.

There was an Uber.

And a phone call.

And lots of angry, vicious ripping.

It takes a moment, but I realize what I've done. I'm sleeping in a sea of faces akin to my old high school cafeteria.

I destroyed my yearbook.

I sigh as a swarm of memories rushes over me. Things I couldn't have possibly said aloud, like blaming Colin for the demise of my writing career.

Wow. I am a grade A asshole.

The light coming in from the window is exceedingly bright; it gives me a headache. I pull the covers over my head to block it, spilling chunks of pages onto the floor. I vow to never leave my bed, to stay engulfed in my own filth and bad choices until eventually I die a slow, painful, lonely death.

I fall asleep this way.

When I wake up hours later, I have to reach around to get my bearings. I find my cell phone in my purse on the floor. I check it for messages. There's only one, from Alisha, making sure I'm okay.

I check my email. Another forward from my mother. This one promises jokes about pirates. *Mom needs a hobby*, I decide.

I raise my arms up over my head and stretch. It's just after noon. I have no job. No plans. No food in the house.

No boyfriend.

I trudge over to the bathroom, where I find a lighter on the sink counter and large black ashes floating in the toilet. It appears I may have lit some of the yearbook pages on fire in my agitated state last night. I pee on top of them and flush the whole mess down the toilet, praying nothing clogs.

Then, I brush my teeth, because nothing's worse than the remnants of yesterday's vomit in one's mouth. I run myself a shower and try to wash away my mistakes, my errors, my missteps, and when I emerge, my body is clean and my hair smells like coconut, but my soul remains shrouded in guilt and regret.

This is no way to live, I tell myself.

I take a deep breath and head over to my computer. Sitting down at the desk, I look up the Starbucks website and print out their job application. I fill it out in my neatest handwriting and decide I'll bring it over to the Starbucks on Emmons Avenue, across from the footbridge.

Maybe I should move back home with my parents, I think. Dad would probably love having me around. It would give him a buffer so he wouldn't have to deal with Mom's brand of crazy all by himself. I breathe into the idea of it. I picture Mom waking me up in the morning, pouring me a bowl of Grape Nuts and waxing poetic about how important fiber is for my digestive system.

So, yeah. That'll be a hard pass.

I lace up my sneakers and sling my purse over my shoulder, then I head over to Starbucks. It's cloudy but warm, and the air by the water smells remarkably of low tide today. Thoughts of Colin pop up like Whac-A-Mole in my brain. I picture him considering how going to talk to Lindsay might help me. *Whack.* I think about his shirtless body bringing me coffee. *Whack.* I remember the look on his face the first time he saw me outside my building. *Whack, whack, whack.*

Thinking about how our situation got so royally fucked up is not going to help me. I try to put it out of my head as I enter the Starbucks, greeted by the aroma of roasted Arabica beans that wafts up into my nostrils.

A hip young girl in a green apron wears a wide grin and several facial piercings. Her head is shaved on one side, and the hair that remains flops across her scalp.

She sounds remarkably professional when she speaks, despite being nineteen years old at best. "Welcome to Starbucks! What can I get for you today?"

A fresh start? I wonder. *A new chance at life?* "A grande caramel Frappuccino, please," I say.

She types my order into the register. "You got it. Anything else?"

I remember why I came. "Um, yes. I'd like to drop off this job application." I hand the application, folded and tucked neatly into a business-size envelope, over to Hip Barista Girl.

"Sweet," she says, tucking it into her apron. "I'll get it to Bess. She's the manager. She'll give you a call once she looks it over."

I nod, looking longingly at her for answers. "Can I ask you something?"

She shrugs. "Sure."

"Do you like it here?"

She laughs. "I mean, it gets the job done, you know? Free drinks, a free meal, good benefits, and some spending cash. The people who work here are chill. Customers vary." She smiles. "Some are cool, but some are pretty pretentious. I feel like if you get their drinks right and you're friendly though, it's all good."

"Are you in school?"

"Yeah. I go to Kingsborough."

Kingsborough Community College is on the easternmost tip of Manhattan Beach. It's an odd location for a school, but the campus is nice, and the views of the water are great, considering it's in Brooklyn.

"Are most of the people who work here so…?"

"Smart? Funny? Put together?" She laughs.

"I was going to say 'young.'" I smile.

"Not everyone. But there are quite a few students."

"Cool," I say, although in my mind, this is the furthest thing from cool. "I'm Grace." I hold out my hand.

She shakes it. "Sabrina," she says. "Nice to meet you."

"Maybe I'll see you around," I say. Three young moms with strollers get in line behind me. I move down to the other end of the counter and wait for my drink.

Back outside, I feel a strange mix of hope and defeat. The sugar and caffeine help me feel a little better physically, but emotionally, I'm all over the map. I'm proud of myself for coming to terms with the notion that I am going to need a job that can help me pay bills, even though I hate the fact that I am an author whose royalty checks make welfare payments seem generous by comparison. I'm also still in complete denial that I'm agentless, that the *Reckless Outlaw* deal is almost 100% no more, and that Colin and I are a thing of the past. These thoughts occupy my mind as I wander over the footbridge and down to the beach, careful *not* to walk past Mrs. A's house. My stomach is still lamenting yesterday's poor choices; there's no way I can handle a heavy meal (no matter how well-intentioned) right now.

On the beach, I sit crisscross applesauce a few feet back from the shore. Staring out at the horizon, I watch the birds dance across the surface of the water and the boats speed by in the distance. I try to focus on my breathing, the way Kiki does in yoga. Before too long, I feel safe. Like if I sit quietly enough, nobody will ever find me here.

"Yoo hoo!" I hear.

I turn, already knowing what fate awaits me.

"You have no chair today?" Mrs. A asks me.

"No," I shake my head. "Just me and the sand."

"Come," she says. "You come sit on bench with me and Olga."

"Who's Olga?" I ask.

"She is neighbor I have. She was engineer in Georgia. Now she live here. We play Sudoku puzzles."

"Sudoku? Isn't that supposed to be a solitary game?"

"Solitaire is only for jail, *devushka*. Any game is better with a friend."

"I see," I say, even though the idea of sharing a Sudoku puzzle with someone else seems maddening.

Mrs. A holds out her hand to help me up off the ground. "You are sick again," she says.

"What makes you say that?" I ask innocently.

"Mela put picture on Instagram. You are looking..." She pauses, thinking. "Drunk as skunk, kids are saying."

I laugh. "The kids don't really say that."

"Well, they should. I show you." She pulls a bedazzled gold cell phone out of her pocket and opens her Instagram account. I consider asking Mrs. A why she needs an Instagram account at her advanced age, but far be it for me to judge. "You see?" She taps her long red fingernail on the screen. "You are look very sick. Big mistake. I see only drinks in picture. No bread. Where is bread?"

I shrug, knowing there's no use in trying to argue. "You're right," I say. "I should've ordered extra bread."

We arrive at a green bench overlooking the swings at the playground. There sits an elderly woman decked out in a Juicy Couture sweatshirt and sweatpants whose coiffed, fluffy, platinum blond hair reminds me of cotton candy, only it is wrapped loosely in a scarf. She is wearing black sunglasses, and the combination bears a vague resemblance to what Susan Sarandon might have looked like in *Thelma and Louise* if she was about a thousand years old.

"I am Olga," the lady says to me matter-of-factly.

"Nice to meet you," I smile.

"This is Gracie," Mrs. A announces proudly. "She is sick from alcohol."

"You need bread?" Olga asks, fishing through her oversized purse.

"No, no. I'm fine, thank you," I say.

"I have breadstick from diner," she says, holding out a crumpled package wrapped in clear cellophane containing a single, four-inch breadstick covered in sesame seeds. "You eat."

I nod, accepting the offer, ignoring the fact that it was stuck to what appeared to be a used tissue in her purse. I know how to behave amongst these ladies. No need to start a thing here on the playground.

"Gracie and Mela are very best friends from college. Gracie live in Babushka's old house."

"Ahh," Olga says, pointing her finger up. "Is haunted," she declares.

"Olga!" Mrs. A says. Then, she rattles off something in Russian, and Olga smiles a pitiful-looking smile at me. "No listen to her," Mrs. A admonishes me. "Tell us, now. What makes you drink to sickness for second time in row?" she asks.

"Just had a bad day," I say.

"You have broken chin?" Mrs. A asks.

"Right," I remember. "Not broken," I say. "I tripped and fell on the corner of Ocean and Avenue Z. Dropped my cell phone in the sewer."

"Poor little *porosenok*," Mrs. A says.

I raise my eyebrows.

"Means *piglet*," Olga says.

Terrific, I think.

"So, you get new cell phone. This is easy fix. What else happened?" Mrs. A asks.

"Well, you remember that guy I told you about?"

"Mister Email?" she asks.

I nod. "We were sort of seeing each other," I say. "But not anymore."

"Why not? He is make baby with somebody else? Like Scott?"

"No, no," I say. "Nothing like that."

Olga reaches out and takes my hands in hers. She closes her eyes and wraps her hands over mine. I sit uncomfortably, frozen but looking around. *Does nobody else think this is weird?* I wonder.

"She is sad. She make mistake. She is regret," Olga proclaims.

Mrs. A claps joyfully. "Olga is studying to be mystic," she says. "First, engineer. Build buildings! Now mystic, seeing future! She is good, no?"

I laugh aloud, then dial it back so as not to appear rude. "Yes, she's very good," I say.

"Why you are sad? Why you are regret?" Mrs. A asks.

I decide it can't hurt to tell them the truth. I have nowhere to go, nothing else to do on this cloudy spring day. So, I begin at the beginning, with freshman science class and the nickname. Then,

I talk about the secret admirer notes, and how I used to day-dream about Colin when I was beholden to Ronald. I share about my writing, and about Scott, and about using my high school yearbook to create characters for a story that could have greatly advanced my net worth. I tell them about Ilana and the baby, my downward spiral into self-loathing and panic, my drunken email to Colin of not even two weeks ago. I spill the details of our brief affair like a child spills milk on the carpet, with innocence and honesty that overwhelms me with catharsis and anguish all at once. I explain about Lindsay, how he called her Elle and how that got us into a tangled mess that ended with the obliteration of my income potential. I end the story with our phone call last night, the awful way I hit below the belt during our fight, the nasty things I said that I can't take back. "I was angry," I explain. "I was hurt. Now, I've lost everything."

When I'm done, Olga says, "No."

"No?" I ask.

"No. You can fix."

"How?" I wonder.

"You are writer, yes? You write for money?"

I nod.

"So, you write this story down in paper."

"It *is* interesting story, Gracie," Mrs. A says. "It reminds me of *Tbilisi Nights*. Is Georgian soap opera about *devushka* named Yelena who is schoolteacher by day and exotic dancer by night."

"How does that relate to my story at all?" I laugh.

"Because she is paying money for sex, yes?"

"I think you mean *being* paid," I say.

"And she is falling in love for one man, but she is teaching his child in school, and he is seeing her in club at night. She is wearing wig—fake hair, yes?—so he does not know she is same schoolteacher for his little boy."

Olga nods her head vehemently. "This is *big* show back home," she agrees.

"Yelena is Yelena in school but in club she is Viktoriya. So the man, Nikolai, he falls in love for Viktoriya but can never be with her because she is exotic dancer and he is noble doctor, important in town." Mrs. A continues.

"Is he married?" I ask.

"Oh, no. His wife is dead from snow avalanche."

"Of course," I say.

"You should watch it. Is very good. You will understand, is just like your story," Mrs. A says.

Olga nods. "You write this all down. Make book from this."

"I don't know," I say.

"Listen to me," Mrs. A says. "In *Tbilisi Nights*, Yelena fall in love with Nikolai, but he is not interested in schoolteacher. He is trying fix Viktoriya, make her life better so she can stop being, how you say, sex worker?"

"Okay," I say.

"Is just same how Colin was trying help you!" she exclaims. "When is last time somebody goes out of their way for you like that?"

I consider the question and shrug.

"Never Scott! He was too much about Scott!"

"That's true," I say.

"This boy is trying love you," she insists.

"But I said such awful things to him. He'll never take me back," I say.

"So, you fix it. He was trying fix for you; now you must try and fix for him!" Mrs. A says.

Olga places her whole palm on my forehead. "Shh," she implores me. Her palm is sweaty and smells vaguely like beef. She closes her eyes and wrinkles her brow. "You are hiding," she says. "For one revolution of the moon, you hide. Give planets a chance to line in order. You plant new seeds, and you see what will grow." She opens her eyes. "This is how it is written in stars."

Mrs. A claps and cheers loudly. "Bravo! Bravo!"

I feel like I've checked into my own personal seaside circus.

I tell them I'd best be going and decline Mrs. A's ample offers for food to take home with me. I carry my empty Frappuccino cup and my wrapped breadstick out of the park with me, and head back towards the footbridge, wondering the whole way why it is that I always think I'll be able to come down to the beach for solitude and reflection. *A smarter person would have learned by now*, I conclude. But I'm smiling, and I feel a little bit better, so it's not all bad.

Colin

I am never drinking again.

I woke up to the sound of a man's voice booming in my ear. "Get up, kid," the voice said. It was accompanied by a three-fingered hard tap on the shoulder.

I was wet. And cold. And I couldn't see. When I tried to open my eyes, I was blinded by white-hot fire trying to burn its way through my retinas.

"C'mon, guy. Don't make this worse than it has to be," the voice roared.

"I can't see," I managed to say.

Suddenly, my eyes felt cooler, and I only saw blackness. I felt a strong hand on my forearm. It pulled me up to a seated position. The raw, slippery brick wall against my back drew attention to what felt like hammers pounding into my frontal lobe.

"You got ID?" the voice asked me.

My hands worked independent of my brain, fishing out my wallet and handing it over. I tried opening my eyes again. This time, I could make out a figure. His oversized silhouette was back-lit by the neon glow of a twenty-four-hour Krispy Kreme.

"You live right here?" he asked, pointing.

I nodded weakly.

"All right, let's get up then."

Again, the grip attached itself to my forearm. It pulled me up to my feet, and my unwilling body slumped against the bricks.

"Now, kid. Up," the voice demanded.

I managed to figure out gravity when he handed me a piece of paper along with my wallet.

"What is this?" I slurred. I did not sound right.

"It's a ticket for public intoxication. And the reason it's *only* a ticket is because you're going straight home now, got it?"

I nodded. "Mmm."

"I'm gonna stand here till you're gone, so hurry it up."

I did my best. It was only about forty steps, but it felt like miles. By the time I opened the door to my building, I looked back, and the cop was gone.

Gripped by panic and surprised by the motion once the door closed, I threw up in the corner of the elevator. I didn't mean to. The wave just plowed over me, and I couldn't control it. Vomit splashed onto my shoes.

Can't take these into the house, I decided.

I kicked them off when I got to my floor and left them there.

A combination of night sweats and wet clothes made me think I pissed the bed when I woke up wrapped in damp sheets a few hours later. The memory of being forced awake by a police officer played through my mind on repeat, haunting me all morning. Maybe for Elle, a night like mine might have been standard operating procedure, typical for a Tuesday. But not for me.

No. In my world, it felt a whole lot like rock bottom.

Consequently, I've been keeping a low profile at the office today. Which isn't easy, especially since it's Wednesday and we have softball practice in about an hour.

Daisy's been great today. She could tell I'd been through the wringer when I came in late. I'm *never* late, unless I have an off-site morning meeting, which is rare. I'm also never hung over, largely because drinking to excess is not a thing in my world. As a result, Daisy's got her Mama Bear persona on full tilt; she started me out with a Starbucks run that got me through the morning, then went to the bagel store and got me a plain bagel with butter. When I kept that down, she went to the deli on the corner and got Cream of Rice, which I haven't had since I was about three years old. She prepared it for me in the tiny staff kitchen/break room/storage closet that houses our microwave, among many other things. It tasted like mildly sweet baby food but made me full without actually feeling like I ate anything substantial. And about thirty minutes ago, she left a corn muffin on my desk when I went to the bathroom to pee.

She hasn't asked me any questions, hasn't pushed me for details, just pops her angelic little gray-haired head in every hour or so to make sure I'm recovering. And I am. Well, physically, at least.

Mentally? That's another story.

I've tried composing about half a dozen different emails and text messages to Gracie, but each one sounds worse than the last. I'm not good at writing like she is. Also, I feel like I already apologized for everything with Elle—and then I went and made it worse—so now, there's just really not much left to say.

Which fucking sucks.

I try not to think about it, because that's easier, sort of. It's quiet at the office, which typically would be a welcome change from Gordy's incessant ramblings, but since he impaled his undoubtedly sub-par manhood with a pencil, he's been MIA. His absence has left me with lots of quiet time to hang out with my thoughts and come up with new ways to permanently obliterate my chances at finding love again. According to Daisy, Gordy needed to go under general anesthesia for surgical repair of said pencil wound and ended up spending the night in the hospital. They gave him pain meds and he's been resting at home since being discharged Monday afternoon.

I suppose the timing has actually been perfect for this nervous breakdown of mine.

There's a gentle knock at my door. "Yeah?" I ask.

It's Daisy. "Want to share an Uber to the field with me?" she asks. "My treat this time."

"Sure," I say.

"And I promise, we don't have to talk at all. Not unless you want to."

I look at her and offer a small smile. "Thank you," I say.

I collect my stuff, shut down my computer, and we leave together. True to her word, Daisy lets me sit in the backseat next to her and mindlessly stare out the window. A horn blares outside, and I realize my headache is gone. It appears my hangover has passed.

As if she's reading my mind, Daisy says, "You okay?"

I nod. "Feeling much better, actually."

"I'm glad," she says. "Because I have to tell you something."

I turn to face her. Nothing good has ever come from a line like *I have to tell you something.* "What is it?" I say.

"Gordon's coming to practice."

"For what?" I ask. "Shouldn't he be—I don't know—resting his one good ball?"

Daisy nods. "Probably, yes. But you know Gordon."

"Master of FOMO," I say.

"What?" she asks, scrunching up her nose.

"Fear of missing out," I explain.

"I don't think that's it," Daisy says.

"Oh, really? Then what's your hypothesis?"

"He's intimidated by you, Colin."

"*Intimidated?* Why on earth would you think that?"

She doesn't answer right away. "Look at you, Colin. I know you're having a rough day, but try and look beyond this moment. You're smart, successful, funny, kind. You're financially stable, good at your job, and you could have any woman in America," she says.

"Right. Except, as I see it, I'm a washed-up, divorced has-been," I counter.

"You're wrong, honey. Try to imagine what it's like to be Gordon. He's your age, no wife, no girlfriend, no family. The guy barely has any friends," she says.

"A personality adjustment would help."

"True. But still."

"Still what? All he does is kiss my dad's ass all the time."

"Also true. But you know that's only because his dad's gone."

I shake my head. "I didn't know that."

"Pancreatic cancer. He died when Gordon was in middle school."

"How'd you find that out?"

"He told me. Long time ago. I thought you knew."

"Nope," I say.

"So, like I said. Intimidated. To him, you've got everything." She shrugs and looks out the window.

This new information makes me feel like a dick.

When we get to the field, Dom, Richie, Courtney, Raoul, Rachel, Jess, and Mark are warming up, and on the bench along the third base line, Gordy is sitting on an inflatable donut.

"You've got to be kidding me," I say aloud. He turns, and I want to smack myself for being too loud. "What's up, man?" I say, intentionally louder. *Good save, Colin. Real smooth.*

"Not much," he replies. "Just came to support the team."

Like half a jock strap—since you only have one good testicle, I think, making myself laugh on the inside. *God, stop being such an asshole. Leave the poor guy alone*, my conscience tells me. "Nice," I say. "How're you feeling?"

"Okay, considering," he says. "The good news is my fertility won't be impacted."

I nod, unable to come up with a normal response. My head is a minefield of adolescent jokes. I try to push them aside. "Did you have to get a tetanus shot?"

He shakes his head. "Just antibiotics. Did you know that number two pencils are not made with lead?"

"Oh, yeah?" I say.

"Graphite," he replies with a thumbs-up.

"Guess you dodged a real bullet there."

"Hey now! Hey, hey, Kiss of Death! There's my team!" my father calls out. His voice is doing that auctioneer-high-on-cocaine thing I love so much.

"Jack Sprat could eat no fat!" Gordy calls back. My eyes automatically roll. Despite my intentions, there is nothing I can do to stop them.

"That's my cue," I say, pointing a finger gun at Gordy and promptly walking away to any other area possible to put down my gear and change my shoes.

My dad and Gordy exchange pleasantries, which I tune out in favor of listening to Dom spill the details of his most recent escapade with a girl he met at an axe-throwing bar.

"What even *is* that, bro?" I ask.

"It's a fusion thing. There's a bar at the front and then further back is the axe throwing, but there's this big wall of glass in between so you can watch people throw instead of, like, watching TV or whatever," he explains.

The image brings me back to Elle's office yesterday. I would be dead right now if the chair she threw at me had been an axe instead, without a doubt.

"Sounds real entertaining," I say. "That reminds me though. Can I file for a divorce modification?"

"For real?" Dom asks. "Why?"

"Because Elle's an asshole, and you were right. I went way too easy on her in the split," I say.

"I'm gonna need to hear *all* the details accompanying this request, dude," he says. His eyes light up, excited for the gossip.

"Some other time," I say.

"Hey now, team!" Dad interrupts. "Let's circle up for a quick chat! Over here by Gordy, so he doesn't have to move," he adds.

"Bench chat! Bench chat!" Gordy yells, clapping his hands in time with the words. He sounds like a damn fool, but I don't say anything. Jess and Courtney roll their eyes and Rachel giggles. Everyone gathers per Dad's instruction, ostensibly to mourn the loss of Gordy's testicle.

"Okay, KOD," Dad says. "We're about to be really challenged. We've got a man down. That means the rest of us have to bring it, every single week, until he gets better. No breathing room. No days off. No slacking. Got it?"

A silent chorus of nods ensues as my father continues to drone on. I zone out, thinking about the axe throwing, and Elle, and Gracie, and the cop, and Gordy's nut, and—

"*Right, Colin?*" I hear.

"Huh?" I ask.

"I *said*, we'll have to treat every game like the World Series. Like elimination is at stake, right?"

"Uh, sure," I reply.

"Which means we can't *waste* our talent with a laissez-faire attitude. We can't walk around like none of this matters."

There is tension in the comment. *Is he coming at me right now?*

I shake it off. *Don't be so sensitive.* But I look over at Daisy, who raises her eyebrows in what looks like concern.

"And if one of you gets hurt, I don't want us to have to call in any more ringers," he continues.

"Why not?" I ask aloud. "Mom did great."

"Your mother got the team out of a pickle," he says. His mouth curves down into a scowl.

"No, for real. She was amazing. We were down by two when you left. Mom brought some much-needed offense to our game."

"Maybe that's what trying looks like," he shoots back at me.

Something snaps in my brain and my mouth opens before I can do anything to stop it. "Are you *trying* to pick a fight with me?" I ask.

"No, Colin. I'm not twelve and this isn't the playground," he says in a condescending tone. "I'm just saying, with Gordon out, everyone will need to try their best."

"Which insinuates that you think we don't play our hardest all the time," I say.

"Colin, honey," Daisy interjects. "I don't think he means anything by it."

"Like hell he doesn't!" I say. "He's shit-talking my mother because she's a better ballplayer than he is! And he's suggesting that I don't work hard out here!"

"That's enough, son," Dad warns. "Don't you dare disrespect me in front of the team."

"The team?" I yell. "This is bar-league slow-pitch softball, Dad. It's a fucking *joke*. I don't know why the hell you care so much!"

"Maybe because you don't care enough!"

"Why should I?"

"You never change, you know that, kid? You don't take *any-thing* seriously! That's why you keep losing!"

"What are you *talking* about?" I seethe. *Is this really happening? Are we having an argument—in public?*

"Well, for one thing, you never took care of your arm. You could've bounced back after your injury, but you just gave up."

"Gave up? Are you out of your mind? Do you have any idea what it was like to sit on the sidelines and watch my team go on *without* me?"

"Amen to that," Gordy mumbles.

"You didn't care—that's why you bailed! Just like you bailed on your marriage!" he continues. "Sports teach valuable lessons, kid, like how to push yourself. But you copped out. You begged to come home, like a little mama's boy."

The team is frozen, or at least that's how it seems in my mind. I am suspended in midair, watching the entire scene unfold.

"Whoa, whoa," Dom says. "John, I think that's enough."

"It'll be enough when he learns how to act like a man," my dad says, his eyes glued to my face.

I feel my fingernails against my palms as I curl and uncurl my fists. I am not in control of my body. The muscles in my arms tense up as a rush of adrenaline shoots through them.

I am going to hit my own father, I think.

But before I can cock my fist back, Gordy stands up, leaving his donut seat on the bench. "Hey!" he calls out. His voice is louder than I've ever heard it. "Leave him alone, Jack! Colin's a very hard worker! He's been giving me a run for my money since day one."

I'm stunned. *Did Gordy just speak out of turn?*

"And you must have zero idea about what his crazy fucking lunatic of an ex-wife did to him," Dom adds. "So, maybe ease up, yeah?"

"You guys don't know him the way I do," Dad says.

"But *I* do," Daisy interjects. "I've known that boy since he was in diapers."

"Daisy, please—"

"That's enough, John. Stop this nonsense talk. You're embarrassing the team." Her voice is firm and commanding, and I am in complete shock.

Still, I can't in good conscience let this continue, and nobody knows my father better than I do. He doesn't back down, ever, even when the odds are fully stacked against him.

"You know what, Dad? You're right. I'm a quitter. I don't care about anything. I half-ass my way through life. Is that what you want to hear?" I don't wait for an answer. "So, you know what?" I go on. "Why should today be any different?"

"What's *that* supposed to mean?"

"Call in a ringer. I'm out."

With that, I turn my back on the whole situation, grab my shit, and march my ass out of the park, towards the subway.

—

About an hour later, my cell phone rings. It's Daisy.

"Hello?"

"Hi, Colin. Sorry to bother you at home."

"No worries, Daisy. How's it going?"

"Well, practice got cut short, so I wanted to give you a call to check in on you."

"I'm fine," I lie. I'm actually in a pretty sorry state at the moment. I didn't want to drink, given my run-in with the law last night, but I also didn't want to be completely sober, so in an attempt to chase any kind of high, I bought myself a tin of Skoal chewing tobacco. The guys on the team at ASU used to say it relaxed them, but moments after I put the first pinch of it in my lower lip, I forgot to spit and instead followed my natural instinct to swallow. The choking that followed caused me no small amount of discomfort. I tried to spit out all of what was left and ended up spending the next twenty minutes in the bathroom, wrestling tobacco particles out of my teeth with my Crest Spinbrush.

"Good," she replies. "Glad to hear it. Listen, I just wanted to let you know, after you left, Gordon continued to stand up for you."

"Huh?"

"To your father. He told John that you're the best player on the team, the smartest attorney he's ever known, and that John was wrong to verbally attack you like that."

"Seriously?"

"Seriously. He actually used the term *unparalleled work ethic*."

Gordy thinks my dad walks on water; I have no idea why he would ever disrespect him like that in favor of standing up for me, especially when we so clearly dislike each other.

When I don't respond, she asks, "You still there?"

"Yeah," I say. "Sorry. I just don't get why he would do that."

"There's more. He quit the team."

"What?"

"Yup. He left right after you. He told John that he didn't want to play for someone who mistreated his own son like that."

"Holy shit. What did my dad do?"

"He told him to take his nut pillow and go."

I laugh. "I can't believe it."

"Just thought you should know."

"Thanks, Daisy."

"Have a good night, Colin. I'll see you tomorrow."

I hang up with her and call Gordy.

"Hello?" he says.

"Hey. It's Colin."

"I know who it is. I think this is the first time you've ever called my cell phone though."

"Probably," I say. "Yo, Daisy told me you quit the team."

"Yeah. I mean, I'm not much good in my condition anyway," he says.

"She made it sound like you…"

"Like I what?"

"Almost like you had it out with my dad," I say.

He's quiet.

"Dude. I appreciate it, but I don't really get it. Why would you do that?"

"I mean," he begins. "I couldn't listen to Jack belittle you like that. It was humiliating. Plus, *you* quit the team first."

"I know, but—"

"Listen, Colin. I know you think I'm a nerd, or a kiss-ass, or whatever."

"No, I don't," I lie.

"Yes, you do. I'm not oblivious to your stupid little comments. But I was raised to stand up for what's right. That's why I studied law in the first place."

"But we're in *estate* law."

"I know. Listen, when I was a kid, my dad died, and he didn't have a will. The state took all his assets because he and my mom weren't married. And I didn't think that was right. Just like today. What Jack did wasn't right. And I wasn't going to sit back and not say anything about it. But I didn't do it so you would *like* me or whatever."

"Shut up, Gordy. I *like* you just fine."

"You can't stand me and that's fine. I don't like you either, if you want to know the truth. But you *are* a good partner and a hard worker. So, if you're off the team, then so am I. And if we don't play, there's no way Daisy's gonna keep playing. Let the divorce guys have the team. I'm sure Dom can fill the empty spots with all the girls he's hooking up with."

I laugh. "Yeah, I'm sure," I agree.

"So, that's it. I'll be resting at home for the next few days, but I'll be back at work next week."

"Okay," I say. "Hey, Gordy?"

"Yeah?"

"You know my dad's name is John, right?"

"Yeah. Jack is a nickname for John."

"Maybe back during the Revolutionary War, but this is the twenty-first century, you know."

"Whatever, Smart Guy. If you think I'm such an idiot, then you won't be surprised when I start referring to you as 'Colon,' you know, since you're kind of an asshole."

I can't help but laugh. "Good one, Gordito."

"That's Spanish, you moron."

"I know. I learned it in high school. It's what you call a small chubby kid."

"I'm not small or fat though."

"I was talking about your busted junk," I retort, snickering.

He laughs too. "You're such a child."

"Just so we're clear, this doesn't mean I like you now," I say.

"Same," he says.

"Feel better though," I offer. "Catch you on the flip."

"Later, Colon."

Gracie

When I was a little kid, maybe about six years old, I had this friend named Robin Rutledge. She lived a few blocks away from me, but we originally met at the playground in between our houses. When I started the first grade, I was happily surprised to find Robin in my class. She was a daredevil—one of those kids who feared nothing, who could easily flip upside down on the monkey bars or stand up and pump her legs on a swing with no problem at all. I think by this point I've discussed my athletic prowess enough that you can imagine that Robin and I were not exactly equally matched. As such, I was often the viewer of her tricks and antics, content to sit on the sidelines munching on Ho Hos while she tempted fate with her crazy stunts.

One day in first grade, our class went out on a trip to Van Cortlandt Park. It was a day not unlike today, sometime in the late spring. Robin brought a skateboard, and I was intrigued. We weren't supposed to leave the perimeter outlined by our teacher, Mrs. Lefkowitz, but we snuck off anyway to an area of the park with a long flight of cement steps that led down to a duck pond.

"Wanna watch me ride my board down the steps?" she asked. In my recall, there were actual flames in her eyes, though I doubt it actually happened this way.

"Sure," replied my naïve, young self.

And sure enough, she hopped on the board, tilted it down over the first step and went off, bumping, bumping down the steps until she hit the ground below. She made it down in one piece and somehow managed to stop the skateboard before careening into the pond.

"Woo hoo!" she called up to me from the bottom of the stairs.

"You're crazy!" I yelled back.

She ran back up the steps with the skateboard under her arm. Out of breath, she said, "Now you."

I shook my head. "Nope. I can't stand on that thing! I'll break my neck."

"Then sit," she suggested.

Even at the fledgling age of six, I knew what I was good at. While speed and balance were not my thing, *sitting* was well within my wheelhouse. And, I had to admit, Robin made *everything* look fun. "Okay," I said. "I can sit."

She positioned the skateboard at the top step, and I sat down on it, tucking my feet up under my behind so as not to hit anything with my knees.

"You ready?" she asked gleefully.

I held on to the sides of the board with my hands and gave her the go ahead. Then, she pushed me ever so slightly, and I began the uneven trip down what felt like a never-ending flight of stairs. With every step, my insides shook and my jaw clenched harder. About halfway down, I decided I could take it no more and I turned my head to look back up at Robin.

This was the exact moment when the front of the skateboard hit a discarded soda can, jamming the wheel and propelling the backside of the skateboard up over my body. I tumbled off it and went down, down, down the rest of the steps, rolling like a snowball on a hill, feeling the burn of my knees and elbows scraping and rescraping, until finally I hit the pavement with a thud.

I was beside myself with embarrassment, shamed and in a good amount of shock and pain. By the grace of God, none of my bones felt broken, likely because I was so close to the ground to begin with. But you know that feeling when something is wrong and you can't quite put your finger on it? That was my experience in that moment. I had a funny taste in my mouth, sort of like metal, and my lower lip was stinging. I stuck my tongue out to feel it and noticed what looked like a ladybug on the ground a short distance away. I took a closer look at it while feeling my face with my hand. Everything felt wet. That was when I realized.

All of my front teeth were gone.

Robin came bounding down the stairs. "You okay?" she asked, cheerfully.

I looked up at her and watched as her expression morphed from joyful to terrified in one quick moment.

"I'll go get Mrs. Lefkowitz!" she cried and ran off.

I sat there alone then, toothless and scared, hurt and anxious. I began to cry. I felt the insides of my mouth with my tongue and my fingers and realized I had lost a total of four teeth. I crawled around on the ground, hunting for them. After all, I was going to *need* those teeth to prove to the tooth fairy what had happened. I scooped up the one that resembled a ladybug, but I couldn't find the others. My tears blurred my vision and made it impossible to see anything clearly.

Hours later, after an emergency visit to the dentist and over an hour of scolding from my mother, I looked in the mirror and smiled. It was hard to adjust to my new face, but Nonna reminded me that baby teeth are meant to fall out, so they can make space for grown-up teeth. I just had to be patient and wait for the big teeth to come in. And eventually, they did. They were a little bit crooked, but they worked just fine and filled out my face nicely enough. Even now, all these years later, my smile's not half-bad.

Sometimes accidents turn out okay, I tell myself when I get home. Then, I pull my calendar out of the junk drawer in my kitchen and try to figure out how many days I've got until one full revolution of the moon passes, per Olga's advice.

Finally, I sit down and start to write.

Prologue

Shawna Carter wasn't a bad-looking girl. She was just a little bit awkward, like most fourteen-year-olds. Her boobs were growing, her face was changing, her hair—oh, her hair—was frizzy and confused about how to act under the gentle motion of a brush. Her clothes were good enough: certainly far from "cool," but also far from "get yourself laughed out of class on the first day of high school."

All Shawna wanted was to go unnoticed. *Just fly under the radar like a stealth jet*, she told herself as she got dressed that morning. *Be nice, be friendly, speak when spoken to. Don't trip or fart or laugh too loud, and everything will be okay.*

She stepped off the school bus and faced the grand entrance of her new high school, Bronx Academy. It was a seemingly huge, almond-colored building with endless red doors for access. Gone were the days of middle school, where Shawna could be a medium-sized fish in a medium-sized pond. This was the big leagues. The last graduating class had over 1,600 kids in it.

In the hallway, kids who looked like grown men and women towered over her, whizzing past en route to class or the lunchroom or their lockers. For Shawna, it was the latter that was the first feat of the day. Locker number B-704 was likely in the basement, leaving her to wander through the maze that included the weight room, the custodial break room, the whole cafeteria, and a variety of random nooks off to the side of the guidance office where some rusty old lockers were left empty. The school was too big, and Shawna was afraid to ask for a map or some directional assistance, so she decided she would be better off holding on to all of her belongings for the day instead of stowing them somewhere. Plus, she was concerned about being late for first period biology, which was in room 4–337. Far from athletic, the thought of climbing up five flights of stairs to the fourth floor of the school seemed akin to scaling Everest.

By the time she finally made it to the classroom, she was able to find a seat way in the back, where no one would pay much attention to her panting, sweating little body or the way her naturally curly hair had already decided to violate the sleek look she'd attempted with the straightening iron earlier that morning. She hoped her deodorant was up to the task of masking any potential body odor. Just before the late bell rang, a boy slid into the desk next to hers. He had floppy brown hair and wore name-brand clothes and Adidas sneakers, which made him look like an athlete.

"Hey, is this freshman bio?" the boy asked Shawna.

Speak when spoken to, she remembered. "Uh huh," she said.

"Oh, thank God," he replied.

He took his binder out of his Jansport bookbag and set it on the desk.

"Good morning, class," the lady at the front of the room said with a smile. "My name is Ms. Kramer, and I will be your ninth grade biology teacher this year." She had dark black hair coiffed perfectly, as if she had come to school straight from the salon. She looked young, but that hair looked like it came straight out of the 1980s; the style was not exactly fashionable for 2005.

The class sat at attention, listening, while Ms. Kramer wrote her name and an assignment on the chalkboard.

"As you can see, I would like you to take the first five minutes of class to partner up with the person sitting next to you." Shawna eyeballed the cute boy to her right and noticed him looking her way as well. "Take a few minutes to share your name, your favorite food, and three fun facts about you. Then, we'll go around the room and share them with each other. Be sure to listen carefully, because the person you're paired up with will be your lab partner this year." Ms. Kramer was exuberant, as if the first day of school was actually *fun* for her.

Shawna turned to the boy, and he said, "You wanna go first?"

"It's fine," she said. "You go ahead."

"Okay." He swallowed. "Well, my name is Cameron Young, but my friends call me Cam for short. Um, my favorite food is probably the bacon cheeseburger from the Bluebird Diner on Grand Concourse. And three fun facts. Hmm." He thought. "Well, I'm on the varsity soccer team, which is a big deal because I'm a freshman."

Shawna smiled in acknowledgement.

"I'm pretty good at drawing, although my dad doesn't want me to focus on that," he said.

"That's cool," Shawna said.

Cameron sat, considering what else to share. "I don't know. My middle name is Howard, which is not exactly cool, but it's the middle name of every male in my family, so it's something." He smiled. "Your turn."

Shawna took a deep breath. "Okay. My name is Shawna Carter."

She thought Cameron might have smirked, but she wasn't sure. *Just don't sound like a tool*, she told herself.

"I like to read and write, which I know sounds pretty boring," she went on. *You're blowing it*, she thought.

"I want to be a doctor, so I spent the summer volunteering as a candy striper at Bronx Memorial Hospital."

"That's cool," he said, nodding.

Thank God, she thought. "And, um..." Her voice trailed off. "I don't know what else."

"What's your middle name?"

"Cora. After my grandma."

"So, hold on. Your name is Shawna Cora Carter?"

"Yeah," Shawna said.

"That's unbelievable," Cameron replied, his face lighting up.

"Why?" she asked.

"Okay, class!" Ms. Kramer called out. "That should be enough time. Let's start in the back. This will test you to see how good of a listener you are," she said. "I want you to introduce your lab partner and say one neat thing you learned about him or her." Ms. Kramer pointed at Shawna and Cameron. "You two can start."

"You wanna go first?" he asked Shawna.

"You go ahead," she said.

"Well, this is my lab partner, and the coolest thing about her is actually her name: Shawna Cora Carter!"

"Oh, snap! Like Shawn Corey Carter!" a kid on the other side of the room called out. "That's dope!"

"Right?" Cameron said.

Shawna looked at him, confused.

"That's Jay-Z's name. Hova? You know, the rapper?" he said.

Shawna nodded. "Of course," she smiled.

"So, I guess my lab partner is the female Jay-Z!"

Ms. Kramer wrote the initials JZ on the blackboard. "Jizz," she said. "What a strange name. Rappers, though, am I right?" She shrugged.

The whole class burst into laughter.

And that was how she got her nickname.

PART TWO

May

Colin

I miss her.

It's Tuesday, and I just finished up a meeting with George Friere. His wife, Lucy, passed away last week and there were some arrangements in her will that were made as a result of family disputes from years ago, back when she was married to her first husband.

Daisy puts an extra box of tissues on my conference table before he arrives. "The men are always in worse shape than the women," she reminds me.

I brace myself for the meeting with an extra cup of coffee around eleven, but really, nothing can prepare me to watch a grown man sob over losing his soul mate.

"She was my life force," he wept. "Lucy made me laugh every single day. Do you know how important that is, Colin?" he asked me.

I nodded in response, as the lump that developed in my throat temporarily kept me from speaking.

In the weeks that followed our series of misunderstandings, I spent a lot of time thinking and waiting. For some reason, my mind often slid between memories of Elle and memories of

Gracie, and it was very hard to untangle the two. I became angrier at Elle than ever; the fact that she slept with someone else and gave me an STD seemed like minutia compared to her dropping Gracie as a client and sabotaging both of their careers.

I busied myself with work, which was easy since much of April was spent dealing with my own marital baggage. On Wednesdays and Sundays, instead of going to the softball field, I got in my car and took myself out driving to clear my head. I'd blast the radio and let my instincts decide where the car should go.

Not surprisingly, I ended up in Brooklyn a lot. I'd pass by Gracie's exit on the Belt Parkway, but I never got off the highway there, because I knew if I did, I wouldn't be able to stop myself from driving past her house and that would look a whole lot like stalking. Still, it was comforting, just knowing that I was near her.

I started leaving work early on Wednesdays just on the off chance that my father showed up at the office. He begged Daisy not to quit the team, and she's a softie, so she stuck it out. Apparently, she and my mom have been hanging out now that Mom's a permanent part of the roster. Dad's not speaking to me at the moment, despite my mother's attempts to get him to see the error of his ways. I've told her I am more than happy to have a little space, but I'm pretty sure that Daisy informed her that I'm having "girl trouble." Which is fine, as long as she doesn't push me for details. It saves me from having to talk about it.

But even though I don't *talk* about my feelings, doesn't mean I don't *have* them. I just haven't figured out what to do about them yet.

I tried "getting over it," and at Dom's suggestion ended up

joining him for a night out at a place called The Meat Market two Saturdays ago. He said it was a pop-up spot that was all the rage in the Midwest. A cross between a traditional bar and a butcher/BBQ place, you go in and pick a piece of meat, which they grill up for you while you drink and mingle with other singles. Dom was like a kid in a candy store. I, meanwhile, was a little grossed out by the scent of dead cow lingering over my Dark 'n Stormy, a drink I chose because I don't think I can ever have whiskey again. Dom tried to get me to talk to a pair of attractive women dressed up as cowgirls, but when I could answer their flirty questions with only one-syllable answers, he resigned himself to the fact that he had a broken wingman and got us a table for two in the back where we carved into our medium-well sirloins and he behaved—if momentarily—like a genuine human being.

"Another girl will come along," he said between bites of steak and garlic mashed potatoes.

I nodded, swallowing. Words were difficult to form, but simple gestures I could handle.

"You know, I'm not really a dick."

"I know."

"Did I ever tell you about Cheyenne?"

"Is that the girl who skipped town on you?"

"Uh huh."

"Not really. You mentioned her once, but never in any detail."

"Well," he said. "I still try not to think about the details, because they suck. Suffice to say, I'm no stranger to heartbreak."

"Does it really help you—y'know, being the way you are?"

"What?" he laughed. "A man whore?"

"I mean, sort of," I replied, not wanting to offend him. "Don't you ever just want to meet a nice girl and settle down?"

"Honestly? Of course. That's the dream, right?"

I took a sip of my drink, listening.

"The thing is, I can't put my life on hold for that. I'm a successful attorney with plenty of money. I've got all the things a woman would want from a good man, but I have no clue where to find the kind of chick who I'd consider wife material. I tried once. It was hard work, giving a fuck like that. In the end, it wasn't worth it." He pauses to wipe his mouth. "But that doesn't mean I don't think love is out there. I think it just wasn't my time."

"So, you never stop and consider that maybe one of these random women who you hook up with might be the one, and you're wasting your shot by being shallow about it?"

He shook his head. "Nope. I think if someone's worth keeping around, I'll feel it in my gut. So far, that hasn't happened since Cheyenne. So maybe I'm just not ready."

"Maybe."

"Do you think Gracie was the one?"

I shrugged, knowing that admitting the truth at that particular moment might lead to the complete demise of my self-esteem. Nothing screams *sexy* like a grown man drying his tears on a bar napkin.

"She may have just been a rebound, you know."

"Yeah. It didn't feel that way though."

"Well then I'd let it play out. Keep a low profile. See what happens. You never know. For a while after Cheyenne left, I thought maybe she'd show up on my doorstep one day, realizing she made the biggest mistake of her life."

"But she didn't."

"Exactly. So I knew I had to move on."

"How long did you wait for her?"

"I wouldn't say I *waited*, exactly. I went out and did my thing. Got back on the horse, so to speak. One day I thought about her, and it didn't hurt the way it used to. That was when I knew I was over it."

"So, your advice is just to do nothing?"

"Nope. My advice is to do *you*, bro. Those chicks who were chatting you up were *fine*. You could've easily gone home with either one. I'm sure you still could. The blond one keeps looking this way."

"I'm good," I said.

"Well," Dom replied, taking the last bite of his meal. "If you're not going to give it a shot, mind if I do?"

"Have at it."

"Cool. You go home though. I'm always down to listen, but your sad-boy persona is a hundred percent cutting into my mojo. You're better off surfing the couch for a few weekends till you feel up to"—he waved his hand in the air—"all this."

With that, Dom took the last swig of his drink, threw a fifty-dollar bill on the table, and gave me a wink. "I'm gonna go see who wants a ride on the Dommy-go-round."

I couldn't help but laugh. I settled up the tab and ordered myself a ride home. By the time I left, Dom was eyeballing a brunette who was loudly yee-hawing atop a mechanical bull, the violent bouncing threatening to set her breasts free from their underwire holster. I shot him a wave before leaving the bar, but he didn't notice.

Since then, I've been spending a lot of time appreciating my La-Z-Boy. Thankfully, May is still sweeps, so there's been some good TV to watch.

The weather's getting nicer too, so I've been trying to make an effort to take walks during the day. Walking helps me clear my head, especially on days like today, where George Friere just about broke my heart lamenting his lost spouse and how she made him laugh.

The sun is shining, so I tell Daisy I'm going out for lunch. I walk down to the East River, grab takeout from Nuevo Vallarta Grill, and head back to the office. A healthy dose of vitamin D along with a Cali-style burrito does me good.

I get back to the office and change out of my sneakers and back into my work shoes. I drag my forefinger along the trackpad of my laptop to wake it up, which is when I notice I've got a new email message.

Holy shit.

It's from Gracie.

TO: Colin Yarmouth (cyarmouth@ yarmouthaycockpc.com)

FROM: Grace Landing (gracie222@mail.com)

SUBJECT: help

ATTACHMENT: ✎ TheBookProposal.docx

Dear Colin,

I know it's been a while since we spoke. I hope you're doing well.

I wanted to tell you that I'm sorry for everything that went wrong last month. I'm well-known for making mistakes. (It's actually one of my specialties.) But I'm also pretty good at apologizing.

So, I'm attaching for your review a new manuscript that I need your help with. I've been working on it incessantly and it's almost done. If you are open to my apology, please read the attached. If not, well, maybe just read the first few pages and hopefully you'll reconsider.

In any case, I hope to hear from you soon.

Xoxo,
Gracie

Gracie

It's amazing how fast you can write when the story is alive inside your head. In fact, I've never put roughly 85,000 words down on paper so quickly in my entire life.

Today marks one complete revolution of the moon. I got a call from Mrs. A this morning to remind me.

"Olga is send me text message to remind me the moon is full circle today," she told me.

"You won't believe this, but I marked it on my calendar," I said in response.

"Of course, my little *khomyak*. You remember because this man is future husband for you."

"What?" I laughed. "I wouldn't take it that far. Colin and I couldn't even make it to two weeks. And what is a *khomyak*?"

"Not sure how you say in English. Like small pet for in cage. Fluffy mouse with fat cheeks."

"Like a hamster?"

"Yes!" she exclaimed. "That is it. My baby hamster. You store love in cheeks for winter like fluffy hamster storing food. This boy is marry you."

"He doesn't even call me anymore."

"Is not my guess, Gracie. Olga is telling me. Olga is study for mystic, so she is knowing what come next in story."

"Well, if that turns out to be true, then I will let you plan the whole wedding." I laughed.

"Yay!" She clapped, and I ended the conversation before she started planning the birth of my fourteen fat babies who would grow up drinking goat milk because that is her milk of choice.

Now, I'm not *really* a believer in mysticism, but you know what? The universe hasn't been so bad to me in the past few weeks since the Lindsay debacle, so I figure it certainly can't hurt to heed the advice of a well-intentioned shaman-in-training. Plus, I've been missing Colin something fierce, and I think his absence has made it easier for me to bust out these pages so fast. I just hope my plan to get him back works.

In the meantime, Gracie 5.0 has been keeping busy, and not just with writing. I started my new job at Starbucks three weeks ago. (My mom's not too thrilled, but she thinks all Starbucks employees are stupid because a barista misspelled her name on the side of her cup *one time*. She has not returned since the "incident." Side note: It's not like *Emina* is the easiest name to spell, either.) The manager, Bess, is a woman about my age, and she's been really welcoming and sweet. The benefits are awesome, and the perks (which include one free drink per day, whether you're working or not, and one free meal per shift) are even better. I spent the first two weeks in training, learning about all the different ingredients that go into all the drinks, and now she's got me on a regular evening shift Monday through Friday, which is amazing because I still have my entire days free to write. The evening shift is also a good fit for me because I'm not as seasoned as the other baristas, and evenings are quieter, so the store is a lot more chill. I've only messed up two drinks so far, and my first paycheck was more than my last royalty statement, so things are looking up in the bank account department.

I used to think Starbucks was super hoity-toity, but that's probably just because I couldn't afford to make it a habit. What I love most about it is the people. Most of them are in school, and boy oh boy, do they bring the drama. It's so interesting to listen to them share stories about who's seeing who, who just got dumped, who's on drugs, and more. The customers are equally fascinating; so many of them sit by themselves, spilling their secrets via Bluetooth for the whole store to hear, and they don't even realize we're listening! Or care, maybe. In fact, just yesterday I heard this one woman have an in-depth conversation about her thoughts on the HPV vaccine for her daughter. It was all going well until she *announced* into her Bluetooth headset that the vaccine is important because "Genital warts are the worst! And trust me, *I* should know." She went on, "What? We *all* had it in high school!"

Did we though? I thought, laughing to myself.

Working at Starbucks has also improved my health—or at least that's what I'm telling myself. In the mornings, I wake up bright and early and stroll down to Emmons to pick up a skinny vanilla latte. It's free and forces me to get out of bed and shower and start my day. Also, it gives me the added benefit of daily exercise and a good, early morning dose of sunshine.

Granted, I don't think it's a forever job, but it's certainly a good-enough-for-now job. And Bess is cool—she actually lives on my block, two buildings down. She has no pets and no spouse, but her boyfriend is the drummer in some band, and she likes to go watch him play on the weekends. She invited me last weekend, but I said no, only because I was committed to finishing up my manuscript by the time the moon had finished its monthly orbit. But if she were to invite me again, I would go. It would be nice to have a friend in the neighborhood who's not over the age of sixty and who speaks English fluently. I'm taking a hiatus from hanging out with Melly, Alisha, and Tori, but not in a hateful way. More in a *I'm here if you need me, but maybe we should cool it on the drinking for a few weeks* kind of way. They're trying to be supportive from afar. Plus, we chat via group text at least once a week, and Melly's mom told her all about Olga's predictions (which she, of course, shared with the group), so they're letting me run with my superstitious foolishness for right now.

If it weren't for the situation with Colin, I would say things have actually been kind of perfect lately. In addition to the steady income, the universe also afforded me the greatest gift I could ever have hoped for exactly one week ago today. I was at home, taking a quick break from writing at about 2:00, when my phone rang. Now that I've become better with the swiping and typing on the new phone, I was able to pick it up on the first try. I didn't recognize the number, but I went for it anyway.

"Hello?" I said.

"My boo!" I heard.

"Evan! To what do I owe this honor? And what is this number? Where are you calling me from?"

"Are you sitting down? Because I have got All. The. News," he said.

I love Evan. He's one of those people who is always smiling, and you can hear his smile through the telephone even when you can't see it. I wish I could be more like that.

"Spill it! I'm ready," I said.

"Well, first of all, you need to take this number down because it's my new office line!"

"New office? What do you mean?"

"You are talking to Table of Contents' Literary Agency's newest Associate Agent!"

"Shut *up*! Evan, that's amazing! I didn't even know you were *looking* to leave Vision Board!"

"I know! I love secrets!" He laughs. "For real though, that place was hella toxic. I couldn't stay there long term. That wouldn't be a good look for me."

"Damn. I'm so proud of you! And Table of Contents is a big deal! They've got some amazing talent!"

"No shit. I fully plan to be New York's next 'it' thing in publishing."

"I'm sure you'll be up there in no time." I smiled.

"No, love. I don't think you understand. I've been doing some digging."

"Oh?"

"*Yes.* Hold on to your hats, boys and girls. I just got off the phone with Danielle Oliver. She's the editor who Lindsay was talking to at Cabaret about *Reckless Outlaw*."

"No way," I said, my heart lodging itself in my throat.

"She was wondering what happened to Lindsay—said she'd called and left messages, but nobody ever got back to her, so she assumed the deal was off the table. She was pissed too. Apparently, she had to fight hard to put up those kinds of numbers in your offer."

I chewed on my fingernail, hanging on every word as my blood pressure threatened the longevity of my new healthy lifestyle with a potential stroke.

"I let her know that due to unforeseen circumstances, Lindsay was no longer with Vision Board and Karlie London was no longer repped by her. I told her that you were now a client with Table of Contents' newest agent, and that I would be more than happy to revisit that deal with her."

"Evan!" I shrieked. "Shut up! What did she say?"

"She's sending me the paperwork now."

"Stop lying!" I yelled. I jumped up and down, the adrenaline in my body producing involuntary movements that would otherwise be unheard of.

"This, of course, assumes that you would *want* a lowly peasant such as myself representing the fine work of one Karlie London," he said.

"Evan! Are you *kidding* me? This is a fucking dream come true! Yes! I mean, of *course*! I would *love* to have you as my agent!"

"Well then, boo. I believe this is the beginning of a beautiful friendship. There is one thing, though. I didn't push for the two-book deal. I figured you might still be sore after everything that happened with Lindsay and Colin. Also, while I loved that manuscript, I didn't want to carry over *any* drama from Vision Board to Table of Contents. Plus, I don't know if you thought about it in hindsight, but…it did kind of feel like a lawsuit waiting to happen." Evan laughs. "I hope you're not mad."

"Mad? I can't thank you enough! I can't believe you didn't tell me."

"I'll send you over an agency contract."

"You are *unbelievable*, you know that?" I asked.

"It's no big thing, babe. I'll just have my people call your people." He laughed.

"Yes, Evan. You do that."

"Oh my God! Speaking of *Babe*, we *did* end up fostering the potbellied pig."

"Really?"

"Yes, and can I just be the first to tell you? Pigs are *life*."

"You have a heart of gold. What's the piggie's name?"

"Wilbur," he announced, like a proud papa.

"Like *Charlotte's Web*. I love it, Ev. So I guess that means you're off the bacon train now, right?"

"I'm actually thinking about becoming a vegan."

I grinned. "So many good changes."

"I'll arrange for the two of you to meet sometime. But for now, keep an eye on your inbox for my contract! Peace out, Cub Scout! I'll be in touch!"

I hung up with a grin on my face and tears in my eyes. *Reckless Outlaw* had a home at Cabaret Books, and I'd have a decent-sized nest egg put away for whatever I decide my next chapter will be.

And all within one full cycle of the moon's revolution around the Earth.

Something else happened too.

You know the saying, *Karma's a bitch*? Of course you do. You weren't born under a rock.

Well, I was minding my own business, finishing up my shift at Starbucks last Friday night. I had no plans other than to get to bed early, because I was getting to a pretty critical point in my new novel and really wanted to keep the momentum alive for the early Saturday writing session I had planned. So, I cleaned up my workstation, went into the back and grabbed my things, then said goodbye to the closing staff and headed home. I was daydreaming about what I might do with my $500,000, other than pay off my condo. I thought about maybe buying a small cottage for myself somewhere near the water, like maybe in Breezy Point, Neponsit, or Belle Harbor, somewhere in the Rockaways where I'd still be close enough to the city to hang out with my girls. I considered getting my driver's license and buying a car. *I'd look cute in a zippy little Honda Civic.* I could buy groceries at the Stop & Shop on 116th Street and live a quiet, easy little life. Just me and Dorian Gray. And maybe Colin, if he'd have me.

I unlocked the door to my building, stopped at the mailbox to get my mail, and was thumbing through the bills on the elevator. When I got to the second floor, I heard sobbing. Not just crying, but all-out *sobbing*. I turned to head down the hall and was shocked—not even surprised, but honestly *shocked*—to see Scott, rumpled-up and sitting on the ground outside my apartment. His head was resting on his denim-clad knees and his arms were wrapped around his legs. As I approached him, I could smell the alcohol emanating from his pores.

"My God. Scott?" I asked.

He looked up. His red-rimmed eyes were puffy and flanked by dark circles.

"What are you doing here?" I wondered aloud.

"I'm sorry, Gracie." He sniffled.

"How did you get in?" I asked.

"I still had the building key. You only took back the key to your apartment."

Aren't you just a clever one, I thought.

"What do you want?" I asked.

"Can we please go inside and talk?" he begged.

I considered this. Inviting Scott into my house was about the last thing I wanted to do, but given the circumstances and the nosy neighbors, I figured it would make more sense than having old Mrs. Jansen down the hall file a noise complaint against me. I helped him up unwillingly, so that I could gain access to my door.

"Ugh. You smell like shit," I said. *No sense in sugarcoating things now.*

"I'm sorry," he said again.

I opened the door and he spilled inside like a fresh sack of garbage down an incinerator chute. Dorian Gray opened one eye on the couch but remained otherwise disinterested. Lucky for him too, because I swear to God, if he would have gotten up and walked his little cat butt over to Scott, that would've been the last time he saw a meal in this house.

"It looks so beautiful in here," Scott slurred.

"Okay. Let's not," I said. "Sit down."

He headed for the bedroom.

"No, Scott. Over here. At the kitchen table. I'll get you a glass of water and that's about where my hospitality will end." I ran the tap. Didn't even offer him the Brita. *Ha!* I thought. *Even Dorian Gray gets Brita water.* I set the glass on the table in front of him and grabbed the garbage can, just to have it close by in case of emergency. Then I sat down opposite him. "What are you doing here?" I asked for the second time.

He burped. *Not a good sign*, I thought.

"Why aren't you home with Ilana and the baby?"

"Ugh," he moaned, loud.

"What's wrong, Scott? Fatherhood not all it's cracked up to be?" I said in my bitchiest tone.

"I haven't slept in forever," he said.

"I've heard that happens when you have a newborn. Still, it's a fucking miracle, right? 'Hashtag best day ever,' no?"

"It's not *mine*," he said, dragging out the word *mine* like it was part of a song.

"What are you talking about?"

"The baby. Lilliana. She's not even *mine*."

"What?" I asked, stupefied.

He took a sip of water. "I kinda had this feeling, you know? She came out all wrinkled and small, and you can't really tell one baby from another because they all look the same."

I shook my head, embarrassed for new fathers everywhere who actually *care* about their adult responsibilities.

"But then she got a little bigger, like after a few weeks, and I sorta noticed something."

"What'd you notice, Scott?"

He hung his head down in humiliation.

"Go on, you came all this way. Might as well spill it."

"Well, she was born with this full head of thick, black hair. And after like a month or so, it all fell out. It was replaced by bright orange hair."

"Is that normal?"

He hung his head lower. "Yeah. The baby doc said kids lose their hair and regrow it pretty often. But, like, no one in my family is a *ginger*."

"What about on Ilana's side?" I asked, pure glee swelling in my chest.

He shook his head.

"No Irish?"

"Uh uh."

Scott took out his phone and showed me a picture of the baby. Cute kid, with little orange ringlets that looked like a crown of fire—appropriate for Satan's spawn—but biologically, she bore exactly zero resemblance to Scott. Or Ilana, for that matter.

"Oh," I said. I couldn't help but laugh. This moment could not have been more beautifully orchestrated by the cosmos.

"So, I went to the drugstore and got one of those at-home paternity tests."

"I never even knew they made such a thing," I said.

"Yeah, well. It wasn't hard. It's just a cheek swab. Like a Q-tip kind of thing. One for the baby and one for the guy. You gotta do it a few times," he said.

"Uh huh," I replied. "And then what?"

He waved his hands around. "And then you send it off to the lab and they send you an email with the results."

"Sounds official."

He sniffs, loud. I am audibly assaulted by the mucus shooting its way up Scott's nose. "You got a tissue?" he asked.

He's so classy. What a shame it is that this one didn't work out.

I got him a napkin. While I was up, I also grabbed a piece of whole-wheat bread from the loaf I had wrapped up on the counter and handed it to him.

"What is this?" he asked.

"Bread. A wise person once told me never to drink without it," I said.

He looked at me, flummoxed.

"It'll soak up the alcohol," I explained.

He took a bite. As he chewed, his lower lip trembled like a thundercloud, threatening to reopen the floodgates.

"Pull it together. I'm sure there's an explanation."

"Oh, there's an explanation, all right. Ilana was sleeping with lots of guys when she first started out in event planning. Anyone she thought could get her a gig, apparently."

"So, who *is* the father?" I asked.

"I don't know, but it sure as hell isn't me! So now, I'm losing sleep every night with this baby who's not even mine crying and wailing and keeping me up until all hours. It's a fucking nightmare, Gracie."

I cringed hearing him say my name like that.

"You still haven't answered my question though. Why are you here?"

He looked at his shoes, studying the laces. Then, he looked up at me, dizzy and stupid, like a high school pothead who's had one joint too many. "You gotta take me back," he said.

"Ha!" I laughed aloud. "Are you out of your mind?" The idea was so preposterous that I felt giddy listening to it. I couldn't help but revel in the fact that suddenly my 24-hour workweek at Starbucks and my sad little royalty checks made me look pretty well put together. Not to mention my half-million-dollar book deal. Whatevs. No biggie, right?

"I mean it, Gracie. What you and me had? It was special." He burped, blowing the odor of old beer and regurgitated nachos into my airspace.

"No, Scott," I said. "It wasn't. It was anything *but* special."

"How could you say that?" he asked, dropping his heavy head down onto the table with a thud. "We were like magic."

If it was magic, I would be able to make you disappear, I thought. Then, I remembered a line from Mrs. A. *It is easier to catch bees with honey than it is with shit.*

I pulled up the Uber app on my phone. "What's your address again?" I asked him sweetly.

"What? Why?"

"So that I can come visit more, honey. I've really missed you," I said, trying to offer a convincing look. "I know I might have sounded a little bit mean, but really, my feelings have just been sort of hurt, you know?"

He gave me a puzzled look, then decided I was serious. "2489 Holmdel Road," he said. "I *said* I'm sorry."

"Right. Of course you did. And I forgive you," I said. "That's in Merrick, right?"

"Yeah. It's not far from the train. I could come pick you up."

Inside, I was dying at the thought of ever visiting this

schmuck at his house with his wife and newly minted *step*child. But I nodded and typed the address into my Uber app. An available driver was only six minutes away. I just had to get Scott's sloppy ass up from the table and out to the curb. It would be well worth the $60 fare to eject him from my house and, of course, to have *this* story to tell in my manuscript.

"We should *definitely* do that sometime. You know, I actually think about you all the time."

"You do?"

I nodded. "You're right. We *were* magic."

"We should get back together. I could move back in with you," he said, but it sounded like "Icuhmoovbakihwihyuh."

"That would be amazing," I said. "For now, I would love it if we could just take a walk. Would you come take a walk with me?"

"A walk?" he asked.

"Yeah. I want you to stay over, but I think you should sober up a little bit first, don't you?"

"I guess so," he reluctantly agreed.

"You have your keys?" I asked. "So we can get back in? I'll leave the apartment unlocked." *Like I would ever do that in Brooklyn.*

"Uh huh," he nodded, jingling the keys above his head. I gently took them from his hand.

"Great. I just need to use the bathroom real quick. I'll be two seconds." I ran off into the bathroom and closed and locked the door, then located the key to my building, slid it off the ring, and slipped it into my pocket. "All set!" I announced, flushing the toilet.

He stood up unsteadily and stumbled to the door, placing his sweaty, clammy hand in mine. "I'm so glad we patched things up, Gracie," he said. "You were always my number one."

And you were always my number two, I thought, laughing at the absurdity of my own stupid joke.

I wrestled him into the elevator and all but carried him out when we arrived on the first floor. I opened the door to the building and a blast of cool damp air hit us. The sudden change in temperature must have affected him, because he ran over to the nearest bush and hurled.

Just then, the Uber arrived. Blade Z., a large tattooed guy with a gold front tooth was driving a souped-up, growling black Dodge Ram with tints that definitely were too dark to be legal, and I waved at him, smiling. *Let's hope Scott got it all out here.*

I walked him over to the car and opened the back door. "I thought we were going for a walk," he said, genuinely confused.

"I called my friend here to drive us instead," I said.

"Oh, yeah? Where we going?" he asked.

"Home," I smiled. Scott put his head back against the headrest and closed his eyes. I closed the door and added a $50 tip to Blade Z.'s Uber account before heading back inside.

I laughed all the way back up to my apartment.

It's been a week since I sent him on his way, and I'm still laughing just thinking about it. Vindication is one of the best feelings in the world.

Now, I'm just stuck, waiting. I've written all there is to write. *The Book Proposal* is essentially complete, with the exception of one thing.

I spend a good chunk of the afternoon hoping for an email

from Colin to arrive. Every time I hear the phone ding, I nearly jump out of my skin. At 4:00, I start getting myself ready for work, and I leave at 4:30 for my 5:00 shift, even though it's only a ten-minute walk. I intentionally move slowly, soaking in the beautiful weather. Birds chirp. A fishing boat returns from a day at sea. The baby buds on the trees have sprouted light-green leaves that sway delicately in the gentle breeze. The air is saturated with hope.

The store is fairly busy for a Tuesday evening. I get a group of girls who are probably in middle school, who grab the velour chairs in the corner and gab ferociously about their love interests. They occupy about ninety minutes of my five-hour shift. A runner comes in for a decaf iced tea; a couple of college kids who know Sabrina come in just to say hi to her. A dog walker gets a cold brew. A pair of women come in well after the sun's gone down and snag two of our remaining sandwiches, along with a cookie and some bottles of water. They sit by the window and chat in curious whispers.

At the end of my shift, I scarf down a protein bar, and on the way home, I realize I'm still pretty hungry, so I swing into the pizzeria.

"Pasta special ends at nine, Gracie, but I'll hook you up if that's what you're here for," a smiling Italian man says as I approach the counter.

"Thanks, Sal. I'll just take a slice to go."

"Regular or Sicilian, bellissima?"

I smile. "Regular, please."

"On the house, Gracie," he replies, handing me a poofed-up

white paper bag. Inside, my single slice of pizza sits on a thin paper plate.

"You sure?"

"I'm closing up in a few minutes. Extra food gets wrapped up for donations. So yeah, kid. It's either you or the church."

"Thanks. I appreciate it."

"Anytime, hon. You get home safe," he says.

I get to my building and head up to my apartment, my pizza slice resting in my palm. I set it down on the kitchen table and say hello to Dorian Gray, who doesn't even bother to open his eyes.

I put my purse on the counter and reach into the fridge for a can of lime seltzer.

And that's when I hear the *ding*.

I grab the cell phone from my purse and swipe right, punch in the code, and open my email. My heart flutters when I see his name. I'm afraid to open it, but I also know that if I wait even just one more second, I will burst into flames.

TO: Grace Landing (gracie222@mail.com)
FROM: Colin Yarmouth (cyarmouth@ yarmouthaycockpc.com)
RE: help
ATTACHMENT: 📎 TheBookProposal.docx

Gracie,
    Come outside, please.

C.

In the second grade, we had a really mean teacher named Mrs. Glugman. She was the kind of awful you never forget. One time, she tossed a boy's desk over because she found an old sandwich in it. She loved to yell, and even though she was small and fragile looking, she had a strong voice and crazy eyes and knew how to terrify children into obedience.

I was known for keeping to myself and not really bothering anyone. I followed the rules, stayed quiet, and hung out with the few little girl friends I had. When it was time for recess, we would sometimes jump rope, or if it was a nice day out, I might bring a Judy Blume or Beverly Cleary paperback book from home and read it on the bench under the tree in our schoolyard.

One particularly nice October day, I was rereading my tattered old copy of *Ramona the Pest* while snacking on Hershey's kisses. You know how sometimes you read a book and just get so deep into it that you lose all sense of what you're doing? Well, that's happened to me since I was very young. As I was eating, I balled up the little tinfoil wrappers and discarded them onto the ground thoughtlessly.

Mrs. Glugman came out to the schoolyard to retrieve us when recess was over and immediately hollered at me from the door. "Grace Landing!" she shouted.

I sat straight up, and a clenching feeling gripped my stomach. I worried I might throw up.

"What have you done?" she yelled.

I looked around. *What did I do?* I wondered. "I, um, I don't know," I said.

"You think this whole area is your personal garbage can? You left candy wrappers *everywhere*," she admonished me.

"I'm sorry," I said, my eyes welling up with tears.

"Don't *apologize*," she scolded. "Stand up! Right now! Get up and pick them up!"

So, I stood up, as scared as I had ever been in my entire short life.

And I peed myself.

I have that exact same feeling right now. This is my all-or-nothing moment. My thinking brain tells me that Colin wouldn't *be* here if he was going to chide me. He wouldn't come all this way to tell me I could shove my apology up my ass. I mean, right? That would be royally fucked up!

But my feeling brain reminds me that I am a sloppy, wretched drunk and the things that came out of my mouth the night that I ended it with him were simply unforgivable.

Then my thinking brain leads me into the bathroom to pee, you know, just in case. And while I'm peeing, my feeling brain causes me to start breathing hard, as if I might have a panic attack.

No! insists my thinking brain. *Just go downstairs and see why he's here!*

So, I do. I wash my hands, wipe them on my jeans, grab my keys, and use the stairs for the first time ever.

I see him from the lobby, standing there in jeans and a T-shirt, holding a brown paper shopping bag. His car is behind him, double parked, and he is looking down at his phone.

I'm immediately struck by the sight of him. He's so beautiful, with those brooding eyes and perfect hair and strong forearms and gentle hands. It's almost like I willed myself to forget about all the tiny things that make him so…Colin.

I push open the door, and he looks up at me.

I walk outside. We stand face to face, about six feet apart.

"Hi," I say.

"Hey," he smiles.

"You're here," I say.

"I am," he replies.

"How come?" I ask.

"Because I read what you wrote."

An involuntary smile creeps across my lips. "Did you like it?"

"I did. But—"

"But what?"

He clears his throat. "You didn't finish it."

"Oh. Yeah, I know," I say.

"Why not?" he asks.

I'm not sure if I can tell him the truth. "What's in the bag?"
I say instead.

"Gyros. Fries. A sampler."

"Baklava?" I ask.

"Of course," he says.

I'm grinning now. I can't help it.

"You didn't answer me," he says.

"I'm sorry. What?"

"Why didn't you finish it?" he asks again.

"Oh," I say. "Because I couldn't."

"You couldn't?" he asks.

I shake my head.

"Why?" he asks.

"Because I needed your help."

"With what?" he asks.

My stomach flutters. "I needed you to tell me how the story ends."

He nods and takes a few steps towards me. "I see," he says.

"I didn't want to write something down and be wrong," I say. "That would be like tempting fate, you know? Like, if I put it out there, I might jinx it."

"I didn't know you were so superstitious," he says.

"I'm not, really," I say.

"Is the part about the mystic true?" he asks.

I laugh. "Yeah. That was real."

"Then I'd say you're pretty superstitious."

I shrug. "I guess."

He looks at me.

"Wait," I say. "You read the whole thing in one day?"

"I did," he says.

"Wow."

"It was the best apology I ever received."

I chuckle. "Thanks," I say.

"And the longest," he says.

I laugh. "Yeah, well. I'm not real good at being succinct."

We are standing close enough now that I can smell the gyros wafting up from the paper bag into my nostrils. The scent obliterates any idea I might have had of eating that lowly slice of donation-bin-bound pizza waiting for me on the kitchen counter. The gyros smell heavenly.

"I mean it, Gracie. Thank you."

"For what?"

"For everything. I mean, you gave me the best ten days of

my life, and when they were over, I didn't know what to do with myself. You know the saying, *If something seems too good to be true, it probably is?*"

"Yeah."

"Well, that's kind of where I put those ten days, once they were over. I didn't want to reach out to you because you made yourself pretty clear in your last phone call."

"Did you know I was drunk?"

"Not at the time," he said. "I do now, of course, after reading this." He holds up his phone.

"I'm sorry, Colin."

He shakes his head. "*I'm* the one who's sorry. I destroyed your career!"

"No! You actually didn't."

"I *didn't?*"

"Nope," I say. "You haven't read the last chapter."

"Why didn't you send it?"

"I *told* you. Because I didn't know how it—"

Colin drops the shopping bag on the ground, places both of his hands on my cheeks, and pulls my face into his. His lips meet mine and my knees go weak. I reach my hands up and place them on his wrists, savoring the feeling of his forearms under my palms, the sensation of his tongue inside my mouth. I unravel right there on the street, shrouded in a moment of inexplicable bliss.

Eventually, he pulls back. "Ends?" he asks.

"Uh huh," I nod. It's all I can muster. I'm swooning.

"That's the thing, Gracie." He looks deep into my eyes. "I'm hoping it never ends."

Acknowledgments

Every story has a beginning, a middle, and an end, with characters along the way who bring depth and meaning (or sometimes humor, or sometimes even just snacks) to the journey. At the beginning of my story, there was my mother, who wished and worked for a better life for me than the one she had to endure. I'd be remiss if I didn't take this opportunity to thank you, Mom—before anyone else—for the Saturday classes at Queens College and the ballet and the sleepaway camp and the expensive school bus to the Bronx when we barely had two pennies to rub together. You're the only one who has been here to witness my story unfold from the very beginning, and I hope you feel like all that wishing and working when I was little has paid off.

In 2019, I had the terrific fortune to be able to go back to school and get an MFA in Creative Writing. It was there that I met Alan Davis, the absolute best mentor I could ever have asked for. He offered genuine constructive criticism of my fledgling writing attempts, allowed me to embrace the world of commercial genre fiction, and taught me the nuances of craft through book recommendations and writing exercises. When I said I wanted to find a literary agent, Al was one of the few people who believed I could do it, and when I began to study the world of publishing on my own, Al supported me, especially when rejections began rolling in. Al, your kindness, knowledge, and willingness to read endless pages of my work has brought me here, to this moment, writing acknowledgements for my very first published novel. From the bottom of my heart, thank you.

On September 8, 2021, after submitting over 300 queries for four different novels over eighteen months, I was offered representation by Elizabeth Copps, who was (and still is) my dream agent. E, the road to becoming your client was long and bumpy, but it was 100% worth it, because sometimes the stars align and dreams come true. I'll never be able to put into words what you mean to me (but that's okay, because I'm pretty sure you already know).

Elizabeth got me a three-book deal with Sourcebooks after being on submission for less than two weeks, and since then, I've had the tremendous opportunity to learn from my editor, Deb Werksman. I'm immensely grateful to Deb, Susie Benton, Rachel Gilmer, Jocelyn Travis, Alyssa Garcia, and the behind-the-scenes Sourcebooks team for their patience with me and their enthusiasm for my debut novel.

To my writing tribe, especially Sam Price, Dane Sawyer, and my sweet friend Valerie Peralta, thank you for being the world's best cheerleaders! To Lee Matthew Goldberg, who I've known since birth, thank you for sharing your industry knowledge with me. To the many talented author friends I've made along the way, especially Shauna Robinson, K.L. Cerra, and Stephanie Eding, and to the #momswritersclub and #5amwritersclub communities on Twitter, thank you for offering encouragement, support, and love. I never had social media before this, and I certainly never expected to create lasting friendships through it.

To my work people, especially Kate Quijano, Anne-Marie Poliviou, Jessica D'Aprile, and Renae Katz, along with Judy Beckman and Melissa Grote, for understanding that literacy lives in my blood, and for reading early pages and drafts, thank you. To the Literacy Nassau Board of Directors (past and present), for your dedication and collaboration in making literacy accessible to the hardest to reach, and to my staff, for living out the idea that everyone deserves to read, I offer endless thanks! And to John and Janet Kornreich, for believing in me over and over again, I am forever grateful.

To my girls Rosie Cook, Sue Flecker, Melissa Golfo, Jessica Cardinali, Valerie Polakovich, and Holly Dorrance, friends like you are hard to find, and I'm more appreciative than you can imagine to have you in my life. David and Ashley Chauvin, you guys make adulting so much easier—cheers to our Zoom drinks, live brunches, and the occasional parenting meltdown!

My life is rich and full thanks to my summers at the Cape. To the Cruz fam, *los amos mucho a todos y ET es muerte*. To Cam Eden, thanks for letting me interview you back in the day and for being so good to my sassy nuggets. And to the Meccas, thank you for being excited about all this book stuff. Roll Caps!

To Chris Fields, for my first set of beautiful headshots, and for a million years of laughs, thank you.

To Logan Ware, I'm so proud of you, and I can't wait to see where the journey takes you.

To Kristan Higgins, you're wicked pissah. I can't thank you enough for being a freakin' gem of a human.

Finally, to my family, the Wares/Judges and the Micciches. Thank you for taking me in and treating me as one of your own. You'll never know how much it has meant to me. Haley and Julie, I can only pray that I've done a good job so far at being a role model for you both. I love you with every fiber of my being, and I hope that watching me chase my dream of becoming an author has taught you that hard work pays off, and that you can do or be whatever you set your mind to.

And to Chris: this book starts and ends with you.

I love you first, last, best, and always.

About the Author

KJ Micciche is a novelist who hails from Queens, New York, where she spent countless hours as a kid curled up under the covers reading *The Babysitters Club* by flashlight way past her bedtime. KJ runs a nonprofit organization that teaches kids with dyslexia how to read. Proud mom of two little girls, she and her family live on Long Island and summer in Cape Cod. Visit her online at kjmicciche.net.